AN
INCOMPLETE
REVENGE

**Center Point
Large Print**

**This Large Print Book carries the
Seal of Approval of N.A.V.H.**

AN INCOMPLETE REVENGE

A Maisie Dobbs Novel

JACQUELINE WINSPEAR

CENTER POINT PUBLISHING
THORNDIKE, MAINE

LT
M
Winspear

This Center Point Large Print edition
is published in the year 2008 by arrangement with
Henry Holt & Company LLC.

Copyright © 2008 by Jacqueline Winspear.

All rights reserved.

The text of this Large Print edition is unabridged. In other
aspects, this book may vary from the original edition.
Printed in the United States of America.
Set in 16-point Times New Roman type.

ISBN: 978-1-60285-126-9

Library of Congress Cataloging-in-Publication Data

Winspear, Jacqueline, 1955-
    An incomplete revenge : a Maisie Dobbs novel / Jacqueline Winspear.--Center Point large
print ed.
    p. cm.
    ISBN 978-1-60285-126-9 (lib. bdg. : alk. paper)
    1. Dobbs, Maisie (Fictitious character)--Fiction. 2. Women private investigators--
England--London--Fiction. 3. Great Britain--History--George V, 1910-1936--Fiction.
4. Kent (England)--Fiction. 5. City and town life--Fiction. 6. Large type books. I. Title.

PR6123.I575I53 2008b
823'.92--dc22

2007051333

Dedicated to my parents,
Albert and Joyce Winspear
With All My Love

"Of all the gifts that people can give to one another,
the most meaningful and long lasting are strong but
simple love and the gift of story."

Clarissa Pinkola Estés, Ph.D., *The Gift of Story:
A Wise Tale About What Is Enough*

If an injury has to be done to a man it should be so
severe that his vengeance need not be feared.

—Niccolò Machiavelli (1469–1527)

There is no revenge so complete as forgiveness.

—Josh Billings, *U.S. humorist* (1818–1885)

PROLOGUE

Early September 1931

The old woman rested on the steps of her home, a caravan set apart from those of the rest of her family, her tribe. She pulled a clay pipe from her pocket, inspected the dregs of tobacco in the small barrel, shrugged, and struck a match against the rim of a water butt tied to the side of her traveling home. She lit the pipe with ease, clamping her ridged lips around the end of the long stem to draw vigor from the almost-spent contents. A lurcher lay at the foot of the steps, seeming at first to be asleep, though the old woman knew that one ear was cocked to the wind, one eye open and watching her every move.

Aunt Beulah Webb—that was the name she was known by, for an older gypsy woman was always known as *aunt* to those younger—sucked on her pipe and squinted as she surveyed the nearby fields, then cast her eyes to the hop-gardens beyond. The hops would be hanging heavy on the bine by now, rows upon rows of dark-green, spice-aroma'd swags, waiting to be harvested, picked by the nimble hands of men, women and children alike, most of whom came from London for a working late-summer holiday. Others were gypsies like herself, and the rest were *gorja* from the surrounding villages. Gorja. More house dwellers, more who were not gypsies.

Her people kept themselves to themselves, went about their business without inviting trouble. Aunt Beulah hoped the *diddakoi* families kept away from the farm this year. A Roma would trust anyone before a diddakoi—before the half-bred people who were born of gypsy and gorja. As far as she was concerned, they looked for trouble, expected it. They were forgetting the old ways, and there were those among them who left the dregs of their life behind them when they moved on, their caravans towed by boneshaker lorries, not horses. The woman looked across at the caravan of the one she herself simply called Webb. Her son. Of course, her son's baby daughter, Boosul, was a diddakoi, by rights, though with her shock of ebony hair and pebble-black eyes, she favored Roma through and through.

About her business in the morning, Beulah brought four tin bowls from underneath the caravan—underneath the *vardo* in the gypsy tongue. One bowl was used to wash tools used in the business of eating, one for the laundering of clothes, one for water that touched her body, and another for the cleaning of her vardo. It was only when she had completed those tasks, fetching dead wood from the forest for the fire to heat the water, that she finally placed an enamel kettle among the glowing embers and waited for it to boil for tea. Uneasy unless working, Beulah bound bunches of Michaelmas daisies to sell door to door, then set them in a basket and climbed back into her vardo.

She knew the village gorja, those out about their errands, would turn their backs when they saw her on the street, would glance away from her black eyes and dark skin now rippled with age. They would look aside so as not to stare at her gold hoop earrings, the scarf around her head, and the wide gathered skirt of threadbare deep-purple wool that marked her as a gypsy. Sometimes children would taunt.

"Where are you going, pikey? Can't you hear, you old gyppo woman?"

But she would only have to stare, perhaps point a charcoal-blackened finger, and utter words in dialect that came from deep in the throat, a low grumble of language that could strike fear into the bravest bully— and they would be gone.

Women were the first to turn away, though there were always a few—enough to make it worth her while— who would come to the door at her knock, press a penny into her outstretched hand, and take a bunch of the daisies with speed lest their fingers touch her skin. Beulah smiled. She would see them again soon enough. When dusk fell, a twig would snap underfoot as a visitor approached her vardo with care. The lurcher would look up, a bottomless growl rumbling in her gullet. Beulah would reach down and place her hand on the dog's head, whispering, *"Shhhh, jook."* She would wait until the steps were closer, until she could hold the lurcher no longer, and then would call out, "Who's there?" And, after a second or two, a voice, perhaps timid, would reply, "I've come for my fortune."

Beulah would smile as she uncovered the glass sphere she'd brought out and set on the table at even-tide, waiting.

Not that a ball made of a bit of glass had anything to do with it, yet that was what was expected. The gypsy might not have been an educated woman, but she knew what sold. She didn't need glass, or crystal, a bit of amethyst, a cup of still-wet tea leaves, or a rabbit's foot to see, either. No, those knickknacks were for the customers, for those who needed to witness her using something solid, because the thought of her seeing pictures of what was to come in thin air would be enough to send them running. And you never scared away money.

Beulah heard a squeal from the tent that leaned against her son's vardo, little Boosul waking from sleep. Her people were stirring, coming out to light fires, to make ready for the day. True gypsies never slept in their spotless vardos, with shining brass and wafer-thin china hanging from the walls. Like Beulah, they lived in tents, hardy canvas tied across a frame of birch or ash. The vardos were kept for best. Beulah looked up to the rising sun, then again at the fields as the steamy mist of warming dew rose to greet the day. She didn't care for the people of this village, Herons-dene. She saw the dark shadow that enveloped each man and woman and trailed along, weighing them down as they went about their daily round. There were ghosts in this village—ghosts who would allow the neighbors no rest.

• • •

AS SHE REACHED down to pour scalding water into the
teapot, the old woman's face concertina'd as a throbbing pain and bright light bore down upon her with no
warning, a sensation with which she was well familiar.
She dropped the kettle back into the embers and
pressed her bony knuckles hard against her skull,
squeezing her eyes shut against flames that licked up
behind her closed eyelids. *Fire. Again.* She fought for
breath, the heat rising up around her feet to her waist,
making her old legs sweat, her hands clammy. And
once more she came to Beulah, walking out from the
very heart of the inferno, the younger woman she had
not yet met but knew would soon come. It would not
be long now; the time approached—of that she was
sure. The woman was tall and well dressed, with black
hair—not long hair, but not as short as she'd seen on
some of the gorja womenfolk in recent years. Beulah
leaned against the vardo, the lurcher coming to stand
at her mistress's side as if to offer her lean body as
buttress. This woman, who walked amid the flames of
Beulah's imagination, had known sadness, had lived
with death. And though she now stepped forward
alone, the grief was lifting—Beulah could see it
ascending like the morning cloud, rising up to leave
her in peace. She was strong, this woman of her
dreams, and . . . Beulah shook her head. The vision
was fading; the woman had turned away from her,
back into the flames, and was gone.

The gypsy matriarch held one hand against her forehead, still leaning against her vardo. She opened her eyes with care and looked about her. Only seconds had passed, yet she had seen enough to know that a time of great trouble was almost upon her. She believed the woman—the woman for whom she waited—would be her ally, though she could not be sure. She *was* sure of three things, though—that the end of her days drew ever closer, that before she breathed her last, a woman she had never seen in her life would come to her, and that this woman, even though she might think of herself as ordinary, of little account in the wider world, still followed Death as he made his rounds. That was her calling, her work, what she was descended of gorja and gypsy to do. And Beulah Webb knew that here, in this place called Heronsdene, Death would walk among them soon enough, and there was nothing she could do to prevent such fate. She could only do her best to protect her people.

The sun was higher in the sky now. The gypsy folk would bide their time for three more days, then move to a clearing at the edge of the farm, setting their vardos and pitching their tents away from Londoners, who came for the picking to live in whitewashed hopper huts and sing their bawdy songs around the fire at night. And though she would go about her business, Beulah would be waiting—waiting for the woman with her modern clothes and her tidy hair. Waiting for the woman whose sight, she knew, was as powerful as her own.

ONE

Marta Jones surveyed her students, casting her eyes around the studio, with its high ceilings and skeins upon skeins of colored yarn hanging from laundry racks raised up with pulleys and secured on the wall, and the six wooden looms pressed against one another, for space was at a premium. Her desk—a battered oak table set next to the door—was covered in papers, books and drawings, and to her right, as she faced her class, an ancient chaise longue was draped with an old red velvet counterpane to hide darnings and tears in the upholstery. Several spinning wheels were set against the wall to the left of the room, alongside a box where she kept wool collected on Sunday excursions into the country. Of course, she ordered untreated wool directly from her suppliers, but she liked to collect tufts from the hedgerows, where sheep had pressed against hawthorn or bramble to ease an itch and left behind a goodly pull of their coats.

She had taken on students with some reluctance. Even though the rent on her studio close to the Albert Hall was cheap enough due to an ancient land law that provided for artists, her commissions had diminished and she was forced to look for additional income. So she had placed one small advertisement in the newspaper, and written to those who had purchased her works in the past, to let them know that she was taking in a "small number of students to learn the art and craft of traditional tapestry." In general, her students were a motley group and definitely better off; the working classes could barely afford to eat, let alone spend money on frivolities. There were two ladies from Belgravia who thought it might be "rather fun" to spend a Saturday afternoon or evening here each week, chatting as they worked their shuttles back and forth, following the sketched cartoon image that lay beneath the lines of warp and weft.

Another two friends, well-funded students from the Slade seeking a class beyond their regular curriculum, had joined, as had a poet who thought that work in color would enhance the rhythm and pulse of his language. Then there was the woman who spoke little but who had come to Marta's studio after seeing the advertisement. Watching her now, the artist was fascinated by this particular student, drawn to the changes she had observed since class began. The woman had explained that she had recently been exposed to the world of art—she said it as if it were an unfamiliar country—and that she wanted to do "something artistic," as her work was far removed from such indulgence. She had smiled and gone on to say that she had never produced a proper painting, even as a child, and she thought she could not sketch at all, but she was drawn to tapestry, attracted to the weaving of color and texture, to a medium that did not present an immediate image but, when one stood back to regard the day's endeavor, a picture began to take form. "It's rather like my work," she had said. And when Marta asked about the woman's profession, she paused for a moment and then drew out a card, which she offered to the artist. It said, simply:

MAISIE DOBBS
PSYCHOLOGIST AND INVESTIGATOR

Marta thought that this one evening each week was the woman's only recreation, but with each class, something about her seemed to change almost imperceptibly, though the artist found the effect to be quite extraordinary. Her clothes had become more colorful, her artistry more bold as she gained confidence. On the evening when they had experimented with dyeing, taking the yarns they had spun during the previous week, pressing them down into buckets of dye, and then pulling them out to hang first over sinks in the studio's own scullery before looping them over laundry racks to dry, she had rolled up her sleeves and simply laughed when color splashed across her face. The Belgravia matrons had frowned and the poet appeared shy, but soon this woman, who had appeared so reticent at first, so slow and measured in her interactions with fellow students, had come to be the lynchpin in the class—without saying much at all. And, Marta thought, she was very good at drawing out stories. Why, only today, while Maisie worked at her loom, her fingers nimble as she wove threads of purple, magenta and yellow, she had asked the teacher but two questions and soon knew the entire story of the woman's coming to England from Poland as a child. In fact, as she answered the questions that Maisie Dobbs put to her, the whole class knew in short order that Marta's father had insisted that his children learn only English, so that they would fit in and not be marked as foreigners. And her mother had ensured the family dressed in a way that did not set them apart from their new friends, who knew them as the Jones family—that most British of names, adopted as they disembarked from their ship once it had docked at Southampton.

Marta smiled, as she watched Maisie Dobbs work at her loom, and picked up her card again. PSYCHOLOGIST AND INVESTIGATOR. Yes, she must be very good at her trade, this woman who had, without any effort at all, encouraged six people to tell her far more about themselves than they would ever imagine recounting—and all without revealing much about herself, except that she was newly drawn to color.

JAMES COMPTON WALKED at a brisk pace past the Albert Hall, taking advantage of the warm September evening. As his right-hand man in Toronto would have said, he had a head of steam on him, frustration with a land purchase that had proved to be fraught with problems. He did not even care to be in London again, though the thought of returning had at first seemed filled with promise. But the Compton family mansion at Ebury Place had been mothballed, and staying at his father's club and spending each evening with crusty old men languishing amid tales of doom regarding the economy and reminiscences that began with "In my day . . ." was not his idea of fun.

Of course, life in the city of Toronto was not all beer and skittles—after all, he had a corporation with diversified interests to run—but there was sailing on the lake and skiing in Vermont, across the border, to look forward to. And the cold was different—it didn't seep into his war wounds the way it did here. He thought of men he'd seen at the labor exchanges, or soup kitchens, or simply walking miles across London each day in search of work, many of them limping, wounds nagging their memories each day, like scabs being picked raw.

But Toronto might have to wait for him a bit longer. Lord Julian Compton, his father, wanted to relinquish more responsibility and was already talking of having James step up to replace him as chairman of the Compton Corporation. And that wasn't all that was bothering him, as he glanced at the scrap of paper upon which he had scribbled the address given to him by Maisie Dobbs during their conversation this morning. His mother, Maisie's former employer and longtime supporter, had always encouraged her husband and son to direct any suitable business in Maisie's direction if possible, so she was the first person he'd thought to telephone when a property transaction began showing signs that it might become troublesome.

"Goddammit!" said James, as he thought of his father's office in the City once again.

"James!"

James Compton looked up, frowning, then smiled, his eyes crinkling at the corners when he saw Maisie waving from the other side of the road. He crumpled the paper and pushed it into his jacket pocket as he walked across to greet her. "Maisie Dobbs! I was so lost in thought I almost walked straight past!" He paused as she offered him her hand. "Maisie, what on earth have you been doing?"

Maisie regarded her hands, then reached into her shoulder bag and brought out her gloves. "It's dye. I couldn't get it out of my hands and should have put on my gloves immediately—but I can't do much about the splashes on my cheek until I get home." She looked into the eyes of her former employer's son, then reached out to touch his arm. "How are you, James?"

He shrugged. "Well, the engagement's off, that's the first bit of news for you. And as you know, I'm here in England on business—duty calls at the Compton Corporation's London office." James consulted his watch. "Look, Maisie, I know I said this wouldn't take much more time than it would to drink a cup of tea, but I am starving, and I wonder—do you have time for a spot of supper? I've been wrangling—"

"Wrangling?"

"Excuse me, I forgot where I was. Let me start again. I've been considering—worrying about, to tell you the truth—this business transaction I mentioned, and I've not eaten a thing all day."

"Well, we'd better do something about that, hadn't we? I'm rather hungry myself."

James turned and signaled a taxi-cab. "Come on, let's go to a charming little Italian dining room I know—just around the corner from Exhibition Row."

"YOU LOOK DIFFERENT, Maisie." James Compton reached for a bread roll, pulled it apart, and spread one quarter with a thick layer of butter.

"The dye has that effect." Maisie grinned, looking up from the menu. "You haven't changed a bit, James."

"Well, the blond hair has a bit of gray at the sides, but thank heavens it doesn't show much. If I can still walk as upright as my father when I reach his age, I will be more than grateful." He poured a glass of Chianti and leaned back. "You seem more . . . I don't know, sort of . . . lighter."

"I assure you I am not."

"No, that's not what I mean. It's your demeanor. You seem lighter *within yourself,* as our Mrs. Crawford would have said." He looked at Maisie, her black hair, cut just above the shoulders to run parallel with the line of her chin, her fringe brushing against black eyebrows that seemed to deepen her violet-blue eyes. She wore a mid-calf-length wool barathea skirt in a rich purple hue, with a red blouse and blue coat—clearly old but well maintained—that draped to mid-thigh.

Her shoes, with a single strap buttoned at the side, were of plain black leather. A silver nurse's watch was pinned to her lapel.

"Oh, Mrs. Crawford. What will you do for ginger-snaps, James, now that your favorite cook has retired?"

James laughed, and for some minutes they spoke of the past, neither shying from the loss of Enid, Maisie's fellow servant at the Compton household so many years past, a young woman who had been in love with James and whom he had loved in return. Enid died in an explosion at the munitions factory where she worked, in 1915.

"So, tell me how I can help you." Maisie glanced at her watch as she directed the conversation to the reason for their meeting. She did not want to make a late return to her flat in Pimlico, for her day's work was not yet done.

As they ate supper, James described the business transaction that was giving him so much trouble and for which he had seen an opportunity to seek her help.

"There's a large estate down in Kent that I want to buy, on the outskirts of a village called Heronsdene. It's about ten or so miles from Tunbridge Wells—and not that far from Chelstone, actually. The estate is pretty similar to many of its kind in Kent—you know what I mean: a large manor house, Georgian in this case, tenant farmers to manage the land, hunting privileges. But this property has something I'm particularly interested in—a brickworks. It's a small concern.

Produces the sort of bricks used in those pseudo-posh neo-Tudor affairs they're building in the new London suburbia. And they manufacture old-fashioned peg tiles for repair of the older buildings you see all over Kent and Sussex."

Maisie set down her knife and fork, reaching for her table napkin. "And you're interested in the brickworks because there's a building boom despite all indications that the economy isn't showing signs of improvement."

"That's right. Now is the time to buy, ready to make a mint when we're on an even keel, even sooner if output can be improved." James pulled a silver cigarette case from the inner pocket of his jacket. "Mind?"

Maisie shook her head.

James continued. "So, despite Ramsay MacDonald being pressed to form a National Government to get us through this mess, and well-founded talk of Britain going off the gold standard any day now, there's still room for optimism—and I want to move ahead soon."

"So what's stopping you, and how can I help?" Maisie waved a hand in front of her face as diplomatically as possible to ward off smoke from James's cigarette.

"I have my doubts about the landowner, a man called Alfred Sandermere. He's the younger son but became heir to the estate when his brother, Henry, was killed in the war. I knew Henry, by the way—good chap, excellent man—but the brother has done nothing but draw funds from the estate, leaving it on

21

the verge of bankruptcy—which of course means I get value for my money. It's essentially a fire sale."

"And?"

James Compton extinguished his cigarette, pressing it into a glass ashtray which he then set to one side, away from Maisie. "There's been some funny business going on down there, and if there is one thing the Compton Corporation likes, it's a clean transaction. We may move fast in circumstances such as these, but we don't get our hands dirty."

"What's been going on?"

"Mainly what appears to be petty crime. There's been vandalism at the house and at the brickworks. The farmers haven't reported anything amiss, and the villagers—many of whom are employed at the brickworks—are keeping quiet about it."

Maisie frowned. "That's not unusual. You *are* talking about rural Kent, after all."

"No, this is different. The locals have been almost silent, no one hurrying to point the finger. And you know how unusual that is, especially when there are diddakoi in the area."

"Diddakoi or Roma? They're different, James."

"Alright, people who travel with caravans. Doesn't matter what they are, the locals are always pretty quick to blame them for all manner of ills—either them or the Londoners."

Maisie nodded, understanding. "Hop-pickers?"

"Last year, yes. Of course, the police from Tunbridge Wells couldn't do much; they tend to let the villages just get on with it. And it's not as if there was any lasting damage. But I don't like these reports, Maisie. If we move on this, I have to ensure that the brickworks is at maximum output from the first day of ownership. We'll expand from there. And given the dependence upon local labor, goodwill and no vandalism are of the essence. Of course, the tenant farmers will remain as such, no plans to change that arrangement."

"So what do you want me to do?"

"I want you to look into matters, find out if there's anything amiss locally that would affect our purchase of the Sandermere estate. You have three weeks—perhaps a month—to compile your report. That's all the time I have now, and it's not much where property of this kind is concerned." He poured more wine for himself, setting the bottle back on the table when Maisie shook her head and rested her hand to cover the top of her glass. "I know it's not the sort of case you're used to," he continued, "but you were the first person I thought to call."

Maisie nodded, lifting her glass of Chianti to her lips. She sipped the wine, then put down her glass with one hand as she reached for her shoulder bag and took out a small writing pad with the other. She made several notations, then circled a number before tearing off the sheet and passing it to her supper companion. "I assume my fee is acceptable to you." It was a statement, not a question.

James Compton smiled. "There's another thing

that's changed, Miss Maisie Dobbs. I do believe you've become a canny business proprietor."

Maisie inclined her head, as James took a checkbook from his pocket. "An advance against expenses." He scribbled across the check and passed it to Maisie. "You'll have your work cut out for you. Hop-picking's about to start, and the place will be teeming with outsiders."

The investigator nodded. "Then it's the perfect time, James, the perfect time. We'll have your report ready in a month—at the latest."

LATER, AT HER flat in Pimlico, as Maisie sat in her favorite armchair looking at the check, she breathed a sigh of relief. Business was still ticking along but wasn't as brisk as it had been. The summer had been slow, and she was grateful that her assistant, Billy Beale, was planning to take two weeks' holiday to go hop-picking himself—it was, after all, a tradition among East Enders. She wouldn't have to pay his wages for those weeks, and at least he'd be earning money and taking a break from the Smoke—the streets of London—and getting his wife and boys away to the country. They needed it, for the family was still grieving for young Lizzie Beale, who had been lost to diphtheria at the beginning of the year. Yes, James had come along at the right moment, the answer to a prayer. In fact, one of the reasons she had indulged in Marta Jones's class, was to do something different and not fret about a certain lack of custom for her business. To balance the expenditure, she'd even minimized use of her MG, understanding the importance of frugality in uncertain times. And she could never forget she had the mortgage on her flat to consider.

Yet, despite the pressures of being a sole proprietor, Maisie knew that the curtain of darkness from her past was lifting. Not that she forgot, not that she didn't still have nightmares or close her eyes and see images from the war in stark relief. But it was as if she were on firmer ground, and not at the mercy of memory's quicksand.

She checked her watch, marked the file of notes that now rested on her lap, and made ready to go to bed. As she reached for the cord to close the blinds, she remembered a dream she'd had twice this week. Dreams that came more than once demanded attention, and even though this was not a fearful dream, she reflected on it and wondered what it might mean. She had been walking through a forest and came upon a clearing bathed in shards of light splintering through the trees. As she walked into the clearing, she saw the still-enflamed embers of a fire, yet there was no one there, no traveler or tramp claiming a home for the night. There was only a loosely tied bunch of Michaelmas daisies set aside upon a fallen tree.

TWO

Maisie Dobbs sat alongside Billy Beale at the table in front of the floor-to-ceiling windows of the one-room office in Fitzroy Square. There had been a pause in their conversation, during which documents were passed back and forth, along with a page of notes sent by messenger from the office of James Compton.

"So, what you want me to do, Miss, is to recce this village to get the lay of the land and let you know what's going on."

"Yes, in the first instance. You'll fit in nicely, being one of the London hoppers, down for the picking."

"Well, that's all very well, but we've been taken on by a farmer a few miles away, not this one. You can't just up and get work at any old farm, not for the 'oppin'; it don't work like that."

Maisie turned to Billy. "Oh, dear. Would you explain to me how it works, then?"

Billy leaned forward and began to scribble a diagram onto a length of wallpaper pinned to the table. These offcuts, from a painter and decorator friend of Billy's, were reversed to form a background for each new assignment's case map, a diagram created with colored pencils upon which Maisie and Billy set down hunches, clues, information and any other points that might help them usher an investigation to its close. Thus far this length of paper had remained untouched.

"You register with a farmer, one who knows you, usually at the end of pickin' the year before. My family's been goin' down 'oppin' since before my grandfather was a boy. The farmer knows which families 'e wants back, the good workers. Then, in spring or thereabouts, you get your brown envelope, with a letter telling you to come on such and such a date for the 'oppin' and that you'll get your hut to live in. So when you get on the train, with all your family and everything from yer sheets down to the tin kettle, you know you've got work and a roof over yer 'ead."

Maisie was silent for a moment. "Do you know anyone going to"—she paused to consult her notes—"Dickon's Farm on the Sandermere Estate? Couldn't you sort of swap with another family?"

Billy shook his head. "No, I don't know anyone goin' to Dickon's Farm, not off the top of me noddle." He paused, rubbing his chin. "But you know what I'll do, I'll 'ave a word with a few blokes I know, see if it can be done. It ain't normal, though. The farmers don't like messin' about with their allocations."

"Good man." Maisie smiled and reached for a file. "Look at this, just like the number twelve bus—none for ages, then three, one after the other. It never rains but it pours, and about time too!"

"More work comin' in?"

"Yes. I came back to the office yesterday evening and there were two postcards and a telegram, all with jobs for us. I've set appointments with the new clients already. There's nothing huge, but it's a good sign and

27

means that, along with my private clients, the business will go along nicely for us, probably right up to Christmas."

"You were worried there for a bit, weren't you, Miss?"

Maisie nodded. "Yes, just a bit." She flipped open the Compton file again. "Billy, I'm anxious to have my planning for this case settled, so here's what I'd like you to do today—after you've completed the notes on the Jacobsen case so I can send our report and issue an invoice. I want you to find out if you can get onto the Sandermere estate as soon as you can." She paused. "I won't have this case eat into your holiday time, and I'll obviously pay you for the work you do while you're down there, so keep a good record of your hours. I just want you to give me initial impressions, based on James Compton's concerns. Then I really want an in for myself—you might find me picking hops with the Beales, if I have to."

Billy laughed. "Miss, I can't get over it—you a Londoner and never been down to Kent pickin' 'ops."

Once Maisie might have nipped such informality in the bud and not encouraged frivolous repartee on a working morning, but since she had known Billy, they had seen much together—not least during their first brief meeting, when he was brought into the casualty clearing station in France where she was working as a nurse in 1916. Her first love, a young army doctor, Simon Lynch, had saved Billy's life, and the man who was now her assistant had never forgotten either of them. Billy's life intersected with Maisie's again when she rented an office on Warren Street where he was caretaker—he had recognized her immediately. After he'd helped her on a significant case, she asked him to become her assistant, a role he gratefully accepted. Now there was an ease in their relationship, though the occasional joke on Billy's part never slipped into overfamiliarity.

"No, I never went down *'oppin'*, Billy, though my father picked hops when he was a boy. Of course, I've seen them growing, seen the men out stringing for the bines to grow up and the women banding-in and training the shoots along the strings in late spring. But I know nothing about the actual business of hop-picking." She paused, remembering. "Instead, we used to spend a week in the summer with my mother's parents, when they lived near Marlow. Granddad was a lockkeeper. He'd been a lighterman on the Thames for years, but my grandmother yearned to be out of the city, and because they both wanted to be near the water he went to work on the waterways eventually—you couldn't keep him away from that river, even when he should have been retired."

"And your grannie? A Londoner, was she?"

Maisie shook her head. "Oh, no, she was a different kettle of fish altogether." She changed the subject, taking up a sheet of paper. "Now then, after a bit of a lull, thank heavens we've some real work to do."

BILLY AND HIS family left London at the weekend, on

29

one of the trains known as a Hoppers' Special. He had managed to effect an exchange of farm employment with another man and his family and, following a swift back-and-forth of postcards and telegrams between the men and the farmers concerned, the Beales were now ensconced in a one-room hopper hut on Dickon's Farm. For her part, Maisie turned to assessing the case in greater detail.

James Compton's notes included a map of the estate, a significant acreage set amid the swath of land known as the Weald of Kent. Heronsdene neighbored the estate at its southern edge, where the village met the perimeter of Dickon's Farm, which Tom Dickon had inherited from his father, and his father before him. And so it went, down through the centuries. Thanks to long leases that were all but untouchable, the farmer considered the land his own, to be kept in the family.

The brickworks was to the east of Dickon's Farm and, as James had said, was doing well. More information on Alfred Sandermere was included, together with a photograph. *Not very flattering*, thought Maisie, as she sized up a man of perhaps thirty or thirty-one. He seemed quite ordinary, though she did not care for his eyes, which were narrowed, bridged by thin eyebrows and swept-back hair with an over-abundance of oil—the photograph revealed an unfortunate shine indicating as much. His lips drew back across his teeth as he smiled for the camera, and Maisie noticed that he held a half-smoked cigar in his hand. *Nothing unusual there.* However, she thought it unseemly, and there was something about his slouch that suggested arrogance and cynicism. She knew she would have to meet Sandermere at some point and did not look forward to making his acquaintance.

A list of crimes committed in the area during the past three years seemed somewhat long, especially those against the estate's property. Broken windows at the brickworks, theft of tools, a fire in the stables—fortunately neither horses nor grooms were lost. Maisie noticed that a number of the incidents occurred in mid-September of each year, at the time when villagers were outnumbered by Londoners and, of course, a smaller number of gypsies. Mind you, that didn't mean a thing. As James himself had noted, visitors were often a convenient scapegoat for locals with crime in mind.

A shorter note pointed to small fires that occurred in the village itself, again during September. There was no indication either of complaints by the villagers or of the source of such events. Billy had commented on the fires, saying, "Perhaps it's all a coincidence, Miss," to which they had then said, in unison, "Coincidence is a messenger sent by truth."

The words of Maisie's mentor and former employer, the noted psychologist, philosopher and expert in forensic science, Dr. Maurice Blanche, were quoted time and time again, though a serious rent in the fabric of the relationship between Maisie and her teacher was far from healed, despite their occasional brief conversations. It was just one year earlier, in France, that Maisie had come to understand the depth of Maurice's covert activities during the war. She took his secretiveness, along with his seeming interference in a case, to be evidence of a lack of trust toward her, and a fierce row had taken place. Maisie had suffered a breakdown of sorts during her visit to France, a deep malaise brought on by unacknowledged shell shock. Though the chasm between Maurice and Maisie had caused her to become more independent of him, fashioning the business as she would have it rather than as she inherited it, there were times when she missed his counsel. But the events of last year remained unresolved.

Maisie wrote the word *Fire* on the case map. There was something about even the smallest fire that was more unsettling than other crimes of a similar caliber. The match idly thrown on tinder can become an all-consuming blaze, while sparks ignored can envelop a mansion if left unchecked. And flame ignited for the sake of malicious damage strikes at the very heart of individual and collective fear, for isn't fire the place where the devil resides?

TO ADD TO a minor but growing unease concerning the case, Maisie wondered about the commission from James Compton. Was it his mother, Lady Rowan Compton, original supporter and sponsor of her education, who had suggested he contact her regarding this latest purchase of land? Fiercely independent, Maisie had long been both heartened and uncomfortable with the former suffragette's patronage. Certainly the gulf between their respective stations contributed to her feelings, although people were generally pressed to place Maisie when it came to conversation, for she was more often taken for a clergyman's daughter than for the offspring of a Lambeth costermonger. But Frankie Dobbs no longer sold vegetables from his horse-drawn barrow. Instead, he had lived at Chelstone since the war, when Lady Rowan's grooms enlisted and he was brought in to tend the horses, a job that was still his, along with a tied cottage.

Maisie decided simply to get on with the work, rather than troubling herself with considerations of its origin. She pressed on with her notes, disturbed only when the black telephone on her desk began to ring. At first, she looked at the instrument without answering, wondering who might be calling; after all, most people still sent letters, postcards and telegrams with their news, requests and demands. She reached for the receiver.

"Fitzroy five—"

"Oh, Lord, Maisie, I don't need you to recite the number, I've just bloody dialed the thing."

"Priscilla! Where are you?" Maisie stood up to speak to her old friend.

"I'm in London, having finally settled—and I use that word loosely—my three toads into their new school. We thought long and hard about it, Maisie, and we're still wondering if we've done the right thing—

they've had such a wild sort of life in Biarritz. But they do need a bit of discipline, or heaven knows what sort of men they'll become. And having just had a long meeting with the headmaster—my dear eldest has already been in a scrap, coming to the defense of his brother—I am sorely in need of a gin and tonic. Care to join me? I'm at the Dorchester."

"The Dorchester?"

"Yes, it's my new quest, to try each new London hotel in turn. This one has been open for six months and is quite spectacular—a telephone in every room, no less. I might well cease my exploration here and now. I'm quite enjoying this, a perfect way to end a day during which I've had to bang heads together. Not literally, you understand, though if I'd had five minutes with them on their own. . . ."

Maisie looked at her watch. "I'll be there as soon as I can. I just have to complete a couple of tasks here at the office, and I must nip home and change. Shall I see you at half-past six?"

"Lovely. You do that and I'll go and complete the task of languishing in a hot bath to ward off the desire for a slug of mother's ruin."

"See you then."

Maisie hurriedly finished her work and was about to leave the office when a postcard arrived via special delivery. It was from Billy.

Dear Miss,
You must come to the farm. Urgent.

Telephone you Tuesday from the kiosk up the road.
Eight.
Billy.

Maisie tapped the card against the palm of her left hand. *It's Tuesday today*. She looked at her watch. An hour or so with Priscilla would be plenty of time for them to catch up with their news, so she could easily return to the office in time for the telephone call. She knew Billy well enough to understand that he would not be sending such a card unless the situation really was urgent. And according to the map supplied by James Compton, the telephone kiosk was a fair walk from the farm, closer to the next village, and could hardly be described as just *up the road*. Indeed, it would be a fair jaunt at the end of a hard working day.

WHENEVER MAISIE WENT anywhere to meet Priscilla, she only had to find a knot of people to locate her friend's exact whereabouts. It wasn't that Priscilla invited conversation, or even knew those around her, but people gravitated toward her, perhaps standing close while speaking with a colleague or waiting for a guest. This evening was no exception, with Priscilla seated in the bar sipping a cocktail and a clutch of guests close to her, each one stealing an occasional glance in her direction.

Priscilla was wearing evening dress, a garment possibly more suited to an al fresco dinner at her home in France. A cream tunic with a wide sash at the hip drew attention to her fashionably tanned skin, and wide navy blue silk trousers with turned-up cuffs enhanced a slender figure. She wore navy shoes of the softest leather and a long white scarf edged with navy around her neck. Though the late summer weather supported lighter clothing, Priscilla was the only guest who would have looked at home on a ship in tropical climes.

"Good Lord, Maisie, darling, you look like Christmas. I don't think I have ever seen you in a color—well, not unless it's something I've insisted you wear. A red dress? I must say, it rather suits you." She was effusive in her affection for Maisie, whom she loved dearly, and was loved in return, though such regard did not prevent Priscilla from giving advice without her counsel being sought. "Now all you need is a black hat with a red band, some daring red shoes, and—if I were you—a black belt to enhance your waist. Waists, Maisie, are coming back in, despite what you see before you."

Maisie rolled her eyes. "I suit myself, Pris. It's so lovely to see you. Please don't start trying to sort out my wardrobe."

"What wardrobe? I don't know how you manage with such a meager collection. By the way, did you dye that yourself?"

Maisie blushed. "Frankly, I couldn't justify a new dress, so, yes, I simply dyed an old one—I've learned how to do it."

"Hmmm, thought I'd seen that cut before. You've made a good job of it, you know."

A waiter approached and Maisie requested a cream sherry, while Priscilla ordered another gin and tonic.

"Tell me about the boys. Which school did you settle on? In your last letter, you said it was St. Anselm's—did you change your mind?"

"No, I didn't change my mind, but I may yet. We'll have to see how they get on." She sipped her cocktail and shook her head as she placed her glass on the low table alongside them. "Three boys—triple trouble. Mind you, I'd take those toads over three girls any day. My parents had three boys, and one girl, and they always said I caused more angst than my brothers put together."

Maisie smiled. There was a time when Priscilla could not speak of her brothers, for they were all lost to the Great War. Priscilla, like Maisie, had also served, though she had been an ambulance driver. That role, along with her loss, had marked her for years.

"As you know, we—Douglas and I both—dragged our feet when it came to the boys' education. They've been so happy in Biarritz; you saw yourself. School in the morning and the beach in the afternoon. It made for all manner of adventures and more than a little freedom. Of course, they mind their manners and can be perfect gentlemen, but any academic or intellectual gifts they may be harboring are definitely still hidden." She reached for her drink again, swirling a single cube of ice around in the cool liquid without lifting the glass to her lips. "Part of it was me wanting them to have the education and upbringing that my brothers had. You know, the rough-and-tumble world of little men, coming home to the country at weekends, lots of friends over for big old-fashioned bread-and-jam nursery teas. But since last week's little fiasco—"

"What happened?"

Priscilla sighed. "They are very much the new boys. Plus, even though they live with two rather English parents and a Welsh nanny—yes, we still have Elinor, though she's in Brecon with her family at the moment—they do have these quasi-French accents, and they are apt to speak in French when they're telling each other secrets, as if they have their own exclusive club. Needless to say, this hasn't gone down terribly well with the other boys, and there's been more than a bit of bullying." She paused to sip her drink. "Now, I'll concede that having to chart the waters of ill feeling can be character building; however, there's a limit. Tarquin Patrick was subjected to a pasting after shooting to the top of the class in French conversation. He was pushed, he ignored it, pushed again, ignored it, then once more, at which point he blacked the other boy's eye—his left hook comes courtesy of some behind-the-scenes training from Elinor's ex, a Basque stevedore and occasional pugilist. Three of the tykes had pounced on him, calling him a filthy frog, a yellow-bellied Frenchie, when along came Timothy Peter, who is equally gifted thanks to the Basque chappie. On the one hand, just as well—big brothers can be handy when you're being beaten—on the other, three boys are now in the sick bay, one with a broken snout."

Maisie nodded. She had come to know the boys well and was always so touched when she heard Priscilla call her boys by both their first and middle names, for each son was also named for one of her brothers. But she was alarmed at the nature of their exploits.

"What will you do?"

"I'm not sure yet. Douglas is in the process of closing the villa but will be coming back to Evernden Place as soon as he can—we've opened up the old house. I've been so terribly excited at the thought of seeing the boys romping across the meadows, building tree forts, and generally getting up to the sort of adventures that my brothers and I embarked upon that this has put a pall on my enthusiasm, and things aren't looking terribly promising. How can children be so beastly?"

"People are often threatened by the unfamiliar, Priscilla, and children are no exception. As you said, they are little men. The fact that Tarquin did not immediately rush to defend himself—the expected response—inflamed the situation. Mind you, subsequent events might have elevated your sons' position now. Fisticuffs are a universally accepted path to schoolroom power, I'm sorry to say." Maisie was aware that she lacked experience in the bringing up of children, so her comments were drawn from an understanding of what it was to be different, treated with suspicion, and regarded with unease, due as much to her work as to her background.

Priscilla looked at Maisie again. "Actually, while I'm on the boil here, there's something else I wanted to talk about too—and not to do with the boys. It's to do with you."

"Me? Whatever are you talking about?" Maisie noticed the change in her friend's demeanor, a squaring of the shoulders, a slight leaning back, as if she was both preparing to break bad news and trying to draw herself apart from the outcome.

"I made a few telephone calls to various friends before coming down to the bar. One of those friends was Margaret Lynch."

Maisie pressed her lips together and found herself mirroring Priscilla's position. *Yes, Priscilla needed to garner strength to broach the subject with me,* thought Maisie, *as much as I need backbone to hear what she has to say.* The Honorable Margaret Lynch was the mother of her beloved Simon, who had been in a special clinic in Richmond since the war, his mind no more than an empty shell following an attack on the casualty clearing station where they had been working together. Maisie was wounded alongside him, though one of her scars was hidden by her hair. The others, no longer aching and livid, remained incarcerated in her soul.

"Mrs. Lynch?"

"She wants to see you. You've managed to avoid seeing her for years—and she you. It was all too much for you both to bear, wasn't it? But I think it's her age now, and . . ."

"And what?"

"Simon is failing. God only knows what's kept him alive since the war. But now the doctors are seeing changes for the first time in eons, and they think it's only a matter of time."

"Oh . . . I . . . Priscilla, I only saw him two weeks ago. Nothing had changed; I looked at him carefully. I was a nurse. . . . I saw nothing to suggest—"

"That was two weeks ago." She reached out and took her friend's hands in her own. "I realize you think me light, Maisie, but hear what I have to say: You can't hold on forever. Yes, I know you didn't visit for a long, long time—Margaret understands completely—but you've gone to the hospital religiously for two years now, to see a man who neither recognizes you nor with whom you can have a conversation. A man who is not alive, except to breathe and take food—just." She rubbed Maisie's hands as she spoke. "See Margaret soon, Maisie. She doesn't think ill of you, you know. I concede you are usually the clever one who understands what people are really thinking, but I'm not above the odd bit of empathy myself. She needs to know someone who loves her son as much as she loves him herself. You were the last person to speak to him before he was lost to us all. You are the connection between Simon then and now. Simply being in contact with you will help her—help you both—to weather his passing."

"His passing? Priscilla, I—"

"Maisie. Look at me. He's dying. There's no clean or kind way to say it. *Simon is dying.* His father is dead; his mother is alone. You are the only other person who visits, and you have burned a torch for him since the evening you met, even though you have courted other men. And much as she might have wanted better—" Priscilla closed her eyes for just a second and then began to plead. "I . . . oh, God, I didn't mean to say that, Maisie. I know how that must have sounded. What I meant was—"

But Maisie was already on her feet, her stance made more bold by the red dress and her dark eyes as she looked down at Priscilla, who remained seated. "She accepted me into her house because it was wartime. She was kind, courteous, but don't you think I knew that at any other time my background would have been a point of contention in the family? What would have happened at war's end, eh, Priscilla? I could never accept Simon's proposal because I couldn't see a future." She took a breath. "Not only because I knew in my heart that something terrible would happen, but because I could feel her dissent, though her words indicated acceptance." Maisie gathered up her coat. "I will write to Mrs. Lynch, Priscilla. And I will go to the hospital as soon as I can. But I am under no illusions as to what was said about me behind my back years ago."

Maisie turned and left the hotel. Priscilla ordered another drink, holding the cool glass to the side of her forehead as she bit her lip and wished she had said nothing. It was unlike Maisie to be so hot-tempered, unlike her to reveal an emotion. She considered her friend's outburst and thought that perhaps it wasn't such a bad thing, though she hoped they would be reconciled soon. "Definitely touched a nerve there," she said to herself, as she placed her glass on the table, gathered her clutch bag, and made her way to her room.

Later, wearing a long silk robe, she sat by the window looking out onto Park Lane, and it occurred to her that she should have known something had changed. After all, that red dress was a dead giveaway. And another thing: When Maisie said that she couldn't *see* a future, that she knew something terrible would happen, she had lifted her hand but did not touch her eye, as one might expect if one were to predict a reflex action. Instead, Maisie touched the middle of her forehead.

UPON RETURNING TO the office, Maisie threw her coat across her desk, dragged a cushion from the one armchair, pulled her dress up above her knees, and sat cross-legged on the floor. *Calm down, calm down, calm. . . .* She repeated the mantra over and over again. She was appalled at herself, disgusted by her outburst. She might occasionally speak stridently where her work was concerned, and of course there was the argument with Maurice last year, but she had never, ever, taken a comment with such passion. Clearly

Priscilla did not mean to insult her. Her friend's confidence in their friendship allowed her to speak honestly, though she knew her error and apologized immediately. *Why did she affect me so?* Maisie breathed deeply, keen to compose herself before taking Billy's telephone call.

As if on cue, the telephone rang. Maisie came to her feet, brushed down her dress, and reached for the receiver.

"Billy?"

"That you, Miss?" The line crackled.

"Of course it's me."

"Sorry, only you didn't say the number—took me by surprise, it did."

"What's happening?"

"I wish I could tell you all of it, but the cat's been put among the pigeons down 'ere, and if this goes on—"

"If what goes on?"

"Two lads from Shoreditch—'op pickers—'ave been nicked for burglary and vandalism up at the big house on the estate. They say they were just outside the gates trying to get at conkers to get a game going, but there were broken windows and some silver's missing so they've been taken into custody. All the Londoners are up in arms about it, Mr. Dickon just wants the 'ops picked, and everyone reckons it was them bleedin' gypsies what done it, which don't make it easy for me and Doreen."

"I'm not following you."

44

"We'd not been 'ere five minutes when Doreen passes one of the gypsy women with a little girl, right little cracker, just like our Lizzie, apart from the fact she's got curly black 'air. So, even though Doreen can barely understand a word the woman's saying, she stops to pass the time of day when they go to the tap for water, and she takes ahold of the baby—Boosul's 'er name; what kind of a name is that?—and so she's looked upon kindly by the gypsies. Nothin' wrong with that, but now me own kind are turning, callin' us gypsy kin."

"Boosul means beautiful. It's a kind of slang, a derivation of the word over the years."

"'ow do you know that, Miss?"

"I've heard it before. What else is going on?"

"The locals are a funny lot, make no mistake. And it's not as if I'm a stranger to this sort of goings-on, but these people are another thing altogether. The ones out 'ere pickin' are sayin' they didn't see anything, but are pointin' the finger at us anyway and at the same time sayin' they don't want the filthy pikeys on the farm neither."

"Sounds like rather a mess to me, and not helped by a lot of unrest among the warring tribes, so to speak."

"You'd've thought we got over that when the Vikings left." He paused. "And it's worse than you think, Miss. These boys could be sent down for a year or more. That Sandermere bloke is askin' for the maximum penalty—as an example, so 'e says. And the man also said there've been threats sent to 'im, so the

45

police've been crawling all over the place. I think you should come down, Miss. There's no one to look out for these lads—only youngsters they are, too young to weather bein' put away. I know their families, they're good people, and they put in a good day's work every day for the sake of their own. You've got the right words, if you know what I mean. You can talk to solicitors and the police, help speak up for the lads—and you're a Londoner. You'll be trusted."

Maisie sighed. She'd hoped the investigation for James Compton might be easier than this, but as it stood there were complications before the ink was dry on the contract. She reflected on the fact that, in her work, the seemingly straightforward cases were often anything but. "Alright, I'll drive down tomorrow morning, straight to the farm. I can stay with my father at Chelstone for a few nights. It should only take me about three quarters of an hour to get there from Heronsdene."

The call ended. Maisie replaced the receiver and returned to her cushion. She decided that, on her way out of London tomorrow morning, she would leave a note for Priscilla at the Dorchester's reception desk, apologizing for her outburst. And she would also pen something to Margaret Lynch, though she would take care with the composing of such a letter. Having made her plans, she closed her eyes, and an image of her grandmother came to mind, as it had during the conversation with Billy. She remembered her mother laughing as her father lifted her from the horse-drawn cart that brought them from the station to her grand-parents' cottage alongside the lock. Her grand-mother's gray hair, which was once as jet as her own and her mother's hair, was drawn back in a long braid. And though her clothes were much like those of other women of the time, she wore rings of gold in her ears, rings that Maisie's fingers sought out as soon as she was swept into her grandmother's arms, always to the same refrain: "Oh, my boosul girl, my boosul little girl, come to see the old old aunt."

THREE

Maisie loved driving, loved the feel of the wind in her hair when the weather was sufficiently fine to draw back the MG's roof, as it was today. There might be a nip of autumn on the breeze first thing in the morning, but the days were balmy, a pleasant warmth with a low sun in the sky that glinted across newly harvested fields as she made her way toward Heronsdene.

Taking the road from Tunbridge Wells to Lamber-hurst, she turned at the sign for Heronsdene and slowed to a crawl when she came to the village, the road flanked by a variety of architecture, from medieval cottages to terraced houses built in Vic-toria's reign. On her left, the beamed exterior of the local inn looked warm and inviting, and farther along to the right a Norman church stood buffeted by the wind as it whipped up the hill from Horsmonden.

There was an assortment of small shops, a butcher, a general store, a hardware shop, and—in the middle of the street close to the church—a war memorial. The road had been divided and rerouted to accommodate this monument, erected to honor the men and boys of the village who lost their lives in the years 1914–1918.

To the left, there was a gap at the end of a row of detached buildings where Maisie might have expected to see another house, or even a shop, but the area was overgrown with weeds and a few clumps of Michaelmas daisies. The daisies were abundant at this time of year, growing along railway lines and on waste ground, and they brought color to an otherwise dull corner of the village. The road intersected here, with a sign to Dickon's Farm indicating a turn to the left.

Maisie swung the car in the direction of the farm, passing freshly picked hop-gardens on her right. The overhead lines from which strings had been woven in spring, up and down, up and down, for the young hops to grow into fully fledged bines, were empty now, with perhaps a lone sprig of hops left high on the wire. Piles of spent bines lay in heaps, the pickers having moved on to the next hop-garden.

Pulling into the farm, Maisie parked the motor car off to the side of the rough road and went ahead on foot. The last thing she wanted was an expensive repair to the underbelly of her beloved MG. She'd prepared for such an outing, wearing a walking skirt of heavy linen with kick pleats front and back, a pair of stout shoes, and a cotton blouse the color of nutmeg. She carried a knapsack in which she'd packed sandwiches, a cardigan, a wedge of index cards tied with string, and a notebook and pen. She'd tucked a small drawstring pouch containing some tiny tools into the front compartment of her knapsack, and her Victorinox knife was nestled in the pocket of her skirt.

She walked on along the sandy farm road, stopping when she came to the oast house. A trailer of filled-to-the-brim hop-pokes was being unloaded, carried in one by one for the hops to be dried in the kiln before being packed in pokes once again and sent to the breweries. The "reek"—a pungent aroma of fresh and drying hops mixed with sulfur—filled the air, and Maisie watched for a few minutes before calling to one of the men.

"Excuse me, but can you direct me to the hop-gardens being picked now?"

The man stretched his back as he answered, taking off his flat cap and wiping his brow with a hop-stained handkerchief. "They're in Railway and Folly—all the hop-gardens have names. Railway runs alongside the railway lines, as you might have thought. Follow this road on for another half a mile, walk through the unpicked garden on your left, and you'll find it. Folly is on the other side of this road. Pass two hop-gardens on your right, and it's the third one you come to." He replaced his cap while taking her measure as he continued. "Looking for anyone in partic'lar?"

"Yes, I am, Mr. and Mrs. Beale and their family—Billy Beale."

"Fair-headed going on ginger? Got a bit of a gammy leg?"

"That's him."

"Railway. He's working there with some other Londoners at the top. Gyppos are at the bottom working their way up, so mind where you go."

Maisie was about to speak but, reflecting upon yesterday's meeting with Priscilla, thought better of it, adding, "I have nothing to fear—and thank you. I am sure I shall find Mr. and Mrs. Beale with no trouble at all."

The man shrugged and shook his head as she walked on, raising her face to the sun to feel the soft warmth on her skin. The hop-garden named for the railway was easy to locate, helped, in this instance, by a train passing. Puffs of coal-laced steam bursting up through the trees provided a marker for Maisie to follow, and soon she was walking along a row of hop-pickers, whole families gathered around a stretcher-length bin made of wood and sacking that could be moved on as they picked. Normally, she would expect to hear laughter, the odd voice calling out, "What about this one?" and the sing-song that followed to pass the day.

She remembered her father's stories of his boyhood, often told as they sat next to the cast-iron kitchen stove on her afternoon off from work, the warmth of both his voice and the coals soothing her. These were the stories he shared in the months following her mother's death, and she wondered, now, if in speaking of his childhood he had been anchored in some way, or perhaps he wanted to draw out her own years of innocence, now that at the age of thirteen she was working long days below stairs at the Ebury Place mansion of Lord Julian Compton and his wife, Lady Rowan. Frankie Dobbs had told of the jokes shared while picking and laughed when recounting the way opinions on the way of the world were exchanged or a jocular back-and-forth interrupted when a wail signaling that a small child—put down to nap on a coat draped across a pile of old hop-bines—had woken from sleep.

Today, though, the temper of the folk picking hops was subdued. For several moments Maisie stood at the edge of the hop-garden, watching, wondering, gauging, for she felt their anger touch her as if their depression were solid, a rain cloud formed of concrete. She continued on; twice she stopped to ask for Billy, each time to be told she was nearly there, he was just along the row, and a hop-stained finger would be pointed in his direction.

Finally, she saw them: Billy and Doreen leaning over the bin picking hops with speed and dexterity, and Billy's aging mother, her arthritis-gnarled fingers taking leaves off a sprig of hops, then using a hand to shuck the clean hops into the bin. The boys, Billy and Bobby, picked into an old laundry basket, which, when full, would be tipped into the bin. Every little bit helped, especially with piecework. Billy drew back his sleeve and checked his watch, then spoke to his wife, who looked around. As Maisie approached them, she heard a deep voice call across the hop-garden, "Get yer 'ops ready!" And each family picked with greater speed, the children being called to pull leaves from the bin, for the farmer wouldn't accept hops that weren't clean.

"Miss!" Billy looked up as Maisie approached. "Just give me a minute, the tallyman's on 'is way and these boys've put in more leaves than they've taken out, I should say."

"I'll help," said Maisie, setting down her knapsack and rolling up her sleeves. She greeted Doreen with a smile and rested a hand on her arm for a second, mindful of the bond formed between them when little Lizzie died. Then she set to work. There were six pairs of arms in the bin now, with hands seeking out the rough, prickly leaves for which the farmer would issue a reprimand.

With the tallyman only two bins away, Billy said, "Right, that's it. I reckon we've got 'em all out," and leaned away to look along the row, his lips silently following the counting. Maisie inspected her hands, already stained after only a few minutes, then watched the tallyman at work.

"And-a-one . . . and-a-two . . . and-a-three. . . ." He would plunge his measuring basket into the bin and out would come a frothy bushel of fresh green hops, which he slung into a hop poke held at the ready by another man; then in went the basket again. "And-a-four . . . and-a-five. . . ."

Maisie saw that as the tallyman approached it wasn't just Billy—everyone was watching, counting along with the counting, making sure that no one was shorted, that the tallyman not only counted without favoring some with a less-than-full basket but that the correct number was entered in the picker's book. And then he moved on. When he reached Billy's bin, Maisie closed her eyes, the full peppery smell of hops enveloping her as the counting began, stirring up pollen and dust and almost banishing the mood that had seeped up under her skin when she walked into the hop-garden.

"Nice lot today, Mr. Beale. Nice picking indeed." The tallyman handed Billy's book back to him and moved on, parting the wave of workers as he approached the next bin. "And-a-one . . . and-a-two. . . ."

"Right, Miss, let's go and brew up a cuppa. Got someone I want you to meet on the way." He nodded to Doreen, who returned his gesture, and then moved on through the rows of pickers. Maisie followed, her knapsack across her shoulder. Billy stopped at a bin close to the edge of the hop-garden, calling across to the man of the family, "George, over 'ere. Come and 'ave a chat with Miss Dobbs, the lady I was tellin' you about."

George touched the peak of his cap. "Right you are."

Maisie noticed the shadows under the man's eyes, at a time when he should have seemed a little more care-free. He reminded her of her father, with his shirt-sleeves rolled up above the elbow, a jaunty waistcoat, and a red kerchief tied at the neck. But his demeanor revealed concern, worry, and—she hated to see such an emotion—a melancholy that suggested defeat.

Introductions were made, and the trio walked toward the hopper huts, where Billy started a paraffin stove and set a kettle on to boil. As she waited, seated outside on an old chair, Maisie looked into the hut. It comprised one small room, a bed at the far end and another along one side. She suspected that the younger boy, Bobby, slept with Billy and Doreen, and the elder with Billy's mother. Opposite the second bed, a washstand held an enamel ewer and bowl, and in the middle a whitewashed table was set with an embroidered cloth and a vase of Michaelmas daisies. The inside of the hut was neat and clean, with the hopping furniture brought from the Beales' cellar and painted each year before the family left London for Kent.

"George, you tell Miss Dobbs 'ere what went on with your Arthur and Joe."

George placed his cap on one knee and reached for the tin cup filled with strong scalding tea that Billy passed to him. He blew across the top to cool the liquid, then set the mug on the ground at his feet. As Maisie watched him, she knew he was buying time, perhaps composing the story in such a way as to shed the light of innocence on his sons—she assumed the boys in question were his.

"'appened Monday. Only been down 'ere three days, we 'ad. We finished pickin' at four on the dot, after the last tally, then come back to wash and start a bit o' grub going." He pointed to a low brick building with a chimney at one end intersecting the hopper huts. "Me and the wife, Audrey, we was in the cook 'ouse—we'd both 'ad a bit of a sluice to get the dust off our 'ands and faces and left the boys to do the same. They're good boys, but they'd been talking all day about the chestnut trees this side of the fence around the Sandermere place—you know what boys are when it comes to a game of conkers. All they want to do is find the biggest conker, polish it up, bake it 'ard, polish it again, and see 'ow many times it'll last when it's whacked by another lad's conker." He picked up his tea, blew across the rim of the mug again, and sipped. Then he drank several more gulps before turning to Maisie once more. "Me missus calls 'em for their tea. No answer. Then again. So out I went lookin' for the little whatsits—they're twelve and thirteen, out of school and workin', but that don't make no difference, they're still young lads." He sat upright, held out one hand, palm up for emphasis, and continued. "Next thing I know, I'm standin' under a tree full of conkers, and there they are, in the old cuffs, off with two coppers who're sayin' they're bein' nicked for breakin' and enterin', theft and malicious damage. The poor little sods are in tears, but that don't make no difference. And there's that Sandermere, mister 'igh-and-bleedin'-mighty, sayin' it'll be a lesson to them, bein' put away, goin' down for a few years." George pressed his chest before speaking

55

again. "My Audrey took a turn, dropped to 'er knees when I broke the news. All we want is to go back to the Smoke now, get away from all this—but we need the money, and we can't get away with the boys in clink."

Maisie nodded, remaining silent for a moment, mainly to gather her thoughts but also to allow the man to say more, if he should need to. When she spoke, it was with a soft voice, measured and slow. "George, I must ask you this question, so please do not be offended, but what evidence do you have that it was *not* your sons and what evidence do the police have that it was?"

"I know my sons, miss!" The man stood up, dropping his tea as he came to his feet.

"Steady, George. Miss Dobbs's got to ask, got to get the lay o' the land, you know, to 'elp." Billy took up the cup, replenishing it half full with tea.

The man settled himself again. "You're right. Best to tell you everything. They've got some local bloke, a solicitor, brought in to speak for 'em, but the man don't look like 'e cares tuppence." He sat down, drank the tea straight back, then threw the dregs out across the sun-baked clay earth. "When the boys were caught, they were searched, and a silver paperweight was found in Joe's pocket and a locket in Arthur's."

"What did the boys say?" Maisie inquired, taking her notebook from the knapsack and beginning to write.

"That they found the silver under the chestnut tree."

"And the police?"

"They say the boys 'ad an accomplice on the other side of the wall, but they couldn't resist keepin' a bit o' what they'd taken with them—and the business of lookin' for conkers was made up when they saw they'd been nabbed."

Maisie nodded. "I see." She reached for the cup of tea she'd placed at her feet when she began to write. "And what do you think, George?"

"Me?" He looked at Maisie, then at Billy, who nodded. "I reckon it was them bleedin' pikeys. Bloody vermin, they are." He turned to Billy again, "And you should watch it, mate, what with your missus gettin' in thick with that Webb woman."

Billy reddened. "It's only the baby, George. Reminds 'er of our little Lizzie. Breaks my 'eart, it does." He looked away.

"It's not as if we don't all know what you've been through, but nothin' good will come of that sort of goin'-on, I tell you." George wagged a finger at Billy, then brought his attention back to Maisie, who had said nothing during the exchange between the two men. "I've seen 'im, the one what don't 'ave no proper name—they just call 'im Webb. I've seen that gyppo over on the hill, looking down toward Sandermere's mansion. Just stands there and watches. And I've seen 'im walkin' around the place, alongside of the fencing. If you want to know who burgled the place, that's where you want to look. Police reckon they've got no evidence, say they can't nick Webb or move the gyppos on, that they ain't doin' anybody any 'arm." He folded his arms and kicked his boot out toward a stone.

Maisie completed a note, nodding her head as she underlined a word, then looked up at the men. "The thing one has to be careful with, in such cases, is rushing in with all guns blazing, so to speak. It's best to take care, though time is obviously of the essence. Where are the boys being held?"

"Maidstone nick—but they're only boys, in with all them villains."

"Don't worry. I would imagine they will probably not be in with the prisoners, just in temporary cells. Not comfortable, but not as bad, either. And where are the gypsies encamped?"

Billy turned around and pointed. "You go back out of these hop-gardens to the farm road, past four more hop-gardens and a field of cows, and you'll see their caravans up on the 'ill close to the wood. There's a sort of clearing in the wood where they've got a big fire. They all sit around at night and 'ave a bit of a sing-song. That Webb plays the fiddle—so do a couple of the other blokes—and they make a right racket up there of a night."

"And who's the matriarch?"

"The what?" Billy and George spoke in unison.

"The eldest woman in the tribe. She'll probably have a caravan set slightly apart from the others."

"The older Webb woman, mother of that dirty thief?

58

I'd watch that one if I was you. Wouldn't go creepin' over there."

Maisie smiled and packed up her things. "I'll go to Maidstone tomorrow, George. And I'll visit the woman today. Do you know her name? Or have they just called her *aunt?*"

Billy and George looked at each other, then back at Maisie. Billy answered. "I can ask Doreen, but I don't think she knows. The woman with the baby girl they call Boosul, that one's name is Paishey—short for Patience, I reckon."

"Yes, that sounds right." She continued to speak as she stood, handing her cup to Billy. "Gypsies tend to have names that are almost biblical—you'll hear Charity, Patience, Faith, that sort of thing." She placed a hand on George's shoulder. "I'll also speak to Mr. Sandermere, though I am not yet sure how I might make his acquaintance. We'll get to the bottom of this soon enough. And I'll see you tomorrow morning, Billy—I'll be out here early."

The men watched as she walked away, stopped to get her bearings, then made her way toward the farm road.

"You sure she can do right by my boys, mate?"

Billy nodded. "Yeah, sure I'm sure. If anyone can find out what went on, Miss Dobbs can." But he wasn't sure that talking to a tribe of gypsies was the right way to go about the job.

MAISIE STOOD AT the bottom of a gentle hill looking up

59

at the knob of trees spread over the brow. As clouds scudded across the sky casting shadows below, the woodland was at once in shade and then as brightly lit as if it were a prop on the London stage. The caravans were drawn close together; she counted five, each with a tent pitched next to it. Then, to the left, another caravan was set apart. Lower on the hill, six stocky cobs grazed on lush grass. Maisie raised her hand to shield her eyes and watched them amble a few yards to a fresh patch, then run together for no reason at all, kicking up their heels before coming back to graze once more. She remembered going with her father to buy a horse at Stow-on-the-Wold, during the gypsy horse fair. Her mother did not come, and later, as she came of age, Maisie realized it was a journey her father would probably have preferred to make alone, but the respite from their daughter's childish energy provided rest for his wife, who was ill, and delight for a girl who had begun to understand that her mother was failing.

As they had walked along the rows and rows of horses and ponies, her father stopping to ask a question or reaching down to run his hands up and down the legs of a cob, she asked, "How do you know which one's the right horse?" And he replied, "Well, we're looking for a thick, strong, hairy leg at each corner and a twinkle in the eyes—and we're waiting for one of 'em to choose us." They came home with Persephone in the goods wagon of the train, then rode her from Paddington to her new home in a warm, cozy stable under the dry arches of Waterloo Bridge.

The horses looked up as Maisie passed, then went on with their grazing. She approached the gypsy camp, calling out, "Hello," though she did not expect an answer, with everyone picking until at least four o'clock. She took care, as she walked past each caravan, and did not pry, for that was not her purpose— not in the way of picking through belongings while the owner was absent, anyway. To her right, just before she reached the caravan set apart, the one she knew belonged to the gypsy matriarch, a path led into the wood. She checked her watch—it was still barely past one o'clock—and walked along the path, emerging in a clearing, with sunlight glinting through tree fronds overhead. A single wisp of smoke snaked up from the ashes of this morning's fire, and with each gentle murmur of breeze the embers radiated their red heat and then grew dim, as if breathing their last before finally crumbling to ash.

Logs had been cut and positioned around the fire, and a black pot with long iron utensils had been pulled to one side. Remembering her dream, Maisie was not moved, nor did she feel fear, remaining in place while she considered the case, which had now developed into more than a simple fact-finding exercise for James Compton. Were the gypsies guilty of breaking into the Sandermere estate? How was the crime linked to other events, as described to her by James and also detailed in his notes? And what of Heronsdene, this place where people were so tight-knit they did not report damage to their property by fire? Yes, she would have to find a way to broach that subject, while at the same time acquiring an understanding of the people. More than anything, she wanted to know why driving through the village had caused her to shiver and the hair on her neck to bristle. Could it simply be a mood of dissent between the landowner and the village, or was it caused by the incoming workers from London and the gypsies?

Maisie turned and shivered again, only this time she felt as if she were being watched. Looking around, she saw no one, so, throwing her knapsack over one shoulder, she moved without haste to the mouth of the clearing, to the sunlit field beyond the canopy of trees. As she stepped out, close to the single caravan set apart from the rest, she felt a clench around her free hand and looked down. A lurcher held Maisie in a viselike grip, yet the bitch had drawn her lips across her sharp teeth, as if she had chosen to do no harm, only to keep the interloper in place until her mistress returned. Maisie breathed in and out slowly, then spoke to the dog.

"There's a good girl. I'll be no trouble to you. But if you're to hold me hostage, then I want to sit down."

No growl issued from the dog, but her small, sharp, glistening eyes did not move from looking up, straight into the eyes of her catch. Maisie had recognized the dog to be a lurcher, the mongrel they called the dog of the gypsies, a first cross between a greyhound and a collie. It was a dog, they said, with the speed of the one and the canniness of the other. *Lur*, as she knew already, means *thief* in the ancient Romany language. And it was no good breeding two lurchers to get a litter either, for only that first cross produced the true lurcher—the gypsies knew their dogs and horses.

The dog allowed Maisie to edge toward the steps of the lone caravan, where she sat to wait, using her free hand to take out her sandwiches. Of course, she could have used her knife or taken tools from the small pouch with an intention to wound the animal, but she knew that, however fast her reflexes, the dog would be faster—and the animal meant her no harm as long as she did not try to move farther. There was no escape to be had, which was likely just as well. She thought she might be expected here, in any case. Leaning back against the caravan door, Maisie lifted the sandwich to her lips to eat, and felt a single wet stream of drool issue from the lurcher's jaws to trickle across her captured hand.

IT MUST HAVE been when the dog released her grip that Maisie awoke. She did not start when her eyes met the eyes of the gypsy woman, standing with her long gray hair drawn back in a patterned scarf, hoop earrings, dark ridges of lines above and between her eyes, and ripples of skin where her cheeks had sagged with age. Instead, Maisie came to her feet and, looking down—for the woman just reached Maisie's shoulder—she simply inclined her head and smiled.

"My name is Maisie Dobbs, and I have come to see you."

The woman nodded and placed a wicker basket filled with freshly picked Michaelmas daisies on the ground. "They call me Beulah." She looked Maisie up and down. "Get away from them steps so's I can get to me vardo." She turned to the other gypsy folk who had gathered around when they returned to find a gorja woman waiting.

"It's *kushti*." It's good. "She's alright. Now get on." Her language was thick on her tongue, her words barely mumbled, yet her instruction resonated though she had not once raised her voice. Without looking at Maisie, she took her kettle out from under the caravan, along with the bowl for washing her hands.

"Carry this for the old auntie you've come all this way to see. You'd better come sit and talk." And with that she whistled for the lurcher, who walked behind her into the clearing, moving from side to side so that Maisie remained in third place and could neither walk beside nor in front of the dog's mistress.

FOUR

Maisie emerged from the clearing as the late-afternoon sun began to give way to a dusky early evening light, the mellow echo of horses nickering as she passed by on her way down the hill. Billy might have expected her to drop in to see the family before she left the farm, but though she could see hoppers gathered around the cookhouse, she was late already and did not want Frankie Dobbs to worry.

Easing the MG out onto the road, Maisie thought the village seemed quiet for a September evening, when folk might be expected to be walking along to the local inn for an ale to talk of the day, the weather, the harvest just in, or the hop-picking. It was the time of year for ease, as barley was cut to form sheaves across the sun-drenched stubble that remained and hay was rolled into bales or set in stooks; for easy ambles along narrow country lanes and memories exchanged of years gone by. It was a time for bottling and drying vegetables for the winter table, and for rich summer pudding filled with berries to be set in a cold larder, the juices to mingle. But there seemed to be little of the season's joy in Heronsdene, a mood, as she'd reflected earlier, that might be connected to the influx of outsiders.

Her thoughts turned to the gypsy encampment and her time spent with Beulah next to the fire. The woman had led her into the clearing and bade her sit on the log next to her. The lurcher nestled at the woman's feet but kept Maisie in her line of vision, lifting her head if she moved even an inch. The animal had no name, and was called, simply, *jook,* the gypsy word for dog.

While Maisie and the woman spoke, heads drawn close so that conversation could be kept low, she knew the attention of the rest of the tribe was upon her, particularly that of the man she understood to be Webb, Beulah's son. He was tall, with eyes of blue and long hair that was not as dark as the others. Maisie knew that many Roma had deep copper glints in their hair, and some were redheads, though most had rich black locks like Beulah or Paishey, Webb's wife. Indeed, they had hair like her own. Webb wore an old shirt and dark corduroy trousers, a waistcoat, and a blue scarf around his neck. A hat with a broad brim partially obscured his face, and he too wore earrings, though not as wide in circumference as those of Beulah or Paishey. Even baby Boosul wore tiny earrings.

From the way he moved, Maisie estimated Webb's age to be about twenty-eight or twenty-nine, just a few years younger than herself, yet in the features she was able to discern he seemed much older. His wife was about nineteen, perhaps twenty. Webb glanced up at his mother every few minutes, as he stooped to light the fire, or when dragging over the heavy cast-iron pot for the women to make a stew of rabbit, with vegetables bought in the village and tasty greens from the forest that anyone other than a gypsy might ignore. Without making her interest obvious, Maisie could tell much about the man from his demeanor. Though she could not emulate his carriage from her seat on the log, she could see the feelings he carried within him, as if a weighted sack were tethered to his body. Webb was not only enraged, he was fearful. Maisie could see both emotions as plain as day. And when she turned to Beulah, she realized the old woman had been watching as the visitor took the measure of her son, and it was clear in her narrowed gypsy eyes that she had seen the conclusion the investigator had reached.

"You here about them gorja boys, from up there." It was a statement put to Maisie with a wave of the hand in the broad direction of London.

Maisie nodded. "That's one of the reasons, yes."

"We di'n 'ave nothin' t'do with it." Beulah took a mouthful of tea and winced as she swallowed the scalding liquid.

"Do you think the London boys did it?"

Beulah looked into the fire. "Not my place t'say. What they do is their business, what we do is ours."

"Your son was seen close to the house on the day of the burglary. Did he see anything?"

"Not my place." She nodded toward Webb, who was splitting logs with an axe. Two other men with him sawed trees that the wind had blown down last winter, wood that would crackle and burn easily, seasoned by nature and a hot summer. "Talk to 'im if you like."

Webb looked up from his work at just that moment, and Beulah beckoned to him. "The *rawni*—woman—wants to talk to you, Webb."

Without first putting down the axe, and with just a few easy steps, Webb came to stand in front of Maisie. Instinct instructed her to come to her feet, for in height she was almost a match for the matriarch's son and she would not be unsettled by him. Her own eyes of the deepest blue could flash a look as intimidating as any glance in her direction.

"Mr. Webb, I am looking into the burglary at the Sandermere house on behalf of the parents of the boys who stand accused of the crime. Though it appears there is more than enough evidence to charge them, I understand that you were in the area of the estate and might have seen what happened."

The man did not move, either to shake his head or nod in accordance with her supposition. He stared for every second of one minute before responding. Maisie did not break connection with his stare, nor did she add any comment to encourage him to speak. Eventually, he chewed the inside of his lip, then began.

"I didn't see anything. I was just walking along, with the dog." His voice was unlike his mother's, lacking the rough guttural low-gypsy dialect.

"He bin to school." Beulah's voice caused Maisie to turn, as the woman deflected her thoughts with an unsolicited explanation. "Learned *your* words, he did. And Webb can write. He does our letters, our doc'- ments, and reads for us, so we ain't ignorant of what's said and what's been writ."

"A useful man to have in the tribe, eh, Aunt Beulah?" Maisie smiled, then turned back to Webb. "Do *you* think the boys did it? Do *you* think they broke into the house, stole the silver, and made off with it?"

Again Webb waited, steady with his reply. "Lads are from the streets of London. They're not stupid, even if they are boys. If they did what the police said, they wouldn't've been caught. Boys like that are light on their feet. I remember when I was that age. I was quick. Had to be." Then he turned and walked back to his task—set a large log on top of another, raised the axe high above his head, and swung it down with force, so that the splitting of wood in one fell swoop echoed throughout the forest.

Beulah sipped her tea, elbows resting on knees set wide as she watched her son in silence. Then she turned to Maisie.

"You from up there?" Again she nodded in the broad direction of London.

"Born and bred."

The woman smiled. "Born but not bred, girl."

Maisie said nothing but looked into the fire, now a heap of blazing wood where there had been sleepy embers just this afternoon.

"Which side, your mother's?"

Maisie nodded.

"But not your mother."

"My grandmother. She was of the water folk. Her family had a narrow boat which, once, they brought into the Pool of London. My granddad was a lighterman, a youngish man, I think, though long out of boyhood. She was barely more than a girl. He asked for her hand, and her father eventually agreed. Her people said it would come to an end, because she was a strong-willed girl, my grandmother. But they were together for the rest of their lives and died within days of each other. I was eight years old."

"And the daughter?"

"My mother died when I was twelve, going on thirteen."

Beulah sipped her tea again, then bent to stroke her dog's head. "Come tomorrow, as the sun goes down. A bit of tea will be here for you."

DURING THE DRIVE to her father's house, Maisie reflected upon her dismissal. She had been asked questions of her life with honesty, without guile, and she had answered in kind. The invitation for tea the following day was more than a request, it was a summons. She would be able to ask more questions, delve more deeply, during the second visit.

Reaching the village of Chelstone, Maisie slowed the motor car and turned left into the grounds of Chelstone Manor, where she turned left again down a small gravel thoroughfare that led to her father's cottage. She had a plan for the following day in mind now: In the morning she would go to Maidstone, to the solicitors acting for the two boys. While there she would visit the local newspaper office, to check on old stories about the village. Then she would come back to Heronsdene, simply to walk along the High Street and gain a sense of the community—and perhaps gather a clue as to why such a dour mood prevailed. Much of what she planned to do revolved around legwork that Billy might have done if they were in London, but Maisie looked forward to getting back to some of the nuts and bolts of investigation that had so immersed her when she was an apprentice to Maurice Blanche.

70

She made a few notes on her pad before emerging from the MG, wondering, in particular, why Webb had been watching the Sandermere mansion with such interest, what it held for him, and what was at the root of his curiosity, if that's what it was. She put her pencil and pad away and gathered up her knapsack; as she stepped from the motor car, her father was already walking toward her, ready to embrace the daughter he loved so dearly.

LATER, AFTER THEY had eaten a tea of corned beef, carrots and potatoes and had washed and put away the china and cutlery, the pair sat together in the small beamed sitting room.

"Soon be time to light a fire of an evening, won't it, love?"

"Oh, let's not rush the summer away, Dad. Winter'll come before we know it."

Frankie leaned back in his armchair and closed his eyes.

"Tired, Dad?"

"No, love. I was just thinking of your mother. She's been dead—what, twenty-one years now, come April? Sometimes it feels like just yesterday that she was with us, eh?"

Maisie fidgeted. If it was Time's task to diminish the yearning for one who has passed, then Time had done a poor job, for Maisie could still see the ache of loneliness for his wife's company reflected in her father's eyes. It was a sadness that caused her to think of

Simon again, though she had been determined to push all thoughts of him to the back of her mind until she visited the hospital in Richmond, a journey she expected to make on Sunday. A brief sojourn away from Kent in the midst of her work would also allow her to reflect upon her findings thus far in what she had come to think of as the Compton case, an investigation that now extended beyond the brief given her by James Compton. During the drive she would also be able to consider evidence regarding the recent burglary at the Sandermere estate.

"Working hard, love? Got much coming in?" Frankie was sometimes uneasy when it came to sparking conversation with his daughter. He was never sure whether such a question might not be prying, or whether she could tell him what she was doing anyway. Sometimes he thought that everyone would have been better off altogether if she'd married and settled down or taken up an ordinary position, something he understood. But on the other hand, he loved Maisie for her individuality and was fiercely proud of her accomplishments.

"It was a bit touch and go over the summer, Dad, but now there's work coming in at a more respectable clip. I'm working for James Compton, looking into matters for him over in Heronsdene. And a couple of other jobs have come in, which will keep us busy for a while."

"Nothing dangerous, I hope."

Maisie laughed. "No, in fact they're all more than

safe, so please don't worry." She paused, then added, "I have to say, though, Heronsdene's a funny place. I have a sense that all is not as it should be in the village."

"Can't say as I've ever really been there, not to stop. No reason to go unless you know folk or you're passing through, I'd say. It's not like you'd go there to do a bit of shopping."

"That's what I thought. Ever heard of this man Sandermere?"

Frankie shook his head. "Not really. I mean, I know he hunts, because I've heard talk about him, and I remember hearing there's folk who think the estate is going to rack and ruin since he inherited. Had some fancy ideas and spent money on expensive machinery that wasn't needed at the brickworks and got on the wrong side of a couple of big customers—your big building firms. Not a businessman like they said his brother was, even as a young man."

Maisie sighed and was about to ask Frankie about the horses in his care when he began speaking again.

"Of course, they had it rough in the war, a bit of a close shave, over in the village."

"What do you mean?"

"Well, you wouldn't've known about it, being as you were over in France, but there was a Zeppelin raid—I reckon the old Boche come over too low on their way to London and thought they'd have a bit of target practice. Anyway, they dropped a couple of bombs—three people killed, far as I know. You never heard much about it, though, not once it was done. Just that it'd happened, and then they just got on with it. I remember thinking it was a bit odd that there wasn't more said at the time—you know how any news is big news in these villages—but I s'pose that was all they could do, really. Just get on with it." Frankie shook his head. "First of all they thought the brickworks was the target—looks a bit like it could be some other sort of factory from the outside—but then, as I said, you didn't hear much more about it."

"When did it happen?"

Frankie shook his head. "Can't say as I remember, rightly—though I think it was during the 'opping season, so probably September 1916." He looked up and nodded. "Yes, it must've been about then, because there was one shot down over London just a week or two before that—you could see the fire for miles and miles—and this wasn't so big, not by comparison."

"I'm going to Maidstone tomorrow, so I'll see what I can find out."

Frankie nodded, and there was silence between them for a few moments.

"Dad, I've been thinking about Nana."

"Your mother's mother? Once seen, never forgotten, old Bekka."

"Didn't you like her? I've only a few memories of her, but they've stuck in my mind."

"She scared the daylights out of me when I first met 'er." He smiled and appeared to look into the distance, as if in squinting down Time's shadowy tunnel he could pluck out memories. "But she loved your granddad, and he liked me, so we were alright, your mother and me, when it came to getting permission to be wed." He laughed. "There she would be, hands on her hips, complaining about this or that, and your granddad would just grin, with a twinkle in his eye, and let her get on with it. Roma, she was, of the water gypsies. She loved your mother, and you were her favorite—even called you Little Bekka when you were a nipper, or Boosul, or one of them names."

"Do you think she missed her people—you know, when she married Granddad?"

"Your mother would've been the one to answer that question, but I remember Granddad saying once that when the water gypsies came through the lock her eyes'd light up and she'd often take a ride with them to the next lock; she'd trail the horse on the towpath behind the barge horse and ride him back home again."

"Did they ever have people turn on them, because of her blood?"

"Oh, yes, according to your mother they did, though Bekka stopped wearing the old gypsy clobber and dressed more like one of us, if you know what I mean. She wouldn't let go of them earrings, though. And your mother said that, when she was a girl, your gran would keep an eye on her all the time, in case she was set upon for her looks. Your mother did that for you, when you first went to school, on account of your hair and the way you might have been seen, but she made sure you spoke proper—she knew how a lady should speak. Mind you, it's a wonder you weren't tormented for that."

"I know, Dad. But I also knew how to use the right tone and turn of phrase at the right time. Mum might have been disappointed, had she heard me at school." Maisie paused. "Did Nana die of old age?"

Frankie shook his head. "No. I mean, she was getting on, but not as old as your granddad. When he went, it was as if there wasn't anything to live for, so she just let go and died. And she was brokenhearted about your mother." He turned to Maisie. "Your mother was poorly then. Old Bekka said she'd seen it coming, that's why she didn't want us to be wed at first. She reckoned it was all her fault, having a child up in the Smoke—as you know, when your granddad was a lighterman they lived in Rotherhithe, before she had her way and he got the job as a lock keeper and they went to live out in the country. She wanted to take your mother back to live with them when you were just a nipper, so she could be near the water and out in the fresh air, but your mother wouldn't move. She took it all on herself, did Bekka, saying it was down to her your mother was ill and still so young. Of course, she didn't say it in front of your mother, but she knew, I swear she knew, that her daughter was dying, even before the doctors said she was."

Maisie's eyes filled with tears, as thoughts of Simon—banished to the back of her mind following the difficult conversation with Priscilla—claimed her once again.

"What's up, love? What's pulling at you?"

Maisie bit her lip, then left her chair to kneel at her father's feet. "Simon's dying, Dad."

Frankie enveloped her in his arms as if she were still a child.

FATHER AND DAUGHTER spoke long into the night, first of Simon, whose demise had been expected years before, in the weeks following his wounding in France. But with the passage of time, his half-life, an existence that saw him lingering between this world and the next, became something to which both his mother and Maisie had become accustomed. Then Frankie asked Maisie if she intended to see Maurice, who was at home in the Dower House at Chelstone Manor. In response, Maisie shook her head, and Frankie chose to let the matter rest, for now.

AT BREAKFAST, FRANKIE broached the subject again, after sliding an egg, two rashers of bacon, and a slice of fried bread onto Maisie's plate, straight from the pan. He served himself, then sat down at the heavy wooden table across from Maisie, as she poured tea for them both.

"I reckon Dr. Blanche would like a visit from you before you leave." He did not look up but cut into his bread and dipped it into a fresh golden-yolked fried egg.

"I'm busy—short on time, Dad."

Frankie set his knife and fork on the plate in front of him. "Maisie, I'll speak plain. You can be a stubborn one when you like, and—I'll give you this—you know your mind and you're usually right. But I don't know about this business with Dr. Blanche."

"Dad—"

Frankie raised a hand. "Hear me out, love. Hear me out." He paused while Maisie fidgeted, cutting into her bacon, then leaving it on her plate as she settled back to listen. Frankie continued. "When you first started lessons with Dr. Blanche, all them years ago when you were in service, I've got to admit I wasn't at all taken with it. I was grateful to 'im and Lady Rowan for giving you the opportunity, but I—"

He paused. A man of few words, Maisie's father was unused to expressing himself with such candor.

"I was a bit put out, to tell you the truth. I wondered if that man wasn't more of a father to you than me, what with all his education. But now I've come to know 'im, since I came down to work at Chelstone. And after my accident, when he made sure I was well looked after, I saw that what he had was respect for you, for what you've done, how far you've come. I don't know what this argument is all about, but though I don't have your learning under my belt, I'm not silly and I can work a thing or two out. All I can say is, if Dr. Blanche kept something from you, it wasn't out of not trustin' you. No, it was for reasons of protectin' you, right or wrong." He lifted up his knife and fork again. "And sometimes you've just got to say *fain-ites*—you've got to call a truce, with yourself as much as anyone else, and then get on with bein' mates again."

Maisie sighed and poked at her breakfast. "I—" she began, but realized that she was about to justify her actions, or lack thereof, again, and simply added, "Nothing. Let's eat our breakfast before it gets cold."

"Right you are. I just wanted to say my piece."

"And I'm glad you did." She looked up at her father, changing the subject. "I think I'll try to stay in Heronsdene tonight, if I can get lodgings at the inn. I want to spend a bit of time closer to my work for a couple of days, but I'll be back again on Friday night."

Frankie nodded and stood up, taking his plate to the sink, where he set it in a bowl of water. He washed his hands, then came to Maisie and kissed the top of her head. "I'll be off to the stables now." He turned to take his jacket from a hook behind the door. "Mind how you drive, round these little lanes. Not like some of them new big roads you've got used to."

"Alright, Dad."

MAISIE DID NOT leave the table for some time. Finally, she sighed and set about tidying the kitchen before she gathered her belongings ready to set off. It was not yet seven o'clock, so she pulled on a pair of Wellington boots and stepped out the back door and into the garden. Long and narrow, the garden was almost entirely given over to vegetables, yet roses grew along the fence on all three sides. The cultivation of roses was an interest Frankie and Maurice Blanche shared, so the men had become friends of a kind across the fence that divided their respective homes, though the Dower House, situated on an incline close to the boundary of Chelstone Manor, was decidedly more grand than the humble Groom's Cottage it looked down upon.

Maisie went straight to the end of the garden, the heavy dew wet across her boots, and looked out at the fields and woodland beyond. She was eternally glad that her father had come to live at Chelstone in 1914 and would be allowed to remain in his cottage until the end of his days. She shuddered to think of such an event, for he was her only family, and he was past seventy.

As she turned to leave, she stopped to look at the Dower House, where she could just about see the roofline and, to the fore, the glass-paned conservatory where Maurice would be taking breakfast, dipping freshly baked bread—his one indulgence—into the strong French coffee he favored. And as she stood there, remembering times past, when they would speak together of a case in hushed tones, she saw movement just beyond the windows of the conservatory. Maurice Blanche was watching her, his newspaper under one arm. He raised a hand to shield his eyes from the searing early morning sunlight that bathed the room, then waved, and after a lapse of some seconds Maisie waved in return. She knew he waited for her to unlatch the gate and walk along the path, across the lawn, and through the rose garden up to the conservatory. He may have already asked for an extra cup and saucer to be brought, just in case she came to join him. But she wouldn't. Not today. She wasn't ready for fain-ites yet.

FIVE

Maisie stopped on the outskirts of Maidstone as soon as she saw a red telephone kiosk alongside a row of shops. The directory inquiries operator found the firm of White, Bertrand and Spelton without much ado, giving Maisie their address as well as a telephone number, though Maisie declined to be connected.

Parking her motor close to the old Corn Exchange, Maisie soon found the solicitors' offices on the High Street. She did not have an appointment and did not want to attempt to make one at short notice, either—such a move would have meant immediate refusal, she suspected. However, though she did not secure an audience with Mr. Spelton, who had been assigned to represent the two boys from Shoreditch, she was able to speak with his clerk, who informed her that the young men were being held on remand at a reformatory school for juvenile criminals and would stand trial for breaking and entering, malicious damage, and theft. With luck, they would serve a sentence of between three to six months, seeing as this was a first offense, though the victim was strongly protesting such a short incarceration. The clerk noted that it was lucky they were not yet of an age—sixteen—where they would be sent to borstal. "Then they'd know all about it," he commented.

Maisie asked a few more questions, then left. As far as she understood, at a reformatory school the boys would not be subject to either a birching if they stepped out of line or a leather across the palm, though the punishment would not be a pleasant experience either. But no matter how seemingly lenient the sentence, her task was to prevent its being passed down.

Turning into Week Street, Maisie's next stop was the offices of the local newspaper, which brought word of events in Kent, whether significant or trivial, to the broad population of the county. A woman receptionist proved helpful, and when Maisie asked if she could speak to one of the reporters who had been at the newspaper for, say, fifteen years or so, she was told that they rarely changed staff, so that would be anyone.

"I reckon the best thing, miss, is for you to speak to Beattie. She's been here since the war and knows what's gone on all over Kent." She paused. "I'd say to speak to one of the men, but they're all over at the King's Arms at the moment."

Maisie leafed through a newspaper while she waited for the reporter to come to the receptionist's desk. She noticed that the burglary at the Sandermere estate had warranted several column inches, including a searing comment from Alfred Sandermere: "Since the war we seem to have been overrun with young ruffians, and they need to be taught a lesson! As if the gypsies aren't enough for us to put up with!" There was another journalistic observation and then a final quote from Sandermere: "I'll see that they are punished to the full extent of the law. Let this be a lesson to others bent on delinquency!"

"Miss Dobbs?"

Maisie turned to see a woman of average height standing before her, wearing a sensible two-piece costume of pale gray lightweight wool with a white blouse underneath. The gored skirt had fashionable kick pleats, and her black shoes demonstrated a choice based both on comfort and demand—she suspected the woman was on her feet for much of the day. Indeed, her clothing suggested nothing threatening and was simple in such a way as to extinguish any immediate rise to opinion on the part of someone she might wish to interview.

"Yes, indeed. Thank you for seeing me, Miss—"

"Just call me Beattie. My name is Beatrice Drummond and my middle name is Theresa. As much as I would have liked to be called Tricia for short instead of Beattie, the middle initial ensured my fate. Call me Beattie." She looked up at a wooden clock that would seem more at home in a Victorian school than a newspaper office. "Would you like to step across the road for a cup of coffee? I can spare about fifteen minutes—then I have to dash."

"Thank you for accommodating me, though I must confess at the outset that I do not have a news tip for you."

Beattie grinned. "Oh, I am sure you do, Miss Dobbs. I am quite familiar with *your* work."

Maisie maintained her smile, though the news was unwelcome. She had seldom been mentioned in newspapers and did not care for such recognition, despite the flurry of business that came in the wake of the spotlight's glare. She would have to be doubly careful when questioning the reporter.

Open casement windows at the front of the coffee shop ensured a cool breeze to temper what promised to be a warm Indian summer day. Maisie ordered two coffees, along with two fresh Eccles cakes, and joined Beattie by the window, where she had already claimed a seat.

"I'm glad to see you haven't brought your official notepad." Maisie was frank, though she couched the comment lightly, as she rested the corner of the tray on the table and placed the coffee and cakes at the already-set places.

Beattie reached for a cup of coffee and an Eccles cake.

"May I ask, before anything else, how you came to be a reporter, Beattie?"

Beattie smiled as she bit off a mouthful of the currant-filled pastry and wiped a crumb from the side of her mouth with her hand. Holding up one finger while she chewed, she swallowed. "I am absolutely starving.

84

Not taken a moment for a cuppa all morning." She reached for her coffee, sipped, and placed the cup back on its saucer. "I came to work at the newspaper in 1916—sixteen years old at the time. Most of the lads in the printing room had enlisted and they had to keep the presses running, so they took on women to do the job. Of course, the print room was run by the older men who were too long in the tooth to wield a rifle, and after a while I ended up as a compositor. I'd always loved books and writing, so I kept asking if I could work in the newsroom, which of course they laughed at, every single time. I even began looking for news, coming in with stories for them to print, but the editor just looked me in the eye and threw my words in the bin."

"How dreadful."

"Ah. I was not to be deterred. I applied for a copy-editing assistant's job when it came along, and again, due to staff shortages, got the position. But still they threw my news stories in the bin. Finally, one day when all the reporters were out—and a right old lot they are, they'll be over in the pub until after closing today, I wouldn't mind betting—I happened to find out about a young woman who had taken her life when she was told her husband had been killed at Passchendaele. I got the whole story in the bag before anyone even knew it had happened—and as you might imagine, this was when it wasn't considered so very bad if you wrote something less than laudatory about the war. But I didn't spend time on the actual war, just the man who had died and his very young wife."

"So you got your break."

"In a manner of speaking. They decided I was good at 'people' stories, which meant I was in grave danger of being relegated to covering flower shows and jam-making contests, to say nothing of Pancake Day races, but I sidestepped a lot of that sort of thing and sniffed out meatier leads. When one of the old boys turns in a big story, they print his name, but they'll only print my initials: B. T. Drummond. They haven't quite grasped that the world has changed in the last ten years. No one cares if it's a man or woman writing the news, just so long as it's written."

"I know what you mean."

"I'm sure you do." Beattie squinted at Maisie through a wisp of steam curling up from the still-hot coffee. "Now then, you didn't come to Maidstone to hear my life story, did you? What can I do for you, Miss Dobbs?" She reached for the remains of her Eccles cake without taking her eyes off the investigator.

"I'm interested in the village of Heronsdene. You've worked at the newspaper since the war, and it sounds as if you've kept your finger on the pulse of the county, so to speak. I know you can't be everywhere, but I wondered if you've any"—Maisie considered her words with care—"if you've any thoughts about the village, any stories or leads that have come your way regarding events there, since about, say, 1916?"

Beattie licked her forefinger and tapped at the

remaining crumbs on her plate, then brushed her tongue across her crumb-encrusted finger again before responding to Maisie's question. "Are you working on a case?"

"In confidence, until I say otherwise?"

Beattie tapped again at her now-clean plate. "As long as I get first dibs on the story—if it's a big one—before anyone else pips me to the post."

"My, my, you're anxious to move up."

"Anxious to move *out,* Miss Dobbs. I want to work on one of the London rags, and I need a big story to open the door. Will I get word from you so I can scoop?"

Maisie nodded. "I'm not sure it will turn out to be anything of note, Beattie, but I assure you that whatever happens I will let you know in plenty of time."

Beattie held out her hand, and the women shook on their agreement. "How can I help?"

"First of all, is it my imagination or is there something *amiss* about Heronsdene?"

The reporter blew out her cheeks. "Straight to the bull's-eye with question one." She sat up straight. "I would say that you've hit the nail on the head there. I do—despite my better judgment—report on local fairs and shindigs, so I know most of the villages across the Weald of Kent, and I would agree with you: There's a different . . . a different . . ."

"Mood?"

"Yes, there's a different *mood* in Heronsdene. Now, I can't speak of what it was like before—I'm Kent born, by the way, in Headcorn—and I can't think of any reason for it, but outsiders say the village hasn't been the same since 1916."

"The Zeppelin raid?"

"Ah, you have another source."

"My father."

"That's alright then." Beattie finished her coffee with one gulp. "Yes, if anything, the raid is the event that seems to have changed the people there, one way or another. I mean, other villages, other towns, had their cross to bear—all the boys lost on one day, families left without a breadwinner—but Heronsdene is different. If that village were a human being, you'd tell it to get on with it, snap out of the malaise. When I go there to report on the annual fete, I feel like an interrogator simply for asking who made the Victoria Sponge at the end of the cake-baking competition table."

"Any idea why they have such a lack of trust?"

She looked thoughtful, for a moment gazing out of the window, watching passersby as if she were mem-orizing every detail of the scene. "Yes, it's a lack of trust." She turned back to Maisie. "It could be the petty crime that's been going on there for some years now—probably ten years. And they've got a local landowner who thinks he's the squire of all he sur-veys, but he's a dreadful businessman—not good news at all when you think of how the village depends on the brickworks. I'm waiting in the wings to report on his financial ruin, to tell you the truth."

"I know about the petty crime. But what about Sandermere? How much does he have to do with the village?"

"Ah—good question, but a better one would be: 'How much does he *want* to do with the village?' "

"What do you mean?"

"Being the landowner, he holds enormous power on a local level, despite what I said earlier. But the people really can't stand him, just cannot abide him, and yet they're careful not to do anything that might rub him up the wrong way. His ownership of the brickworks doesn't explain the acquiescence, to be perfectly honest with you. Frankly, we all gave up trying to get a story about the crime there—especially the fires—because the villagers don't report them to the police. Of course, Sandermere is always calling the police for this or that at the mansion, which doesn't go down well with the Tunbridge Wells constabulary, but he's the only one. You get the impression that the locals would prefer it if he showed half their stoicism when it comes to these acts of delinquency."

"You can't ignore crime, though."

"They do, most of the time. Mind you, we've got a nice little story with those two London boys. The readers love that sort of thing, mainly because in every village they think the Londoners are better off up there in London—though they don't mind the custom in the shops and the pubs. And at least they're not gypsies. Nobody wants the gypsies, so any story where a pikey gets pulled by the boys in blue is worth a string or two."

Maisie looked at her watch, as did the reporter. "One more question for you, Beattie. Do you know who was killed when the Zeppelin bombed Heronsdene?"

The woman squinted, as if looking at newspaper columns stretching back years. "It was a shopkeeper, if I'm not mistaken. I can check on the details for you."

Maisie stood up. "Don't worry, I can look into it myself."

Beattie laughed. "Yes, I am sure you can." They walked out into the sunshine. "But if you're at the inn, talk to Fred Yeoman, the landlord. Go easy with him, perhaps buy him a half of light and bitter, and he may just remember a thing or two."

"Right you are. Thank you, Beattie."

"Remember—I've got the scoop, alright?" She waved and turned, walking with an assured purpose back to her office. As she watched, Maisie saw the reporter take a small notebook from her pocket and begin to make notes. She was not concerned, though, as she made her way back to the MG, for she was sure that B. T. Drummond would not have gained the confidence of ordinary people across the county, or maintained her place on the newspaper's roster of reporters, without some level of honesty, some degree of trustworthiness.

MAISIE REACHED HERONSDENE just after lunch, idling the MG as she drove through the village, where she parked opposite the inn. Last orders had not been called, though she guessed the inn would be open all day for residents to come and go, even if drinks were not served.

Opening the ancient oak door and dipping her head to avoid the low beam, Maisie entered where a sign read RESIDENTS, which led into a small, comfortable sitting room where an extension of the main bar allowed the landlord to respond to calls from both regular patrons and visiting guests alike. Leaning across the wooden counter, Maisie saw the landlord serving pints in the noisy public bar, where a group of men were playing darts. The air was thick with smoke, filtering into the saloon bar, situated between the residents' sitting room and the public bar. The womenfolk who accompanied men to the inn would usually sit in the saloon bar. A sign behind the bar mirrored one that Maisie noticed outside: NO GYPSIES.

"Excuse me." Maisie waved to the landlord, who nodded and smiled, to let her know that he had seen her waiting.

"Sorry to keep you . . . miss." He wiped his hands on a towel and glanced at her ring finger. "They're all trying to get a round in before last orders. Can I help you?"

"I'm touring the area and wondered if you might have a vacancy for two nights."

He reached under the counter and took out a ledger. "Two guest rooms still vacant—not that we have that many, mind, just the four."

"I'll take one, if I may."

"Right you are." He reached for the pencil balanced behind his ear. "Lovely time of year to come down to Kent. From London, are you?"

"Yes, though I know the county well."

"Just sign here, miss, and put in your details." He continued speaking as she wrote. "See a lot of young women these days, touring like yourself. Specially since the government brought out them billboards telling everyone to get out into the fresh air and hike for health! Don't see so many traveling alone, though."

Maisie was not fond of using her past to gain an ally, but sometimes she found it was a valuable tool. "After I was in France, during the war, I thought that if I could face that trial I was up for anything in my own country. And what could there possibly be to cause me fear or harm in your delightful village?"

The innkeeper nodded, looking at Maisie with a regard he had not exhibited before. "Nurse, were you?"

"Yes, I was."

"Fred Yeoman, at your service." He reached behind the bar for a key, which he dangled in front of him as he looked down at the register. "Best room in the house. Follow me please, Miss Dobbs." Yeoman lifted the counter's wooden flap, stepped through to the sitting room, and pointed toward another small door between the inglenook fireplace and the diamond-paned windows. He unlatched the door to reveal a narrow staircase snaking toward a landing lit by a shaft of light from a dormer window set into the roof.

Maisie followed and was shown into a room with windows looking out to the back of the inn.

"The bed's soft but comfortable. You'll find it might be noisy of an evening—the hoppers can get a bit rowdy at the end of the day—but it's quiet by eleven. We're not what you'd call a drinking pub, if you know what I mean, so we don't attract the Londoners anyway." He rested his hand on the door handle. "My wife serves a hot breakfast in the residents' sitting room at eight, and if you want a supper put out for you, just let us know. She'll pack up some sandwiches as well, if you want."

"Thank you, Mr. Yeoman. I'll be having a cooked tea later on, so I doubt I'll be hungry. This is a lovely room."

"My wife made the curtains and counterpane." He surveyed the room with pride. "Now then, the WC is along the landing, to the right, so there's no going out-side to an earth closet in the middle of the night. Will you need towels?"

"I've brought my own, thank you, Mr. Yeoman."

He passed the key to her. "Fred. You can call me Fred, miss."

"Thank you, Fred." Maisie smiled as Yeoman left the room, closing the door with barely a sound.

The room was neither small nor spacious, and the rug-covered wooden floorboards creaked under her footfall as she stepped toward the window. From the outside, she had dated the inn at around 1350, of typical medieval hall-house construction. The upper floors would originally have been simply a galleried landing where people slept; she suspected the division into rooms probably took place in the seventeenth century, with water closets and gaslights being added during Edward VII's reign. Electricity would likely be next, and she thought Fred Yeoman might look to adding a bathroom for guests, so they weren't completely dependent on a single washbasin in the room for their personal hygiene.

The window provided a perfect vista across the farmlands beyond, and in the distance Maisie could see the roofline of the Georgian manor house at the center of the Sandermere estate. If she craned her neck, she could also view the hop-gardens and even the train chugging toward Paddock Wood. The room, she thought, would be perfect for a couple of nights. She locked the door behind her as she left, slipping the key into her jacket pocket. Waving to Yeoman as she departed the inn, she decided to walk along the High Street to get her bearings.

To the right, as she walked, there was just one shop, a general store selling all manner of goods, from groceries to oil for lamps, from kitchen cutlery to baby clothes. A few houses followed, then a common where, she thought, cricket would be played in summer and the local fete set up on a sun-filled June day. She imagined Beattie Drummond walking back and forth, trying to get even the most mundane story from the locals, to no avail. Considering the villagers, she looked about her and realized that few people were out and about on such a fine afternoon. Early closing was yesterday, so perhaps the shopkeepers had only just opened again following their midday meal.

THE VILLAGE SCHOOL was set at the far end of the common, and the muffled but high-pitched singing of a folk song signaled a music lesson in progress. Beyond the common, farther down the street, an old outbuilding with smoke belching from the chimney suggested a blacksmith at work, and as she walked closer she saw two draft horses waiting to be shod, flicking flies from their hefty rumps with their long tails or occasionally turning to nip an insect from their flanks. She watched for a while, then walked on. A strip of fallow land came next, with neither house nor sign of recent harvest, and there was no indication that it was used for grazing, which she thought strange, for country folk are not given to wasting land.

Maisie retraced her steps and reached the smithy just as the farrier came out to collect one of the drafts, reaching up and taking it by the halter.

"Excuse me," Maisie called, taking advantage of the farrier's being outside, away from the clanking bellows.

The man cupped his ear with his free hand as he looked around the horse to see who had spoken.

"Over here." She walked toward him, gentling the horse with a hand to his neck as she approached. "Sorry to bother you while you're working."

"What can I do for you?" The man was not curt, but neither was he making an effort to be courteous.

"I'm visiting Heronsdene and wondered about the land next door to you. Does anyone own it?"

"Me. And I ain't selling."

"Oh, that's alright. I was just curious, wondering why it wasn't used."

The man shook his head and turned toward the blackened inner sanctum of his smithy. "Not used since the war, since the Hun bombed out my barn. Lucky to save my business, I was, but everyone pulled together, everyone helped."

"I'm terribly sorry, that must have been dreadful. Will you build another barn?"

"When I get the money, per'aps I will. Until then, I've left it fallow. Now then, miss, I've got to get on." And with that he turned away from her, in such a way that, had she not stepped sideways with speed, the horse might have caught her foot with his own.

Maisie stood for a moment or two, watching the farrier as he maneuvered the horse into stocks and tied the lead rein to a ring on the wall. Though the horse turned his great head to look at her, the man did not speak again or cast his eyes in her direction. She crossed the road and went back through the village, passing her motor car and the inn as she walked in the direction of the church.

Three people were apparently killed in Heronsdene, but the smithy had not even mentioned the tragedy when he spoke of the Zeppelin. She considered this as she looked first at the Norman church, then at the ancient lych-gate and the graves beyond. She tried to ignore the war memorial close by but thought the people killed in the bombing might be listed among those from the village who were lost in the years 1914–1918. Maisie sighed and walked over to the memorial. She barely cast her eyes over the list of names, not wanting to inspire memories that came on with the same ferocity as a searing headache might be visited upon her by a too-bright light or a piercing sound. There was no mention of the three who perished here.

Maisie looked around and once more took account of the waste ground she had seen when she first arrived. She crossed the road to better look at the rectangular lot, set apart from other houses in the village, and stood for a while at the edge of the land, for she had realized she was reluctant to step forward onto the ground and was aware of a definite perimeter, even though it was overgrown and no margins of any building that might have been there remained. She closed her eyes as she felt a sudden shaft of cold air, even in the midst of a sun-filled September day with morning's early chill long banished. It was not a cool breeze borne on the promise of autumn that made her shudder, but a sensation akin to an icy finger laid upon her skin, accompanied by a dark shadow that descended into her waking consciousness. *Oh, my God, what happened here? What terrible thing happened here?* Maisie staggered backward. The horn from a passing motor car blared as she almost tripped into the road, a sound that served to prevent her fall and caused her to stand upright and regain her balance.

This is where they died. Maisie knew in her deepest being that life had been lost in this place, that an act of aggression had touched the very earth across which she cast her gaze. She shivered, surveying the barren ground, a wasteland except for the Michaelmas daisies. It was then she remembered her grandmother again, remembered the gift of a bunch of the bright mauve blooms she'd gathered while walking with her father. "Ah, St. Michael's flowers, brought to me by my boosul little angel herself," said her grandmother. And she cupped Maisie's cheek with her hand, liver-spotted and wrinkled, and bent forward to smell the musty aroma of Michaelmas daisies, flowers that always bloomed in time for the old festival of St. Michael, the warrior saint of all angels.

MAISIE TURNED TOWARD the church, the cold air diminishing as she made her way along the cobbled path to the entrance. It took both hands to wield the latch and gain entrance, and at once she felt at ease, comforted by the smells of ancient flagstones underfoot, of fresh blooms arranged by the village womenfolk, of damp foxed prayer books and worn woolen knee cushions. But she came not into the church seeking the tranquility offered amid the prayers of ages. She was looking for some sort of marker, some commemoration of the three who were lost when the Zeppelin released its deathly cargo. Names of villagers from earliest times were immortalized on the walls of the church, plaques placed following a timely donation by heirs centuries ago. But there was nothing, no honoring of the dead of a most terrible disaster. She emerged into the day once again, then began walking around the churchyard. Gravestones giving up the weight of years leaned toward one another, moss- and lichen-covered so that names could barely be read. A small contingent of stones in one far corner were those of prisoners of war from Napoleon's time, given their due and buried with the blessing of God upon them.

Then she found a trio of small stones together under a yew tree, set apart from the rest. The stones were of more recent design and plain in appearance, the names not heralded with curls and loops. Three names, of the same family: Jacob Martin, Bettin Martin, Anna Martin. The date was half buried in weeds but indicated the three had met their fate in September 1916. An inscription followed:

Forgive them; for they know not what they do.

—Luke 23:34

SIX

The hop-pickers had moved on since Maisie last saw Billy and his family. Now the hop-garden where they had previously been picking was barren, a field of rusty spent bines and parched khaki soil. Holding her hand to her forehead to shield her eyes, Maisie squinted across the heat-drenched acres of clay to the hop-gardens beyond and located the pickers moving along abundant rows of hops. Making her way closer, she could see the Londoners at the top of the garden, separated from the gypsies at the bottom.

Once again she tramped along in the midst of a flurry of activity until she came to Billy and his family, snatching hops from bines freshly tugged down to lie across the bin. They were working silently, though Billy looked up and smiled at her approach.

"Miss, 'ow are you, then? Any luck findin' out about George's boys?"

Maisie noticed that Doreen had turned away from Billy, as he began to speak, and had her back to him now. She had only issued a brief smile upon greeting Maisie, yet her demeanor did not suggest she thought ill of her husband's employer, rather that she was more than a little annoyed with her spouse.

"They're being held on remand, currently at the boys' reformatory school outside Maidstone. They will be charged with the theft of valuables from the

Sandermere estate, malicious damage, and breaking and entering. At the moment, the fact that they have no 'previous' will stand them in good stead—if you can call it that—and they will serve, if found guilty, only three to six months."

Billy frowned and threw down the hop-bine that he'd been picking. "But I thought you could get them out!"

"Not so fast, Billy." She held up her hand. "They stand accused of a crime for which there is evidence of their guilt, and though we believe there is cause for doubt, we have to prove them innocent, which takes time. I should add that they seem well represented, as far as it goes. We must, however, do all we can to locate the stolen goods and find out who might have conducted the burglary in the first place."

Maisie looked at Doreen Beale, who was biting her bottom lip as she picked hops into the bin with short, sharp movements, ignoring both her sons, who were much too quiet, and her mother-in-law, with whom she had always enjoyed a warm companionship. It was clear that the couple had exchanged harsh words, though the discord might be the result of a minor squabble that had escalated in tone or some act or retort on behalf of one that was seen as more than a minor infraction by the other.

"Billy, I'd like to talk to the boys' father again and, if your family can spare you, I'd like you to come." Maisie smiled at Doreen, who looked back at Billy and nodded.

"*He* can do as he likes," said Doreen, a bladelike edge to her reply.

Billy ignored the comment, passed his half-picked hop-bine to his sons, and motioned for Maisie to follow him. "Over 'ere, Miss. George is this way."

They had walked only a few yards when Maisie whispered to her assistant, "Look, Billy, I know it's none of my business, really, but may I ask—is Doreen upset about something?"

They passed the last cadre of pickers and walked on through untouched hop-bines draped like rich green curtains across the rows. Though no one could hear them, Billy kept his voice low. "I had to put me foot down, Miss. You know, about Doreen talkin' to them gyppos."

Maisie frowned, and though she understood the folly of coming between man and wife, she could hear her annoyance as she replied, "What did you do that for?"

Billy stopped and looked at her. "Not you too? What with me mum, and now you." He plucked a single hop from an overhanging bine and crushed it between his fingers. "I was alright, like, when it came to Doreen stoppin' to 'ave a chat with that woman, Paishey Webb, what with 'er 'avin' the little girl. I was worried, mind, because I could see Doreen was sort of *making* their paths cross—she was always there when the woman went over to the tap or back up the road. And you never know when someone might turn, might reckon there's somethin' wrong with my

Doreen." He shook his head. "I know what it means to 'er, bein' able to hold the litt'lun every now and again, but you never know what people might think."

"You're worried about other people?"

"Well, you've got to be, 'aven't you? It's all very well sayin' what others think ain't important, but you've got to get along, got to live with people. Them gyppos will be gone in a few weeks, off back to Wimbledon Common or wherever it is they go when there's no more work down 'ere. But it turns out I *know* most of the people pickin' around us after all, grew up with 'em; they come from round our way. And what with this business with George's boys, and 'im reckonin' it was really the gypsies—nah, ain't worth it, puttin' up with the talk." He barely paused to take breath. "And what else you've got to consider is that them old pikeys might take a funny turn to it, you know, 'er stoppin' to look at one of their babies. You never know what they might do to Doreen."

Maisie sighed. "I do wish you wouldn't call them gyppos and pikeys. They're people, you know. They might look a bit different, dress a bit different, and sound nothing like you or I, but they've got their own codes of behavior, and it may interest you to know that by their standards *we* do things that are considered beyond the pale."

"I don't know about that, Miss."

They had stopped walking by now and were conducting their conversation in the middle of the hop-garden.

"Well, I do. Take that enamel bowl in your hut. Use it for water to wash the boys in the evening, do you?"

"Yes, but—"

"And then you rinse it out and fill it with water to clean the plates after you've eaten?"

"Yes, but—"

"And I bet you fill that bowl again when there's a bit of laundry to be done."

"What're you gettin' at, Miss?"

"Gypsy folk think that's disgusting beyond measure. They have a different bowl for each task, and they never mix them up. You'd never see a gypsy filling a bowl to have a shave and then use it later to wash some clothes."

Billy looked at his feet. "That's all very well, but there's more."

"Yes?"

"Doreen's 'eard about that woman, the one they call Aunt Beulah. Says she wants to go to 'ave her fortune told, that the woman knows all about what's going to 'appen—you know, in the future."

"I see." Maisie was calm now. "Yes, I see what you mean."

"It can only end in tears, Miss. I don't reckon that woman can see any farther than you or me, and I don't want Doreen goin' there for false hopes, wantin' to know if we'll 'ave another little girl, wantin' to know if we'll ever leave for Canada, wantin' to know if we'll ever . . . get over it."

"Doreen is grieving, Billy. Your Lizzie hasn't even

been gone a year, and both of you have gone through hell. She's looking for a light at the end of her tunnel, and the other women's stories have given her a glimmer of hope, the possibility that there might be good news on the horizon."

"I know that, Miss, but I don't want 'er led up the garden path, neither." He shoved his hands in his pockets and kicked at a clod of earth. "What makes people think that gypsies can tell the future anyway? What do they know that we don't?"

Maisie held out her hand to indicate that they should walk on. "I'm not sure they do know more than anyone else, though here's the difference—they spend a lot of time out here in the country. Their ways are simpler. I know this might sound fey, but they are more inclined to pay attention to the thoughts and feelings that herald an event than we are—even if they don't know they're doing it. You could say they use that particular muscle a bit more than we might. That trust in what they perceive to be a mark of what is to come means they are more inclined to intuit events than you or I."

Billy shrugged. "Well, more than me, anyway. You're more like them, in that way, if you don't mind me sayin' so." He paused. "D'you reckon I should give Doreen me blessing, let 'er go?"

"That's not for me to say, Billy." She paused, thoughtful. "However, I do have two observations. First, you and Doreen have gone through too much for this discord to drive a wedge between you. And second, perhaps it would be a good idea for you to have a chat together, about whether you really want to know what might happen in the future." Maisie waved to George in the distance, who had seen them walking in his direction; then she turned to Billy. "How much better it would be for you both, to sit down and talk about what you would like to see happen in your family and then go about discovering what might be done to point your ship in that direction, if you know what I mean."

"All very well, if you've got the money."

"It doesn't take money to use imagination, Billy."

"It does if you want to go to Canada."

GEORGE WAS VISIBLY relieved when Maisie informed him that his sons were not being held at His Majesty's pleasure in Maidstone Prison, though the thought of them in a boys' reformatory kept him unsettled.

"So now all we've got to do is prove they didn't do it."

"That's more or less what needs to be done. There must be a cache of stolen goods somewhere—the question is where?" Maisie turned to Billy. "Normally, I would refrain from the widespread search of a property—it can be time-consuming at a point when manpower might be better utilized elsewhere. However, in this case I think it's better than nothing. Billy, the boys found the silver close to the chestnut tree where they were collecting conkers. If we make an assumption that whoever made off with the goods leaped over the wall and then dropped the locket and paperweight as he landed and ran, more items might have been lost or a trail might still exist."

"I doubt that, Miss."

"Any better ideas?"

Billy shook his head.

"Right, so you and George—not now, when the sun's still high; wait for dusk—map out a trail from the chestnut tree, across the road, and then see if you can get a sense of which way the thief might have run."

"Better than nothin', eh, George?"

George seemed doubtful but nodded accordance. "Can't do any harm."

Maisie checked the watch pinned to her jacket lapel. "I've just enough time to try to see Alfred Sandermere. Then I have an appointment to join a friend for a nice cooked tea." She paused before proffering a word of advice to Billy. "Oh, and when you cross the road, try to suspend what you *think* for a moment and see if you can just go where you *feel* might be the right direction."

"Alright, Miss."

Maisie left the two men, who watched her walk away before speaking.

George frowned toward Billy. "What's she mean, Bill?"

"Nothin'. Come on, let's get back to work for an hour or two."

• • •

MAISIE PROCEEDED OUT onto the farm road, then back toward the MG, parked at the entrance of Dickon's Farm. Starting the motor without delay, she pulled out onto the main thoroughfare in the direction of the Sandermere manor house. She didn't think Billy and George would have any luck today, but there was a lot to be said for keeping people busy when they might otherwise get in the way.

"MISS DOBBS, DELIGHTED to meet you. The solicitors acting for Viscount Compton informed me that you would be visiting, though I thought I might have a little more notice." Alfred Sandermere descended the staircase and held out his hand toward Maisie as he walked across the black-and-white checkered tile hallway. As they stood facing each other, Maisie thought they must look rather like chessmen, each waiting for an opportune move. She was surprised not to be shown into a reception room to meet her host, but it seemed that Sandermere had responded to the news of her presence with speed, coming straight from his study on an upper floor to greet her.

Sandermere was dressed as if he had only just dismounted his horse. He was wearing beige jodhpurs, Viyella shirt, and waistcoat, with a rich tweed hacking jacket and a silk cravat at the neck. His hair had been flattened by a hat, the ridge along his forehead suggesting he wore a flat cap when out riding. His brown leather boots, clearly polished to a shine before the ride, were now dusty—she could not help but feel sorry for the maids who cleaned the house of a man who tramped dirt into the carpets, though such a habit could be attributed to many of his station. She wondered if James Compton was any different.

"I have been in the village for two days and thought I would drop by, on the off chance that you might be able to accommodate a meeting for a few moments. I am most grateful to you for seeing me."

Sandermere looked Maisie up and down, rather as he might judge a hunter. "Let's adjourn to the drawing room." He turned to his butler. "Mason. Tea in the drawing room." The instruction was punctuated with neither *please* nor *thank you.*

Maisie suspected the drawing room was exactly as it had been when Sandermere's parents were still alive and may not have had even a lick of paint since the turn of the century. The room seemed cluttered, with a worn brown leather chesterfield and an assortment of armchairs drawn close to a fireplace, now hidden by a needlepoint screen. Long, musty red-velvet drapes obscured a calm green view from the windows out toward the farms, the woodlands, and, to the right in the distance, the village of Heronsdene. Maisie thought the brickworks was probably not visible from the part of the house it faced but was instead surrounded by trees so the gentry's view would not be sullied by such a thing as a factory.

Sandermere sat down on the chesterfield with something of a sprawl, leaning back into the corner of the seat and putting his boot-clad feet up on the low table upon which the butler would doubtless place a tea tray. He inclined his head and held out his hand toward an armchair with worn covers. Maisie rested her black bag alongside the proffered chair and sat down.

She was about to speak when the butler entered, set a tray to the side of his employer's feet, and poured tea for both Maisie and Sandermere. Maisie made a point of smiling broadly and thanking the butler but, again, Sandermere barely nodded toward him.

"Mr. Sandermere, first of all, I would like to clarify the reason for my visit. I am here at the request of Viscount Compton of the Compton Corporation to conduct certain inquiries that will support the company's purchase of the estate, except, of course, your residence and the immediate gardens and land. I am not here to discuss the division of the land prior to sale or issues such as rights-of-way."

Sandermere raised an eyebrow, sipping his tea with an audible slurp. Maisie bristled but continued. She already felt slighted by his manner and fought the pressure to descend into immediate mistrust.

"I am, however, interested in incidents of small-time crime that seem to have beset the estate, with particular acts of vandalism at the brickworks and in the stables here—I understand you were lucky not to lose your horses." Maisie looked down at papers she had drawn from her black bag. "I take it, though, that you were recompensed by insurances."

"Indeed, Miss Dobbs, without which I would not have been able to bring the brickworks back to full output or provide shelter for my horses."

"And your insurers are Lloyds."

"Yes, that's correct."

"Now I also know something of the unfortunate burglary that took place last week."

"Blasted Londoners! Lord, I know the farmers need them for the hop-picking, but what do you expect when a tribe of ruffians from the East End of London is set loose in the country? I'm amazed I didn't lose more—but at least the two louts who broke in are in custody now."

"Yes, that must be a weight off your mind, Mr. Sandermere." Maisie paused. "Two small items were recovered—the culprits were caught with the goods on them—but I understand a significant haul is still missing."

"Yes, all family heirlooms, not the easy-to-carry trinkets those London boys kept on them. A list has been submitted to the police and also to Lloyds."

"It's unfortunate that such family treasures cannot be replaced by money alone."

"Yes, indeed. I am saddened beyond measure at their loss."

Maisie reached for her tea, which she had set down when the interview began. She sipped; then, continuing to rest the saucer in her hand, she held the cup to her lips but did not drink. When she sipped again, she looked directly at Sandermere. "You do appear to have been victimized. I must ask if you have any idea, any thoughts as to who might have initiated the fires? The theft is more easily explained, as you have said yourself, a couple of London ne'er-do-wells. But what about the fires? There have been a number of fires in Heronsdene over the years. Do you think they are connected?"

"To be frank, I believe each fire in the village has an explanation. Perhaps a saucepan left on a stove for too long, or a chimney fire as a result of an overzealous villager loading up the logs—probably cut from my forests without permission! No, I'd be willing to bet those fires in the village are all coincidence, with nothing to draw them together at all. And the fires here?" Sandermere leaned forward, his eyes narrowing. "To be honest with you, Miss Dobbs, I own everything you see when you stand at that window. In years gone by, my ancestors owned Heronsdene itself—owned every man, woman and child." He leaned back, smiling, though it was not a warm smile of grace and inclusion, but one of arrogance. "Of course, feudalism died centuries ago, but most of the people who live in the village have their roots as intertwined with this house as with their own humble cottage. In fact, with a few exceptions, most of the villagers pay rent to me."

"I see." Maisie put down her cup and brought her attention back to her notes, then to Sandermere. "So what you are saying is that the fires on the estate are really the result of history's follies seeping into the present. Bad blood from the past finding an outlet here, in 1931."

"If you want to put it like that, yes."

"Would you envisage that, should a sale go through, there would be no cause for the new owners to be concerned about continued delinquency?"

"No, no cause whatsoever. Once the act of retribution has had the desired result—for whatever the perceived infraction on the part of some long-lost ancestor—the need for more of the same is negated."

Maisie pushed the clutch of papers into her black bag and stood up. "Thank you, I think that's all for now, Mr. Sandermere."

Sandermere came to his feet, pushed his hands in his jacket pockets, and walked to the door with her. "I suppose that when you've completed your reports, I will hear from Viscount Compton's solicitors to move forward with the purchase."

"I am not privy to the details of the purchase, Mr. Sandermere. As you have already been informed, my role is to complete a more informal report on the area and, indeed, to look at recent events in the vicinity of the estate and brickworks that might have an effect on the smooth takeover of a considerable acreage and a vital manufacturing asset."

"Very good." Sandermere nodded.

The butler stepped forward to escort Maisie to the door, and she bid good afternoon to Sandermere. She was about to cross the threshold but turned, calling to Sandermere, who had just set foot on the staircase.

"Oh, Mr. Sandermere—one quick question."

"Yes?"

"I'm curious—were you at all familiar with the Martin family, Jacob, Bettin and Anna?"

He shrugged. "I am familiar with them only because their lives were lost when the village was bombed by a Zeppelin during the war, Miss Dobbs. I was not in situ at the time, having returned to school." He turned and continued walking up the stairs.

Maisie made her way back to the MG, settled into the driver's seat, and shut the door. She chewed the inside of her cheek while surveying the mansion, then drove toward the main road, halting at a place she thought would not be visible from the house. Stepping from the motor car, she walked around the perimeter of the landscaped grounds toward the stable block. The stables, with stalls for seven horses, were quiet when she entered. There was no sign of the groom. Maisie suspected that he was probably in a tack room, applying saddle soap to deep brown leather or preparing buckets of bran mash for the horses—she'd counted three bay hunters and two gray carriage horses. One of the hunters glistened with sweat and smelled of liniment. She laid her hand to his flank and knew he had been galloped to the point of exhaustion. She could see that a groom had walked him cool, then covered him with a soft flannel sheet packed with dry hay to absorb the moisture that still ran from his body. The horse searched for a sweet treat in her hand as she touched his nose, and she whispered to him while reaching up to rub his ear, "He wouldn't dare do that if Frankie Dobbs were his groom—he'd soon see who's boss!"

She walked on until she came to the part of the structure damaged by fire, passing the tack room on the left. The groom was not there. A tarpaulin was drawn across a gaping hole in the roof and down the side of the building, where repairs had yet to be completed. She looked up into the rafters, then closely at the remains of a wooden stall, now charcoaled and splintered. The detritus left by fire was not something about which she claimed to be an expert. However, she did know when she'd been told a deliberate lie—or two.

SEVEN

Maisie walked up the hill toward the gypsy encampment and stopped, as she had before, to survey her surroundings. The horses were clustered in a corner of the field, and when she looked up, she saw clouds in the distance, moving in from the coast. The pickers would not be put off by rain but would soldier on through any downpour, sheltering under tarpaulins drawn capelike across their shoulders as they worked.

Gypsy vardos were not the gaily painted horse-drawn caravans of common fairy-tale mythology but more workmanlike in appearance, of deep and earthen colors. This tribe's vardos, with their accompanying tents, were all maintained well, and even now, close to teatime—not the afternoon tea of ladies in well-to-do homes but the more common hearty after-work repast—the *rom,* gypsy men, were tinkering with wheels and repairing roofs.

Maisie came closer and saw the lurcher emerge from the clearing, sit back on her haunches, and stare in her direction, nose held up to a breeze that gave notice of the visitor. When she reached a boundary visible only to the lurcher, the dog stood up, moved forward, and, without giving voice, walked silently alongside Maisie as she entered the clearing.

The black rotund cooking pot had been drawn across a blazing fire. Paishey and a woman Maisie knew as Esther were adding greens gathered from the hedgerows, first leaning forward toward the pot and then turning back to plates that held different ingredients. Maisie thought Esther even more gypsy-like than Paishey or Beulah. Her ruddy skin was framed by hair that had been pulled back at the crown, then pushed forward with carved wooden combs, giving the impression that she was wearing a mantilla, with jet-black tresses piled on her head before cascading veil-like across her shoulders. Each woman wore a copious white apron covering her waist-gathered skirt. The apron, Maisie knew, was worn less to protect clothing from stains and splashes than to provide a barrier between the body of the cook and the food to be eaten. In gypsy lore, if food came in close proximity to a woman's body, it was considered *mokada*—sullied—and not worth the eating.

Beulah was sitting on the same log as before, so Maisie stopped to wait for the old woman to become aware of her presence. The dog moved toward her mistress and nudged her elbow, and Beulah turned, beckoning Maisie to sit beside her. The lurcher settled at Beulah's side, remaining ever watchful.

"Sit, *rawni*," instructed Beulah. "Jook caught us a nice couple of *shoshi*." She nodded toward the pot. "You'll have a full belly tonight."

"I'll be glad of that," said Maisie. She did not have a deep knowledge of the gypsy dialect but knew enough to understand that the dog had caught a brace of rabbit. Maisie waited to be spoken to again.

"So, you've been to see the *sap* up at the house." Beulah nodded toward Sandermere's mansion.

Sap: snake.

"Yes, that's right."

"What'n be your business?"

"I know a man who wants to buy the whole estate." Maisie swept her hand around to indicate the breadth of the buying. "He wants it to be a clean *chop*." A clean sale. She knew this sale wouldn't be sealed gypsy-fashion, with a banging together of knuckles to bind the agreement and barely a word spoken. Instead there would be offers and counteroffers, punctuated by pages of land law utilizing long-outdated vocabulary, and mazelike codicils to protect both parties. Indeed, if trust had been involved at all, she would not have a job.

Beulah reached into her pocket and pulled out a piece of wood. She held it to her mouth and began to chew. She was quiet for a moment, then regarded Maisie, shaking her head. "The *moosh* is a *dinlo*." The man is a fool. She stopped chewing and put the wood back in her pocket.

"Have you had dealings with him?" asked Maisie.

At that moment, Webb came into the clearing holding an armful of wood. He set the fuel alongside the fire and nodded to his wife, Paishey, and to Esther. The women took a couple of logs each and added them to the fire, holding their white aprons lest they be caught by sparks spitting out from the wood.

Beulah shook her head. "Not directly." She pronounced it *direckly,* her eyes on Webb as she spoke.

Maisie turned and found that, once again, he was watching her, this time with eyes narrowed as a gust of wind pushed gray woodsmoke in his direction.

"Hello, Mr. Webb." Maisie smiled, just enough, she hoped, to break the shell of ice that always seemed to envelop Beulah's son.

He touched his hat in greeting and left the clearing, returning with more wood. She thought it might be better if she delayed the asking of questions until bellies were full and the warm fire had worked magic on aching backs. She had only picked for a short time, but already she felt the soreness in her hands and arms where rough hop-bines had scored the skin, leaving welts that stung when she washed. These people—men, women and children—had worked for days, and even after the picking was done the women had gathered flowers to bind into bunches, or made lilies of colored tissue paper to sell door-to-door, while the menfolk hunted or fashioned clothes pegs from wood to take to market.

Soon the rich aroma of a broth well simmered teased Maisie's taste buds and caused her stomach to rumble. The women brought enamel plates from their respective vardos and gathered to dish up the meal. At the edge of the clearing, children lined up to be washed from bowls set aside for the purpose, and the men began to come in from their work.

Maisie followed the conversation, spoken in an English that was scoured of embellishment and peppered with dialect. For the most part, their stories mirrored those of the Londoners. They spoke of the hops in this garden or that, of the farmer, the tallyman, and how much they had earned. They talked of the clouds in the distance and were glad their tarpaulins were at the ready. Beulah complained of a toothache that had spread to her jaw, and one of the children squealed when a hot, wet flannel cloth was rubbed along his arms.

She heard Paishey telling Esther that the *gorja-rawni*—the woman who was not a gypsy—who had smiled upon her little Boosul, had turned her back today as they passed on the way to the tap. Esther put her hands on her hips and shook her head. She wagged a finger, telling Paishey that the woman wasn't any different from all the rest of them and would probably cook her baby for tea if she had the chance, because she was—as likely as not—a *beng,* a devil. Maisie stared into the fire. Was it worth putting the story right? Should she tell them that the woman grieved for her own lost daughter, had felt warmed as the gypsy baby nestled in her arms, and was now shrouded in a chill of prejudice that enveloped her because her people didn't trust the gypsies and were wary of them? No, probably not. She would keep her counsel. After all, the tribe suffered too, from the virulence of fear.

Paishey brought a plate of rabbit stew with a wedge of bread for Beulah, who pointed to Maisie and nodded, indicating that a plate should also be offered to their guest. A portion was brought for the outsider, and as steam wafted up from her food, Maisie's mouth watered and she smiled at Paishey. "Thank you. This smells lovely." Paishey said nothing, acknowledging the gratitude with a brief nod, and continued handing round enamel plates, with those of the men holding a good third of a measure more than the women.

There was little talk as the company devoured the awaited meal. Then the empty plates were cleared and slops from the pot taken to the edge of the clearing for the dogs, though Beulah's jook was fed first, on account of her catching the tribe's end-of-day meal.

Maisie made her move. "Why are the people in the village so afraid, Aunt Beulah?"

Beulah laughed, though it came out as a cackle, making her sound like a *chovihanni,* a witch. "Them's

120

too afraid of their own shadows. Them's looking over their shoulders, waiting for the ghosts to see them."

"What ghosts? What do you mean?"

Beulah shook her head. "Them ghosts that feed on all of us, the ghosts of them as we've done wrong by."

"But that could be anyone anywhere. There's someone in every village who has done something wrong, but those places don't feel like Heronsdene."

Now the gypsy woman sighed, and Maisie, drawn to look over her shoulder, saw Webb walking toward them. Beulah turned to her and said, "It's all a long time gone, but not what they hold of it."

Webb leaned forward to whisper in Beulah's ear, and Maisie watched as some of the gypsies, men and women, went to their tents, returning with fiddles and tambourines, wooden sticks and whistles. Paishey emerged from her vardo with a violin case in her arms, which she passed to Webb. Maisie noticed that the other rom carried their fiddles with much less care than Paishey and Webb had demonstrated. And even as Webb clicked open the case and lifted his violin from the faded golden velvet in which it was cocooned, it was with reverence, as if the instrument were a religious icon.

He lifted the violin to his ear, picked at the strings, tensioning them to tune, and then pressed it under his chin, to sound chords and test the notes. The other gypsies were creating a cacophony of sound, yet Webb had closed his eyes as if they did not exist, as if the world around him had receded like the tide, leaving only soft, untouched sand. Then he opened his eyes and looked at the company. Silence fell upon the group, as Webb lifted his bow to the strings and teased out notes that caused tears to form in Maisie's eyes. So skilled was Webb that it was as if he had become, in an instant, one with the violin, its fine maple tinted with a reddish-gold varnish reflecting flames that leaped up between the musicians and their audience. He played a lament, and as she listened it was as if the whole forest had become silent, had stopped to listen to the gypsy and his violin. He quickened the pace, his foot now tapping out a faster beat, his head moving from side to side, as he sawed the bow across the strings. Then he looked up, nodding to his fellow fiddlers as the lament became a jig. They joined in with strings squealing as bows were pushed back and forth, back and forth, all of them keeping pace with Webb, like pilgrims following their master along a winding and leaping path.

Two gypsy women emerged into the clearing, their tambourines flying, their feet barely touching the ground as they leaped in dance. Children banged sticks together, or rattled stones in a can, and soon most of the company were yipping and pounding their feet to the rhythm set by Webb. There was no pause, no lingering between this tune and the next, just a glance from Webb to his band, who were now playing and dancing along. Only Beulah and Maisie remained seated, the old lady clapping her hands on her knees, while Maisie felt the beat seep up from the ground and into her soul. The music was raw and tumultuous, swollen with the rhythm of passion, the taut scream of exhilaration. Oh, how she wanted to dance, how she wanted to feel each note in every cell of her being as she stamped her feet and clapped her hands. How she wanted to belong to the moment, as the gypsies did with their dance.

She saw Webb meet his wife's eyes with his own and, still dancing, Paishey made her way around the fire to Maisie. With leaping flames reflected in her eyes, she took Maisie's hands and tried to pull her to her feet, into the group of gypsies. Maisie shook her head, protesting that she could not dance and was happy just to listen, to watch, but her words were drowned by the music. With the gypsy still grasping her hands, and on the verge of panic, she looked around to Beulah, who motioned with her hand that she should join the dance. She felt the barrier of fear paralysing her, fear of what might happen if she gave herself to the music, to the power of the gypsy dance.

Paishey pulled on Maisie's hands again, this time drawing her into the throng. There was no going back without causing offense, nothing to do but allow all reticence to fall away. She felt the throbbing pulse of the music echo up from the forest floor into her bones, making its way straight to her heart as she danced a dance that was primitive and unreserved. This was no gentle fox-trot, no metered modern swing, and she gave herself to it. Time and again she danced, for even when the tempo changed, the music did not stall but went on and on, to the edge of night.

Later, when Beulah looked up to the stars and motioned to her son, the gaiety came to an end and it was time for Maisie to leave. Knowing they needed to rest now, Maisie insisted that she did not need a chaperone to accompany her to her motor car. Two gypsies would have had to leave the group, for they did not hold with a woman being alone with a man who was not her husband, nor with a gypsy woman returning to the tribe alone. Smiling and still a little breathless, Maisie thanked one and all, for her meal and for being included in the evening's dancing, and then made to leave. As she turned, Beulah whistled and then pointed to the lurcher, who came to Maisie's side. She raised her hand in acknowledgment and left the clearing, the dog at heel.

Across a field damp with evening dew, a sign of tomorrow's looming showers, Maisie walked on, the lurcher's paws soft on the ground, her cold nose reaching up to touch Maisie's hand every few steps. Soon they reached the MG, the dog standing back as Maisie unlocked the door and took her place behind the steering wheel.

"Go on now, jook, go home." Maisie pointed toward the field they had just crossed. The lurcher turned and slinked away into the night, though as Maisie drove to the road and glanced back, she could see the animal's eyes, glistening like crystal beads in the darkness as she waited until Maisie was gone.

• • •

WAKING IN THE middle of the night from a deep and dreamless sleep, her eyes heavy, her heart slow, Maisie was sluggish in establishing her bearings, and it was some seconds before she remembered that she was in her room at the village inn. But what had woken her? She turned and then sat up, now wakeful and alert in her pitch-black room. She raised her nose to smell the air. *Smoke.* She drew back the covers and ran across to the window to see whether the smell might be lingering in her clothes, which had absorbed the aroma of the gypsies' campfire. She'd washed her blouse and left it to hang by an open window, along with her skirt, hoping the night breeze would blow away all traces of wood smoke. Reaching for the fabrics, she pressed her nose to them—barely a memory of the evening lingered within the threads.

The acrid odor became stronger now, and as she leaned out of the window, she saw flames at the back of the inn. This was not a cozy campfire, controlled and alluring, but a ravaging conflagration borne of deliberate combustion. The coal shed was on fire, close to two outbuildings, including the one in which barrels of beer were stored. And in the distance, running from the inn's long garden to the fields beyond, Maisie saw a man—or perhaps a woman.

Without wasting a moment, she grabbed her dressing gown and opened the door. "Fire! Fire! Wake up and get out! Fire!" There was not a moment to lose. Down the corridor she ran, banging on doors, and through another door that she supposed led to the quarters of the landlord and his family. "Fire! Fred—where are you? The inn's on fire!"

There were voices behind her as she found the stairs by touch and made her way down. Light from the flames outside now illuminated her way, and she ran straight to the kitchen, then out to the scullery. A heavy mop bucket stood in the sink. Maisie twisted the tap and left it to run as she searched for another bucket. Fred was soon behind her, along with his wife.

"Get everyone out, Mary! Out to the front, and raise the alarm!"

The next twenty minutes passed in a blur, as she and the landlord, soon joined by villagers summoned by the tolling of the church bell, came to help, buckets in hand. Back and forth they ran, then, when enough people had gathered, a chain was formed, passing buckets of water to the flames. At first, it seemed as if the fire would never abate, as if Loki, the god of fire and mischief, were dancing among them, taunting and snickering, igniting the flames as soon as they were doused. Then they began to win, and the water chain was drenching the blackened smoking ruin.

Exhausted, spent, Maisie, the landlord and the villagers who had come to help stood in silence in front of the remains of the coal shed and an outbuilding. Waterlogged wood hissed and sizzled, and no one moved.

After first allowing the stillness to temper emotions that she knew would follow such an attack, Maisie touched the innkeeper on the arm. "Fred. We'd better not let this linger. It should be checked, then we should clean up."

"Right you are, Miss Dobbs." He looked around, then up at the inn. "I would've lost the lot if it weren't for you. I owe you everything."

"You would have smelled the fire soon enough."

"A fire can do a day's work in a minute." He pursed his lips. "No, you've got a calm head on your shoulders, and we owe you. The men will help now, you go on back indoors. Mary will get a bath out for you." He gave a half laugh. "She's banking up the stove for more hot water now. Better tell her to go easy with the logs, eh?"

Maisie was silent for a moment longer. Still no one moved. "Why wasn't the fire brigade called?"

"Takes too long. No station here—they would have had to come over from Paddock Wood."

"But that's not far. Who has a telephone in the village? The damage should be inspected, to ensure all traces of fire are gone, and the police must be called so that the person who did this is caught."

"You go in to Mary, miss. We'll look after it all now. These things happen. I've been building up the path here at night, with ashes from the fireplaces inside the inn. Like as not, it's my fault for not making sure the embers were dead. Only takes a spark to get a fire going, especially near a coal bunker." He stood straighter and squared his shoulders. "No, I blame myself. I should have known better."

127

"But I saw someone, running down to the end of your garden, then off across the field."

The innkeeper shook his head. "No, miss, I doubt you did. There's a vixen that comes a-hunting for food at night, around our dustbins at the back. She's a right one, that fox-bitch, and what with this moon"—he pointed to the sky with the forefinger of his blackened right hand—"the shadows would've made her look like a person."

"No, I don't think—"

"You go on in now, miss. There's Mary at the door, she's got a nice hot bath waiting. We're grateful to you, all of us. But we can do what needs to be done now."

Maisie looked at the villagers standing by, men and women listening to the conversation. She nodded, acquiescing, and walked to the back entrance to the inn. Just as she dipped her head to avoid the low-beamed back door, she turned. The women were moving away but the men were clustered, looking at the waterlogged and smoking ruins, their heads drawn together as they spoke of the fire.

IN A ROOM next to the kitchen, decorated with floral wallpaper and white wainscoting, Mary had filled a tin bath with piping hot water and, on a chair next to the bath, set two white towels still infused with the memory of the warm breeze that had dried them on the washing line outside. The innkeeper's wife had also left a freshly ironed flannel nightgown on a chest of drawers in the corner, along with a dressing gown. As she was about to remove her clothes, Maisie caught sight of herself in the oval mirror hanging from an olive-green picture rail. Her face was almost black, her hair was slicked against her cheek, and her eyes were red and stinging from soot and heat. She looked down at her pajamas and dressing gown and saw that they were fire-soiled beyond repair. Sighing, she undressed and eased herself into the bath, reaching for a brick of green Fairy household soap that Mary had placed upon the towels.

The fire had been ignited deliberately, of that she had no doubt. But why was her observation of the person running away across the field denied by the landlord? Why did he decline to summon the fire brigade? The church bells ringing in the middle of the night should at least have alerted people in the next village that there was something amiss. Why did no one come? There had been fires before, one a year for some years, according to James Compton's report. Were the people of nearby villages immune to the call for help? Or did they offer help once, only to have it turned away?

Questions filled Maisie's head as she soaped away the soot and sweat of the night. Her nails were broken and her knuckles grazed from filling the buckets with water, then running back and forth before the chain was formed. *All those silent, ashen-faced people.* Maisie closed her eyes and imagined their collective demeanor again, saw the message written in their eyes. There had been no surprise registered, no shock at a tragedy averted by a hair's breadth of time. Instead, she had once again seen the emotion she was becoming familiar with in the course of her work in Heronsdene: fear. And something else: resignation, acceptance. As if the events of the evening were expected.

EIGHT

Breakfast was a quiet affair. The other guests had left as early as possible, their curiosity regarding the fire far outweighed by their desire to depart from the site of a troubled night. Maisie understood that, though they were not consciously aware of such a sensation, the mood of the village and the nature of the "accident" had driven them away. But she was hungry for the plate of eggs and bacon served by Mary, and relaxed as she tucked into toast and marmalade and poured another cup of tea. She was also waiting. Waiting to speak to Fred Yeoman again, to gauge, if it were possible, the depth of his silence on the matter of the fires. She heard him in the cellar, changing the barrels of beer and grumbling to himself as he made his way back to the bar, where he began preparing the inn for opening time.

"Hello, Fred," Maisie called out, turning toward the bar.

Fred's hobnail boots clattered on the stone floor as

he came along to the bar in the residents' sitting room.

"Morning, Miss Dobbs. You don't look any the worse for wear. I hope we didn't keep you awake with our clearing up out there."

Maisie dabbed the corners of her mouth with a table napkin and shook her head. "That hot bath worked wonders. I slept like a log as soon as my head hit the pillow." She paused. "How bad is the damage?"

"Not as bad as it would have been if you hadn't raised the alarm. I won't be charging you for your stay here, on account of that."

She was about to shake her head and protest, then reconsidered. The innkeeper wished to thank her in a tangible way, and this was likely his only means of doing so. It would be foolish to decline the offer. "Thank you, Fred, that's very kind of you."

"Not at all." He remained at the bar, wiping a cloth from left to right across varnished oak that centuries of beeswax polish had brought to a rich hazelnut-hued shine.

"Don't mind me saying so," said Maisie, as she reached for the teapot, "but even if they are accidents, you seem pretty unfortunate in Heronsdene when it comes to fires. Didn't you say that Mr. and Mrs. Smith's conservatory was destroyed last year?"

The innkeeper shrugged. "Whyte. It was the Whytes," he replied, as if looking into the flames once more. "And it was their summer house." He looked up again, shaking the memory from his mind. "I wasn't aware that we had more accidents here than anywhere

131

else, and I didn't know it was anything to talk about."

Maisie shrugged. "I know there's been at least one fire for each of the last ten years or so." She lifted her teacup to her lips and let it remain there without sipping from the rim as she continued. "And always at this time of year."

Fred rested his hands on the bar and shook his head. "I wouldn't mind betting them Londoners—or the gypsies—have been up to some mischief over the years. I don't allow the gyppos to come in here, shady buggers if you ask me. We let the Londoners in, but I don't know—they're just as bad, looking for trouble." He paused, then continued running the cloth across the bar. "The truth is, no matter how much I don't like them, this fire was down to me, and like I've said before the other fires have been on account of carelessness. It's not as if there have been that many, not when you look at it, and certainly not every year, like you said."

Maisie pushed back her chair and stood up. "I'd better get going now, or I'll be late." She walked to the bar. "Are you sure I can't pay for last night?"

"Positive."

"Well, thank you again. I'll be seeing you next week, I daresay." Maisie smiled, opening the door that led upstairs to her room, where she collected her belongings and walked out into a morning of showers. With one hand she pulled the collar of her tweed jacket up around her neck and held on to her hat as she ran across the road to the MG and stowed her bag.

Lifting the bonnet, she went through the motions of starting the motor and took her seat behind the wheel. The innkeeper had not realized that in the midst of their conversation, when Maisie had mentioned last year's fire, she had not known who had suffered a loss of property and had used the name Smith, because most villages have a family of that name. Without thinking, Fred had corrected her. She would find out where to find the Whyte family from someone else.

HER FIRST STOP this morning would be the hop-gardens, to tell Billy she was leaving for Maidstone, followed by Chelstone and London, and planned to be back on Tuesday. There was the visit to see Simon, and there were questions to put to James Compton. In the back of her mind, something about this assignment was bothering her. James claimed his reason for retaining her was to ensure a clean sale, that events in the village and the estate were investigated to reveal their importance or lack thereof. However, though she could see why a company accorded utmost respect in the world of commerce would want to do nothing to besmirch a fine reputation, it occurred to her that the very same events that might give rise to controversy in the city would reduce the value of the property. On the one hand, an owner such as Alfred Sandermere would now be in a position to make repairs and improvements financed by insurance claims, but on the other hand, the mere fact of the fires and acts of delinquency could bring down the selling price—so the Compton

Corporation would be positioned to make a pretty penny by purchasing property from a financially compromised owner and then selling at a later date.

She drove through the village toward the war memorial and was about to turn left toward Dickon's Farm when a flash of color caught her eye. She wound down the window and looked across to the waste ground where the Zeppelin's bomb had fallen. There, among the weeds, was a bouquet of flowers. She stopped the motor, reversed back to a safe parking place, then stepped out from the MG and crossed the road.

The shower was not cold but, instead, added to a sticky morning humidity. Yet once more Maisie felt chilled by her proximity to this piece of land. She closed her eyes and, as she had done many times before to ensure her protection in such circumstances, she imagined a white circle of light enveloping and protecting her from spiritual harm. Opening her eyes, she took a deep breath, stepped forward, and felt as if she had entered a house built with bricks of ice. Moving toward the bouquet, she knelt down to inspect the flowers, searching for a message, a sign, something to indicate who had left the blooms. Judging from softness in the stems, and limp petals, the collection of dahlias and chrysanthemums had been there for some time. Overnight, perhaps. There was no message. Maisie looked up and around; coming to her feet, she walked farther into the waste ground, stopping where the foundations and low remains of walls long fallen stood proud from the ground. She pulled back weeds and reached out to touch fire-blackened stone, the telling remains of the blaze that had taken the lives of a family.

Maisie turned to leave and realized she had an audience. Three children stood watching her, their eyes wide. There were two boys, each wearing short trousers with braces over cotton collarless shirts too big for them, battered leather lace-up boots, and flat caps that made them appear like old men. The girl wore a floral dress and old leather sandals that were a size too large, likely hand-me-downs from an older sibling. Her fair hair was tangled, as if she had been playing in the woods, and a long forelock had been pulled to the side and tied with a ribbon to keep it from her eyes. As Maisie made her way to the pavement, walking toward them, they screamed and ran, with the little girl almost left behind, squealing, "Don't leave me, don't leave me. It's a ghost, it's a ghost. Pim's come to haunt us, Pim's come to haunt us."

Maisie laughed to herself as the children ran, and even called out, "It's alright, I'm a person, not a ghost!" Returning to the MG, she was sorry they had not stopped, for she was curious to know who Pim might be. An immortal of local legend, perhaps? A storybook character akin to Scrooge or Magwitch? Or perhaps a presence conjured up by parents trying to keep curious children away from dangerous waste ground, where a fall on debris might cause a deadly infection? Or was the ghostly Pim someone far more important?

MR. AND MRS. Whyte were not hard to find. They lived in a Georgian villa with a front garden accessible from the High Street. Maisie knocked at the door, which was answered by a housekeeper, and upon asking for the residents, the housekeeper informed her that they were out for the day.

"When might they be home, if I may inquire?"

The housekeeper paused before answering. "They will probably be back late tonight. They've gone down to the coast for the fresh air." She nodded toward the inn. "They both went straight over to the inn last night, to see if they could help, and this morning, Mrs. Whyte said their constitutions needed a good old clean out and the sea air would do it."

"Quite right." Maisie frowned, showing concern. "It was terribly brave of them to lend a hand, especially after what happened to them last year."

The woman crossed her arms and moved closer. "That's what I thought. Takes a lot of gumption, that. Mind you, they know what it's like, fire. And in a village like this, we all pull together."

"Of course you do," said Maisie, edging forward as if sharing in a conspiracy. "How did their fire happen?"

"Accident. Left a paraffin stove in the summer house on a chilly night, on account of the plants, and it caught one of them fancy blinds. Got too hot, it did, and then *whoomph!* The whole lot went up. Lucky I was upstairs and heard something go."

"They're lucky indeed. Same time of year, wasn't it?"

The housekeeper nodded. "Same day." Then she began to draw back. "Well, then, I must be getting on. Shall I say who called?"

Maisie shook her head. "Not to worry. I'll come back another time, perhaps." She paused, then moved forward once more. "May I ask you, Mrs.—"

"Marchant. Mrs. Marchant."

"Mrs. Marchant, you must remember the Zeppelin raid, in the war."

The woman pursed her lips. "Terrible, it was. That's why we try to forget, here in the village. Terrible thing to have happened. Now then, like I said, I'd better be getting on." She closed the door.

The same day. Maisie walked to her motor car, sat in the driver's seat, and made a note to visit Beattie Drummond once more.

"WELL, WE DIDN'T find any stash of silver and valuables, Miss." Billy looked up from picking hops. "And we didn't find any sign of a new path beaten through the woods." He raised one hand and tapped his temple. "We was usin' a bit of nous while we was about it, and still we didn't find anythin'."

"It'll be alright. The boys won't come to any terrible harm while they're in the reformatory. We'll prove them innocent, don't you worry."

"You seem pretty sure, Miss."

"I didn't say it would be easy, Billy."

Billy sighed. "Rotten luck, it is. Them boys've both got apprenticeships—and you know how 'ard it is to get a job these days. Mind you, they don't 'ave to pay an apprentice much to do the job of a man, so it ain't surprisin'—anymore than it's surprisin' that women are in jobs before men, on account of their wages bein' lower."

"And there are many women wanting for jobs too, Billy, a good number of them widows from the war with children to feed."

"I tell you, Miss. What kind of a country are we livin' in, eh? Where there's people feelin' pain in their bellies where food should be, and widows left wantin'—and little children dyin' for need of the hospital."

Maisie saw Billy's anger and pain from his daughter's death rising again, along with his dissatisfaction with his lot. *The grass is always greener, Billy.* She was about to speak when he began again.

"And as for them down there, where did they all come from, anyway? They certainly ain't from this country, and there they are, picking fruit and 'ops what we—we who come from 'ere—want to be picking."

"I'm sure the people of Kent feel the same about Londoners, Billy."

"Hmmph!" He looked down at his work again, without commenting.

"Well, I have to return to London tomorrow morning. I'm following some leads, Billy, so don't lose heart." She made to leave, then reached out to her assistant, placing her hand on his shoulder. "And don't harden your heart, either, Billy. That heart is the finest part of you."

IT WAS AS she left the hop-garden that Maisie reached for her old nurse's watch. She usually pinned it to her jacket, and when she did not feel the cool silver at her touch, she realized it wasn't there. She gasped. How could she not have noticed it missing? The watch had been a parting gift from her patroness, Lady Rowan Compton, before she left for nursing service on the battlefields of France in 1916. It had needed repair only once. She thought of it as her talisman, for it had remained with her even when she was wounded, when the casualty clearing station in which she was working was shelled. Simon was caught by the same shell, though his wounds had taken his mind, whereas hers had seared a welt into her scalp and a deeper scar into her soul.

She began to retrace her steps, walking an exact path back through the farm, searching around the area where she had parked the MG, and then, with a certain reticence, she picked her way across the waste ground again. Nothing.

Returning to the inn, Maisie entered via the residents' door in time to hear raised voices in the public bar.

"Are you refusing to serve me?"

Maisie recognized the voice straightaway. It was Sandermere.

"I was just saying that you might have had a bit too much, that's all. Now, if you'd like to take a seat, we'll bring you a nice cup of tea."

"I do not want *a nice cup of tea*, I want a double whisky. Either pour me my drink or I will come over there and get it."

"Now, Mr. Sandermere—"

"Don't 'now Mr. Sandermere' me, you worm." The man's voice was thick, his language slurred. "I own this whole damn place, and I shall do as I please." At the last word, there was the sound of breaking glass as a whisky tot hit the wall. "Now, get me my drink— and Whyte here will pay for it!"

She heard the drink being poured, then a few seconds elapsed, during which, she guessed, he had drunk the alcohol straight back. He cracked the glass down on the bar and left, saying, "That's better. We've all got to stick together here in Heronsdene, in our loving little community, haven't we? I'll see myself out the back way—I'll have a look at the remains of your sheds on the way."

Maisie allowed a moment to pass, then went to the door, which she opened and shut again, before calling, "Hello! Anyone there?"

Fred came to the bar in the residents' sitting room and greeted Maisie with cheer, though he seemed quite shaken, with ashen skin and trembling hands.

His jaw was set, and his eyes were reddened.

"Ah, Miss Dobbs, I know exactly why you're here." He reached under the bar and brought out her watch.

"Oh, wonderful! I don't know where I would be without that. I am so glad you found it."

"It was where you left it, miss, on the side table in your room. Mary came down as soon as she found it, saying it looked important, not your ordinary watch." His eyes met hers. "Been through a lot, has that, judging by the date on the back."

Maisie nodded and reached for the watch, which she began to pin to her lapel. "Yes. It's been with me since I was a nurse in France. I was at a casualty clearing station."

"You saw enough, then."

"Yes, I saw more than I want to see ever again." She paused. "Bit like living through your Zeppelin raid for twenty-four hours each day."

He sighed and shook his head.

"Are you alright, Fred?"

"Just thinking." Another sigh, then he looked up at her. "How do you feel now? You know, about *them*— the Germans."

Maisie paused. "We treated many of them in the clearing station. In fact, we had two German doctors working alongside us—prisoners of war. Doctors who were captured always went to work straightaway, just as our Allied doctors who were POWs went to work for the Germans." She shrugged. "If your calling is to save life, it takes precedence over killing." Another pause. "But here's what I saw, Fred. I saw wounded soldiers who cried for their loved ones, wherever they were from. I held the hands of dying young men, whether they were British, Allies, or German. It's war itself that I have an opinion about, not the origin of those who fight."

"Even now, even with some of the business we're hearing about, you know, going on over there? There's them as says we'll be at war again before this decade's out."

"Perhaps not if it were down to the ordinary people, Fred." Maisie smiled. "Now then, I must be on my way. I have to go into Maidstone again today."

"Right you are, miss. I daresay we'll see you again next week, like you said."

MAISIE LEFT THE village with two more pieces to add to her puzzle. That Mr. and Mrs. Whyte had not left for the coast today but were very much ensconced in Heronsdene. Secondly, she now understood that Sandermere wielded some leverage, some coin of influence, in his relations with the villagers. Of course, in a feudal system—and many small villages still resonated with the echoes of times past—he would be very much the country squire. "He who must be obeyed" seemed an apt description, and Maisie had already deliberated upon his aura of entitlement, of ownership, when it came to the town. But she sensed something deeper, a mutual connection that went beyond an imagined master-servant relationship. She sensed that whisper of fear once again, a dependence, perhaps, on a shared truth.

AS SHE CAME to the outskirts of the village, she passed a woodland that had been newly coppiced, the trees thinned and pruned, with the younger branches and twigs bound together and leaning in stooks, waiting to be gathered by the farmer. It was there she saw Beulah, walking with the lurcher, the dog stepping with care in her wake, for the woman was making her way deliberately, step by step, where only days ago men had worked with saws and axes. In her hands she held a forked branch, each hand holding an end, with the fork in the middle. Maisie slowed the MG, knowing Beulah could not see her, though the lurcher looked up in her direction, then back at the heels of her mistress. As she watched, the fork dipped, and Beulah stopped, bent over to squint at the ground, and then reached down to brush fallen leaves aside. She picked up something, perhaps a threepenny-bit, possibly a lost trinket, which she rubbed on her skirt and scrutinized, holding it sideways to better catch the light. Then she put it in her pocket and began again, dowsing for coins lost when a handkerchief was taken out, or a small treasure dropped as a forester bent over to gather up twigs.

Maisie watched for a moment more, then pressed the motor car into gear again and drove on her way. *So Beulah was a practitioner of the ancient art of dowsing.* She should have guessed. It was a skill worth knowing about.

• • •

BEATTIE DRUMMOND CAME as soon as she was summoned to the inquiries desk. "I'm the only one here—Friday afternoon, and the boys have gone home. You never know, that scoop I've been waiting for might come in. Got one for me?"

"Not yet, Beattie. I'm hoping you can help *me* again."

"And you've nothing I can print?"

Maisie shook her head. "Nothing—yet. But I do have a question for you, that I think you may be able to answer, though it will probably take some time for you to go through your notes. I take it you keep all your notebooks."

"Of course."

"It's about the fires in Heronsdene over the years. You said you could not write much of a story on them, given the less-than-helpful attitude of the villagers."

"Yes?"

"Do you happen to have a list of names of those who suffered damage, and the dates? I have some general reports, but they do not give specific times."

Beattie raised her eyebrows. "That's about all I did manage to get on each of them, and it was like pulling teeth from a horse. But date, time and name doesn't make much of a story without a comment here, an aside there, some real meaty background on Granny's heirloom china lost or a portrait burned to a cinder."

"I'd like those names and dates. The information I have from my client isn't as full as I would like. Also, if it's possible, can you find out anything more about the family who were lost in that Zeppelin raid in the war?"

Beattie nodded, making notes as she did so. "Anything else?"

"Not at the moment—oh, yes, one more thing. Is there a vicar in the village, do you know?"

"Ah, I can answer that one—already been down that road myself. The village can't support a vicar of its own anymore; the diocese concluded it's far too small, so there's a sort of locum who does the rounds, comes in every Sunday morning and for the usual hatch, match and dispatch work. I should write about the state of English churchgoing, shouldn't I? It's not as if he can draw a crowd as soon as the bell tolls."

"I thought so. Has he been there for a while?"

She shook her head. "No, not very long. Old Reverend Staples, the last vicar, moved on a few years ago, which was when this new chappie came in."

"Do you know where he went?"

"I can find out for you."

"Thank you."

"As long as—"

Maisie interrupted the reporter. "Yes, I know. I won't forget your scoop."

SITTING BEHIND AN ancient oak desk in an office lined with shelves of law books, the solicitor's clerk with whom Maisie had spoken previously, regarding the two London boys who stood accused of breaking into the Sandermere estate, had some promising news.

"It looks like the police might have a problem making the case stick, despite the fact that the boys are outsiders and the influence that the Sandermere name carries—or, I should say, *once* carried."

"Alfred Sandermere?"

"Yes, brought the family's reputation into disrepute."

Maisie guessed the solicitor probably had as much, if not more, information as either Beattie Drummond or even James Compton when it came to Sandermere. "Bit of a ne'er-do-well, isn't he?"

"Bit of one? That's an understatement. He was never an angel, even as a boy, and now he's become something of a boorish opportunist who appears to believe in an England that hasn't existed for years."

"Why are the police having trouble with their case?"

"There's no other evidence to show the youngsters were ever in the house. They had the sense—the police—not to take the stolen goods in the Londoners' possession at face value, and sent in the lab boys to gather fingerprints from the mansion, which they compared to the accuseds' dabs taken when they were charged. We could get them out of custody within twenty-four hours, if we're lucky. Mind you, they may have to remain in the area—they were still in possession of stolen goods, and the judge might not believe they thought it was manna from heaven."

"That's good news indeed. Sandermere will be beside himself if they're released, though."

The young man looked at Maisie over half-moon spectacles, an accessory, she suspected, worn to underline a certain gravitas. "Put it this way: I wouldn't want to be on the estate when he blows his top. That temper's been his downfall since he was a boy."

"How do you know so much about him, if I may ask?"

The clerk smiled. "I was at the same school, though he was a few years older than me. Alfred Sandermere would have been at home in *Tom Brown's Schooldays*—and not as one of the nice lads, either. He was eventually kicked out for good, expelled for bullying. He'd had numerous suspensions, and I believe—not exactly sure, because it was before my time—that he was once sent home, then got up to some mischief with a local lad. Of course, his father pulled strings, ensured the Sandermere name was kept above the mud, but the other boy carried the can, so to speak, all the way to a reformatory. I think he was too young for borstal."

Maisie chewed the inside of her lip. "Where were you at school, if I may ask?"

"Smaller school, in London. St. Anselm's. Excellent academic reputation, which is why parents send their boys there, along with their so-called emphasis on the arts as well as Oxbridge entrance." He paused. "I suppose it all builds character."

"You say that with an air of regret."

The man shook his head. "It was alright, really. I just

kept my head down and tried not to attract the attention of bullies—there are always bullies in a boarding school. Wonder what kind of men they become, don't you? Look at Sandermere." The man pulled a pocket watch from his waistcoat. "Now, Miss Dobbs, I know your questions are in the best interests of the boys concerned, however, I shouldn't have revealed quite so much—though the papers will have it soon enough, especially with Beattie Drummond snooping around. I really must go now—work to do."

"Thank you, you've been most kind."

Maisie opened her umbrella as she left the solicitor's office. She decided not to drive back to the farm to give George the news that his sons might be released as soon as tomorrow—it was always best not to tempt Providence. She was more keen, now, to be in touch with Priscilla. Though the revelation that Alfred Sandermere attended the very school now charged with educating Priscilla's three boys was something of a surprise, it did not take her aback. There are only so many boarding schools to which the landed gentry, the men of commerce, the aristocracy, foreign diplomats, and reigning monarchs of Europe and Asia might send their sons to be educated, and if one preferred a smaller school, the list became shorter. It may not have been a startling coincidence, but it was a stroke of luck.

NINE

Frankie Dobbs was not at home when Maisie arrived at Chelstone, so, after settling her bag into her old room, she dressed in worn corduroy trousers, a pair of stout walking shoes, a white shirt that had seen better days, and carried an aging cardigan, along with her umbrella. Rain at this time of year tended not to be the cold drops that fell needle-like on the skin in winter but a warmer shower, what her father called a clearing rain to take the edge off an end-of-summer humidity.

Frankie was exactly where she thought he might be: in the stable yard, walking a mare and her foal back into their stall. The mare seemed to lean toward Frankie, while her foal followed, keen not to lose sight of his mother. Maisie loved to watch her father with his charges: the precision of his movements when he was working, the way he used different brushes, the flat of his hand, and a scarf-sized scrap of velvet to bring a gleam to the most mud-encrusted coat. Horses would lift their feet willingly to be picked clean, and Frankie rarely had to raise his voice, except perhaps to a mischievous colt feeling his oats. And that one reprimand was all that was needed when Frankie Dobbs laid down the law.

As soon as the mare was stabled, Maisie called out and walked toward her father. "Can I help?" She reached forward to kiss his stubbled cheek and looked around the yard. "Jester is still out. I take it James Compton is hacking."

Frankie nodded. "Should be back any minute, if he knows what's good for the horse. That sun goes down fast this time of the year, and what with all his time over there in Canada he forgets." At that moment, the sound of a horse's hooves, echoing like slow castanets, clattered across the cobblestones. "Talk of the devil." Frankie winked at Maisie.

Unlike Sandermere's horse, Jester had been given a cooling walk before being brought into the stable yard. Standing tall at the withers, the horse was a prize hunter, and James was ensuring the gelding's fitness for the coming hunt season, for which he had decided he *might* remain in the country.

"Nice ride, sir?" Frankie took hold of the reins and, out of habit, held his hand to Jester's nose, to feel his breathing, and then to his flank. "He's doing well, this one. Stamina good?"

"Didn't show any signs of fatigue, so I think you've got the feed just right, Dobbs. I'm amazed how he's come along since I was last at Chelstone." James dismounted and reached into his pocket for a sugar cube, which he held out on the flat of his hand for the horse to take. "Maisie, can't say I'm surprised to see you here. Do you want to see me?"

"Yes, I do." She paused, as Frankie led the horse away to his stall. "Would it suit you if I helped my father here for a while? Then we can speak when you've had a chance to change."

James looked down at his hacking jacket, breeches and boots, all splattered with a dusty mud kicked up by fresh rain and sandlike topsoil. "Not a bad idea. Come over to the house at seven. I am sure my mother would like to see you."

Maisie nodded accordance, while James turned and walked across the yard toward the manor house. Frankie was using a damp cloth to clean the horse, then brushes and a soft towel. Maisie picked up a cloth and worked on the opposite flank. The horse turned to nuzzle her while she worked, and she gave him a playful tap on the nose as she brushed.

"It still makes you feel a bit odd, me going up to the house, walking in the front door, and sitting down with the Comptons, doesn't it, Dad?"

Frankie sighed. "Can't say as it sits well. Makes me wonder about my station, though I should be used to it by now, what with all they've done for you and, on the other hand, what you've done for them. Thinks the world of you, does Her Ladyship."

"And she'll never forget that you saved her hunters in the war, Dad. Look how you've advised her on breeding racehorses. You're not the head groom here so much as her racehorse expert, and she knows it."

Frankie looked up from his work. "Well, like you said yourself, it still makes me feel a bit odd. I'm best when everyone knows where they stand. Reckon most folk are like that, even if you're able to do things differently."

Maisie said nothing, and soon her father stood back,

rubbed his hand down the horse's neck, and said, "Now then, mate, I'll get your bucket and you're done for the day."

FRANKIE, LIKE MOST of those who work on the land, had his tea as soon as he could eat after the day's work was done. And, like the gypsies and those who picked the hops, tea was a hearty meal with meat and vegetables, a repast cooked to replenish energy stores for another day of toil ahead. After sharing her father's evening meal, Maisie walked across the lawns to the back entrance of Chelstone Manor. There was no reason why she could not use the front door, for her position as a professional woman had given her the confidence and leave to make her entrance in an appropriate fashion. However, she enjoyed seeing old friends and the place where she once worked herself—though that was in her salad days when she was green and young, like a sapling that can be bent and twisted to all manner of shapes. It had taken years to find a mold that was her own. Indeed, she felt as if she were bending and twisting again, finding some truth to who she was before the juice ran from the branch and she was finally formed.

Mrs. Crawford, who had been cook when Maisie first came to work for the Compton family, was now retired, but the butler, Carter, was still a prominent member of the household staff, though likely to leave his employer soon, for he was finally showing his age. The once-stalwart bearing now seemed burdened, the sergeant-major shoulders less able to fill his tailored jacket, and he had to lean forward and cup his hand to an ear when spoken to. Maisie knew Lady Rowan would never give him notice, for the woman who once would provoke an argument at a supper party, just to wake everyone up, had come to dislike change, feeling more comfortable with the status quo.

"Maisie Dobbs! The stranger returns!" Carter came toward her and took both her hands in his own.

"Mr. Carter, it's lovely to see you. Sorry I've not been in to visit you, but each time I've come down to see my father, I've barely had the time."

He shook his head. "I still look at you and see that young girl who almost cost me my job." He turned to the new cook, a thin woman who had none of Mrs. Crawford's ample welcoming folds that had comforted Maisie when she returned from war, wounded and spent. "Reading in the library at two in the morning, she was—and caught by Her Ladyship," he continued, looking now at Maisie. "But it turned out alright, didn't it?"

Maisie laughed and looked at her watch. "I've a few minutes before I have to go upstairs to see Master James, so I'll have a cup of tea, if the kettle's on." James Compton was still known as Master James to the older staff at Chelstone Manor. The protocol appropriate for his position in childhood had been extended by his father when, years before and on the cusp of manhood, James had demonstrated particularly juvenile behavior. His father at once decreed that he should be known by his boyhood nomenclature until further notice. Maisie thought that James Compton, though wounded in the war, and now an accomplished businessman, still earned the title Master on occasion.

The cook nodded to Carter and turned to the stove, and in the meantime staff came through the kitchen to greet Maisie. When the tea was ready, Carter invited her to join him in his office—a small room adjacent to his quarters—where the tea tray was set between them, and Maisie poured.

"I still can't get over how well you've done, Maisie. I suppose I should call you Miss Dobbs and be very proper."

"No, you shouldn't, Mr. Carter." She handed him a cup of tea, then thought to ask a question. "Mr. Carter, I wonder, do you know anything about Heronsdene? You've lived here for years now, and even before that, before the household moved to Kent, you were here on and off throughout the year, weren't you?"

"I should say that Mrs. Crawford would have been the one to answer that question. She knew more about the village. I was completely taken up with the estate and with the comings and goings of the house, generally overseeing—well, you know my job. But Mrs. Crawford knew who was who on account of having to order food for the estate. She only wanted the best suppliers, the ones who delivered when they said they would, with prices you couldn't beat if you tried, and who could come up with a miracle if Her Ladyship suddenly decided to invite the Prime Minister for supper—which as you know, she does when she wants to have one of her political arguments, with everyone talking at odds across the table and all thinking they're the only one who's right."

Maisie frowned. "I'm just curious about the village, and I thought you might know something about it."

Carter shrugged. He'd been leaning forward to hear Maisie, but not having quite caught her words, he continued on. "She swore by the bakery there. Swore by it. Couldn't say enough about Mr. Martin and his breads and pastries. Remember that cake, the one we had here for your leaving party when you went up to Cambridge? Mrs. Crawford ordered it 'specially. She said she couldn't do any better herself, that the prices were good, and he never let her down."

"Jacob Martin?"

"Yes." He paused, stirring his still-untouched tea. "Then of course there was the tragedy, the Zeppelin—you would have been in France when it happened—and they were all gone." Carter lifted his cup to his lips, then set it down, continuing to speak before Maisie could ask another question. "Terrible thing to say, but I reckon it was just as well the son was killed too, over there in France. Imagine having to come back and find all your family gone. Terrible. Terrible."

"There was a son?"

Carter nodded. "Yes, he used to talk about his children to Mrs. Crawford, did Mr. Martin. Can't say as I knew much myself."

They were interrupted by a knock on the door, which then opened to reveal James Compton. "Apologies for intruding on your domain, Carter, but I thought I would find Miss Dobbs here." He looked at Maisie. "I've booked a telephone connection to Canada for half-past seven, so perhaps we can have that chat now. If I'm going to get my directors to talk to me, I had better be on time—Toronto's a few hours behind us here in England, you know."

Maisie stood up. "Of course." She turned to Carter. "Thank you very much for the tea, Mr. Carter. It was lovely to see you."

Leaving Carter's belowstairs fiefdom, Maisie smiled when she heard the new cook complain. "I've never worked in such a house, where no one knows their place. First there's a maid who's come up in the world, with such a fine idea of herself she thinks she can just walk in here and march upstairs. Then there's the Viscount, coming down here and looking for gingersnaps—gingersnaps! Coming into my kitchen without a by-your-leave and saying Mrs. Crawford always made them for him. Well, I'm not Mrs. Crawford and I don't know if I can stick this. I like a position where people know their station and stay there."

Carter's reply was simple. "Beg your pardon, Cook, didn't quite hear you."

MAISIE FOLLOWED JAMES into the library, a less grand room than the library at the now-mothballed London home of the Compton family at number 15 Ebury

Place. The ceilings were lower, and the room had a warmer, more welcoming sense to it, though the tomes held within were no less impressive, especially as many had been transferred from the London home.

James motioned to a chair adjacent to a mahogany secretaire, while he sat down in front of the pulled-down writing surface that was laden with full-to-over-flowing folders. "Sorry about this." He waved his hand across the pile of work, tipped in the chair, and balanced it on its two back legs. As he spoke to Maisie, he tilted forward to grab a manila folder, then teetered back again.

The motion interested Maisie, for it suggested a familiarity with imbalance, a comfort when the status quo was just out of reach, or a propensity to create such a lack of stability. She had come across such a trait before in men of commerce and thought it akin to generating a constant wager, wherein the thrill of the chase, the tumult of a less than smooth business deal, was more compelling than an effortless negotiation.

He spoke again, interrupting Maisie's thoughts. "I am anxious to close this deal in about ten days. Perhaps you can bring me up to date with your progress—and I take it you have some questions for me."

Maisie recounted details of her investigation into the issues of vandalism and crime in Heronsdene and suggested that indications as to the source of the troubling acts were both close at hand and, at the same time, hidden from view. She added that she was confident that she would get to the root of the problem in the time allotted.

"However," added Maisie, "as you said, I do have some questions for you."

"Go on." James tilted the chair back and forth within a narrow margin of error, outside of which the chair would most certainly have crashed backward or fallen forward.

"The first is an issue of insurance. Sandermere is insured, as one might expect, by Lloyds, but looking at the stables, it would seem to me that repairs to the standard required by the terms of a compensatory payment have not been met. Are you aware of this?"

James held the edge of the desk, then reached for a file, coming back to his teetering position while he flicked through a few pages. "When our surveyors visited the estate, Sandermere's insurers had already given him permission to begin repairs, which were expected to commence within a couple of days. They should have been completed by now."

"I have yet to visit the brickworks," said Maisie, "but as far as the stable block is concerned, virtually nothing has been done and there are tarpaulins spread to keep out the rain. Fortunately, there has been little in the way of inclement weather in the past month or so, but I would imagine that's about to change."

James nodded. "Of course, the stables will remain in Sandermere's possession. The boundary of sale, as I explained before, extends from the immediate gardens and what we would call domestic outbuildings, to the perimeter of the mapped estate."

"But surely you do not want any ambiguity in the final transaction, which may occur if questions remain regarding the integrity of Sandermere's dealings with his insurers."

James reached for a pen. "Good point."

"Also, James, I have another question that is outside the purview of my work with you but about which I would like to have some clarity in any case."

"Yes?"

"I completely understand the need for, as you said, *a clean sale*. Yet is it not also true that the estate's compromised reputation, along with that of the village, renders the selling price even more negotiable than before?" She inclined her head. "Don't you have more bargaining power, in consideration of events at the Sandermere estate and in Heronsdene?"

James tilted his chair forward, almost but not quite to the floor. "Yes, that's true, to a point. But it's not something we would set out to do."

Maisie deliberately relaxed her shoulders and allowed her hands to rest in her lap, crossing one leg over the other as she did so. "No, I wasn't suggesting you would. I have undertaken work for the Compton Corporation before, and understand the integrity inherent in your procedures. However, you will negotiate a lower selling price, won't you?"

James paused. "Of course. I'm a businessman, and even though we will not court controversy, there is an opportunity here for a revised deal to be brokered."

Maisie nodded. "Yes, I thought so."

"Does your question pertain directly to the brief?"

Maisie leaned forward. "In a way it does. If I am to reach any conclusions, or present a comprehensive report, I must understand the nature of the relationship between the Compton Corporation, your representatives, and the Sandermere estate. Your answers have simply raised more questions in my mind about Sandermere's actions."

"What do you mean?"

Maisie sighed. "In military terms, James, I have a sense that he is in the process of shooting himself in the foot."

"Good for us!"

Maisie stood up. "Ah, not if you want that clean sale, it isn't—and certainly not in the period of time you'd like." She held out her hand to James. "I will be in touch. In the meantime, it's a bit late to see Lady Rowan now, I expect she's with Lord Julian in the drawing room, sipping sherry." She stepped forward, placing her hand on the back of James Compton's chair. "You know, you really must be careful, James, you'll come a cropper if you keep teetering back and forth." She smiled. "Don't summon Carter. I'll see myself out."

DEEP IN THOUGHT, Maisie meandered slowly back to the Groom's Cottage, her father's home. Carter's knowledge of the dead Martin family in Heronsdene had piqued her interest, not least because of the tragic consequences the war had laid upon them. An entire family wiped out by conflict, three at home, one overseas. Yes, perhaps it was a blessing the son was lost. She imagined how it might have been had she returned from France, with her wounds as they were, only to find herself orphaned. Just the thought brought tears to her eyes, and she ran to the cottage, colliding with her father, who had just walked out into the night to collect wood for the fire.

"What's all this, what's all this, Maisie?" asked Frankie, as she enveloped herself in her father's embrace. "What's happened to upset you so, love?"

"Nothing, Dad. I was just thinking, that's all."

"Well, you're home now, so you can stop that—I never did hold with too much thinking. Now then, help me with some wood. The nights are beginning to blow up a bit chilly, 'specially with this rain coming out of nowhere. A nice fire will set you right, you'll see."

TEN

Maisie remained at Chelstone until Sunday morning, when she left early to be in Richmond by eleven o'clock. Morning visiting hours ended at noon at the convalescent hospital where Simon had been cared for since the war. She would have one hour to be with a man who could not respond to her conversation, who did not see her, and who was not aware of her presence.

As was her habit when she visited, she parked the car close to an ancient oak tree at the far end of the graveled turning circle close to the former mansion that was now a place of retirement and care for those soldiers, sailors and airmen who had lost their minds to war. Most of the patients had been infantrymen, many of them officers, as the clinic was a private concern for those with families who could afford such attention.

Maisie made her way along the gravel and, as always, walked across the lawns to a stone wall overlooking the Thames, from which the mansion, built on a hill, commanded a panoramic view. She rested her hands on the wall, closed her eyes, and breathed deeply. Maisie had been well tutored in the stilling of the mind, in the practice of drawing strength of spirit in quiet contemplation. Now she sought to dampen the stirring of doubt, the sense that she could no longer face the young man she had loved at a time when life was slipping from him. She leaned forward and rested her head on her hands. *But we are neither of us young anymore.* Though she knew very well that the years were drawn on Simon's face, when she thought of him, it was that boyish man she saw, the newly minted military doctor with whom she had fallen in love, and he with her. And when she slipped into the chair alongside his bed, closed her hand around his, and whispered the words, *It's me, Maisie, I've come to see you,* she would lean over and kiss his forehead at the very place where fragments of shell had burrowed into his skull and he had been lost to her forever.

A breeze blew up from the river, and Maisie moved away from the wall, took one more deep breath, then turned and made her way back to the main door of the clinic.

"Good morning, Miss Dobbs. Not very nice out, is it? Sign here, please, and I'll call staff nurse. The captain's been moved; he's in another ward now." The receptionist enunciated every word in her singsong voice, framed by lips coated liberally with cherry-red lipstick, which, as always, matched the long nails that clicked on the telephone dial as Maisie completed the visitors' book.

Maisie signed her name and pushed the book back to the receptionist. "Thank you. I see I'm the only visitor today so far."

"Yes, though his mother does try to get in every other day."

Maisie nodded, then turned, as she was greeted by the staff nurse. "Good morning, Miss Dobbs. Follow me, and I'll take you to Captain Lynch."

They walked along corridors with polished wood floors, bouquets of flowers set in white jardinières, and a fragrance free of the usual hospital hallmarks— the odor of human wastes masked by disinfectant and bleach. Passing the entrance to the hospital conservatory, formerly the winter garden where the ladies of the house would take a turn when frozen weather forced them to remain indoors, Maisie thought back to other times and past visits, when she would sit with

Simon close to the fountain, or perhaps alongside an open window. With his pale blue pajamas and navy dressing gown, and a rich tartan blanket across his knees, he was a silent partner to her conversation. She would speak of her cases, knowing the confidence would be kept, and tell him about her father, and perhaps even speak in lowered tones of a man she had dined with, or accompanied to the theater. And always she spoke of those years when she did not come, when her fears and reticence following her own convalescence caused her to stay away. At the heart of her angst had been the shell shock she suffered. Like a dragon, leashed and sleeping, it threatened to rear up at any time, to take her by the throat in its enflamed jaws and crush every part of her with memories of what had gone before.

It was just one year ago, in the midst of a case, when the dragon began to emerge from the hibernation of her control, that she had sunk into the very depths of an abyss from which her emergence had been fragile for months afterward. But she now understood that to control the dragon, she had to look into his eyes and back at her past. Only then would she begin to be free.

Simon lay in a bed in a private ward in which he was the only patient. His breathing was labored, sustenance delivered to his body via a single tube inserted into his arm. Such equipment was unknown in the hospital where Maisie had trained as a nurse, but wartime had brought new tools to medicine.

The staff nurse took Simon's limp right hand and

counted his pulse, then felt his forehead. His breathing would be regular for some seconds, followed by several labored gasps before becoming even again. "I'll be honest with you, Miss Dobbs, I don't know what's kept him going all these years. Amazing what the body can do, isn't it?"

Maisie nodded and, as the staff nurse moved aside, sat in the chair for visitors set by the bed. She reached for Simon's hand.

"Only fifteen minutes today, not your usual hour, Miss Dobbs."

"Yes. Of course." As the nurse turned to leave, Maisie called after her. "Staff nurse, I wonder—can you tell me, how long do you . . ." Her words faltered.

The nurse shrugged and blew out her cheeks. "To tell you the truth, if you had asked me last week, I would have said a day, perhaps two. Now he's still here, I wouldn't like to say, but—" She paused, pursing her lips for a second and shaking her head. "It won't be long now. I would say he'll be gone before the week's out."

Maisie had become used to the honesty with which the nurses spoke to her, as if, by having been a nurse herself, she was admitted into a confidence of plain speaking, a forthright response where, with family, such opinions and observations were administered only by doctors.

"Thank you, staff nurse, I appreciate your candor."

The nurse stepped back into the room for a moment and pressed Maisie's shoulder with her fingers, a gesture Maisie returned by squeezing the woman's hand before she left the ward.

Maisie sighed and reached toward Simon once more. "I think I ought to say my farewell today, Simon, just in case. I might not be here when—" And she looked down at their joined hands.

SHE LEFT THE clinic fifteen minutes later and walked directly to her motor car. She took her place in the driver's seat and grasped the steering wheel, resting her head on her hands and closing her eyes. Several moments passed. Then there was a sharp rap at the window.

"Priscilla! What are *you* doing here?" Maisie opened the door and stepped out of the MG to embrace her friend.

Priscilla held Maisie to her, then pulled away to look into her eyes. "This must be wretched for you, darling. I mean, it's bad for all of us who knew Simon—I've known him since I was a child—but you loved him."

Maisie shook her head, reaching for a handkerchief in the pocket of her mackintosh. "I'm alright, Pris. But what *are* you doing here?"

"I'm here to see you, actually. I knew you'd be here, you usually come on a Sunday, so I caught a taxi-cab knowing I'd find you. And there you were, in your minuscule MG. Let's go down into Richmond for a bite to eat."

"Aren't you going to see Simon?"

Priscilla shook her head. "No. I can't. The Simon I

knew died in 1917." She walked around to the passenger door, opened it, sat down, and turned to Maisie. "Now, then, let's get going, squashed as I'll be in your little motor car."

PRISCILLA DIRECTED MAISIE to a hotel lower down the hill and closer to the river, where the grill room offered diners a calm vista across the water. A waiter showed them to a table for two set in a corner offering two outlooks.

"I'll have a gin and tonic—and please, don't drown the gin." Priscilla pulled off her gloves, fingertip by fingertip, as she ordered.

"And a ginger ale for me, please," added Maisie.

The women consulted the menu and, having made their selections, sat back.

"You should have had a drink."

Maisie shook her head. "No, not me. The last thing I want to do is drown my sorrow."

"It'll take the edge off."

"I need that edge, Pris." Maisie thanked the waiter, who had just set their drinks on the table. Priscilla waited for him to leave after taking their luncheon order, then reached into her handbag for her silver cigarette case and lighter.

"Here we go. Let's upset the matrons, shall we?"

"I don't know if anyone gets upset about a woman smoking anymore."

"More's the pity."

"So, how are the boys?" Maisie inquired.

Priscilla rolled her eyes. "I'm off to the school again tomorrow, on the verge of pulling them out."

"More bullying?"

"Yes. And it's made even worse by the fact that all three of them don't want to be seen as cowards with Mummy and Daddy running to the rescue."

"How serious is it?"

"Frankly, it sounds dreadful, according to the letters I've received. I know a lot of parents would probably say that it will pass, it builds character, and if we take them out now they will never learn how to weather life's storms. But as I see it—and so does Douglas, only he's still in France—there's plenty of time to learn men's lessons when they're men." She shook her head and sighed. "I don't know, perhaps it's me. In the war, I helped collect the bodies of boys only a few years older than Timothy Peter is now, so to see my sons fighting and hurt touches a rather raw nerve." Priscilla blew a smoke ring and flicked ash from her cigarette into a crystal ashtray. "I mean, make no mistake, those three could quite cheerfully kill each other in their rooms at home; however, there's something rather wicked about being set upon for being different, don't you think?"

Maisie nodded, then put a question to Priscilla. "May I come with you, to the school?"

"Whatever do you want to do that for? Believe me, if you want to experience motherhood by proxy, this is not a route I would recommend."

"No, it's to do with a case—and you know I can't

say too much about it, so please don't press me. But I need to ask some questions about a former pupil of St. Anselm's—and I'm going back a few years; you won't know him—so an introduction to the head-master by a parent might help oil the wheels of dis-covery."

Priscilla pressed her cigarette into the ashtray as a trolley with two plates topped with silver covers was wheeled to their table. "The trouble with that plan is that the parent in question might be persona non grata after five minutes with the headmaster." She leaned back to allow the waiter to serve lunch. "However," she added, "I could say that I want to see my sons before our meeting, to allow you time to have a chat. The headmaster's name is Dr. Cottingham and he's been at the school for at least twenty-five years. He came as a young teacher before the war, and he's def-initely the sort to remember every single old boy, especially the bad ones."

"Thank you, Pris." Maisie paused to thank the waiter once more; then, when they were alone again, she lowered her voice. "Do you know if Mrs. Lynch will visit Simon today?"

"I'm sure she will. She's there as often as possible these days, and it's troublesome for her, with her rheumatism. I told you she wants to see you. Would you like to go back up to the clinic after lunch, during afternoon visiting hours?"

Maisie shook her head. "No, that's alright, not today."

"There might not be too many more 'todays' for Simon."

"I know."

Priscilla nodded. "Just don't leave it too long, will you?" She smiled, reached out and squeezed Maisie's hand, then picked up her knife and fork. "Well, better tuck in before it gets cold. By the way, I'd love a lift back into town, if you don't mind—I'm looking at a house today, a base for us in London, in Mayfair."

Maisie began to eat, her mind on neither her case nor Priscilla's house, but the prospect of seeing Margaret Lynch after so long.

FOLLOWING LUNCH, MAISIE drove Priscilla first to an estate agency in Mayfair, the principal of which had agreed to see his new client on a day of rest, in anticipation of a lucrative outcome for his trouble. From there, Maisie returned her friend to the Dorchester before going to her office. There was some post to attend to, but otherwise there seemed little to do on a Sunday, except return to her flat in Pimlico. She attended to a few outstanding matters, finally unpinning the almost-blank case map that she and Billy had started before he left for Kent. She would work on it at home this evening.

The flat was cool when she entered, and she found that she missed the company of Sandra, a former maid at the Comptons' Ebury Place home who had lodged with Maisie for several months earlier in the year. She had chosen to leave the Comptons' employ and remain in London when Lady Rowan decided that the mansion was not used enough to keep it running, so it was closed until such a time as James Compton made his home in England once more. Most of the staff left to work at Chelstone Manor, but Sandra was engaged to be married and was looking for suitable accommodation until then, so Maisie offered her the box room. Though the women were separated by age and education, Maisie enjoyed Sandra's presence and found the companionship comforting. But Sandra was married now and living in a one-room coldwater flat above the garage where her new husband worked.

She rested her bag on the dining table which, along with four chairs, had been found at a sale of second-hand furniture by Sandra, who knew a thing or two about driving down the asking price on anything from food to clothing. The case map, rolled and carried under her arm, was unfurled and set in place with books at each corner, and Maisie took out the colored pencils she had brought from the office. She went into the small kitchen, put on the kettle for a pot of tea, and returned to the case map. Only then did she remove her mackintosh and hat. She set to work.

In truth, Maisie did not know what she was searching for and felt a shiver of excitement as she set about her business. This was the challenge she loved, the myriad paths ahead that might lead to an answer to her question—in this case, what exactly was happening in Heronsdene? What truths were being hidden from view? Who was at the heart of the crimes and the fires? She knew that, like a river with many tributaries, there was one source, one spring from which the flood came. Who or what was the spring? As she mapped out the information gathered thus far, she knew one path would come to the fore—but would it be the right one? Or would her feelings, her observations, and her own preconceived notions of right and wrong—her prejudices, perhaps—color and cloud her vision?

Maisie went to bed early and, after leaning back and listening to the silence of her flat, she slept. The bell connected to the outside door began to ring just after midnight. Like a cat woken by a predator, Maisie was alert, running to the door while pulling on her dressing gown. She left the door on the latch and made her way with more caution toward the glass outer doors, standing behind a wall to view the visitor summoning her at such an hour. It was Priscilla.

Maisie opened the door. "Whatever is wrong?" she asked of her friend, her stomach knotted for fear of the answer.

"Get dressed, Maisie, there is no time to lose. There's a taxi waiting to take us to Richmond." Priscilla continued to talk while Maisie pulled on her walking skirt, a white blouse, warm tweed jacket, and a pair of brown walking shoes. "I received a telephone call from Margaret Lynch. Simon is not expected to last the night."

Maisie nodded, feeling the tears prick her eyes. There was nothing to be done except follow Priscilla.

She would think later, in the morning, when it was over. When it was finally over.

At the late hour traffic was light, ensuring an easy and swift drive to Richmond. Priscilla had linked her arm through Maisie's as they sat, silent, in the back of the taxi. Maisie felt as if her journey were not through west London but instead through time, the veils of years past being drawn back, one by one, for her to look, to take some account of who she was, who she had been, and how she had come to this place now, a woman approaching her middle years who had kept the light of love alive—a love ignited when she was just eighteen—even though others had come to claim her heart. Who would she be without Simon, without the scar on her soul? What would have happened had they both returned from war, unscathed except by experience? Would there have been a fairy-tale ending, the glass shoe fitting perfectly? Or would the disparity in their stations have come between them? She drew her hand across the window, clearing it of condensation, and caught her reflection in the glass. She was her own woman now, not a girl in love. With his passing, Simon was setting her free, in his way. How might she be changed by his death, an event that had not come and gone, taking its place in her history, but had lingered alongside her like a weary shadow?

The taxi scrunched to a halt on the gravel, and Priscilla put her arm around Maisie as they entered the hospital. A night watchman, sitting at the reception desk, looked up from his newspaper.

"Can I help—"

"Mrs. Priscilla Partridge and Miss Maisie Dobbs, to see Captain Lynch. We're expected." Priscilla waved her free hand to indicate she knew the way, and together she and Maisie began to run down the corridor. They stopped outside Simon's room.

"Alright, deep breath. Now, go in." Priscilla pulled out her cigarette case and pointed toward the door. "I'll be outside."

Color from the exertion of running drained from Maisie's face. She nodded, pulled at the hem of her jacket, ran her fingers across her hair, and opened the door.

Margaret Lynch looked up from her place, sitting next to her son's bed. The staff nurse acknowledged Maisie with a brief nod and a watered-down smile, then left the room without speaking. Maisie remembered meeting Margaret Lynch for the first time, when Priscilla had taken her to a party Simon's parents had thrown for him, on the eve of his departure for France. She was a woman of bearing, of understated elegance, with her aubergine gown and her hair drawn back in a chignon. She had greeted Maisie with such grace, as a friend of Priscilla Evernden. It was as she stood with Priscilla to watch the dancing that Maisie had looked across at her hostess and saw her gazing at her only son, saw her raise her hand to her mouth, her face filled with dread. Now, years later, her hair, still styled in the chignon, was gray, and she wore a woolen dress of pale blue which seemed to reflect the prominent veins at her temples. Her eyes were red rimmed, and a handkerchief was crumpled in one hand.

"I am so glad you're here, Maisie. So glad you came." She stood up and held out her hands toward Maisie, and Maisie leaned down to kiss her cheek, as if she were indeed the daughter-in-law she might have become, had the fates not ruled otherwise.

Maisie nodded, grasped Margaret's hand, and walked to the bed. Simon's breathing was even more labored than it had been earlier in the day. She helped his mother to the chair, then reached across to lay her fingers on his forehead. His eyes were closed but seemed to flutter as she touched him, though as she drew her hand away, there was no movement, no indication that he had felt her touch. She walked to the end of the bed and looked at the clipboard with notes attached. There was no reason to think he was uncomfortable while death made ready to claim him.

The staff nurse returned with another chair, and Maisie drew it close to Margaret. They sat for a while, both watching Simon, the rise and fall of his chest, listening to the breath catching in his throat, the sound reverberating into his lungs, before echoing back like a slow rattle.

"You've been good to come these past two years, Maisie."

Maisie bit her bottom lip, once more at a loss to explain her earlier absence. "I—"

"It's alright, my dear. I know, I understand. You were both so very young, you saw so much. I might

175

have not been able to comprehend your not visiting when he first came home, but time has tempered me, has given me leave to appreciate how the war touched you, too." She turned to look at Maisie, her eyes watery with age but her vision still acute. "I don't know how I would have dealt with such a blow, had it been me. So, yes, I am glad you have come."

"Thank you, Mrs. Lynch."

"Things are very different than they were in my day," she continued in a whisper, with respect to the hour and Simon. "And I confess, Simon's father and I, though we thought you delightful, were rather worried—I shall be frank with you, Maisie, I am too old now to do otherwise—that you would not be suited to marriage with Simon. But it was wartime, and we loved our son, so we sought to do nothing until he was home again." She shook her head. "Now, of course, I wouldn't care whom he married, what he did, if only he were here and not like this." She raised her handkerchief to her mouth.

Without giving a thought to protocol, Maisie placed an arm around the woman's shoulder and allowed her to lean against her. "I know, I understand. We neither of us know what might have happened, but we are both here now, and we are here for Simon, for your son."

Simon's breathing became louder, his eyes at once wide open, as his body automatically responded to the pressure of his failing lungs. His chest raised up, twisting his spine, and he convulsed. Maisie stood up and held his shoulders down, spoke gently, though he could not hear, as Margaret Lynch wept aloud. "Simon. My son, my son . . ."

He became calm, and though he continued to breathe, in troubled raspy breaths that sounded like a barber sweeping a blunt blade slowly back and forth across the strop, he looked not at Maisie or his mother but at a place above and in front of him, staring wide at a vision only he could see. Then all movement ceased and there was nothing. No more abrasive breaths, no life in his eyes, just the shell of a man lost to war in 1917.

Maisie reached over and drew her fingers across his eyelids, then took his hands and rested them on his chest, as if to protect his heart. She turned to his mother. "Stay with him, Margaret, while I go to the staff nurse. And . . . don't be afraid to talk to him, to say your final farewell."

"What about you, Maisie?"

Maisie looked back at Simon. "I said my farewell this morning." Her voice was low as she turned to face the bed where Simon lay. "It's alright—we've said our goodbye." She squeezed his cooling hand and left the room.

ELEVEN

Maisie and Priscilla remained with Margaret Lynch while formalities concerning Simon's death were completed before accompanying her back to her London home in a taxi-cab. They saw that she was comfortable and her household alerted to her loss before taking their leave. Margaret Lynch had bid farewell to Maisie with an affection laced with melancholy, holding her hands as if she were unwilling to release this young woman who had known and loved her son. Maisie accepted an invitation to visit. She knew that, for the first time, Margaret Lynch would ask her to describe the tragedy that had led to both Simon's wounds and her own and that, in telling the story, there might be healing for them both. Priscilla insisted on escorting Maisie to her flat, and as soon as she left, Maisie went straight to bed and descended at once into a deep and dreamless sleep.

ARRIVING AT THE Dorchester in something of a rush later that morning, for she had overslept, Maisie saw Priscilla waiting for her outside the hotel. She was dressed in black, as was Maisie. A doorman opened the MG's passenger door, and Priscilla waved him off quickly with a tip so they could continue on to St. Anselm's in haste.

"For goodness' sake, Maisie, when will you have a

telephone connected in your flat?" Priscilla wound down the window and lit a cigarette.

"I have one at the office, and that's an extravagance, Pris."

"We might have been late."

"But we're not. We'll be at the school on time. What's wrong with you? Too many bad memories of being called up in front of the Head for a strapping?"

Priscilla laughed and waved a plume of smoke out of the window. "I suspect you're right. I detest this sort of thing, makes me wonder whether we ought to just leave London for the estate and take on a tutor for the boys—but that rather defeats the object, doesn't it? So much for my vision of a houseful of boys down for the weekend, games of tennis, and building forts of branches and leaves in the forest. Looks like my three will be outsiders forever if I don't sort something out."

"Does it have to be boarding school?"

Priscilla shook her head. "We'll see. I'll have to talk to Douglas after I meet Cottingham this morning. And speaking of my absent spouse, thank heavens he'll be in London next week. We miss him terribly."

"Here we are." Maisie maneuvered the motor car through the gates of the school, parking alongside one other motor car in the semicircular carriage sweep. "And with five minutes to spare."

"Look, you wait in the entrance hall, and I'll go in to see Cottingham. I'll tell him you'd like to meet him, then suggest that I see my boys while you are in con- ference, which will give me a chance to find out what they've been up to and assess the damage. Let's hope he's in an acquiescent mood." Priscilla stepped from the MG, and as the women made their way to the entrance, Maisie handed her a calling card. The plan went smoothly, and Maisie was called in to see Dr. Cottingham, while Priscilla was escorted to a room where she would be able to see her boys, who would be brought from their classes to join her.

"Dr. Cottingham, how very kind of you to see me this morning, and without prior notice." Maisie extended her hand to greet the headmaster. She was surprised to find him quite young for such a post, and calculated that he must be in the region of forty-five. She had envisioned a rather crusty professorial character, with a balding pate and eyes narrowed by constant vigilance for the less-than-sterling behavior of his charges. Instead, Cottingham wore a tailored pinstriped suit, crisp white shirt, and silk tie. His shoes were polished to a shine, and his gunmetal-gray hair was swept back. The gown that a master usually wore had been draped across a chair, ready to be donned should a boy be brought to him for punishment or, less likely, praise. Clearly he had no need of such accoutrements to impress or intimidate parents. Yet he gave the immediate impression of being a fair man, which inspired Maisie to wonder how bullying could survive in any environment in which he worked. Or perhaps that first impression was a blind.

"It's no trouble at all, Miss Dobbs." Cottingham took her hand and smiled, then returned to his chair behind the polished oak desk. "Please, be seated." He paused. "Now then, how might I assist you? I understand that you are"—he reached forward to take up her card from the desk—"a private investigator and a psychologist. Very impressive, if I might say so. Where did you study?"

"At Girton and at the University of Edinburgh's Department of Legal Medicine."

"Well, well, well." He set the card back on the desk. "Please, go on."

"Our conversation must be in confidence."

"Of course."

"I would like to ask some questions about a former pupil—and you will have to cast your memory back a few years, I'm afraid."

"Who?"

"Alfred Sandermere."

"Oh, lord!" Cottingham rolled his eyes. "Once seen, never forgotten. If I were to pick three or four boys from my days here who might attract the attention of either the police or a private investigator, Sandermere might be at the top of the list."

"Really, why?"

"Dreadful boy, such a chip on his shoulder. Typical second-son behavior, but multiplied by ten. Possibly because his older brother was definitely a top-drawer scholar, with first-class performance on the sports field—multiplied by ten!" He looked at his watch. "If you will excuse me, I'll have his file brought up."

Cottingham left the room, leaving Maisie on her

own. It was the first opportunity she'd had to be in wakeful solitude since Simon died, less than twelve hours earlier. She stood up and paced to the window, which overlooked a quadrangle where boys congregated between classes. To the right a stone wall marked the perimeter of the headmaster's house, beyond which, she suspected, a walled garden gave the impression of being in the country, rather than in west London. Had Simon attended such a school? She frowned. It occurred to her that she had little knowledge of his life before they met, except, perhaps, the snippets shared by Priscilla, for he had been a family friend and a cohort of her three brothers. Maisie's entire knowledge of him was, more or less, limited to their time together and to life since then, a life spent grieving for a man not yet dead but lost to war all the same. And now he *was* dead, except that the true mourning had already been done, and there was little more to do now, except respectfully wear black until after the funeral. How would she fill the place he'd occupied? How would she use such freedom, now that it was hers? It was as if she were a seeding ground that had lain fallow for years and had now been freshly tilled. How, then, might she grow, now that he was gone?

"Ah, we're in luck. My secretary found Sandermere, A.'s records with the greatest of ease. Terribly efficient, our Miss Larkin. Now then, let me see." He resumed his place without questioning the fact that he had entered his study to find Maisie at the window. She sat opposite him once again.

"Not a terribly impressive academic record. Good at sports, but not what you would call a sportsman—he was a bad loser. Never could make him captain of the cricket or rugger teams, though he certainly had the physical accomplishment." He turned a few pages.

"Can you tell me, specifically, about his suspensions?"

"That I can." Cottingham reached for a sheaf of papers clipped separately into the folder. "I have the exact dates of suspensions, until, of course, his final expulsion from the school." He unclipped the list in question and passed it to Maisie. "You may make a note of those dates. We released him to his father. As I understand it, he languished at his parents' estate in Kent to consider his wrongdoings."

"Bullying?"

"I wish it were as simple as that. It was intimidation, really. Rather sophisticated, even for a boy like Sandermere. There wasn't much I would put past him. Mostly it was to do with money—it's not as if he needed it—but he would find out what other boys had been getting up to, you know, their petty little infractions, and demand money." He looked at Maisie. "Yes, *with menaces,* as they say in police parlance."

"Did he harm anyone?"

"That's what a menace such as Sandermere does. Hard if you fight back, hard if you don't." Cottingham looked at his watch. "Can I help you with anything else, Miss Dobbs?"

Maisie gathered her notebook and placed it, along with her pen, into her black leather document case. "No, you've been most kind."

Cottingham walked her toward the door and held out his hand, which she took, asking a question at the same time. "What about the Partridge boys? They're being bullied here, and understandably they're fighting back. How will you deal with that?"

"I think *bullying* might be too strong a term for the Partridges' teething problems here at St. Anselm's. If we give it time, they'll deal with the occasional ribbing themselves, Miss Dobbs. Staff step in if it looks as if the damage will really hurt someone. But every boy gets a black eye or a split lip now and again. Do bear in mind, the rugger field is a far more dangerous place than the dormitory." He frowned. "The thing is, they're different. When they fit in a bit more, the teasing will stop—they'll be part of the pack. You see, they can be whoever they want to be at home, or back in France, but here in school it's like an army. Everyone has to march to the same drum."

"Thank you, once again, Dr. Cottingham." Maisie left the office and shivered.

"GOOD HEAVENS, WHAT'S happened here?" Maisie looked at Priscilla, who raised an eyebrow and shook her head, then looked again at the three boys seated beside their mother outside the Head's office. The eldest, Timothy, was sporting a black eye, the middle son, Thomas, a nasty graze to the cheek, and the youngest, Tarquin, was running his tongue back and forth through the gap where four front teeth used to be.

"At least they were his milk teeth, Maisie. Can you imagine what I would do trying to find a dentist to make a plate for a boy who had just lost his adult teeth? I really don't know whether to bang their heads together or just pull them out of here."

"But, Maman—"

"Not a word, Tarquin, not *one* word." Priscilla held up her index finger as she spoke.

The youngest slumped in his chair. "Wasn't my fault, Tante Maisie. That boy picked on me first." He continued his explanation in English peppered with French, as if he had no conception of the point at which one language ended and the other began.

"Yes, but you didn't have to slug him back, did you?" Priscilla raised an eyebrow as she looked sideways at her son.

Maisie smiled and whispered, "Yes, he did, Pris."

"Don't encourage them, Maisie, unless you want to come and live with us and teach them instead of being an investigator."

Maisie winked at Tarquin, then smiled at Priscilla. "I think I'll have a walk around, while you're in with Dr. Cottingham."

"Probably for the best. Then you won't have to listen to a screaming mother on the other side of the door."

Maisie stepped away. When she looked back, she

saw Priscilla draw her glove from her hand, lick her fingers, and try to slick down each boy's unruly fringe. She heard the door open and close behind her, and suspected the meeting might only be a short one. Nevertheless, she walked around the entrance hall, stopping to look at various plaques commemorating the school's achievements.

One huge marble engraving held the names of each headmaster since the school's founding in 1640, and another a roster of sporting achievements since the century began. Then another, with a single red poppy placed on top, a list of boys from the school who had given their lives in the Great War—boys who had left school to join Kitchener's army and had, most likely, lied about their age. She ran her finger down the list of names until she came to the one she wanted: First Lieutenant Henry Arthur Crispin Sandermere, V.C., July 1916.

"WELL, THEN, THAT'S that." Priscilla marched toward Maisie, her face flushed, her arms outstretched around her boys, like a mother hen shielding her young with her wings. "We're off to the Dorchester now. The boys will *not* be coming back to St. Anselm's. I'll send a driver for their trunks and tuck boxes later." She feigned a glare at her sons. "Not one giggle, one comment. This is only the end of this school, not of your education. Come along, let's go to Tante Maisie's motor car."

Maisie walked briskly alongside Priscilla. "Pris, it's

a two-seater. I don't think I can fit—"

"Nonsense. These two can squeeze behind the seats, and this one will sit on my lap. Somehow, we will all get into your MG."

Not wanting to contradict her friend, Maisie acquiesced, rolling back the roof to better accommodate her passengers. Fortunately, the sun was shining as they drove along, slowly, so as not to lose a boy. The two older boys were seated precariously on the collapsed roof, while Tarquin Patrick sat on Priscilla's lap, still poking his tongue through the gap in his teeth. Not being able to stop herself, Maisie began to laugh.

"Don't laugh, you'll start them off," said Priscilla, the corners of her mouth twitching as she endeavored to counter the urge to giggle. It was a battle lost within seconds.

Maisie delivered the Partridge family to the Dorchester and went on her way, smiling. She was glad the boys were no longer at St. Anselm's. She didn't like a place where prejudice was tolerated, and violence between boys, who would one day be men, explained away as the result of not hearing the drumbeat of one's peers.

CHECKING HER WATCH as she entered her flat, Maisie decided to add a few notes to the case map before collecting her bags and setting off for Kent. Once more she would stay with Frankie this evening, and then at the inn until the end of the week, by which time, she hoped, her work would be done and some sort of explanatory report could be submitted to James Compton.

She logged the dates of Alfred Sandermere's boyhood suspensions from school alongside a list of dates germane to the case, then read through the notes taken shortly after her visit to meet him. He had made a point of informing her that he was away at the time of the Zeppelin raid on Heronsdene, yet according to the tally of dates, he was very much at home, as Cottingham had said, "languishing at his parents' estate" soon after the term had begun. She wondered what a boy of fifteen, almost sixteen, might do with time on his hands in a place where there was little to amuse him. Some boys were joining up at this age, and even younger, though it appeared that Sandermere, A. was not one of them.

Maisie worked for a short while longer, making plans to meet more of the villagers in the days to come, taking into account that she was waiting for additional information from Beattie Drummond. The reporter was an interesting woman, thought Maisie, someone who searched high and low for news and who worked ten times harder than her fellow newspapermen to get the story. And of course Beattie wanted the big story, the scoop that would jettison her to *The Daily Express* or even *The Times.* As she packed up the case map and gathered her belongings for the trip, Maisie wondered to what lengths B. T. Drummond might go to get what she wanted.

She was about to leave, when she set down her bags

and went again to the dining table at which she'd been working. She drew a box of fine vellum and matching envelopes toward her and took out her fountain pen, tapping the end of the barrel on the blotting paper as she mentally composed her letter. Once satisfied she had the words in her mind—though she would eventually compose and discard several versions of the letter—she began: *Dear Margaret . . .*

IT WAS AGAIN suppertime when Maisie arrived at her father's cottage at Chelstone Manor and, as before, Frankie had prepared a hearty repast for his daughter. Maisie remained concerned about her father's health, though his recovery from an accident some eighteen months earlier had been considered excellent by the local doctor. But he was getting on in years. It had often occurred to Maisie that, with the exception of Priscilla, those closest to her were in their twilight years, and she dreaded the losses that might come in quick succession. Her attempts to broaden the scope of her friendships were, in part, due to such fears.

Frankie dished up dinner almost as soon as Maisie walked in the door.

"Been a man here asking for you." He ladled a hearty helping of stew into the broad-lipped soup bowls, while Maisie cut and buttered bread in the thick slices her father favored.

"Me?" She held the knife suspended above the bread.

Frankie nodded. "Not what I would call a nice chap,

either. What was that man's name? S . . . Son . . . San—"

"Sandermere?"

Frankie pointed the ladle at her. "That's it. Sandermere. The one you asked about the other day, and I said I'd heard of him. Well, he came here on a big bay hunter. Fair sweating it was. I offered to walk the horse around, cool it down while he had a cup of tea—don't like to see a horse in a state like that—but he just went off again, cantering down the road like a highwayman. I thought to myself, *Who does he think he is*? Coming in here like he's Dick Turpin, all steamed up and having had a few, if I'm not mistaken."

Maisie frowned. "I wonder how he knew where you lived. And that I might be here." She began to cut the bread again. "More to the point, I wonder what he wanted."

"Well, I didn't like the man. A fella who treats an animal like that is a man to keep clear of, as far as I'm concerned." He lifted up his knife and fork. "And Dr. Blanche didn't take to him either."

"Maurice?" Maisie sat down, picked up her spoon, and began to sip the broth before starting on the thick wedges of brisket.

"He was walking back from the manor when that bloke turned up. I saw him, just watching, taking it all in. Then, when he rode off on that poor horse of his, Dr. Blanche came over and asked me about him."

"Did he say anything else?"

Frankie reached for a slice of bread and looked at

Maisie directly. "As a matter of fact, he did. Said that, if you've time, he'd like to see you. Seemed very . . . *concerned,* I think is the word. Yes. Didn't like what he saw. And to tell you plain, neither did I."

Maisie looked at the big round clock on the wall and then back toward her father. "If it's alright with you, Dad, I think I might wander over to see him after we've had supper."

"Don't mind me, love. In fact, if you've to deal with the likes of that man who came today, and Dr. Blanche can give you a spot of advice, I reckon you should go and see what he has to say."

Maisie nodded. "Yes, I'll do that." She smiled. "The stew's lovely, Dad."

WHEN FATHER AND daughter had cleaned the kitchen following their meal, and Frankie was seated by a fire with his newspaper, Maisie pulled on her jacket and walked toward Maurice's house via the garden entrance. She made her way up to the house and saw Maurice silhouetted against the windows of the conservatory. He would have seen the torch she carried.

The main door was already open by the time she arrived at the front of the house, and Maurice himself was waiting for her on the threshold.

"Ah, Maisie, I am so glad you have come." He reached out to her with both hands, which she took in her own.

"It *has* been a long time, hasn't it, Maurice?"

"Come, let us go to the drawing room—a fire's just

191

been lit. We'll have an after-dinner drink together, and we can talk." He turned to her as he walked, "Like old times."

Even as they walked the few steps from the door to the drawing room, Maisie knew that Maurice Blanche was gauging her emotional well-being, was mirroring her pace, her stance, her demeanor, to ascertain—what? Her stability? Her strength? She knew he would want to know exactly how she was feeling, as that information would dictate how he opened their conversation. Only this time she would be the one to begin speaking.

"I have some news, Maurice." She sat down as he pulled a cord to summon his housekeeper. "Some sad news."

"Yes, I know. You carry the weight of bereavement, of loss."

She nodded. Though she had also carried, for almost a year now, a resentment regarding Maurice, this animosity was rendered weak under the weight of her desire to speak of the events of last night. "Simon is dead, Maurice. He's gone."

Maurice handed her a glass of port and sat opposite her in his favorite wingback chair. He set a crystal glass with two fingers' worth of single-malt whisky onto a small table at his side and reached for his pipe, which he tapped against the brick of the fireplace before taking up his tobacco pouch. Then he responded to her announcement. "It was past his time, the poor man."

Maisie nodded. "Yes, it was." She spoke quietly. "I don't know how I feel, Maurice."

Her former employer and mentor regarded her, then turned to his pipe, pressing the bowl against the tobacco in the pouch and filling it so as not to waste even a strand. "Do not expect to know how to feel, Maisie. You buried your grieving for years, not only for Simon but for your own lost innocence. And the death you saw as a girl in France—that is the most terrible loss of innocence." He paused while he held a match to his pipe and drew against the flame. Then he looked at Maisie. "Last year was a watershed for you, your collapse in France reflecting a weight of emotion, of remembrance, that could not be borne any longer. Do not try to second-guess your responses. Otherwise you will encounter guilt if you have reason to embrace laughter, or you will draw away from those things that bring you joy, because you will be trying to feel a certain way, a way expected by a broader society."

"I was with Priscilla today, and we were laughing at her boys. When it came time to write to Margaret Lynch, I found I was taking myself to task for those moments of lightness."

"The challenge with death is that it can lift a burden, and we feel those two sensations—the lightness you speak of, along with melancholy, of loss. You have already suffered one, Maisie, so do not be taken aback when there is only one remaining and it is the one that brings with it moments of levity." He paused, as if taking care to look for stepping-stones as he negotiated difficult terrain. "Cast your mind back to the time when you were seeing Andrew Dene." Maisie sat straighter in her chair, as if to brace herself, but Maurice continued. "Though you had happy times, and he certainly could make you laugh, you always carried the obligation you felt toward Simon. Of course, I understand that there were other difficulties, but do not underestimate your feelings, and don't draw back from doors that open, now that the one closed for years has locked forever. Simon's spirit is at peace. Allow yours to be free as you live."

Maisie sighed. She would consider Maurice's words later, in her room in her father's house. For now, though she had opened the subject, she wanted to deflect the conversation away from Simon, for his death was ground upon which she, too, stepped with care. "My father said you saw the man who came looking for me today."

Cradling the pipe by its bowl in one hand, Maurice reached again for his single malt. "Not a particularly nice character, if I may say so."

"Far from it, I'd say. I wonder how he might have known my father lives at Chelstone."

"You're working for James Compton, I take it?"

"Yes, but—"

"That man came here to see James. He came to the front of the house. I had been visiting Lady Rowan and was about to leave when he arrived, looking for James. When informed the Viscount was out on his hunter, the man mounted his horse and made for the back of the house. I can only assume one of the groundsmen confirmed that James was out and, when asked when he'd left, said 'Mr. Dobbs would know.' Then the horseman of course realized that there was some connection between the Dobbs who was the groom and the Dobbs who had been breathing down his neck."

"I wouldn't say that I was breathing down—"

"The man kept running his fingers around his collar, which was not tight. It suggested an outward demonstration of his state of mind." Maurice sipped the malt and placed the glass back on the table. "Can you tell me more about the case? Would you like to discuss your findings?"

Maisie saw that Maurice was again treading with care lest he cause offense. She had claimed a measure of independence since last year, and knew her mentor anticipated that she would not be willing to concede significant ground. However, she valued a dialogue that would help marshal her thoughts on the case.

"James is about to purchase a large estate in Heronsdene, about ten or so miles from here."

"Yes, I know."

"He's really interested in the brickworks, to take advantage of the increase in building, despite the slump. The only parts of the estate that will remain in the owner's hands—and that was him who came to Chelstone today, a man called Alfred Sandermere— are the house and the immediate gardens, plus the stables. James is concerned about instances of petty crime that have been plaguing the area for years, especially a spate of fires set deliberately."

"Fires?"

"Yes. And there's a mood in the village, a sort of scar formed following a tragedy that happened in the war. Three people were killed in a Zeppelin raid, and that event, as much as the loss of their young men, seems to have been a catalyst—for a change of heart, if you like. Of course, one expects such a thing to leave a mark, to lead to different behaviors, but that was fourteen years ago."

"The heart does not know chronos time, Maisie."

"Yes, I understand." She paused. "I don't trust Sandermere, even though I know I should refrain from such conclusions. I believe he's embezzling his insurers, and I have a sense that he's trying to pull a fast one on this deal with James. Perhaps with more bad publicity, the news of a likely lower price on the estate will bring in more potential buyers, which will drive up the price again. It's counter to what one might otherwise believe, but we both know that once people are bent on acquisition, they continue, even if it comes close to breaking them."

"Yes, indeed. Tell me more about the villagers and what you've sensed."

"It's hard to get a clear reading at this time of year. The hop-picking brings in the Londoners, plus a tribe of gypsies, so there's no cohesive community, just different camps all filled with mistrust. The locals hate the incomers, but they don't mind the extra business, while the Londoners think the villagers are all turnip bashers who get up to goodness knows what and put the blame on them. And then there are the gypsies, who keep to themselves and who are actually not bad people, though no one wants to pick near them. The women go out, selling flowers and clothes pegs door-to-door, and the villagers buy goods from them, then turn their backs—but there's a few who go find the old matriarch to have their fortunes told."

Maurice's laugh was short, and he shook his head. "The double standard."

"Yes." Maisie sipped her port, set down the glass, then went on. "And the land where the bomb killed three people has no marker. It's overgrown, and—cold."

"Oh, dear."

Maisie nodded. "Michaelmas daisies grow wild there. As far as I can tell, it's the source of supply for the gypsy women who make bouquets for sale."

"Purple flowers, the color of mourning."

"Yes, but these are wild. No one planted them."

"Not that you know of."

"Indeed, not that I know of."

There was silence between them. Maisie knew that Maurice did not want to offer advice that might be unwelcome and was cradling their reunion gently, like sand in cupped hands, in case she left, offended, not to return for some months. Thinking again of those she loved who would be taken from her by time's passage, and how close she had once been to her mentor, Maisie began to soften, though she was not yet ready to relinquish the feeling of being slighted.

"What will you do next, if I may ask, Maisie?"

She inclined her head and stared into the fire. "I will keep the counsel of our earlier years together, Maurice. I will ask questions and more questions, for as you've always maintained, the power is in the inquiry, not necessarily in the answer."

"Good."

Maisie set down the glass of port. "You've a heavy hand with the decanter this evening, Maurice. I can't finish my drink."

"No matter." He stood to see her to the door. "You will contact me if . . ."

"Of course."

"And you will visit again?"

Maisie allowed him to take her hands in his, as she had when she entered the house. "Yes, I will."

As Maurice was about to close the door, Maisie called to him. "Maurice?"

He opened the door and squinted, to better see her in the dark.

"Do you happen to know anyone who is knowledgeable about violins?"

"Actually, I do. He's in London, has a small music shop in Denmark Street. He's an expert on stringed instruments and has a particular interest in violins. I'll send my housekeeper around with his name and address tomorrow morning, if you wish."

"Thank you. I am much obliged to you."

Maurice watched as Maisie switched on her torch and made her way back to the Groom's Cottage. He knew he was not quite forgiven.

TWELVE

Maisie left Chelstone soon after Maurice's housekeeper came to the cottage bearing an envelope for her, with a note from Maurice and the name of the luthier in Denmark Street who would, she hoped, be able to tell her more about the violin she had witnessed Webb playing with great skill.

The showers had abated, and morning once more held the pepper-and-herb fragrance that seemed to be ingrained in the breeze at hop-picking time. Verges alongside the road were still full of hogweed, showing off cream-colored fronds of tiny petals, interspersed with the delicate shepherd's purse, its fragile heart-shaped leaves shimmering as the motor approached, as if to hide behind the last of summer's pink common mallow. She had the road to herself, which offered an opportunity to plan her visit to Sandermere's brickworks, her first stop.

According to James Compton's notes, the foreman was Pete Bracegirdle, who had been employed at the works since he was twelve, starting as an apprentice. He was a master craftsman who could fashion any type of brick or tile and, before he became foreman, could turn out peg tiles—used in the repair of the many cottages built in medieval times—at a fair clip and with fewer breaks or seconds than any other artisan, making him a valuable worker. In addition to Bracegirdle, the brickworks employed some twenty-four men, a few of them apprentices.

Maisie drew the MG to a halt just inside the main gate to the works. In appearance, the factory itself looked more like a farm, with timber-framed out-buildings with tiled roofing, but minus the many smells and sounds of a farm. The entrance itself was not grand, a simple wooden five-bar gate of the type that might be found at the opening to a field of sheep or cattle. To the left, a sign, crooked and misspelled, pointed the way to the "Ofice."

The door was open, and two men stood behind a dust- and paper-laden desk, poring over an order. At first they did not see her.

"They definitely said they wanted the bricks by the end of October, so if we get them to Paddock Wood by—"

"Good morning."

Both men looked up, simultaneously wiping their hands on their mustard-colored workmanlike heavy cotton coats.

"I'm looking for Mr. Bracegirdle."

The shorter worker thumbed toward the man holding the order, who tucked a pencil behind his right ear and set down the sheet on top of a pile of papers. "I'm Mr. Bracegirdle." He was about to hold out his hand to greet her when he noticed the dirt ingrained in his palm. "I'm sorry, I can't—"

Maisie shook her head. "That's alright. Do you think you might be able to spare me ten or fifteen minutes of your time?"

Without inquiring as to the purpose of her visit, the foreman looked at his deputy, who touched his flat cap. "Right you are, Pete. I'll get the boys working on that order."

"I'll come out to the kilns as soon as I've had a word with this lady, Bert." He turned to Maisie, then came around to the other side of the desk, removed a pile of papers from a chair, flapped the papers back and forth across the seat to remove the dust, and held out his hand. "Take a seat, miss."

Maisie was grateful that she'd worn her heavy linen skirt, which, being khaki, would not show any dust lingering on the chair.

"What can I do for you?" Bracegirdle leaned back against the table and folded his arms. "You haven't come here for bricks or tiles, I'm sure."

"You're right. I'm working for the Compton Corporation, who are—as you've probably heard—in the process of finalizing arrangements to buy the business side of the Sandermere estate."

"Yes, we were all told when the works and the land went up for sale. Bit worrying, in these times. You never know whether you'll still have a job."

"I think I can say with a relative degree of confidence that, should the sale progress to completion, the

Compton Corporation wishes to expand the works here, develop the range of bricks and tiles, and make a significant well-considered investment in new equipment and practices."

"Well, we'll wait and see. That all sounds very nice, but you do hear about these—what do they call them?" He rubbed his chin.

"Asset strippers?"

"That's it. They take a business, sell it lock, stock and barrel, and then everyone's out of a job."

"Not a brickworks, and not when there's so much building going on."

"We can hardly keep up with the orders."

"Which is good news, for you and for buyers."

"Well, it's not all good news. We need investment to make sure we meet those orders. In fact, we've needed the right investment for a long time."

Maisie frowned. "I understood that Mr. Sandermere put a lot into the brickworks, more than could comfortably be afforded."

Bracegirdle pulled a cloth from his pocket and began rubbing his hands. "Not for me to speak out of turn, but to be honest with you, there are people who buy something new just for the sake of it. And half of what he paid good money for isn't what we wanted. I told him, I said, 'Here's what we need.' But he went for the goods the fast talkers pushed—with more than a dose of toadying up to him, I shouldn't wonder—which is why he bought, feeling like the big businessman. Lot of what we really want, you can get secondhand. I hope I manage to have a serious word with whoever buys the place so we can get what we need—and a bit more in the wage packets wouldn't go amiss, either."

"Quite." Maisie paused. "Mr. Bracegirdle, wasn't some of the expenditure on the works to replace equipment damaged in a recent spate of malicious destruction at the estate?"

"No, the spending came before the shop was got at. We've managed to repair a fair bit, and of course we lost a lot of inventory, but I got the boys working round the clock and we were able to fill our orders. Of course, Mr. Sandermere said he'd ordered some new parts, but I've yet to see them. We make do and mend when we have to, don't we?"

"Of course." Maisie shifted on the seat. "Have the insurers come to view the works?"

"Mr. Sandermere had them in straightaway, and of course they were interested, being as the stables went up in flames as well. They insisted a police report be made. Mr. Sandermere hadn't called the police, saying it was probably some local lads out on the beer and the police couldn't do anything anyway. And he wasn't wrong there—they came, had a sniff around, took a few measurements, paced back and forth from the door to make it look like they knew what they were about, and then off they went."

"I see."

" 'Course, it would have been different if his brother was the boss."

"I understand he was a different kettle of fish altogether."

"Very fair. Knew the business. I remember him coming in here when he was just a lad, wanting to learn how to make bricks. Took him round myself, I did. And he knew the farmers, made it his business to know about farming. We have a bookkeeper from the village, a Mr. Soames, who comes in of a Friday." He laughed. "I have to do a bit of tidying up on Thursday night, so he don't get upset on account of the mess we've made." He smiled. "Anyway, Mr. Henry came every Friday, even when he was back from his school in the summer, to sit with Mr. Soames and make sure he understood what went on here."

"And Alfred's not the same."

Bracegirdle gave a half laugh that came out as a derogatory snort. "Oh, he's interested in the bottom line, alright—because he likes to spend anything that isn't spoken for."

Maisie nodded. "Have there been any other incidences of vandalism?"

"We get the odd nipper from the village with a pot of paint who reckons himself an artist with a bit of a flair for walls, but other than that, no, just that one."

"But when you add it to the vandalism in the village and the fires, it all mounts up."

Bracegirdle moved around to the other side of the desk. Maisie watched, curious, for his move had placed a substantial piece of furniture between them at the mention of the problems in the village.

"Don't know much about the village, not specifically."

"Oh? I assumed you lived in the village, Mr. Bracegirdle."

"I do, yes, but I don't know much about the fires." He shrugged. "Mind you, there was the accident at Fred Yeoman's the other night—silly bugger threw out the ashes and started it himself."

Maisie knew there was little to be gained from the conversation, though she wanted to press the foreman just a little more. "Do you remember the Zeppelin raid?"

"Don't forget a thing like that."

"No, I shouldn't wonder. I understand the local baker and his family were killed when a bomb hit their shop, for of course they lived upstairs."

"That's right."

"And no one has ever built on the land. Or even put up a memorial."

He shrugged again. "Best left as it is. They're buried in the churchyard."

"I know, but I thought—"

Bracegirdle looked at the clock on the wall behind him. "Well, I haven't got the time to sit about, got work to do. If that's all, miss—"

"Of course." Maisie stood up, brushing her hand across the fabric at the back of her skirt to remove dust. "Thank you for seeing me."

He nodded and turned to leave, via the door leading into the works.

• • •

MAISIE HAD NOW confirmed the impression she had of Sandermere, a spendthrift who was likely entranced by the thrill of expenditure and the attention that accompanies the impression of having considerable wealth. He liked spending money. He liked being a man of commerce, of land, but he had no aptitude for either and no wise counsel to direct him—if he had cared to listen. She was in no doubt, now, that her suspicion—as put to James Compton—that Sandermere was embezzling his insurers was correct. He had probably received compensation for both the stable fire and for the damage to the brickworks. And what of the items lost when the mansion was burgled? Had he claimed already for that loss? There was a police report, though the suspects were probably released by now, so there might be a lapse of time before he received those funds. How desperate was he? Maisie suspected that the man's weakness was akin to those who are unaware of their limits with alcohol, except his addiction was to money and, more particularly, to the thrill of profligacy and to the attention such behavior garnered. If he had nothing, he would be like the addict deprived of his drug—what, then, might he do next? Would his craving for attention, which she thought might be the root of his character deficiencies, lead him to set fires, to pyromania? Or would other aspects of his life suffer a descent, due to lack of control?

She brushed off the back of her skirt again, before

she took her seat in the MG, and drove out of the brickworks and across to the farm where Billy and his family were working. Taking her knapsack, in which she'd placed a flask of hot tea, she locked the motor car and began walking toward the hop-gardens, following the sound of voices in the distance, like a dog nosing a scent. The hop-gardens already picked seemed desolate. Where there had been a full, rich, green crop, a hundred or so pickers hard at work, and the noise of talk, laughter and singing filling the air, the land now seemed bereft, with only the ghostly remains of a verdant harvest. There was a shallow incline on the path ahead, on the other side of which, set to one side, was a tap where people came throughout the day to fill a bottle or a kettle or to wash the knee of a child who had fallen while playing. She was surprised to come across Sandermere's horse, grazing on the verge, and thought that perhaps the landowner had stopped to quench his thirst. But as she came over the hill, she heard a scream and was just in time to see Sandermere take Paishey Webb by the arm and pull her to him. At first, Maisie could hardly believe the scene before her or what the man was thinking to do such a thing. Each movement seemed to be in slow motion, but barely a second passed before the gypsy shrieked again and again, trying to escape Sandermere's grasp. She kicked out at him, her scarf pulling back as he took hold of her hair, then put his finger to her hooped earring, and dragged it through the skin of her lobe. She cried out in pain and kicked again, desperate to save herself.

Maisie lost no time in running toward the pair, shouting, "Leave her alone! Stop!" And then, louder, "Help! Help!"

But Sandermere did not stop, pulling Paishey to him as if to press his lips to her neck, even as blood ran from her torn ear to his mouth. Another voice, stronger and louder, joined Maisie's. Billy Beale had just walked up the hill from the hop-garden toward the tap. Dropping the kettle he had brought to fill, he launched himself at Sandermere and dragged him away. Though he was not the stronger man, Billy was faster and drew back his fist before Sandermere could even curl his fingers. The punch struck home, smashing Sandermere's nose so that blood sprayed across his shirt and down his face.

"You nasty git, you bleedin' nasty piece of work. I don't care who you are, you bugger off out of 'ere before I kill you! So 'elp me, I'll kill you, you bastard!"

As Sandermere staggered away, pulled himself onto his horse, and galloped off along the farm road, Maisie took Paishey in her arms. More people, locals and gypsies alike, came running from the hop-garden, drawn by the screams and shouting. Webb was in the crowd, pushing others aside when he saw Maisie and Billy with his wife.

"You, gorja! What—"

"He saved my honor, Webb," said Paishey. "Leave'n

him and her alone." She wiped her hand across her face, smearing the profusion of blood.

Maisie pulled a handkerchief from her knapsack, ran cold water onto it from the tap, and held the cloth to Paishey's ear. "Come sit on the verge, and let me have a look."

Paishey allowed Maisie to lead her, while Billy explained to Webb what had happened. Maisie saw Webb turn as if to go after Sandermere, but Billy braced himself against the gypsy. "I know how you feel, mate, but calm down. He'll have the law on you like a ton of bricks if you go after him now. You can't win—you'll end up inside for the rest of your life. Then where will your little nipper be, or your missus?"

Webb raised his hands to either side of the crown of his hat and then let them slump at his sides. He turned away from the crowd and screamed as if to a god who could not hear. It was a loud, impassioned cry that came not from the throat but from deep inside his body, and it was enough to begin to disperse the onlookers. Paishey ran to her husband and Webb held her to him, his fingernails white with the pressure of his grip. Then she pulled away, taking his hand, below which a scar crossed the inside of his wrist, and she held her own wrist, her own scar, to it, so that the place where their blood had run together on the day of their marriage was joined once more.

Billy shook his head. "I'd scream too, if I was 'im. Fine 'ow-do-you-do, this, ain't it? Probably won't 'ave a job come morning, me *or* 'im."

As she rinsed blood from her handkerchief, ready to hand it to Paishey once again, Maisie realized she was shaking. "I can't believe what I just saw. That a man would act in such a way is unconscionable—and in broad daylight!"

"I better not see that bloke again, that's all I can say."

"I'm so glad you were here, Billy. Are you alright?"

Billy nodded. "I knew 'e could punch me into the ground with one good one, drunk as 'e was, so I 'ad to get in quick with the old one-two. I 'aven't got enough go in the old legs to get into a bout with someone like that." He rubbed his knuckles where they had connected with Sandermere's nose. "Lucky I came along when I did. Doreen 'ad seen the gypsy walking to the tap and picked up the kettle to go over there. I knew what she was thinking, that she'd 'ave a word, explain why she 'adn't been passin' the time of day or makin' a fuss of the baby, and thought I'd better go myself. Not as if you can explain a thing like that, but I didn't want any trouble." Billy shook his head. "Found trouble alright, though, didn't I?"

Webb and Paishey walked across to them and Webb held out his hand to Billy. "You saved my wife's honor. I am in your debt."

"No, you're not, mate. You would've done the same, anybody would."

Webb shook his head. "No, they wouldn't." He looked at his wife, then back at Billy. "Sometimes it's

210

like the morning hate when we come out to work."

Billy frowned, pausing before saying more and with his head to one side, as if considering the man's words. Then he changed his expression and reached out to grip Webb's shoulder. "Just promise me you won't go after 'im." His smile was one of irony. "Not unless you take me with you, anyway."

Webb nodded, and Maisie reached out to help Paishey clean more blood from her face and neck.

"Aunt Beulah will doctor me now. She'll mend my ear."

Maisie drew back, respectful of the gypsy ways, but she was curious to know what events had unfolded just before she came upon Sandermere attacking Paishey. She rested a hand on the woman's shoulder so that she might not pull back, fearful, when asked about the attack. "What happened, Paishey? What did Sandermere say before he went for you?"

The woman looked at the ground as she spoke. "I'n came for water, and the *rye-moosh*—the boss man—came up to the tap while I was filling the kettle. He'n told me to move, to let him in, and I told him my kettle was nearly filled and I'd soon be done. I said *sir* out of respect." Maisie saw a flash of the gypsy's independence as she spoke. "Then he'n lifted his stick and went to thrash me, and he'n was saying I was nothing, that he would have us all sacked for our trouble, and the whole farm was his, all the hop-gardens and the tap and all the water what comes from it. Then he'n went for me, just as you come along. Said everything was his, me an' all, and he'n be takin' what he wanted."

"And there was a stink on 'is breath, couldn't miss it," added Billy. "'e'd been at the bottle, no doubt about it. It's a wonder 'e could get up on that 'orse."

Maisie nodded and said they'd probably all better be getting on, and Beulah should look at Paishey's ear. Together they walked back to the hop-garden, where Webb and Paishey joined their people, before gathering up their daughter and leaving the workers. Maisie knew they were returning to the clearing, which, although temporary, represented the lair that any animal would escape to when harmed or threatened.

BILLY PAUSED BEFORE walking along the rows to join his family. "What d'ye think that was all about, Miss, Sandermere actin' like a lunatic?"

Maisie thought for some moments before speaking. "The man is losing the very underpinning of his life—the land that has been in his family for centuries—and it's all his fault. The estate has given him a certain status to bolster him, and now it's slipping through his fingers, so he's clutching at whatever he can. And the drink is keeping his anger well oiled." She paused. "There's a sadness to him, as despicable as he is. A man who acts in such a destructive manner is himself harmed."

Billy shrugged. "Well, 'e'll be 'armed a lot more if I see 'im tryin' on that sort of thing again, make no mistake. Like I said, I reckon we'll be lucky to still be in work tomorrow. I don't expect to be seein' that ugly dial again as long as I live—and I'm glad of it."

They continued in silence for a while. Then, as she walked alongside Billy, back to the bin where his family worked together, Maisie broke the news of Simon's death. Simon had saved Billy's life in the war, a memory forever fresh in Billy's mind. He shook his head.

"After all this time. Gaw, blimey, Miss, I kept wishin' it was the other way round, that 'e'd come back to what 'e was, before the shell got 'im." He looked at her. "You alright, Miss?"

Maisie felt her eyes moisten. She nodded. "Yes. I don't know whether I'm shocked or not. It was as if his very life had been playing wolf with us, so that when the time came for him to . . . to go, I couldn't quite believe it. It's as if we've been tricked by hope ever since he was wounded."

Having stopped to talk, Billy walked on and Maisie kept pace, her head lowered. "You'll feel better after the funeral, Miss. When that's done there's nothing more than to get used to it. Once our little Lizzie was laid to rest, we could only remember her and try to— you know—just go on, day by day, one foot in front of the other." He paused again, unused to speaking of his feelings. "Sometimes I feel as if, when you throw that big clod of earth onto the coffin, you're not just startin' to fill the 'ole in the ground but the big gapin' one that's been blown in your life."

213

As they reached the bin, with the tallyman close at hand, her thoughts were deflected by the rush to clean the hops of leaves. She had wanted to ask Billy why he had looked at Webb so intently when they were speaking after the encounter with Sandermere, as if something had taken him aback, just for a second. Instead, she steeped her hands into the hops and began to pull out leaves.

Once the tallying was finished, they spoke of the London boys just released from police custody. As soon as they had returned to the hop-garden, George and his family had packed up their belongings and gone home to Shoreditch. "Shame," said Billy. "They needed the money, and the farmer's not duty-bound to pay you your wages unless you see out the picking to the end. Pity they couldn't find it in them to stay." When they began speaking of Sandermere's attack on Paishey Webb, Maisie debated whether to visit the gypsies again today. She had planned to but now wondered if her presence would be unwelcome at such a time. But it struck her that the risk of retaliation by Sandermere, owner of the land where they had made camp, might encourage them to move on, and she wanted to see Beulah again. So she chatted briefly with the Beale family and took her leave, once again carrying her knapsack over one shoulder as she walked at a brisk pace toward the hill and the clearing. If she was not welcome, she would leave with haste.

THE LURCHER CAME down the hill, walked with her

until they reached the vardos, and then ran across the clearing to Beulah. Maisie waved as she came into the shade, her eyes seeing only outlines as they adjusted from the day's bright light. Beulah raised one hand and beckoned Maisie to her.

"I wanted to find out how Paishey is." Maisie took her place, seated on a fallen tree next to Beulah.

"She'n be better when we leave, now. Only another week, then we'll go."

"Where to?"

"Up'n there." She thumbed to the north, meaning London. "We'll go to the Common for the winter. No more work on the land afore year's end, not for us anyway."

Maisie nodded. "What about her ear, where the ring was taken from her?"

Beulah called to Paishey, who was sitting on her haunches, chopping vegetables into a bowl. She set the task to one side and, light of foot, approached the matriarch. "Show'n her." Beulah pointed to the younger woman's ear.

Paishey drew back her black hair to reveal the lower half of her left ear, encrusted with a deep green paste molded to her flesh. Beulah motioned for her to lean forward and, as she came close, reached up with her vein-strapped hands and picked at the paste until it fell away. The lobe was no longer livid and swollen, and there was no division in the flesh, just a single line of no more than a hair's breadth where the earring had been dragged free.

"She'n be wearing gold again, come morning."

Maisie smiled at Paishey, taking her hand. "And your heart?"

The young woman nodded accord, to say she was well. "I've my Boosul and my Webb. If 'n I let my heart break over an old sot, Webb'd go after 'im, and I don't want that. We'n be good people, don't want trouble." She waved as she returned to her bowl of vegetables.

"I saw you out in the woods last week," said Maisie, turning to Beulah. "You were dowsing, with a forked hazel twig."

Beulah cackled. "Least you knew it were hazel."

"Can you teach me?"

"No. Can't be taught. I can tell you how, but I can't teach you to feel, to listen to the rod."

"I want to try."

Beulah placed her hands on her knees and levered herself to standing position. Maisie stood up, too, and thought the old woman might rest her hand in the crook of her arm. Instead she walked upright, not stooped, toward her vardo, motioning for Maisie to follow her. She reached underneath the vardo to pull out a wooden fork cut from a hazel branch and cleared of leaves, then walked toward the field where the horses grazed. She stopped and looked out across the land, breathing in the late-afternoon air, as the sun traveled down toward the horizon, bathing the stubble in a pale orange-red shimmer. Beulah handed the fork to Maisie. Then, placing her hands on top of her pupil's, she gave weight to the rustic divining tool.

"This'n be how it'll feel, when it's pulling."

"How does it know what I'm looking for?"

Beulah shook her head. "You'n know the answer, girl. You does it all the time. You hold it here." She tapped Maisie's head. "If 'n you want coins, you hold coins. If 'n you want water, you see water. And if 'n you want silver, you think silver." And when she said the word *silver* a second time, with a movement as sudden as lightning, she removed the watch from Maisie's jacket lapel and threw it into the field.

Maisie clutched her lapel. "Oh, no! Why did you take that? We could have used something else. Why my watch?" She looked down, clutched the fork's handles, and moved forward.

"Slow, girl, slow. Let'n the fork tell you how to step."

Maisie felt the woman's hand, light, on her arm. She had not seen where the watch was thrown but listened with her fingers to the rod's counsel and held the watch in her mind's eye. Taking one carefully gauged step after another, she made her way across the grass. Without looking up, she knew the horses had stopped grazing and were ambling in her direction. Beulah walked behind her, along with the lurcher. She offered no words of advice, no instructions, only her presence as witness.

She turned once, the weight between her fingers pulling her to the left and then in a straight line. The horses were closer now—she could hear them nick-

217

ering behind her. She wondered why Beulah did not chivvy them away, then thought it was to test her resilience to distraction. Never, since her apprenticeship with Maurice, had a lesson been so keen.

The rod pulled again, the weight trying her balance. Her watch was close. Then, as the rod pointed downward, the heaviness in her hands diminished. She knelt down, pushed the stubble aside, and claimed the watch.

"Thank God!" She held it to her chest, closing her eyes, then stood up, turning to Beulah.

The woman regarded Maisie in silence, with the horses leaning close together behind her and the dog at her side. "Now'n you know. Now'n you can dowse."

"It was a sudden lesson, Aunt Beulah."

Beulah was frowning and came to Maisie, taking the watch from her. She held it in her hand, as if to feel its weight. "Get rid of it."

"What do you mean?" Maisie stepped back, as she might if threatened.

"That watch has been too close to death. That watch holds too much pain to be worn so close to your heart. Its time is done now. Get rid of it."

"But it was a gift, from someone dear to me. I can't just—" She took back the watch.

Beulah stared. "Yes'n you can. Hold on to time, like that"—she pointed at the watch—"and you stay in time." She turned and walked back up the hill, stretching out her arms to send the horses away, while the lurcher followed, stopping only once to look back at Maisie.

LATER, MAISIE RETURNED to the inn, where she was shown to the same room she'd occupied before. She ached for a hot bath and, when she inquired, found that the Yeomans could not do enough for her. Once again she steeped herself in a tin bath filled with hot water, leaning back to rest her head as the steam filtrated into every pore.

A letter had awaited her arrival at the inn, a brief note from Beattie Drummond written in a matter-of-fact manner to let her know she would be coming down on the train from Paddock Wood the next morning, arriving at Heronsdene station at nine o'clock. She asked if Maisie would pick her up, as she had information of interest regarding the case. *The case.* She thought Beattie's tone somewhat proprietorial, as if she was claiming part of the case as her own. Maisie had encountered such behavior in the past, in other instances where the interest shown by a source of information crossed a line. The reporter's enthusiasm was a direct result of her hunger for some acclaim in her field, but Maisie could not allow it to stall her progress, which she felt was already hampered enough—by herself.

Later, as she lay back in bed before allowing sleep to claim her, Maisie replayed the day in her mind, watching as certain events and encounters came to the fore. There was Sandermere's drink-inspired frenzy, his lack of control. Then Beulah, taking her watch, the talisman that had gone to war with her, and throwing it away. And her warning: *That watch holds too much pain to be worn close to your heart.*

She cleared her mind so she could rest. The last thing she saw before she fell asleep was a vision of Simon, sitting in his wheelchair at the convalescent hospital. She remembered, once, leaning over him, her arm around his shoulder, his head pulled into the crook of her neck. There was a point at which the edge of her scar met his.

THIRTEEN

Beattie Drummond stepped down from the train, once more wearing businesslike attire, a blue-gray skirt with a white blouse and, on her feet, black shoes smart enough for the street yet stout enough to wear out to a farm, should it be necessary. She carried a jacket to match the skirt, and a brown briefcase with both buckles broken, so the flap lived up to its name. She moved the jacket and briefcase to her left hand when she saw Maisie and held out her right hand in greeting.

"How are you, Miss Dobbs?"

"Very well, thank you, and you?"

After shaking hands, they walked to the MG, where the reporter squinted into the sun as she waited for Maisie to open the passenger door. "Might I call you

Maisie, seeing as we're working on the same case?"

Maisie waited until Beattie was seated and then turned to face her. "Of course you may. But look, Beattie—" It was time to set a boundary between her work and the newspaperwoman's business. "I am grateful for the information you are finding for me, and I will most certainly keep my word and ensure that you are the first to know if I encounter anything that amounts to a scoop for your newspaper, but I have only one assistant."

Beattie was firm. "I thought, seeing as he's not with you at the moment, you might need a bit of help with the legwork."

Maisie shook her head. "Ah, but he *is* here. And I have found that I make more efficient progress alone, or with just my assistant working on other aspects of a case, in tandem with my inquiries." She paused, so that her words might have an effect. "And though I am at present looking into events that have piqued your interest for some time, it is not yet what I might term a *case,* not in the way you might think."

"Oh, yes it is. You're sniffing at this one like a hound following a scent, and I want to be there when you chase down the culprit."

"Then if you wish me to execute my duties effectively, you must return to Maidstone when we have completed our conversation and leave me to do my work. Rest assured I will keep my promise to you."

Beattie Drummond looked down at her hands as she clutched the top of her briefcase. "I want to be out of here so much. I want to be taken seriously by a news-paper and not have to go to one more school fete."

"Yes, I know you do, Beattie, and I give you my word that you will have your scoop."

Beattie nodded. "Is there somewhere we can talk?"

Maisie started the motor car and drove slowly away from the station, stopping at the edge of a field. She reached behind the seat for a blanket and a bag with a flask and two beakers.

"Come on, let's have a cup of tea."

They set the blanket at a point overlooking the soft undulating patchwork-quilt fields and ancient wood-lands that were a hallmark of Kent's High Weald. Sitting down, each with a beaker of tea, they discussed Beattie's findings.

"Here's a list of seven houses where miscellaneous fires have broken out. There have been at least three more according to my records, but I don't have the details. As you can see, they take place around the same date each year. You have the family names there, though I have only given the head of household and spouse, not the names of all the children—with one exception."

"Which is?"

Beattie leaned across, still holding her beaker of steaming tea in one hand. "Phyllis Mansell, now Phyllis Wheeler. She and her husband live with her parents, though they have two children of their own, and a new baby, I think—last time I came to the vil-lage for the paper, she was up like a balloon. Anyway, she was supposedly best friends with the girl who died, Anna Martin."

"How do you know?"

"Snooping. Asking questions to make things easier for any private inquiry agent who happened to come along."

Maisie raised an eyebrow and smiled, taking the comment in the spirit of a quip, rather than a bitter retort. "Thank you. I appreciate it. Do you know anything else about the Martin family? How long had they been here?"

"They had been here for some years. The parents had been in London, then came to Kent because Anna had trouble with her breathing. They thought that getting her out of those pea-soupers would be just the ticket. You can imagine it: 'Come to the country air, breathe in dust and hay!'" Her mimicry reflected recent government advertising campaigns to get more people out and hiking, for better health and to fight disease. However, Maisie was intrigued when she mimicked an accent, rolling her vowels and using a singsong cadence.

"Why are you speaking like that?"

"Well, they were Dutch, the Martins."

"Dutch?"

"Yes, only one generation back—something like that."

"So the original name was probably Maarten." Maisie looked into the distance, seeing the name written in her mind's eye. "Hence the names Jacob and Bettin."

"And Willem."

"Yes, of course." Maisie was reflecting upon Carter's description of the baker in Heronsdene and how Mrs. Crawford always ordered from him, because he was the best. But he hadn't mentioned that the family were from the Netherlands.

"Did they have discernible accents, do you think?"

"I don't think so, despite my impersonation, though I understand Dutch was spoken in the home. I once had a Dutch friend who spoke five or six languages. She liked to travel and told me, 'No one speaks my language, so I have to speak everyone else's if I want to be understood.'"

Maisie was thinking about Priscilla's boys, hence "I see" was the sum of her reply.

"Anyway, you'll find Phyllis rather loath to talk about her friend—I know. I tried collaring her for a chat during the pancake races one Shrove Tuesday. Clammed up very tight, she did."

"I'll try to find out if she has any thoughts about the fires."

"I doubt she can tell you much, really. I was just sniffing around, wondering whether to write some sort of In Remembrance piece when the ten-year anniversary of the Zeppelin raid came around. No one wanted to think about it, talk about it, or otherwise bring it back. So that little idea was shot down in flames, as so many before them." She sighed. "Anyway, here's the Reverend Staples's address. He was the village vicar. As you can see, he lives in Hawkhurst now, at Easter

Cottage, down the road from the church, St. Laurence's at The Moor, which is the old part of the village, up on the hill. He's not the vicar there, but old habits die hard—he can probably only sleep if there's a church clock on his doorstep clanging away all night. Do you need directions?"

"Please, if you don't mind."

"He's a good sort, really. Rather fond of chamber music. In fact, while he was vicar he started a quartet here in the village." Beattie noted the directions on the sheet of paper she had already prepared for Maisie and handed it to her.

Maisie folded the paper and placed it in the black document case she'd brought with her from the motor car. "You've been very kind and incredibly helpful, Beattie." She paused, then reached out and placed her hand on the reporter's shoulder. "You really will get your chance, I promise. As soon as anything concrete surfaces, I'll be in touch. I give you my word."

Beattie nodded and glanced at her wristwatch. "Well, this will never get the eggs cooked, will it?" She looked at Maisie. "Where's that lovely nurse's watch you were wearing last time we met?"

Maisie shrugged. "I forgot to put it on today. I'll have to use the sun as a timepiece."

As the women returned to the MG, Beattie expressed annoyance at having missed the two London boys who had been released by the police. "I thought I would be able to interview them with their people, you know, among the hop-pickers, get some other bits and pieces to give some local color. Heaven knows, they didn't hang around once they'd been let off."

"The parents wanted to get them back to London, back to work before news of their arrest filtered northward and they lost their apprenticeships," said Maisie, easing the MG back onto the road.

Conversation was lighter as they drove toward the station for Beattie to catch the train to Tunbridge and from there to Maidstone. As Beattie alighted from the motor car, Maisie leaned toward the passenger window. "Beattie, I had some good advice from a friend yesterday. She told me that if you want to find silver, you have to think silver. There's no reason why it wouldn't work with your business as well. If you want success, you have to hold it"—she tapped the side of her head—"as vividly as you can, up here."

Beattie frowned, then smiled. "Oh, I see. Imagine myself sitting at the guv'nor's desk."

Maisie shook her head. "No. Really see yourself at one of the big newspapers. Think silver, Beattie."

MAISIE DROVE DIRECTLY from the station to Hawkhurst, a journey that once again took her through village after village resplendent in the midst of a varied and colorful harvest. She saw apples almost ready for the picking as she passed the orchards, with sweet Cox's Orange Pippins hanging heavy on branches and hearty bitter Bramleys just waiting to be sliced into a pie. Alongside an orchard of nutty-brown russet apples, she stopped, idling the MG while she slipped through the fence and twisted one from a branch, and then drove off before anyone caught her in the act of scrumping.

Entering Hawkhurst, she drove up toward The Moor, past the grassy common, the village school, and the church, before parking outside Easter Cottage. She pulled on her jacket, smoothed the linen skirt she had selected that day, and on her head placed a soft straw hat with a purple grosgrain band and low broad brim. She put a clutch of index cards into her shoulder bag, not wanting to use the document case, lest it seem intimidating, too formal. Then she locked the MG, walked up the path, and rang the bell.

The Reverend Staples opened the door, calling out to his wife, "It's alright, Jane, I've answered it myself." He turned to Maisie. "May I help you?"

"Reverend Staples? My name is Maisie Dobbs." She paused to hand him a calling card. "I am working for the company currently in the process of purchasing a large tract of land, plus the brickworks, from Alfred Sandermere in Heronsdene."

The vicar, who still wore his white clerical collar, along with a V-necked maroon cardigan that had been darned at the elbows, frowned as he read her card. "I'm sorry, but I don't see how—"

"I'm completing a report on the village's recent history, a factor the purchaser always takes into account, as a local business is so much a part of the adjacent community. Given your very close associa- tion with the village, I thought it would be a good idea to seek your opinion on a few points."

He stepped aside, holding out his left hand. "Of course, do come in." He closed the door behind her. A woman came from the drawing room, through which Maisie could see French doors leading to the garden, where whitewashed cast-iron furniture was set on a lawn. The woman wore her silver-gray hair in a tight permanent wave and looked very much the quintessential vicar's wife, clad in a simple knitted cardigan with a string of pearls at her neck and a skirt that brushed her calves just above the ankle. "Ah, Jane, this is Miss Maisie Dobbs. She represents the company buying most of Sandermere's estate. Wants to find out a bit more about the village."

The woman clasped her hands in front of her waist as she replied. "I'm glad to hear it. That brickworks needs to be properly run, and the interests of the village in the business that employs most of the men should be taken seriously." She paused and smiled. "Might I bring some tea to your study, dear?"

The vicar replied that tea would be very nice indeed, and Maisie suspected that Mrs. Staples had spent much of her married life making tea for those who came to see her husband.

Reverend Staples led Maisie to his study and held out his hand toward a chair as he closed the door behind him. "Please, take a seat."

Once more, Maisie was seated on the guest's side of a wooden desk more suited to a room three times the size. With a ream of unused paper to one side of the blotting pad, and a scribbled-upon haphazard collection of notes on the other, it seemed that the vicar was working on a manuscript of some sort.

"You're a writer, Reverend Staples?"

He waved his hand as if to dismiss the thought, then used an arm to sweep the written-upon papers to one side. "I thought I might be. I've been working on an autobiography of sorts, a recollection of my days as a country vicar. I thought I might blend witty anecdotes with a treatise on the pastoral care of a small community. However, I have discovered that I am not a born writer, and that those little scenes of rural humor do not stand the test of time. But the work gives the impression of getting on with something and assuages the guilt that accompanies a stroll across the road to watch the cricket."

Maisie smiled. She was glad the conversation had mellowed, so much the better for her questioning. "I think I should come to the point. My client has been concerned regarding the instances of petty crime in Heronsdene over the past—say—ten years or so, including a spate of fires. Have you any . . ." She paused, seeking the right word. "Have you any *insight* that might shed light on the causes of such vandalism? I should add that the fires—which seem to happen on an annual basis—are of particular concern."

The vicar ran his finger around his collar and rubbed his chin. *Hot around the collar*, thought Maisie, as Maurice's words echoed in her mind. The door opened, and Jane Staples brought in a tea tray. She made a comment about the garden while pouring, then passed cups of tea, to Maisie first and then her husband, who seemed relieved at the interruption.

As the door clicked behind her, Maisie repeated her question. "Your thoughts on the vandalism, sir?"

"Of course, I've heard about the *petty crime,* as you call it. You no doubt know the lion's share of those incidents were after my time, so I cannot exactly lay claim to having my finger on the village pulse. Certainly, such events do seem to coincide with the hop-picking, and the coincidence cannot be ignored. High jinks by London boys in particular."

"And the fires?"

His cheeks became pink once more. "Yes, the fires. I'm sure that, to an outsider, the fires might look suspicious—generally the same time of year and so on. However, you people really mustn't make a mountain out of a molehill. It's a busy time of year. People are working in the fields all day—if not in the hop-gardens there's often a second threshing of the hay, then the apples and pears, and that season follows the picking of summer fruit, strawberries, cherries, blackcurrants—so workers are tired, they ache from the day's labor, and they make mistakes. A chimney's set on fire because the stove's been banked up for more hot water, a saucepan alight on the hob because someone's fallen asleep, or a paraffin lamp's been left untended—no one in the village has the convenience of electricity, my dear."

"So you believe ten or more small fires, generally at

the same time of year, are the result of household accidents?"

Staples leaned forward and began folding the edge of a sheet of paper, first one fold, then another, until the paper was triangular in shape. He spoke while his hands were busy. "Yes, I do, Miss Dobbs. If you list them it seems hard to believe, but Heronsdene is a rural farming community, with the addition of a factory. The people are not strangers to accidents. They take them in their stride, help one another out. They are very close-knit, as you have no doubt discovered. It is a blessing that no one has been hurt."

"Some weeks ago a fire almost took the lives of Mr. Sandermere's hunters."

"Well, that might be one fire to take a second look at."

"I have already."

"I'm sure."

Maisie smiled, encouraging Staples to soften before presenting another question she knew would challenge him. "Can you tell me about the Martins?"

He scratched his right ear and reached for his hitherto untouched cup of tea. "Of course. Very nice people. Churchgoers. Musical family—Mrs. Martin played the church organ, Anna was a pianist, and Jacob quite a respectable violinist."

"A violinist?"

"Yes, tragic loss, with the Zeppelin."

"Indeed. You were of course in the village when the tragedy happened, weren't you?"

He cleared his throat. "I had just returned from London earlier in the day. I had church business at the archbishop's office at Westminster. While I was there, I was also on an errand for Jacob Martin."

"What sort of errand?"

"Well, he'd told me several weeks earlier that he had taken his violin to be repaired by an expert in Denmark Street. He was a very busy man, so when I knew of my appointment, I offered to collect it for him. I arrived back in the late afternoon and had not had an opportunity to return the instrument before the bombing."

"Do you still have the violin?"

He shook his head. "No, unfortunately not. It was stolen from the rectory in Heronsdene."

"I thought you said the petty crime came after your time."

He deflected the question. "The thieves were probably London boys, inexperienced in their trade. Had they been less callow, they would have known that the items taken—the violin, a small clock, a brass toasting fork—were of almost no consequence. There were more valuable ornaments in a display case that was left untouched."

"London boys? So the burglary took place at hop-picking time?"

"Yes. As I suggested, if something untoward is going to happen, it will be during the hopping."

"What did the police say?"

He shook his head. "We did not summon the police.

There's no local constabulary, so the police have to come some distance, and seeing as it really was very petty, with no great loss, we thought best simply to let it go and let God be the judge of the perpetrators."

Maisie was about to speak when there was a light knock at the door and Jane Staples came into the study. "I'm so sorry to interrupt, Miss Dobbs." She turned to her husband. "Telephone for you. It's the bishop's office."

"Oh, dear." Staples stood up. "Do excuse me, Miss Dobbs. I shall have to bring our conversation to a close. One doesn't keep the bishop waiting, and—between us, please—he can go on a bit."

"Thank you for your time, Reverend Staples."

The vicar's wife showed Maisie to the door, while her husband walked toward the drawing room.

Maisie returned to her motor car and drove a short distance, to park again close to the pub. She doubled back toward Easter Cottage on foot and, careful not to be seen, walked around the perimeter of the vicar's house and gardens before making her way back to the MG once again. As she passed the pub, a beery warmth wafted out, along with patrons leaving, having been turned out following the afternoon's last orders. She was thirsty, having taken but one sip of tea, and could almost taste an ale rich with hops and barley teasing her tongue. Pulling onto the road, she drove toward Hawkhurst's white-painted colonnade of shops, where she bought a cherry-red Vimto to quench her thirst. And for a while she sat to consider why a man of the cloth had lied to her—for as she had suspected, there was no telephone connection at Easter Cottage.

BY THE TIME Maisie returned to Heronsdene, it was mid-afternoon. Several hours of daylight remained, so there was no time to be wasted in contemplation. She had work to do. She engaged in a cordial conversation with Fred Yeoman, then went to her room to change into her walking skirt and brogue-like leather shoes. She had remained in Hawkhurst only long enough to drink her bottle of Vimto and make notes on the wad of index cards, which she now placed in her leather case. She put several fresh cards into her knapsack, along with binoculars and her Victorinox knife, reached across the dressing table to pick up her nurse's watch—but stopped. Her fingers lingered over the watch and then she took it up, placing it in the front pocket of her knapsack instead of pinning it to her jacket, next to her heart. She would heed Beulah's warning, but she still needed to know the time.

Leaving the MG parked outside the inn, Maisie set off on foot for a walk of two miles or so, to the tree where the London boys had hoped to claim a couple of tenners—conkers that would be so strong in competition with other boys that they would smash at least ten lesser conkers to pieces. Instead they had found silver and a week in police custody.

Hiking along a woodland path, Maisie first searched for a specific tool: a slender hazel branch she could

234

cut just below the fork, to use as a divining rod. Standing on tiptoe to take hold of a worthy branch, she drew back the leaves to better view the diameter of the still-green wood. She let the branch snap back up, took out her knife, pulled open a suitable blade, and reached up to the branch again. Cutting through the sinewy fibers, she soon brought down the section she wanted. She sliced off the leaves, tested the rod, and smiled. Now all she had to do was think silver.

She had earmarked two locations where the cache of Sandermere silver might be stowed or buried. The first, down by the stream, was less compelling, but she had to search the area to ensure her investigation was completed to the most thorough degree. For Beattie Drummond was right: It *was* an investigation, no less important or significant than any case she had worked on before.

Walking farther, she doubled back through the woods and up toward the horse chestnut tree. She hid her knapsack behind the tree, so as not to be encumbered on her way, then closed her eyes and envisioned a collection of silver—spoons, goblets, platters, teapots, chafing dishes. She held the hazel rod, with the fork in the branch facing in the direction of the woods opposite, and walked on.

With branches hanging low and brushing against her face and undergrowth hampering her progress, Maisie struggled to become attuned to the rod. She knew the image of silver was becoming fogged, as if shrouded in the mist of disbelief, and any powers of divination to which she might have laid claim were being drawn away, just as water is sucked from the shore by the tide's pull. Following the rod's direction, she came close to the stream, her brow glistening, her arms filled with ache.

"Well, I won't find anything here!" She slumped down next to the stream. Resting the hazel rod on her lap, she watched the water run up around the roots of an ancient oak, eddying along, carving through the clay, leaving visible layers of strata in its meanderings. Maisie sighed, the water soothing her, encouraging her to go to the second place now, where the encroaching eventide shadows might camouflage her presence. She came to her feet, brushed down her skirt, which she knew was in dire need of laundering, and looked one last time at the stream before turning to go. But something stopped her, something at the edge of her vision caused her to halt, to wait, to regard her surroundings once again.

Trees overhung the rushing water, and the undergrowth was a rich green, with ferns and bindweed covering the peaty ground. Closer to the stream, the heady aroma of wild garlic tested her senses as she looked back and forth and around her. Then she saw, hidden in the greens and browns of the woodland, a collection of four or five old and rusty one-gallon cans. They had been thrown some four feet in from the bank, not carelessly, but with some speed, otherwise they would not have been found at all. Ferns had been pulled across, to disguise the rusted tin as far as could be managed. Maisie knelt down and unscrewed the top of one can, flinching as metal rasped against metal. Yes, they had once contained paraffin oil, a most flammable liquid.

Maisie spread the ferns back across her find and left the woodland, wondering who had used the liquid. She entertained the thought that its purpose might have been innocent, with, perhaps, simply a careless dumping of spent metal. But a paraffin can was useful, not something to throw away. She wondered if the liquid had been used to set the fire on Sandermere's property. Perhaps even for those in the village. Yet each of those fires represented too small a conflagration for such an incendiary substance to have been used.

She left the wood, returning to the chestnut tree to claim her knapsack. It was still warm, and too light to do anything more, so she walked along the road, looking for a place to sit, to complete more notes. Consulting her watch, she thought it might be an efficient use of daylight to call upon one or two of those who had been the victims of arson—or merely fiery accidents—in recent years. She found a fallen tree trunk at the side of the road, its head of leaves and branches sawn away to leave a welcome seat—for a walker or for one who just wanted to rest for a while. As Maisie sat down and looked out across the land, she realized her chosen place commanded a view over the wall of Sandermere's immediate property and on toward the house and stables. A shallow hill rose to the right, and as she continued to cast her eyes over the property, she saw Webb, his broad-brimmed hat marking him, standing on the hill, watching Alfred Sandermere's house. He did not move for some moments, remaining still as if transfixed by the mansion. Then he turned and walked away.

FOURTEEN

Upon reflection, Maisie considered it best to confine her visits with the victims of "accidental" fires to the hours of one day, rather than begin knocking on doors in the evening. In a small village, word of her presence would doubtless travel with speed from house to house, from person to person, like a bumblebee hovering from one bloom to the next, though in this case the work at hand would not result in a honeyed sweetness.

And though she had been tempted to go to the gypsy camp, drawn by the music and dance that was still smoldering within her, she knew a pall had enveloped the tribe since Sandermere's attack on Paishey, and a quiet stillness had descended upon their sojourn in Heronsdene. Sandermere, as far as she knew, had not been seen since the incident. She was tempted, also, to join the Beale family and the other Londoners this evening, knowing they would be preparing tea in the cookhouse before sitting around a fire to tell stories, to reflect on hop-picking in years past—and to talk, now that there was but one week or so to go of the harvest, about returning to London, to the Smoke. Instead, she remained at the inn.

The residents' sitting room was empty when Maisie came down for supper, other guests having not yet returned from their walks across the countryside or forays into the surrounding villages. Fred Yeoman served a plate of hearty shepherd's pie with fresh vegetables from the garden and stopped to pass the time of day with her, to talk of the weather and how they had been lucky, with only one or two days of rain throughout the hopping. But as their talk lulled, and Fred looked out of the window to comment on a flight of ducks passing on their way to warmer climes, the conversation from the public bar became louder and within hearing.

"I'll be glad when that property's sold and we all know what's what around here," one voice piped up.

"Pity Sandermere isn't going too, as far as I'm concerned. The war took the wrong brother, no doubt about it."

"Can't do nothing about that now, Sid. Twenty-five boys and men were taken from this village, half on the same day, and we can't do nothing about that either."

There was a general jawing, a chewing over of times past, then another comment. "We'll breathe a bit easier when they've all gone: the Londoners, the pikeys—and that woman! Asking her questions about *them,* down the road. Wants to know a bit too much, if you ask me."

At first, Fred Yeoman seemed paralyzed by the overheard conversation, but then he hurried to remove Maisie's plate while raising his voice to a degree that was unnecessary in the small room, a level that ensured he would be heard in the public bar.

"Enjoy your pie, Miss Dobbs?" He barely paused while clearing her plate. "We've some lovely fresh apple tart with custard, made this afternoon. Got any room for just a slice?"

There was silence in the bar, as if Heronsdene itself was waiting to learn whether Maisie Dobbs, a Londoner, wanted fresh apple tart or not.

She shook her head, blowing out her cheeks. "I'm fit to pop, Fred, thank you. Tell Mary the shepherd's pie was the best I've ever had—bar none."

"Right you are, miss. Anything else we can get for you? I expect you'll want to turn in, what with you being so busy. Think you'll be finished soon?"

"With my report for the buyers? I daresay I will, Fred. I daresay I will." And with that Maisie left the residents' sitting room. As she ascended the narrow staircase, she heard the buzz of conversation strike up again in the public bar, though she could discern no more references to "that woman."

In her room, Maisie reread a postcard that had arrived for her earlier. It was from Priscilla, confirming that Simon would be laid to rest in two days, and they would need to meet to discuss the arrangements. Maisie shook her head, for her friend, as always, could not resist offering an opinion as to how

Maisie should travel, suggesting she come by train to avoid tiring herself in advance of a long and difficult day. But essential work in London, together with the fact that she could only afford a short time away from Heronsdene, meant that Maisie would be driving back and forth despite a mounting fatigue every time she thought about the funeral.

She worked on the case map for a while, noting points she had gathered but had not previously added to the map. Using colored pencils, she joined words, circled a name, and drew a line to another name, making connections, crossing them out, then making them again. If Billy were with his employer at their office in Fitzroy Square, he might have smiled at exactly this stage. Then he would look at Maisie and say, "You've known all along, haven't you, Miss?" And she would comment, in return, "But there's more to do, Billy—still more pieces to slot into place."

As she rolled up the case map and placed it in her bag, she knew her work was almost, but not quite, done. There were still questions and, as she knew only too well from her years of apprenticeship with Maurice, just one question could lead to many responses, and each one of them was part of the story. Tomorrow she would uncover more threads to be woven into the picture that was forming.

The image of threads played on Maisie's mind that night as she lay in bed. She thought of Marta, her weaving teacher, and the fact that she bore a name that denied her origins, denied her the color and texture of

241

her people. She had become a Jones, a name her father chose, like a cape with which to cover a garish costume. She was a Jones to fit in, the truth of her heritage enveloped in someone else's name.

THE FOLLOWING MORNING, Maisie's first stop was to a "two-up-two-down" terraced house close to the village school. Mr. and Mrs. Pendle lived alone, though Maisie suspected that Mr. Pendle would be out at work when she called. She had only to knock once, and the door was opened by a woman in her early sixties, wearing a gray skirt with a blue cardigan and a floral sleeveless wraparound housecoat fastened with a length of cord around the waist. She wore knitted stockings that had gathered at the ankle and black lace-up shoes. Her hair was tied back in a bun so tight it seemed to pull at the corners of her eyes. In her hand she wielded a feather duster. She reminded Maisie of the women who worked at the coffee shop she sometimes frequented on Oxford Street, the one she always said was more caff than café. They were women who called you dearie while wiping the table in front of you, lifting your cup and saucer, and paying no mind to the fact that you were still eating toast as they went about their business of wiping, lifting, and tut-tutting about the way some people leave a mess behind them.

"Mrs. Pendle?"

The woman frowned. "Yes?" Her response came out as *Yerse*.

"My name's Maisie Dobbs. I represent the company

242

in negotiations to purchase a large tract of land on the Sandermere estate. The buyer is very keen to know more about Heronsdene, especially as men from the village are employed at the brickworks, so I'm taking the opportunity to speak to a few of the people who live here. Could you spare me a moment or two?"

The woman stepped forward and looked both ways on the street. "I should think you'd be best to come when my husband gets home."

"Is he employed at the brickworks?"

"No, he's a plumber, working over in Paddock Wood."

"But I am sure you can still help me, Mrs. Pendle."

The woman looked back and forth again and stepped aside. "You'd better come in then."

Maisie entered a shadowed passage, with dark brown wainscoting and brown and pink faded floral wallpaper. A brown picture rail some nine inches from the ceiling ran the length of the passage, with family photographs of different sizes hanging from it like marionettes. On the opposite wall, three plaster mallard ducks were positioned to give the effect of flight into the sky, though one had come loose and was poised for a nosedive toward the polished floor. Maisie suspected the wavering mallard might be the source of some nagging by Mrs. Pendle toward her husband.

"To the right, Miss Dobbs, into the parlor, if you don't mind."

Maisie stepped into the parlor, which smelled of

lavender and beeswax polish. A piano stood against the wall just inside the door, and a settee with two matching armchairs, covered in a prickly brown wool fabric with patches darned along the arms, were situated in front of the fireplace. In the bay window, a mahogany table was set with a lace doily, on top of which an aspidistra drooped, its pot settled in a saucer overfilled with water.

The wallpaper was the same as that which decorated the passageway, and a mirror hung over the fireplace from the picture rail, along with several more photographs on each wall. On the mantelpiece, three pewter frames held sepia photographs of two young men and a girl.

"Do take a seat, Miss Dobbs."

"Thank you." Maisie sat down on the settee, while her hostess perched on the edge of the chair next to the fireplace, as if not quite happy to be using the room, which was no doubt only occupied on Sundays, and perhaps at Christmas and Easter.

"Now then, what can I do for you?"

"My employers, the company who hope to complete purchase on the estate, have been somewhat concerned about petty crime in Heronsdene and about the fires that seem to occur here with some regularity. I understand you and your husband had a fire here a year or so ago."

The woman rolled her eyes. "Oh, that! Nothing untoward about that, I can tell you. Chimney fire, caused by my husband."

"How did it happen?"

"He thought he'd be clever and collect coal along the railway lines. Lot of people from round here do it—walk along the lines, pick up coal dropped when they're filling the engines. Saves a bob or two, I can tell you, and we all need to do that, don't we?" The woman laughed. It was a short laugh, dismissive in its way. "Anyway, he came back with a big sack of coal over his shoulder, dumped it in the bunker out the back, and then we used it for the stove in the kitchen." She leaned forward as if drawing Maisie into a family secret. "But clever boots, my husband, didn't stop to think that boiler fuel that can pull a locomotive from here to London, would probably cause an almighty blaze in our chimney—and that's what happened!"

"That's an extraordinary story, Mrs. Pendle. Who would believe such a thing?" Maisie leaned forward too, allowing the impression of being drawn into the tale. "And you never reported the blaze? Not even to your landlord?"

The woman waved her hand. "No, no point. We sorted it all out ourselves and made repairs. Good as new in next to no time. We all help each other in Heronsdene, you can depend on that. People came. It's not as if the fire got out of hand and hurt anyone."

"Well, I'm glad the whole house didn't go up." Maisie paused. "Can you tell me about the night of the Zeppelin raid, Mrs. Pendle?"

The woman sat back. "Whatever do you want to know about that for?"

"Oh, not for the sale of the estate. No, I heard about it from the smithy and became interested. I understand it took a whole family—the Martins. Dutch, weren't they? You must have all been terrified when it happened."

Mrs. Pendle had rested her hands in her lap and now she wrung them together, her fingernails grazing paper-thin flesh and swollen veins. "Terrible thing, it was. Not that I ever knew they were Dutch beforehand, though I knew they came from somewhere over there." She faltered, leaning forward again. "The airship came over just a day after we found out about the boys, you see."

"What do you mean?"

"Well, half the men and boys in the village had joined up together and were with the West Kents, and we lost them in 1916. The Somme, it was. Then, just one day—or it might've been two; it all runs together now, when I think back—before the raid, six or seven more families had word that their sons were gone, killed in action. Brought it all back, you know, to those still mourning. It was like they went all at once, us all being so close." She looked up at Maisie. "We're not a big town, just a small village, and look at how many we lost, boys and men born here, who worked here and would have died here, at home. Men who had families or sweethearts, boys you'd've seen grow into men, who would've had families of their own. Instead they were dead, in France, killed by them Germans."

Maisie began to speak again, but the woman went on.

"I mean, it must have been the same, over there in Germany—I know that now, don't I? But then, all I could think about—all anyone could think about—was how our village had lost so many. And then, to add insult to injury, along comes that Zeppelin."

"It must have been dreadful for you all. Especially to see the Martin family killed."

The woman picked at a loose thread in the arm of the chair. "Yes, well, it was very sad, yes."

"And their boy gone too."

She nodded, her face flushed.

"Did *you* lose a son, Mrs. Pendle?"

She nodded again. "That's why I can't tell you much about the Zeppelin raid. We still couldn't believe our Sam had gone. His brother was at home, wounded, when we heard, and our daughter was working at the hospital in Maidstone. I can't say as I remember as much as some might be able to."

Maisie nodded. "Thank you, Mrs. Pendle, you've been very kind to answer my questions."

"Yes, well . . ." She glanced at the clock on the mantelpiece and stood up. "I'd better get on. No peace for the wicked, eh?"

Maisie stood up and moved toward the door. "The people here must have been very angry when the Zeppelin went over."

"Oh, yes, we were angry alright. But it's sometimes like that, isn't it? Instead of feeling heartache, all you are is filled with temper."

. . .

MAISIE MOVED ON to the next house on her list, on the opposite side of the street to the smithy. A man recently widowed lived at the cottage, which was another example of medieval architecture, with low beams and a thatched roof. Once again, the door was opened following the first knock, and Maisie explained why she was calling. This time she was led into a small kitchen not unlike her father's. A black cast-iron stove was set into an inglenook fireplace, beside which a threadbare armchair with several worn cushions—to make up for a sagging seat—provided a convenient resting place for an ample cat with a neck as wide as its girth. The cat looked up at Maisie, yawned to reveal every needle-like tooth in its head, and went back to sleep.

"Better not disturb Mildred there. You wouldn't want to sit on that chair, on account of the hair, and she'd only want up on your lap anyway."

Instead, the man, George Chambers, pulled out two wooden chairs from a pine block of a table that was bowed in the middle from decades of use, dusted off the seat of one chair with the palm of his hand, and beckoned Maisie to sit down.

"Now then, what do you want to know from me? I can't see as an old fella like myself can be of any use to one of those concerns in the city bent on buying from his nibs over at the estate."

Maisie smiled. She liked Mr. Chambers, though she suspected he knew—probably the whole village knew by now—that she would come to see him. But though she understood that no one person would ever tell her the whole truth, if at each house she came away with one small nugget of information, it would help her color the story that had already been outlined, in her mind and on her case map.

"Mr. Chambers, would you be so kind as to tell me about the fire you had here, about five years ago?"

"Fire?"

"Yes, I understand a fire broke out in your living room under suspicious circumstances, yet you did not inform the police."

"Suspicious circumstances? Where did you hear that?" His laugh was phlegm-filled, as if something were caught in his chest. Maisie thought he would be well advised to spend fewer hours sitting beside a stove fueled by anthracite. "We got it so quick, it wasn't worth even calling out the fire brigade—I daresay you know by now that the nearest is in Paddock Wood."

"So what started the fire?"

"Boys. Always the same. The little blighters start collecting or making fireworks about now, in time for Guy Fawkes night."

"But that's not until November fifth."

"That it might be, but those nippers think ahead when it comes to Bonfire Night."

"And you think they—what? Threw a banger or a Catherine wheel through the window?"

"That's about the sum of it, miss."

"I have to say, Mr. Chambers, that you seem rather sanguine about it. Why, where I grew up you would have had your hide tanned for such antics and been called upon by the constabulary."

He shook his head. "Oh, no, not for a bit of high jinks. And the neighbors came quickly, and everyone helped put it right."

"And you never caught the children responsible?"

The man shook his head. "Per'aps we were a bit soft on them, but that's how we've come to be here, us who lost our sons in the war. My wife passed on last year and was glad to go, to be with her boys—neither of them came back, you know."

"I'm terribly sorry, Mr. Chambers." Maisie paused. "I was a nurse in France."

"Then you know, don't you. You know."

"Yes. I know."

The man's eyes grew moist, and he pulled a soiled handkerchief from the pocket of his corduroy trousers.

"I've heard from some of your neighbors about the Zeppelin raid. Can you tell me about it?"

He blew his nose, sniffed, and inspected the contents of his handkerchief before crumpling it again and returning it to his pocket. "I reckon it was either going toward London, and for some reason had to turn back and so dumped its bomb here, or it was on its way out of London, hadn't found the target it wanted, saw a light—even though we had the blackout—and then dropped it."

"And it happened just after some of you had

received word that your boys had been killed in France?"

"That's right. We lost Michael and Peter early in 1916, but it was still here." He pressed his fist to his chest. "And of course you'd learn about this one gone, and that one. But then came the telegrams telling of more, on the same day. And we all see the nippers grow up, so it's like losing your own all over again. Then that balloon went over and we copped it. Insult to injury, like I said."

"And you lost the Martin family."

"Yes. Though they were outsiders, you know, not born and bred here. Only been in the village about twelve–thirteen years. They were from over there, you know—Europe."

"They were English, as I understand it. At least the children were born here."

"But not *here*." He pointed to the ground. "Not in Heronsdene. But it was bad, all the same."

Maisie was just about to ask another question when a knock at the door interrupted her.

"I'd best get on now, miss, if you've nothing else to ask me."

Maisie shook her head. "Thank you for your time, Mr. Chambers."

He led the way toward the front door, which he opened to reveal Mrs. Pendle, standing on the doorstep holding a tray covered with an embroidered cloth.

"Oh, hello, Miss Dobbs. Didn't know you were here. I hope I'm not interrupting."

"Not at all, I'm just leaving." Maisie turned to Mr. Chambers, thanked him again, and went on her way. As she stepped back onto the pavement, she heard Mrs. Pendle announce in a loud voice, "It's a nice oxtail soup today, with dumplings." When she looked around to wave goodbye, she saw Mrs. Pendle hand over the tray and step inside the cottage, her arms folded. She smiled to herself. Her grandmother had once said that you always knew when a neighbor woman was about to stay for a chat, because she'd fold her arms, ready to lean on your fence. But time spent with the villagers had been more than worthwhile, especially the conversation with Mr. Chambers. He'd given more than two nuggets' worth of value with just one unguarded comment, as she suspected he might.

Considering the list again, Maisie decided that at this stage she would visit only one more house, the home of Phyllis Wheeler, née Mansell, the girlhood friend of Anna Martin. It was located about a quarter of a mile past the smithy, on the right. An Edwardian villa set back from the road, the house was shabby despite being younger, by several hundred years, than many in the village. Two bay windows flanked an olive-green front door, the color of the house reflecting the livery of the local railway company who owned the property, so Maisie concluded that Phyllis's father worked at a local station. She hoped Phyllis would be at home, seeing as she had two children and a new baby.

She was walking along the path toward the door when it opened and a woman began struggling to maneuver a perambulator across the threshold.

"Here, let me give you a hand." Maisie stepped forward and pulled the front of the baby carriage, while the woman pushed from inside the door.

"Thank you very much. I usually leave it outside, but with all these Londoners and gypsies about, you never know, do you?"

Maisie smiled. "Mrs. Wheeler?"

"Yes."

Maisie explained the purpose of her visit, at the same time concerned that it might be met with a negative response. Instead the woman agreed to answer a few questions, especially if it helped to get the brickworks in better hands, because her husband worked there.

"Are you going shopping or just for a walk?"

"Bit of both, if I've time before this one wants his feed. The elder two are in school, and by the time I've cleaned up the kitchen, I'm dying to get out of the house for a bit. My father leaves early, working on the railway, and my mother's up at the Sandermere place, so I'm alone all day until the children come home."

"Well, shall we walk down to the crossroads and then back toward the village again? It's turning quite warm now, isn't it?"

The woman agreed, and they began strolling away from the village. The baby slept, the pram's white summer canopy casting shadows on his sleep-blushed cheeks. For a moment or two, Maisie spoke of the weather, of the apples hanging heavy on the trees, and of the beauty of Heronsdene. She was grateful to be walking, not least because it gave her the opportunity to gain a deeper understanding of the woman. In mirroring her gait, the way she moved and held her hands—even though she was pushing a pram—Maisie would absorb, for a moment, some of the emotions the woman experienced as she answered her questions. And with movement of the body came movement of the mind and of the voice, so Maisie thought the conversation might be fruitful.

At first they spoke of the estate and of the brickworks, with Phyllis repeating stories of the daily ups and downs of his trade that her husband brought home, especially criticism regarding Sandermere's ownership. In the set of her shoulders, her jaw, even the manner in which her walk became brisk, she indicated dislike of Sandermere and perhaps something even deeper. Maisie pressed her to reveal her feelings.

"To tell you the truth, I can't stand him. He's the one who should have died in the fire, not Anna."

"You mean the fire following the bombing?"

"Yes. Yes, that's what I mean."

"Was he in the village, then?"

"Everyone was in the village, we were all there."

"How old was he at the time, fifteen, sixteen?"

"I can't say as I know, exactly."

"But you were about the same age, and from what I've seen of Alfred Sandermere he would have paid attention to a pretty girl in the village—especially as any other suitors a young woman might have, had all enlisted."

"Well, I didn't like him, but Anna did."

"She did?"

The young woman stopped, reached into the perambulator to pull a soft white blanket up around the baby's chubby legs, and then crossed her arms, allowing the handle of the carriage to rest against her hip.

"Oh, make no mistake, Miss Dobbs, man and boy he could be all sweetness if he wanted. To tell you the truth, she'd set her hat for Henry, the elder son. Mind you, it's not as if the likes of them would ever look at the likes of us, not for anything but a—you know—not a serious courting."

"I understand."

The baby whimpered in his sleep, so they began walking again.

"Bit of a Sarah Bernhardt, was Anna, very given to being dramatic. She was besotted with Henry, but she wasn't much more than a girl when he left for war. He'd come into the village in the dogcart and tip his hat to her. 'Good morning, Miss Martin,' he'd say, and she would swoon. He did the same thing to every woman in the town, out of being polite, but she thought it was all for her." She shook her head. "She was a funny one, Anna, made me laugh. And I loved her for it." Phyllis reached into her pocket for a handkerchief, and when she couldn't find it, Maisie took one from her black shoulder bag and handed it to her.

"So"—she sniffed, dabbing her nose—"after Henry went back over there, along came Alfred—and you have to remember, Anna was a very, very pretty girl."

"I see."

"Well, there's more to see yet."

A change in the woman's movement caused Maisie to pay more attention. She moved ahead with an urgency to her step. *She wants to be free of a burden,* thought Maisie.

"She was a bit of a will o' the wisp," Phyllis continued. "Couple of times, Mr. Martin sent Pim round to—"

"Who?" Maisie rested her hand upon Phyllis's arm. "What did you say?"

"Pim. That was her brother. That was his nickname." She shrugged. "It's what the Dutch call someone with the name of Willem."

Maisie nodded, slowly. "So Mr. Martin sent Pim round. Why?"

"Because they didn't know where she was. Called high and low for her. And I couldn't lie, could I? But Anna had lied. She'd told them she was coming to see me of an evening, when she was out." She shook her head. "Later on, when we'd had word that Henry was dead and she was seeing a lot of Alfred, I told her, I said, 'You'll get into trouble if you're not careful.' She said he wanted to marry her, and I told her not to be so silly, he would never marry below him, never marry someone who wasn't a toff like him, who wasn't his sort."

Maisie smarted, trying not to think of Simon, of Mrs. Lynch.

"I told her that the likes of Alfred Sandermere would never marry one of us. No, he'd marry one of his own."

"Then what happened?"

She sighed. "Doesn't do any harm to tell it, now she's dead and gone. But she came over one day, about a week before the Zeppelin, and we went for a walk, like we're doing now, down to the crossroads, and she told me she'd got herself into trouble. She was in the family way."

Maisie nodded. "She must have been terrified of anyone finding out, in a small village like this. Of the shame."

"Oh, you might have thought as much, and first off she was a bit scared. But you know the silly thing? She thought he would marry her. She thought that baby would put her in the big house and give her the—I don't know, the . . . what did she call it?—*belonging,* that's it, the belonging she wanted."

Maisie understood. "Then what happened?"

"Next thing, Alfred's telling her he knows of a woman in Tunbridge Wells who does for girls in her condition. He had the name from a friend. But what friend? That's what I wanted to know. I begged her not to do it, to tell her parents and get it over with. I told her she could go away until after the baby was born and no one would know, not for definite. But instead she told him she wanted the baby, she wanted them to get married, and according to what she said to me, the last time I spoke to her, he said something would have to be done if he had to do it himself."

"He said that?"

She nodded. "And that was that. Then she was dead anyway."

"Did Alfred . . . ?"

"I'd better turn back now, Miss Dobbs. The baby's stirring and he'll be wanting his feeding soon." She stopped for a moment, pulling her dark blue coat across her still-swollen stomach, and flicking back chestnut hair that had come loose from the combs used to push it back into a twist. "I can't tell you any more than that. That's all I can tell you about Anna. The Martins were very nice to me. I was always welcome in their home, up above the bakery—I remember how it smelled, all warm and sweet. Doughy." Phyllis shook her head. "She was my best friend since I first went to school, and we stayed that way right until the day she died."

They walked in silence until they reached the house. Maisie offered to help maneuver the perambulator through the doorway, but she declined.

"What was Pim like, Phyllis?"

"What's any younger brother like? He was a little toe-rag when we were girls, always sneaking up on us, teasing, pulling ribbons from our hair. The other children tormented him at school, more than they did

Anna, it being she was so lovely. Not that Pim was ugly, mind, but you know what boys are like. It was his name, and the fact that he and Anna would speak in Dutch to each other. They didn't do it to be sneaky or anything like that, it was just their way. But people eavesdropped on them all the same." She nodded, looking down toward the school. "Yes, he took a fair bit of it, when I think back. Then, when that Alfred Sandermere was sent home from school a few times— oh, there were other stories told to the servants, so it would get around the village, but we all knew the truth—he started looking for friends around here, and Pim became his little companion. He was younger than Alfred, and talk about look up to him! Mr. Martin didn't like it at all. We all saw that Pim changed, you know, started getting up to mischief, on account of Sandermere pushing him to do this and that. It was through Pim that he and Anna met, though it wasn't long before Pim was sent away."

She paused, placing her little finger between the baby's gums as he began to wriggle. "I put it down to all that teasing, all that trouble in school, and then Sandermere, a nasty evil boy, he was." The child stirred, wimpering, as if working up steam to wail.

"The long and the short of it was that they got up to something serious, and it was Pim who went down for it, to the reformatory. The next thing you know, he was in the army—and only thirteen at that. Then he was killed. Vicar said the telegram arrived the day after the Martins died, so it was just as well they didn't know, none of them, what had happened."

"The vicar?"

"Yes. When the postman came with the Regret to Inform telegram, he didn't know what to do, so he went to see the vicar, being as we all knew each other here."

The baby wailed, pitching his scream to meet the grumble in his stomach. Phyllis moved to push the perambulator away. Even though she had accomplished far more in her questioning than Beattie Drummond predicted, Maisie needed to press her with just one more question.

"I've heard village children talking about seeing Pim Martin's ghost. Do you know why?"

Phyllis shook her head. "It's just kids, trying to scare each other. But if he did have a ghost, it would haunt Heronsdene. Goodbye, Miss Dobbs, I hope the walk was worth it."

"Yes, it was, and I think for you too."

Phyllis pressed her lips together, and as she turned, bending over to soothe her infant, Maisie saw the tears running down her cheeks.

FIFTEEN

Maisie went straight to the hop-garden to see Billy. She passed the gypsies, waving to Beulah, Webb and Paishey. As she walked by, she thought the scene would not be out of place in a Thomas Hardy novel—

the women's long skirts and Webb, with the broad-brimmed hat he always wore when he was out working, and his loose uncollared shirt, rendering the image more akin to a Victorian pastoral tableau. All that was needed was the tragic character—a Jude or a Tess—to complete the story.

She found Billy and his family working hard, with the usual banter between the Londoners in full swing.

" 'allo, Miss, we was just wonderin' where you'd got to, didn't see you yesterday."

"I've been busy, Billy. Have you got a minute for a quick chat?"

"Right you are." He put his arm around his wife's shoulders and kissed her on the cheek. "Won't be long, love."

Maisie and Billy walked back toward the farm road, heads bowed as they spoke.

" 'aven't seen that Sandermere since I bopped him one. Thought we'd be kicked off the farm, we did."

"I think he's gone to ground at the mansion, probably nursing a broken nose, if that swing was anything to go by."

Billy shook his head. "No, if 'is *breath* was anything to go by, 'e'll be in 'is cups. Anyway, one of the locals came across yesterday—they didn't mind seein' 'im knocked over, that's a fact—and told me that, according to someone who works up at the 'ouse, 'e's not been out of 'is rooms since 'e got back there. Bet that 'orse is enjoying a rest."

Maisie nodded. "Billy, I wanted to let you know

261

how I've been getting on with the investigations, even though you're on holiday. And I'm going back to London later today."

"Blimey, you're goin' back and forth for this one, ain't you?"

Maisie nodded. "I know, but it won't be for much longer. Now, let's walk along here. There's something I want you to do while I'm away."

An onlooker might have been intrigued by the pair as they strolled on. The man, revealing a slight limp, his wheaten hair rendered almost white-blond by the sun, leaned toward the woman as she spoke. And the woman, tall, slender, wearing a straw hat to protect her skin, would sometimes use her hands to emphasize a point. Some might have thought them conspirators, though a more acute observer would have seen the man nodding his head—and on two occasions wide-eyed surprise registered on his face.

"Right, Miss, don't you worry, I'll find a way to get what you want, without anyone givin' it a second thought. You said her name was Beattie Drummond?"

"Yes, that's right. And be careful—she's sharp and she's after a big story. I'd go to Phyllis again, but I believe her to be overwhelmed, especially having a babe-in-arms."

"Poor woman. Mind you, she told you as much as she could, didn't she?"

"It was enough, in a roundabout way, along with the other grains of knowledge. As usual, there's that leap

262

of the imagination, which is why there's more to do. Now then, I must be on my way."

"And you reckon they'll see you at the reformatory this afternoon?"

"I hope so. I may have to grovel."

"Best of luck, Miss. See you the day after tomorrow."

MAISIE HAD OFTEN rolled her eyes at what she and others referred to as *the old school tie,* those connections forged and sealed in the boarding schools of youth—for those of a certain station—that would bond boys together as they came of age, so, as men, a favor could be asked, a door opened, even a loan settled or a crime forgotten. For her there was no old school tie or any other claim to some association, except that of being a Londoner, or the thread of familial relationship that rendered her welcome by Beulah and thus by the gypsy tribe. It was therefore a stroke of good fortune that the man who happened to be governor of the reformatory displayed on his desk a photograph of his wife as a young woman.

"Ah, your wife was a nurse, in the war, I see," said Maisie.

"That's where we met. I was a medical orderly at the same general hospital."

Maisie smiled. "I was a nurse too, at a casualty clearing station."

The man nodded. There was no need to say more, to share a reflection or a memory. He simply smiled and said, "And how can I be of service to you, Miss Dobbs?"

When she explained the reason for her visit and described the information she was seeking, he lifted a set of keys from his desk and replied, "We'll have to go down to the records office. I can leave you there with the files for half an hour. Will that be sufficient?"

"Thank you—that will be plenty of time."

Not quite the old school tie, but a lifelong bond all the same.

MAISIE LEFT THE reformatory for London in the late afternoon, glad to depart the dour smoke-stained red-brick buildings, to hear the gate locked behind her, and to silently bid adieu to the sullen boys, all dressed the same in blue overalls, working in the gardens, marching across the parade ground, and cleaning the windows. Though the reformatory was not a hardscrabble borstal, it was nevertheless an incarceration.

She drove all the way back to London with the top down on the MG, glad to feel the balmy air cross her skin, prickling her senses alive and shaking off the dark mood of the reformatory. She had gleaned more information than she thought possible, which, as she knew, would only beg more questions. To her list of tasks to be accomplished, she added a visit to the repository for war records, but she would need an introduction to open those doors, as she was not a relative of those whose records she sought. With luck, she could draw upon her relationship with the wearer of an impressive old school tie.

On the outskirts of London, she stopped to pull up the MG's roof. Following some delay on the Old Kent Road, where a costermonger's barrow had overturned, pitching fruit and vegetables into the street, she was keen to see her flat again. She had already sent a telegram to Priscilla to let her know that she was driving up this evening and would pick her up tomorrow morning for the journey to Margaret Lynch's London home, from which the funeral cortege would leave.

Maisie spent the evening quietly, except for one excursion, out to a telephone kiosk to place a call to James Compton, to whom she gave a résumé of her investigation to date. She informed him that she estimated a final visit to Heronsdene of only two more days, perhaps three, after which she would submit her report and recommendations. Then she asked if he knew where she might be able to reach his father.

"He's here at the club this evening. We've been in conference with the directors all day, talking about expansion and also—right up your alley—security at our offices in Toronto. Can't have one without the other."

"Of course."

"Hold on a minute, I'll get him for you." James set the telephone receiver on the table, and Maisie heard voices in the background as he informed the porter to hold the call. The voices receded, there was silence, and then a voice came closer again, thanking the porter.

"Maisie, how are you?"

"Very well, Lord Julian, and you?"

"Better when James has the reins well and truly in his hands, but I think it'll be difficult to have him come back from Canada for any significant length of time, even though I'm trying my best. I thought he would stay for the hunting, but now I'm not sure." He cleared his throat. "Now, what can I do for you?"

"I need a door opened at the war records repository."

"How soon?"

"Tomorrow afternoon. I want to view two records."

"Consider it done—but I'll need the names."

MAISIE'S SECOND TELEPHONE call was to Priscilla, at the Dorchester.

"Maisie, I am so glad you telephoned. Where are you?"

"In a telephone kiosk in Pimlico."

"Oh, dear God, a public telephone kiosk, and in the dark? Anyone could be watching you, ready to strike."

"Don't be melodramatic, Pris. There's no one watching me, and I'm perfectly alright. How are the boys?"

"I'm making progress. I've summoned Elinor back from Wales, so she's here with us—and probably glad to be back. Half her family are miners, and life is bleak for them." There was a brief pause. "Oh. I seem to have found the perfect London house, and I may have settled the question of my sons' education."

"Will they board?"

"No. The boys will become day pupils at a London lycée where they teach in both French and English. It's popular with diplomats from the far reaches of the empire who want their sons to have a solid British education, so everyone's different. And when they come home at the end of the day, I will have Elinor to keep them on the straight and narrow if I need a moment to myself."

"Where's the property?"

"You will never guess. Margaret has decided to vacate the London house for now and live permanently in Grantchester—you remember, where they had Simon's party?"

"Of course." *How could I forget?* thought Maisie.

"We discussed the lease when she telephoned with details of the service tomorrow. And speaking of the service, it's not quite what we may have expected."

"What do you mean?" Maisie rubbed her hand across condensation forming on the kiosk's window-panes and peered out to see if there were passersby.

"Hold your breath, Maisie." Priscilla paused. Maisie drew away from the window and looked up into the small mirror behind the telephone. "Simon's being cremated."

"Cremated?" She saw her eyes redden in the rust-spotted mirror.

"Yes. Margaret is being terribly modern—and it's

not as if cremation has been seen as quite the devil's work ever since the Duchess of Connaught was cremated in 1917—first member of the royal family into the fire."

"Oh, Priscilla, how could you?"

Priscilla drew breath but did not apologize. "Maisie, do try to be less sensitive. I know this is a terribly difficult time, but one has to keep some perspective. The Simon I knew would have been first to laugh at such a quip." She sighed. "Margaret thought—rightly, I have to say—that it's what Simon would have wanted, having lingered for so long. She said there can be a proper goodbye before his ashes are sprinkled across the fields close to his home where he played as a boy, and she won't have to fret about who might look after his grave when she's gone."

"But—"

"No, you can't, Maisie. You can't commit to grave visiting, I won't allow it. When he's laid to rest—or whatever they call it when you're cremated—it will be a rest for those close to him as well. I agree with her wholeheartedly that it represents a release, a letting-go for all concerned."

Maisie said nothing.

"Hello? Hello? Can you hear me?"

"I'm here, Pris. And I think she's right too, though it came as rather a shock at first."

"Yes, of course it did. Now then, I am going to lounge in a deep bath this evening, seeing as Elinor has the boys back under her thumb once more and all is well in my world. My darling Douglas will be here soon, along with my motor car, and my cup will runneth over."

Maisie nodded, though there was no one to see her. "Good night, Priscilla. See you at half-past nine tomorrow."

"Sleep tight, dear Maisie. And don't fret, it will soon be over."

Maisie walked slowly back, glad to return to the flat that she now saw as a cocoon. She thought about what Billy had said, about throwing on the clod of dirt, of releasing something of the memory into the earth. What did one release with a cremation? Where was the ritual, the ending of the story, when there was no grave to visit, no place to set down a posy of primroses or an armful of fresh daffodils? She sat for a while, and though the evening was not cold, she placed a florin in the gas meter and ignited the fire. She felt chilled to the bone, yet when she considered Margaret Lynch's decision, she could not help but feel it was a good one, and wondered if she had settled upon it, in part for her sake.

MAISIE STOOD TALL when the final hymn was announced, feeling the numbness in her feet, which had been cold since she went to bed last night. It was no ordinary cold but a deep seeping dampness that could not easily be countered by exterior warmth. It was bitter and clammy and, in truth, it had been with her since France, since the war, and there were days

269

when she thought it would freeze up through her body and turn it to stone.

Margaret Lynch stood between Maisie and Priscilla, and as they opened their hymnbooks to the correct page, she felt Simon's mother lean against her. Maisie closed her eyes for a moment and rooted her feet to the ground, so that Margaret might share her strength, and then, though it might be considered presumptuous, she linked her arm through the older woman's to offer greater support. Margaret Lynch patted Maisie's hand and nodded, and as air gushed from the organ's bellows, the introduction began and voices rose up in unison.

I vow to thee, my country, all earthly things above,
Entire and whole and perfect, the service of my love;
The love that asks no question,
the love that stands the test,
That lays upon the altar the dearest and the best;
The love that never falters,
the love that pays the price,
The love that makes undaunted the final sacrifice.

As the second verse began, the coffin was moved back through a divided curtain toward the incinerator. When the curtain closed again, Simon was gone from them forever. Maisie felt his mother increase the pressure on her hand, and she in turn drew her closer.

Later, following an early luncheon at the Lynch

house in Holland Park, Maisie and Priscilla waited until the other guests had departed before taking their leave.

"Are you sure you'll be alright, Margaret?"

"Yes, of course, Priscilla. I am in need of rest, so I will go to my room and put my feet up." She reached out toward Maisie and Priscilla. "I am so glad you were both here."

Priscilla kissed the air next to Margaret's left cheek, while Maisie stepped back. Then, just as Maisie was about to hold out her hand to bid the bereaved woman goodbye, Margaret took her by the shoulders and looked directly into her eyes.

"Please come to visit me, Maisie. I shall be here in Holland Park for a week or two while my belongings are packed up and sent to Grantchester. So, please come."

"Of course. I would be delighted."

"Thank you." She held Maisie's hands in both her own. "Thank you. For all that you were to him."

HAVING DEPOSITED PRISCILLA at the Dorchester once more, Maisie pulled her watch from the black document case and checked the time: two o'clock. She had to be at the repository at half past three; in the interim, she would go straight to Denmark Street, a mecca for London's musicians.

Andersen & Sons, Luthiers, was halfway along the narrow street, just off Charing Cross Road. A brown awning kept the sun's rays from the window, in which a gentleman mannequin, garbed in evening dress, was seated on a chair with a cello positioned ready to play. The bow had been tied to his hand to hold it in place, and it looked as if he might come alive and draw it across the strings at any moment.

A bell rang above the door as Maisie entered the shop. All manner of stringed instruments were positioned around the four walls. Guitars were hung from hooks, as were lutes, balalaikas, ukuleles, violas and violins. Two harps were set on the floor, along with a cello and a double bass. Mahogany counters flanked either side of the shop, displaying strings, clamps, an assortment of plectra, and other tools of the string musician's trade. Just inside the door, a stand held a selection of sheet music that had become dusty and curled. And at the back of the shop, through a velvet curtain tied to one side, she saw two men working at facing benches. Each surface was illuminated by two electric desk lamps, though the shop itself was dimly lit, probably to save money and to protect the instruments. The older of the two men also used a substantial magnifying glass, which had been bolted to his workbench.

As the door closed, the younger man rubbed his hands with a cloth and came out to greet Maisie.

"Can I help you, madam?" He executed a shallow bow as he spoke.

"I wanted to speak to Mr. Andersen, if I may?"

"Which one? There are three, with only two of us here today."

"Then it would be Mr. Andersen, Senior."

The man, who was about thirty, went back to the workshop, calling "Dad, lady to see you," and pushing the curtain aside as he returned to his work. The older gentleman, his shoulders hunched from years of leaning across the workbench, came to greet her.

"May I help you?" He spoke with an accent, which Maisie identified as being Danish or Swedish.

"I have come to see you about a violin you repaired, some years ago."

The man smiled, his gray-blue eyes kind, while the white woolly curls on his head made him seem endearing, like a favorite uncle in a child's fairy tale. "I keep perfect records, and I remember my customers, though I am more likely to remember their instruments."

"The violin belonged to a man named Jacob Martin, but seeing as he was Dutch, it may have been Maarten." Maisie emphasized *ten,* her tongue touching her teeth as she spoke.

Andersen frowned. "I remember Jacob well. His surname was originally van Maarten."

"Van Maarten?"

"Yes. He changed it when his daughter, Anna, was born. Jacob was born and bred here, and he wanted his family to be *assimilated.*" His pronunciation of the word was deliberate, syllable by syllable. "He came into the shop often, as his bakery was close to Covent Garden, so he would stroll up after the market folk had come for their pastries in the morning, the traders for their coffee and sausage rolls. We had a shared love, you see, of the instruments." He paused. "But why do you ask of him?"

"Before he died, Mr. van Maarten brought a violin to you for repair, and it was collected by the vicar of the parish, I believe, on the day he was killed, in a Zeppelin raid."

Andersen frowned. "Let me get my order book, and I will be able to tell you exactly."

Maisie waited while the man went back into the workshop. Standing alongside a harp, she stretched out her hand and ran her fingers across the strings, the tumble of notes reminding her of a shower on a bright day, of primrose petals bending to the weight of rain-drops. She regretted never having learned to play an instrument.

"Yes," said Andersen, as he came back through the curtained doorway and into the shop. "He brought the violin to me in August. He liked to bring it in once a year. It was like a child to him."

"What can you tell me about it? I know very little about musical instruments."

Andersen looked up at Maisie, smiling as if remembering the features of a much-loved friend. "It was an exceptional violin, a Cuypers—Johannes Cuypers, the father, not one of the sons, who were also luthiers. It was an earlier model with the most exquisite reddish-golden finish, as if candlelight were reflected in the wood. The violin was almost one hundred and fifty years old, and Jacob—" he pronounced the name

Yaycob—"inherited it from his father, and his father before him."

Maisie took a deep breath. "Was he a proficient player?"

The man took off the spectacles he had donned to better read the ledger and pointed a bony finger toward the shop's entrance. "Let me tell you, when Jacob picked up his violin, people would stand at that door to listen. He was an artist. It was a great loss." He shook his head and looked down at the ledger once again, then turned it to face Maisie. "It may be my own writing, but my vision has worn with the years, and of course with my work. Your eyes are younger than mine. Look there and you will see when it was collected. I confess, I do not recall the man who collected the violin speaking of the Zeppelin, so it must have been before the tragedy, as you said. I myself received word of it some weeks later, when a mutual friend came in to tell me that he had perished, along with his family. It is best, I believe, that the boy was killed in the war. He was close to his father. It would have destroyed him."

Maisie nodded and, squinting in the diminished light, made a note of the date of collection on an index card. "Thank you, Mr. Andersen."

As she made a final note before placing the card in her bag, Andersen continued speaking, his affection for the van Maartens evident in memories shared. "They were a musical family, their own little orchestra. The boy was his father's son, though given

275

that he was but a child, his violin was a lesser model. I would not be wrong if I said that he would have become the better player, which would have pleased Jacob; mind you, the boy was troubled as he came to the edge of manhood, there were difficulties at school, so Jacob told me. It concerned him, as he had tried to avoid such problems." He shook his head. "I often wonder what happened to the Cuypers. It was a delight to hold, such balance, such workmanship. And such beauty."

Maisie held out her hand to Andersen. "And you never changed your name, Mr. Andersen? It seems something of an accepted practice among those from foreign lands."

"I never needed to. The Vikings were kind enough to leave their names behind centuries ago, so my name is not unusual in this kingdom. Indeed, to me, an Andersen in Denmark Street seemed a perfect match." He shrugged. "It is surprising, though, to have an acceptable name that originally belonged to marauding and cruel invaders."

Maisie smiled. "Thank you, Mr. Andersen, you've been most helpful."

The man inclined his head and shuffled back to his workbench.

SHE SAT IN the MG for some moments before moving on to the war records repository. The cards were falling into place. It was one thing to know, in some way, what had happened in a case such as Heronsdene, but another to understand the layers of truth and the web of lies that held a story together. Now she was acquiring a transparency, more able to interpret a chain of events in a manner that made sense. She sighed, checked the flow of traffic, and pulled out into the Charing Cross Road. One thing was clear, and that was that the man of the cloth had told another lie, for the violin was collected two days *after* the Zeppelin raid, when the Reverend Staples had known that both Jacob van Maarten and his son were dead and there were no descendents to lay claim to the valuable violin.

Maisie had visited the War Office Repository on Arnside Street before and was struck again by how much it reminded her of a library, with its polished dark wood floors and whispered conversations between visitors, who sat at refectory tables while poring over manila folders and onionskin papers. Today there were two couples and a woman on her own. Maisie thought the couples might be parents of soldiers lost to war or taken prisoner, and hope had kept them searching for a sign, perhaps one word, a sentence, a comment by a commanding officer that might give hope that their son was alive somewhere. Then again, it could take years to face up to the truth of a loved one's loss—how well she knew that her-self—and perhaps the lone woman was at last curious, after years of widowhood, to know the circumstances of her husband's death on a foreign field.

Maisie placed her hand on a bell mounted on the

counter. Less than a minute after the chime, a young man appeared, a pile of large envelopes under his arm. Maisie gave him her name, and explained that she had received a clearance to view two records. The man placed the envelopes on the counter and ran his finger down a list of names.

"Ah, yes, there you are." He pointed to a table by the window. "If you take a seat, madam, I'll fetch the files for you."

Maisie thanked him and sat at the table indicated while she waited. There was no view to speak of, simply rows of rooftops extending off into the distance. Sun glinted off skylights, and she watched pigeons swooping back and forth, and sparrows alighting on gutters, and listened to the sounds of the river in the distance. It occurred to her, as she waited, that she would try to see Maurice on the way back to Heronsdene. Of course, she would see her father, but she wanted to talk to her former mentor, as in their days together.

Until now, she had avoided reflecting upon the cremation this morning, busying herself with those aspects of her investigation that must be accomplished before she returned to Heronsdene. Though she had at first been taken aback by Margaret Lynch's decision not to have Simon laid to rest with a gravestone at his head, she had come to understand both the wisdom and the sacrifice inherent in that choice. And she was filled with admiration, all other feelings having burned away within her as Simon's mother leaned against her, seeking her support. And she wondered about that movement, and those often elusive events, conversations, or thoughts that rendered the path clear for forgiveness to take root and grow in a wounded soul.

"Here you are, madam, Sandermere and Martin, though as you can see we have two names for the corporal, on account of his being enlisted under one name and then taking another—which, according to the record, was his in the first place."

"I understand. Thank you. I shan't be long."

"Take your time. We close at five o'clock."

Maisie had handled such records before, had spent time at the repository searching for clues, inconsistencies and truths in the papers of those, alive and deceased, who had served in the war. But when she came to the moment of opening the records of the dead, she undertook the task with a deep respect and reverence because, whatever might have been said about the man by his commanding officer, he had given his life for his country. Whether that gift was given willingly, perhaps with regret, or with anger was not relevant, once that life had been lost.

She discovered that Henry Sandermere had been killed by a sniper in the Somme valley shortly after his return from leave, in early July 1916. The report from his superiors was complimentary, and he would soon have received a promotion to captain had he lived. Nothing about the death was unusual. Officers were, for the most part, drawn from the families of the landed gentry, the aristocracy, families of wealth and privilege. Centuries of advantage, of—at the very least—better nutrition, had resulted in such men being, on average, taller than the rank and file. It was no surprise, then, that the sniper found an officer an easy target. And the regular soldiers were canny, learning quickly to keep their heads away from the parapet.

Corporal Willem van Maarten's file was somewhat fuller, given that notes had followed him from the reformatory. Maisie had known that many boys and men incarcerated at His Majesty's Pleasure were enlisted with the promise that their service would render sentencing void, unless they committed criminal acts while in the army. Youth did not spare one the opportunity to serve, though van Maarten's record contained two letters of complaint from the boy's father, who was concerned at his son's age upon enlistment. An official note had been attached to the letter, to the effect that the boy wished to remain in the army and to serve in France. She shuddered to see a letter from the reformatory with the words RELEASED TO THE ARMY stamped across it.

There were also notes pertaining to the issue of whether Corporal van Maarten had been taken prisoner and then confirmation, in September 1916, that he was presumed dead. The telegram to his parents had been sent just one day after the Zeppelin raid. The final comment by his commanding officer had described his service record as exemplary.

Maisie did not need to make notes on an index card, for she had already garnered the information required, and those details she wished to retain were lodged firmly in her mind. She replaced all notes in the manner in which they had been given to her, collected the folders and her belongings, and walked back to the counter.

"Got everything you want?"

"Yes, thank you."

"Well, if you need anything else, you just come back and we'll help you out."

Maisie looked around the room, at the solitary woman holding her hands to her forehead, leaning forward as she read, shaking her head. She would prefer never to have the need to come to the war records repository again, but she knew that, given her work, it was a faint hope.

It was half-past four when she left London. If she had a good run down to Chelstone, she would arrive by six o'clock. Time to see her father and walk across to the Dower House to visit Maurice. She planned to be in Heronsdene again by nine o'clock. Then she would lay down her head and rest, for morning would herald a formidable day.

SIXTEEN

Following supper with her father, Maisie walked across to the Dower House to see Maurice Blanche. She guessed he had seen her motor car pull in through the gates of Chelstone Manor, and she knew in her heart that he hoped she would come to see him again. She made her way though the gate that divided the properties, up the path past the conservatory, and around to the front entrance. The housekeeper, a short woman who always wore a black skirt and a white blouse with a cameo at her throat, was waiting with the door open to greet her.

"You'll find the doctor in his study. He asked for port to be brought for you, and there's some nice Stilton with biscuits on the trolley—I always think port's too harsh on its own."

"That's lovely. I'll go straight through."

Maurice was sitting at his desk as Maisie entered the room, and he looked up, smiling, as she closed the door behind her. She tried not to notice how he had aged of late. There seemed to be a strain in his standing and locomotion, and he reached for his cane more than he might once have done. Had sadness wrought such changes? One year ago they traveled to France together, and though there was no doubt about his age—he was in his seventies—there had been more of a spring to his step. Had his work begun to take its toll? The events of last September, when she was brought in secret to the house in Paris to be told that her investigations had crossed the path of the intelligence services, proved his knowledge was still in demand and that he played a role of some significance in matters of international importance.

"Maurice, are you feeling unwell?"

He shook his head. "Do not concern yourself with my health, I am simply demonstrating the effects of age. Those falls and scrapes one has in earlier years come home to roost. Take that as a caution, Maisie."

Maurice kissed Maisie on the cheek and then held out his hand toward her usual seat by the fire, opposite his well-used armchair. A trolley was positioned between the two chairs, and Maurice poured a glass of port for Maisie and a single malt for himself before easing himself into his customary place. He reached to the side of the fireplace, selected a pipe and his tobacco pouch, and began to speak as he went through the motions of filling and lighting the pipe.

"You wish to talk about the case in Heronsdene?"

"Yes, I do. But first—"

Maurice looked at Maisie, inclining his head as he drew upon his pipe.

She continued. "Simon was cremated and—oh, dear." She rested her head in her hands. "I can't believe it was just this morning. So much has happened."

"I take it you fell to your work soon after the ritual of that final farewell? No doubt you busied yourself with appointments germane to your investigation."

Maisie nodded. "I allowed only a day in London; I have to return to Heronsdene tonight. I'll drive back to the inn when I leave here."

"Was that necessary, the rush?"

"It was best. There is a momentum, and I am under some pressure to secure an end to my work there within the next day or so."

"I see." Maurice shook the match and threw it into the fireplace. "Tell me about the cremation."

"At first I was taken aback, but I realized that Margaret—Simon's mother—had made the best decision. Simon had remained alive for so long, yet it was not Simon, not like we all remembered him. But I had never been to a cremation before. I was"—Maisie pressed her lips together as she searched for the word to describe her feelings—"unsettled. Yes, I was unsettled, knowing his body was being consigned to an inferno."

There was a silence as Maurice looked into the fire, considering her words before speaking again. "He was wounded in the fire of shelling, and he has been laid to rest in fire. There is a rhythm to the decision, as well as a practicality for an aging woman alone."

Maisie remained silent, holding the glass of port in both hands, turning it around in her fingers and watching the alcohol's film run along the rim of the glass.

Maurice began to speak again. "The concept of such an end brings to mind the phoenix, the sacred firebird, who at the end of life builds a nest of cinnamon twigs, which he ignites, and goes to his death amid flames that will bear new life." He took one sip of the rich amber malt whisky. "Of course, a new young Simon will not walk through that door to greet us, but I sense that seeing him go in this way, knowing there will only be ashes to sprinkle on the breeze, is a gift that has been given you, if you choose to take it." He smiled. "This is one of those times, Maisie, when you must not think, must not dwell and search for meaning. You have done those things, you have held Simon in your heart, and you have taken steps into a future that you might never have imagined in 1917. He is gone now. Think of the newborn phoenix and embrace it."

She said nothing. In her mind's eye a bird with gold and red plumage struggled amid flames of its own combustion.

"It is also worth knowing that tears from the phoenix were said to heal all wounds."

Maisie looked up at her mentor, placing her port on the trolley. "Thank you, Maurice. I'm glad I came to see you."

"You are no longer my pupil or my assistant, Maisie. You are accomplished in your own right. You have little need of me now, I understand that—"

"But—"

"Allow me to finish. Our relationship has changed, as it should. I hope, however, a new friendship will develop between us, and that you might allow an old campaigner to share in the excitement of your investigations, if only afterward, in a story by the fire."

Maisie came from her chair and kissed him on the cheek. "You have been so kind to me, Maurice."

As she stood back, Maurice reached for his cane once more. "I will walk you to the door."

"But the case—"

He held up his hand. "You don't need my counsel, Maisie. You know what must be done."

SHE ARRIVED IN Heronsdene later that evening, parked the MG outside the inn, and walked down toward the waste ground that was once the site of the van Maartens' house. She thought of the fear, the terror, the sheer unimaginable suffering they must have endured, their lungs festering with smoke and fumes, skin searing back from the bone, as unconsciousness and death claimed them. She wondered about the house, a bakery with a dwelling above, and imagined this home, a place of security, the lair to which a family cleaves, as instead a flame-filled inferno that consumed three human beings who had lived, breathed, worked, made music, and loved. Then there was nothing. *Nothing.* Nothing but an eerie cold, a bitter aura that kept a village at bay—except one soul who seeded the land with a profusion of Michaelmas daisies and who had come back, on the night of the fire at the inn, with a humble bouquet. It was as if a message had been left: *There, it is done, you are remembered.*

THE FOLLOWING MORNING, Maisie left the inn early, having asked only for tea and toast, though her taste buds were tempted by the rich aroma of eggs, bacon, tomato and mushrooms being fried ready for the guests. Fred had offered to pack a hot egg and bacon sandwich, but Maisie declined. She had to be at the Sandermere estate at a time when the groom might be out exercising the horses—it was widely known in the village that Alfred Sandermere had still not emerged from his rooms on the first of the mansion's upper floors. According to local talk, trays left outside his door were being dragged inside when servants left the corridor, only to be pushed outside again in the middle of the night. An empty brandy or wine bottle indicated that a fresh supply must be brought to the room, but it was said that Sandermere had not left either clothing or bed linens to be laundered, nor had he allowed servants into the rooms to clean.

She parked the MG some distance from the estate, in a lay-by from which she could hike through the woods and climb over a fence on the way to her destination. She had deliberately worn her brown corduroy trousers, brown leather walking shoes, and a dark brown cardigan over her blouse. She wore a brown felt hat, pulled down as low as she could, and hoped she had enough camouflage to avoid being detected. Along with her knapsack and Victorinox knife, she brought the hazel divining rod she had fashioned herself.

Soon she was on the perimeter of the Sandermere property, making her way toward the stables. She looked about her, ran from the security of overhanging trees to the rear entrance, and listened for movement. The only sounds audible were those of horses, pacing a stall, munching on hay, or nickering at the sound of someone close by. She did not hear a groom talking to the horses or walking back and forth with pails of water, nor did she hear the scratching sweep of a brush being drawn back against a horse's coat. She looked around the arched entranceway to the stables and stepped inside. She counted the horses—one was missing, so the groom was out. Stepping with care along the brick walkway that divided the stalls, she reached out to each horse as she went by, perhaps to offer a sugar lump—she was Frankie Dobbs's daughter and never went anywhere near a horse without a treat—or to rub a soft equine nose or the side of a horse's neck. She reached the far end of the stable block, where tarpaulins still flapped against the side of the building, and took out her divining rod. She slipped her Victorinox knife into her pocket and hid her knapsack on the ground behind the door of the tack room, which was drawn back and tied to prevent it from slamming shut. Unencumbered, she walked out beyond the stables, holding the divining rod in the manner taught by Beulah. She closed her eyes. *Think silver.*

She felt the heft of the rod in her hands, not light as the branch had been when she cut it from the tree.

Now it had substance as she clasped it, and she recognized the weight of its power as it drew her on. She had thought it might lead her to the tarpaulin, to the foundation recently disturbed and pulled apart. The ground was gravelly and uneven where workers had been reconstructing the stables before Sandermere had called a halt—it was this unfinished work that had brought her back, suspecting it might be evidence of more than a job awaiting completion. But as she walked toward the site of the rebuilding work, the fork seemed to become small and delicate in her hands. Holding the image of silver in her mind's eye, Maisie turned, trying to find that vein of energy again, that line of influence where the hazel would come alive, like a fish on the line.

The rod became strong as she turned and stepped onto the cobblestone floor of the stables. Now she felt the draw, now she and her divining rod were engaged as she placed one foot in front of the other. It was as if the rod itself were formed of that sacred ore, magnetized toward shared mystical properties, as she was pulled back toward the archway through which she'd entered the stables. Then, just as she was about to step out of the building, she felt a drag on her hands, a wilting, so she turned first to the left, and almost cried out in frustration as the rod became loose, unharnessed as it rested on her fingers. Maisie turned to the right, and sighed with relief as the leaden sensation returned. Now she was looking straight into the eyes of Sandermere's hunter. The horse responded to her hand, blowing soft sweet air onto her palm, and then reached out to investigate the rod with his nose.

"Oh, no, you don't, laddie." She unlatched the half door of the stall, pushed back on the horse's chest with her left hand, and waited as he moved away at her touch. She latched the door again and paced around the stall.

Resting her hand first on the horse's flank and then his withers, she moved him back and forth, pushing fresh straw aside so she could check every inch underfoot. She stepped to the right, to the left, and to the back of the stall, kicking away straw and pressing down on the square paving stones with her feet. She used her divining rod again, and as her fingers took the weight, so she was drawn toward the raised water trough in the corner. It was a plain brick and enamel trough, akin to a square scullery sink but deeper and longer. Underneath, a support had been built of the same slate slabs as were used on the floor. Maisie knelt, aware but not afraid of the hunter behind her. The horse seemed as curious as she, his warm breath close to her neck as if he too wanted a closer look.

She took out the knife, selected a blade, and began to run the tip along the pointing between each slab. One slab came away with ease. Soon she could grasp it, her fingers working carefully to pull it free. She checked the security of the water trough. It held firm, likely supported by bolts or bricks underneath.

Hearing horses' hooves and a voice coming closer, she held her breath.

"Right, then, Humphrey, that's you done!"

Maisie listened as the groom dismounted, his boots clattering against the cobblestones.

"Nice and easy does it, eh, old fellow? None of that racing all over the place, just a nice little trot, that's good enough for us." The groom spoke kindly to the horse. "We'll get all this lot off you, a bit of a rub-down, and then we'll take you down to the bottom field. How about that, my friend?"

Maisie heard the groom pat the horse's neck and the sounds that accompanied the removing of saddle and bridle, of the horse's hooves being picked out and cleaned, one by one.

"Fontein, you're next, so don't you stand there getting in a state, alright, guv'nor?"

Maisie listened, still as stone against the water trough, as the groom made much of the horse just exercised. At last she heard the horse turned around and sounds indicating the groom had left the stables once more, to put the horse out to pasture.

She continued with her endeavor, finally easing away the slab and using all her strength to pull it aside and lean it against the wall that separated the hunter from his stablemate. She had no torch with her, so was dependent upon the shaft of light that came in through the archway and was now being blocked by the horse.

"Move over, lad. Come on." Maisie stood and pushed the horse back once again, reaching into her pocket for more sugar lumps, which she hid in the hay remaining in his manger. "There, that'll keep you busy."

Kneeling down next to the water trough, Maisie peered into the space revealed by the slab she'd removed, feeling with her hands for something loose, unexpected. Soon her fingers alighted on fabric of rough texture; using one hand to brace against the side of the trough, she pulled it out. The sack was dirty and damp, tied with string at the top. She lost no time in untying the closure to inspect the contents. *Silver*. The sack was filled with so much silverware that Maisie thought it looked like a priest's ransom. There were goblets, decanters, cutlery, all manner of goods marked with the etched insignia of the Sandermere family: a large "S" set in a shield with a heart in the center and a single sword across.

She reached in again and found another sack, this time containing items indicating theft from places other than the estate. There was an empty wallet, a watch, a roll of money, jewelry. Maisie stood up, took off her hat, and wiped her hand across her forehead. Instead of taking the sacks with her, she secured them as she had found them and heaved the slab back into place. The groom was no thief, of that she was sure. She replaced her hat, while the hunter, who had eaten all the sugar, nuzzled her for more.

She pushed him aside. "If you're not careful, I'll have a soft spot for you, you big lug."

Maisie checked the stall and, listening for the groom's return, let herself out and latched the half door once again. The hunter's blanket had been hung over a bar on the outside of the door, obscuring his nameplate.

"Well, well, well. *Merlin.* I should have known." She patted him once more. "Only you and I know that your master is a thief."

MAISIE GATHERED UP her knapsack, relieved that the groom had not even noticed it in the shadows, and made haste back toward the woods, once more climbing the iron fence and claiming her MG. She drove away from Heronsdene, into the next village to find the telephone kiosk, and lost no time in placing the call.

"James?"

"Maisie—gosh, you sound out of breath."

"Just a bit. I have some information for you that I believe you must act upon without delay."

"Go on."

"I've found the missing Sandermere silver and a few other things besides. And I know the culprit."

"Who?"

"Alfred Sandermere."

There was a pause. "I might have known. I never trusted that man, from our first meeting. And the fires?"

Maisie took a deep breath. "That's something different. But I will have news about them for you shortly. In the meantime, I should recount the events of the past week, concerning Sandermere."

When she had finished giving him all the necessary information, James sighed. "What do you think should be the next move?"

"Call the police, James. You now know where the silver and the other items are hidden. I suspect he was waiting for a while before selling his hoard via underworld contacts. It was likely a scheme to keep his creditors at bay. Do warn the police that he is a volatile man and may need to be restrained."

"Of course. I shall also speak to my solicitors."

"Indeed. Now I must go, James. I have no doubt I shall see you soon."

Maisie allowed herself a short time alone in the MG, leaning her head back against the seat. Her stomach grumbled, and a warmth rose up in her chest that took her breath away. Was she sickening for something? Beads of perspiration trickled down the side of her nose, and she reached for her handkerchief to wipe her brow and cheeks. *I am on fire.* She opened the door to allow a breeze to waft into the motor car and recognized that she was unsettled about the feelings rising within her.

Soon the sensations subsided, the inferno that had gripped her insides extinguished by logical consideration and fresh air. In some way she thought the lingering image of Simon's cremation had played a part in her indisposition. She shook her head and once again set off for Heronsdene and the farm.

THE PICKERS WERE only two hop-gardens from the end

of their work on the farm, and many were already talking of the packing up, the journey back, and welcoming autumn's snap, then winter's chill. Billy saw her approaching from a distance, waved, and came toward her, stopping to pick up his jacket on the way. They dispensed with the pleasantries of greeting.

"I went into Maidstone on the train yesterday mornin' to see Beattie Drummond. Blimey, she's a bit of a one, eh?"

"Push you for a story, did she?"

"Not 'alf, but I was ready for 'er when she said you'd promised she'd be the first to know when you've done your bit."

Maisie nodded. "So, did she find anything?"

Billy pulled an envelope from his pocket and passed it to Maisie. "She came out and gave me some photographs taken in the village before the war. I didn't let on, didn't say what we was lookin' for—or who."

"Right." Maisie opened the envelope and flicked through each photograph with some speed, until she came to one image in particular.

"Here we are."

"I can smell the bread from 'ere. I reckon that was taken on Empire Day, what with the flags and bunting outside the shop, and Mr. Martin standin' there with a big loaf of bread shaped like the British Isles in 'is 'ands—I mean, that's clever, ain't it? You can cut the dough in the right shape, but to get it to turn out how you want it after you've put it in the oven—that takes a lot of skill, I would've thought."

Maisie nodded, squinting at the photograph. She reached into her shoulder bag and pulled out a magnifying glass, leaning over to better consider the subject.

"Shall I post 'em back to 'er?"

"Yes, if you don't mind."

"Got what you want, then?"

"Yes. I just wanted to double-check something, before I go any further."

"Do you want me to come with you later on?"

Maisie smiled. "No, you've done enough. You're on holiday, remember?" She paused. "Oh, and when you're in touch with George, tell him his boys are well and truly off the hook. They won't be summoned back to Kent."

"Just like you thought, was it?"

She nodded. "More or less. Want a hand with the picking? I can help out until packing-in time, then I have to go up to see Webb."

MAISIE WELCOMED AN afternoon sojourn among the hop-pickers, the smell and grainy stain on her hands, the way the bines were pulled down, opening up the blue afternoon sky, as if a canopy were being drawn back to reveal clouds puffed up with white importance, a backdrop for rooks cawing overhead and swallows calling from on high. This, she knew, was the calm before the storm, the clouds a portent for the events that must unfold in all their grayness.

The tallyman came around, and as the last count of the day was completed at each bin, the pickers moved off, either toward the hopper huts if they were Londoners or to the village for the locals, while the gypsies wandered toward the hill, the women's skirts catching in the breeze, a profusion of color moving from side to side with the sway of their hips.

"And-a-one . . . and-a-two . . . and-a-three. . . ." The tallyman continued his count at the Beales' bin. Maisie smiled, for each member of the Beale family mouthed the number as the tallyman, sleeves rolled up above the elbow, pushed his flat cap on the back of his head and plunged the bushel basket in again and again. "Nice work, clean picking, that's what I like," he said, then took his pencil from behind his ear, and noted the afternoon's accomplishments.

Maisie waved to the Beales as she left, walking toward the hill that led up to the gypsy camp and the clearing they had used as a gathering place since before the hop-picking began. When the jook came down the hill to meet her, she stretched to rest her hand on the dog's shoulder until she reached the vardos.

She went first to Beulah and greeted her before asking, "Is Webb back from the hop-gardens?"

The old woman was holding an earthenware cup filled with a translucent green broth that she sipped before replying. "Gone for wood. Jook brought us hare again." Then she rubbed her chest.

"Are you feeling ill?" asked Maisie.

Beulah winced. "Not holding my food well today. It's sitting on my chest, on account of the bread."

Maisie sat next to her. "Do you have any other pain?"

"Don't need none of your doctoring. I'll see to myself."

"What are you drinking?"

"Mixture. Helps the food go down. Now then, girl, never you mind about me. There'n be nothing wrong with Beulah."

At that moment, Webb came back into the clearing, along the path on the opposite side of the ring of stones that marked the perimeter of the fire.

Beulah called to him. "Webb. Come, son, the rawni wants to talk to yern."

Webb dropped the armful of wood alongside the stones and brushed his hands down the front of his trousers. As he came forward, he removed his hat and ran his fingers through the mane of brown curls that was now almost shoulder-length. "What do you want, miss?"

Maisie stood up, still concerned about Beulah. "I'd like to ask you a question or two, if you don't mind."

The man shifted his position, moving his weight from one foot to the other, crossing his arms and raising his chin just enough to reveal defensiveness. "Depends on the questions."

Maisie wondered how she might tread lightly, how she might couch her questions in a manner that was not inflammatory. "I have a friend in London, a luthier. His name is Mr. Andersen, and—"

"Don't know no Andersen." Webb had taken a step back.

"Of course, but I was telling him about your beautiful violin, and when I described it he thought it might be worth—"

"You reckon I stole that violin, don't you?" Webb's shoulders were hunched now, his eyes flashing like those of a fox with the hunt at his tail.

"Of course not, of course I didn't think to suggest that you stole the violin."

Webb came closer.

"Webb!" Beulah had come to her feet, still clutching the green liquid with one hand while she rubbed her chest with the other. "No wonder my food's stuck in my gullet with you a-goin' on like that. Now then, my son. Listen to her."

But Webb was not to be cut off. "You're just like the rest of them—no, you're worse. You come here, eat our food, dance to our music, and act like you know us, and now you've shown your colors as a true diddakoi, not one of us and not gorja but half and half, and they're the worst—they'll stab a back before it's turned."

"Webb! Now, then. You pull your neck in, my boy!" Beulah nodded toward Boosul, who was swaddled in her mother's skirts, for Paishey had come to sit beside Beulah.

Maisie looked from Webb to Beulah, then shook her head. She had been wrong in her timing, off in her choice of words, and she knew she should leave. "I know the truth, Mr. Webb. *I know.* And I can help you." She squeezed Beulah's hand and began to walk away.

She had gone but a few paces when she heard Paishey scream, followed by Webb shouting, "Beulah, Beulah!"

By the time Maisie reached the woman's side, she was wide-eyed, gasping for breath, her words barely audible. The gypsy clan gathered around, as Paishey knelt behind Beulah and rested her head in her lap.

"Move back, she needs air!" Maisie heard her own voice echoing in her ears as she waved her hand to add weight to her words.

"Do as she says," urged Webb. "Give her room to breathe."

Maisie felt for Beulah's pulse, her fingers barely moving against a throb that was neither strong nor rhythmic. "It's her heart, Webb."

Paishey had loosened the gypsy matriarch's silver-gray hair, which lay down across her shoulders. Now, as the lines and wrinkles that marked her age diminished with each second, the woman raised her arm and motioned to her son to come to her. Maisie moved aside, allowing Webb to crouch beside his mother, then looked on as the dying woman wrestled against the weakness in her body to grasp the cloth of her son's shirt and pull him closer. Webb cradled her in his arms, while Paishey remained at her head, and he leaned forward to hear the words his mother strained even to whisper. He nodded, his eyes reddened, yet his grip remained firm.

"Listen to her, son. She'll free you," was all that Maisie heard. Then, calling upon all reserves of energy remaining in her body, she spoke loud enough for the clan to hear. "He is *my son*. Follow'n *him* now."

Webb began to sob. "No, Beulah, please, no. Stay, don't go."

But Beulah was smiling, holding up her hands as if to one who was reaching down to her, and saying her final words with a gentleness Maisie had not heard before. "Set yourself free, boy. Set yourself free."

Maisie stepped forward, kneeling to feel her pulse and then to listen for her breath. There was nothing. She sat back to look at Beulah, then turned to Webb and Paishey. "She's gone. I'm so sorry."

Leaning forward, Paishey placed her hands on each side of Beulah's head and used her thumbs to close her eyelids. Then she kissed each closed eye before reaching into her pocket for two copper coins to lay on the motionless lids. Webb moved away, and the women came forward, Esther helping Maisie to her feet. "We'll'n look after her now, miss. You go on home. She belongs to us. We'll'n take care of her."

Maisie walked once more to the edge of the clearing, where even the horses had gathered, their heads up and intent. She pushed them aside to pass, and as she made her way down the hill, she heard the heartsick wail of a dog howling. It was not an ordinary call, the yelping that might answer a vixen's midnight screech, but the timeless baying that country folk called a death howl. Maisie stopped to listen, was still so the dog's cry could move through her, so she could feel the vibrations she had never been able to voice, that had caught in her chest so many times.

SEVENTEEN

As she walked away from the encampment, Maisie knew the keening had started, a sound that would grow ever louder as the gypsies gave vent to their loss. There would be no time to speak to Webb until after Beulah's funeral, for which she would return in a few days. It would be a narrow opportunity—the gypsies would move on with haste now.

Not wanting to be on her own, Maisie walked to the hopper huts, where Tilley lamps burned outside to beckon her forward, for the sky bore the rose tint of sunset and dusk was but minutes away. The doors of the huts were open, and Londoners had brought chairs outside so they could sit and talk now that the day's work was done. Billy's mother was seated outside the family's hut, shucking peas, the colander on her lap held steady by her knees.

"Is Billy here, Mrs. Beale?"

"Him and Doreen are in the cookhouse." She pointed toward the whitewashed brick building and went back to her task.

Maisie stopped to talk to Doreen, noting the gaunt pallor that had clung to her skin since the death of her daughter was now disguised by sun-kissed cheeks.

Billy walked outside with Maisie, where she told him about Beulah's death.

"Well, that'll put the tin lid on that, won't it?"

Maisie nodded. "It certainly makes things a little trickier." She paused. "You know, there's one thing I've been meaning to ask you, Billy. I want to know what you heard after Sandermere attacked Paishey, when you restrained Webb. He said something that appeared to flummox you—then you seemed thoughtful, as if what he'd said wasn't quite right."

Billy nodded. "It was when 'e said *mornin' hate.*" Billy pronounced the h—a consonant that was usually absent in his cockney accent. He was emphasizing the word *hate.*

"What does it mean?"

He shrugged his shoulders. Maisie understood that he did not care to speak about the years of his soldiering. "It's what we used to say, in the war." He kicked his foot against the clay-like earth, folded his arms, and looked down as he spoke, staring at the sandy patterns left by his boot. "There was times we knew the Hun didn't want to be there any more 'n we did, and they knew we didn't want to be there either. These weren't the big shows but the sort of in-between times. We'd be in our trench, like ants, and they'd be in theirs. Bein' a sapper, I was with the lads what 'ad to get out there and mend the wires, lay communication lines, that sort of thing. But of course, the 'igher-ups, theirs and ours, didn't like us all just sittin' there, not doin' anythin' but brewing up a cup o' char, so we 'ad to fire off a few rounds every mornin' and again at night, just to show we were still after the enemy." He shook his head. "And it was as if we all knew what we 'ad to do, them and us. Someone would call out to us, 'Guten Morgen, Britisher,' or we'd call out to them, 'Wakey, wakey, Fritz,' and then we'd go at it for a while, prayin' that no one copped it. Don't know what *they* called it, but we called it the *mornin' hate* and the *evenin' hate*. Sort of summed it up, shootin' at each other to show—to prove—that we *hated*."

Maisie nodded.

"And for what? That's the big question, ain't it? For what?" Billy shrugged.

She placed her hand on his arm. "I'd better go, Billy. I'll leave you in peace with your family. Not long to go now, eh?"

He looked up at the spent hop-gardens. "Next year'll soon roll round, and we'll all be out 'ere again." He pulled a packet of Woodbines from his trouser pocket, along with a box of matches. "Puttin' the money away, we are."

"Your passage to Canada?"

"If we can do it, Miss. I used to just say it but didn't reckon I'd ever want to go, not really, not being a Londoner born and bred. Now, what with Lizzie gone and Doreen not gettin' over it at all, we need a new start." He lit a cigarette, closing his right eye against a wisp of smoke that snaked upward. "Don't know whether me old mum will come with us, but I won't want to leave 'er. And I don't know what sort of work I can do, but—well, I'll 'ave a go at anything."

Maisie nodded. "I know you will." She smiled encouragement. "But in the meantime, I need a good assistant, so don't think of going anywhere too soon, will you? Now then, I'm off, back to the inn. I'll see you tomorrow."

ARRIVING AT THE inn, Maisie stopped to greet Fred Yeoman before climbing the stairs to her room. She was not hungry and had declined supper, saying she would have some bread and cheese and an ale on a tray, for later if she was hungry. At least the ale would help her sleep.

She opened the curtains wide, the better to see out to the clear night sky as darkness descended. Pulling her chair to the window, Maisie sat down and closed her eyes. How would she ever bring the case to completion now? She could point to Sandermere as being responsible for much of the petty crime in the village, but without the evidence of confession she could not throw light on her other suspicions.

A knock at the door caused Maisie to start.

"Sorry to bother you, miss, but there's a man to see you."

Man, not gentleman, thought Maisie.

Yeoman cleared his throat. "It's one of the travelers, the pikeys. Don't know what the fellow wants, but I told him to wait outside. Name of Webb. Wears a big hat."

305

Maisie nodded. "Right you are, Mr. Yeoman. I'll come down straightaway."

Closing the door behind her, Maisie held on to the banister as she hurried down the winding, narrow staircase and through the doorway to the street, lowering her head as she went to avoid the beam.

"Webb, what a surprise."

He nodded and touched the brim of his hat. It was almost dark, and she could only just see his eyes as he turned toward her and was bathed in warm amber light from the inn's outside lantern.

"Beulah would have wanted me to come. I talked to Paishey—she's with the women—and she said I should."

Maisie frowned. "Is it alright for us to speak without one of your womenfolk with us?"

"Because of how it is, and that we're here in the street, we can talk."

"Would you like to walk, just down to the church perhaps?" Maisie knew such a stroll would entail passing the site of the old bakery, which was opposite the memorial and the church.

"Beulah said you were expected. That she'd asked for help, and you came."

"And do you believe that?"

He turned to walk, and Maisie fell into step alongside him.

"You mean, do I believe that, seeing as *I'm* gorja?"

"Yes."

Webb pushed his hands into his pockets and, as they

walked, spoke with an eloquence not apparent when he was with the gypsy tribe. "I *do* believe. Beulah saved me, looked after me, so I'd have done anything for her, and I've seen enough to believe her." He looked sideways at Maisie. "You know who I am, don't you?"

"I do, yes, but I'll still call you Webb, if you like."

"Yes, that is my name now."

"And I'd like to know your story."

"But you know it already. I've seen it in your eyes. And you saw me leaving the inn's garden. And there are the questions you've been asking."

"I know your story, Pim van Maarten, only inasmuch as I have facts. I would like to hear it told in your words."

Webb looked down at the ground and shook his head as they continued walking. "Haven't been called by that name in over ten years." He stopped as they reached the waste ground, then turned toward the church, where a gaslight was glowing over the gate, and to the side was a bench. "Let's sit down over there."

When they were settled, he began to speak again.

"We came down here when I was a baby, because my sister couldn't breathe right, not up there in London. To tell you the truth, I don't reckon she breathed right down here, but she grew out of it anyway. My grandfather was from the Netherlands, where he was a baker, like my father, though he came to London after he was married and before my father was born. They spoke Dutch at home, and we did too. It was my father who dropped the *van* from our name and changed the spelling. He said he didn't want us to be different, he wanted us to sound English. My mother—who came over from the Netherlands to marry my father—worked hard to lose her accent, but we kept to some of the old traditions, like celebrating the visit of Saint Nicholas and Black Peter in December."

"You were a happy family," said Maisie, encouraging him to continue.

He nodded. "We were. It was my fault that everything changed. Children can be harsh, Miss Dobbs. They can be hurtful. One of the boys at school had heard us speaking Dutch at home, and for some reason—I never understood why it began, it could have been because my reading was better than his—he started to tease me, and the teasing went on, and it got worse, until I didn't have any friends at all. I was the whipping boy, the one who was always left out. The one who was bullied."

"And your sister?"

"Ah, Anna was beautiful, so for her it was not too bad. And she tried to protect me, but as soon as she was twelve and matriculated, she left the school to help in the bakery. Then later on, I met him: Alfred Sandermere."

"And he offered you friendship, but at a cost?"

"Yes. I was to be his cohort, the younger sergeant-at-arms who would get into mischief with him."

"And the mischief grew more serious."

He nodded, leaned forward, and rested his head in his hands.

"My father was so diminished by my behavior. He tried everything to help me but was lost, trying to deliver me from the path I'd chosen. I was not the man I am today. I was a boy who made a poor decision, a boy who wanted to be of some account, and Alfred gave me what I needed. He gave me friendship."

"Then you were caught."

"Yes." Webb leaned back, his cheeks wet. He removed his hat and ran his fingers straight back through his hair. "We had committed a crime, a robbery—Alfred was a seasoned thief, but there were dogs, and we were discovered."

"And you took the blame."

"His father, the name, connections—you know, the magistrate who goes shooting on the estate—Alfred's time in custody was over like that." He snapped his fingers.

"But you were sent to the reformatory."

"Yes." He wiped the back of his hand across his eyes. "My father came whenever he could to visit. He brought me books, he brought me my old violin, which he had to take away again because they would not allow me to have it. He was ashamed of me, his son, but he never failed to visit. He blamed himself for what I had done."

"When did you enlist?"

He sniffed, composing himself. "They came to me

when I turned thirteen. They looked at all of us of a certain age. I was solid for my years. Working in the gardens and in building jobs at the reformatory had given me muscle. I could have been taken for nineteen, and that's all they wanted, boys who would pass the medical and could be listed as fit for service." He took another deep breath and blew it out through pursed lips. "I was told that enlisting would absolve me of my crime, that my record would be destroyed. I signed the necessary papers, and off I went. By the time I was fourteen, I was in France, in the trenches. I was a soldier, a fighting soldier. And there were others, other boys who passed as older. Some of them had enlisted with their fathers, some wanted to get away from home, and there were the boys like me who had been released from the reformatories or borstals."

"Yes, I know."

"I saw terrible things there."

Maisie nodded.

"I saw things I never want to see again."

She allowed a pause before speaking. "And you were listed as dead."

"I didn't know what I was listed as until I was sent home. I was in a shell hole, my mates shot or blown to pieces and gone, the rats crawling all over me. I was scared to put my head up, scared to do anything but cry—cry because I could, because it was the only thing left for me to do. Then, the next thing I knew, there was sky no more, so I looked up, and there were five big Germans leaning into the hole with bayonets fixed. Then one of them said, 'He's a boy, a big boy. They have sent boys to do the work of men.'" Webb turned to Maisie. "I also speak some German and some French, so I knew what was being said. I was taken prisoner. And because I thought they would kill me, I pulled off my tags and threw them in the hole, so that my father and mother might have word of me. I thought that even though there was no body—and that wasn't unusual, the way men were blown up in the shelling—when my pals were found, they would know that I, too, was dead."

"Yes. I understand."

"I was released after the war and repatriated. Then came demobilization, and all I wanted to do was come straight home." He gasped, a cry issuing from his lips, as if he might break down. "I walked from the station and came into the village before dawn, when people were still in their beds. I'd returned a man, not a boy, and though the war was written in the lines on my face, in years I was still a youth. I was proud of myself. I had a clean record. I could take on anyone who went for me, and I could turn away from Sandermere. I wanted to be my father's son again, I wanted to see my family."

They were silent for some moments, until the man, his voice breaking, began speaking again.

"I walked down this street—there was no memorial then, no division in the road to accommodate the list of fallen from the village. Most of the older boys who had made my life a misery were gone. Dead. I have

311

seen others, though, seen them with their arms missing, in their wheelchairs, or with their faces scarred." He shrugged. "Then I came to this place, expecting to walk through the front door to wake my family, expecting to be received with their love, but there was nothing. Nothing but the burned shell of a building that was gone, incinerated. I could not speak, could not think. My breath left my lungs. The only thing I could think to do was to go to my sister's friend, to see Phyllis. I waited in the woods close to her house. I could not go in, could not trust myself to speak to anyone, could not even have mustered polite conversation with her father. I waited until they departed the house one by one, until I saw Phyllis, in her maid's uniform, leave the house to walk up to the estate. And I stopped her." He gave a half laugh. "She thought I was a ghost."

"And she told you everything."

"Yes, everything. And she told me who was involved. I knew I would never forget them."

"How did you meet Beulah?"

"I told Phyllis not to say a word about seeing me. Then I ran. I ran, my kit bag across my shoulder, until I couldn't run anymore. I half walked, half fell into the woods and collapsed. I have no memory of the days and nights that followed. I do not know what happened. When I awoke it was to the smell of broth and wood smoke. I was laid out in that clearing up on the hill. It was summertime, 1919, and they had come for the fruit-picking and the hop-picking."

"And Beulah claimed you for her son."

"Her real son had died as an infant and would have been about my age, so, yes, she took me for her son. And I was willing to be adopted, for I had no one, nothing except a need to make them pay." He turned to Maisie. "You see, I understood revenge. And I understood that if that was what they had wanted—revenge—then the job was left half done, because I was still alive. Pim van Maarten was alive, and I wanted my pound of flesh, from *them*"—he pointed back toward the center of the village—"and from Alfred Sandermere, because my father, mother and sister would still be alive if it hadn't been for him."

"Yes, I know." Maisie paused. "So you hounded the villagers with fires, each year, on the anniversary of your family's death."

"I surprised myself, you know. I thought I would be able to take the life of every one of them, make them feel what my family felt. But I must have seen too much killing in France. All I could do was scare them. I only caused damage to bricks and mortar."

There was silence, broken when Maisie spoke again.

"Your father would have been proud of your mastery of the violin. You are a worthy successor—and you favor him, though not with the hair."

Webb smiled. "Yes, he would be proud. And though I look like him, I am not half the man. He would have found it in his heart to understand."

Maisie allowed a few seconds to pass. "How did you

know the Reverend Staples had the violin?"

"Stroke of luck, it was, going to the vicar's house with Beulah, selling flowers. When he opened the door I saw it there, lying on a table. So I went back later and took what was rightly mine. I remembered some things from Sandermere, such as how to break into a house or just walk in while the doors to the garden were open."

"And what will you do now, Webb?"

He looked again toward the waste ground that was once his home. "We'll bury Beulah, do what we have to do with her vardo, her belongings, and then we'll go." He turned to Maisie. "Will you come? To her funeral, and to the afterwards?"

She nodded and said she would go, though she did not reveal how much she dreaded the *afterwards*.

After bidding Webb farewell and returning to her room, Maisie leaned back in her chair and looked out into the blackness. A faint light rose up from the kitchen below, and she could hear the bubbling of talk in the public bar. She knew that Webb would not rest until he had received some acknowledgment from the villagers, and she understood that secrets long buried were not easily brought to the surface. She would try to see Sandermere tomorrow, but first she would visit the Reverend Staples.

She stood up and reached out to close the window against the unrelenting howl of the dead gypsy's lurcher. *We'll do what we have to do with her vardo*. She wondered if she could bear to witness the ritual.

● ● ●

AS MAISIE LEFT the village next morning, bound for Hawkhurst, she passed two police Invicta motor cars traveling in the direction of the Sandermere estate. Clearly James had made his report. She wondered what tack they would take. Would Sandermere be summoned from his room for questioning, or would there be a softly-softly approach, with the police claiming they were acting on a tip-off, perhaps, and knew where the silver was hidden? How would they link Sandermere, except by accusation? His fingerprints would be expected to be on such items as were hidden in the horse's stall, which led her to believe that they would question him until he confessed, wearing him down with suppositions that would eventually prove to be true.

She paid little attention to the surrounding countryside today, wanting only to complete her confrontation with the retired former vicar of Heronsdene parish church, and arrived at Easter Cottage in time to see Mrs. Staples leave the house with a large basket, then continue walking toward the houses on the other side of the green. There would be no phantom telephone calls today. Parking along the street, Maisie locked the MG, walked back to the cottage, and rang the bell.

"Miss Dobbs, what a surprise." The vicar seemed flustered, holding a copy of *The Times* which he began to fold and fold again as he spoke to her. He was wearing exactly the same garb as at their previous meeting and seemed crumpled and uncomfortable at having his morning disturbed, especially by a woman who doubtless would broach a subject he would rather not dwell upon.

"Good morning, Reverend Staples. I was just passing and thought I would drop in to see you. I have some information you might find interesting."

"Do come in." He led the way to the study. "Please, be seated." He waved the newspaper toward a chair and sat down when Maisie was settled. He leaned back, placed the newspaper in the wastepaper bin, and, as if trying to find a comfortable position in which to brook an unwelcome conversation, he leaned forward, resting his elbow on the desk. Finally, he sat up with his arms folded in front of his ecclesiastical cross. "Now then, what's all this about?"

Maisie smiled, confident in her composure. She was used to being lied to, but not by a religious man.

"I had cause to travel up to London this week and by chance was close to Denmark Street, so I popped in to see Mr. Andersen—Senior, that is—the luthier to whom Jacob Martin always took his precious and very valuable Cuypers violin to be tuned and generally reconditioned."

The vicar frowned. "Cuypers? Precious? You must be mistaken. And valuable? I doubt it."

"The luthier, whom I believe to be something of an expert, said the violin was one of the most beautiful he had ever seen and that Jacob was an accomplished musician."

"Well, I never." The vicar shrugged.

"Reverend Staples, please do not be vague. I believe you know perfectly well why I am here. There is nothing I can do now regarding your crime—for what you have done constitutes looting and is thus a criminal act—but I can at least be an advocate for the dead and tell you that I know what you did."

"I don't know what you mean!"

"Yes, you do. Jacob Martin—and you knew that the family's real name was van Maarten—told you he had taken the violin to London, to his friend Mr. Andersen, in Denmark Street. After the tragedy, indeed, *after* you received the telegram with news that Willem, *Pim*, was presumed dead, you went to London to claim the violin, saying nothing to Mr. Andersen of what had happened, only that Jacob had asked you to collect his property. Weren't you afraid he might ask what you intended to do with the instrument? Or that he might know a relative with a claim to it?"

"I—it wasn't like that."

"Oh, I think it was, Reverend Staples. And, as I said, what you did amounted to looting, which is beneath your calling."

"But it would have languished there; it would have not been played. It was a beautiful thing, a work of art."

"And it didn't belong to you. It was meant to be passed on, father to son."

"But the son was dead."

"As far as you knew, he was *missing*."

"But he—" The man stopped speaking and looked at Maisie, his eyes narrowed. "What are you trying to say?"

"Before I try to say anything, I have one question for you."

"And that is?"

"Why didn't you stop it? A man of the cloth could have put a stop to what went on in Heronsdene."

"But I—"

Maisie inclined her head, watching the white pallor of fear rise up on the vicar's face. "Your expression has told me all I need to know."

"You don't know what it was like. The chaos, the fear, the terror."

"But aren't you supposed to walk up to that chaos and challenge it, Reverend Staples? Isn't that what you are called to do, rather than be part of it?"

The man leaned forward, his shoulders slumped. Then he looked up and sighed deeply. "The violin was stolen from me anyway, so what does it all matter now? It's in the past."

"You retired several years ago, didn't you?" She did not allow him to reply, but continued. "I suspect because you could not stand another hop-picking season and the fires that came with it. You probably thought you were being haunted, didn't you? Haunted by the ghost of a young man who had lost his entire family in one night. Haunted by the young man who might one day come for the violin that was rightly his."

There was silence. Then the Reverend Staples spoke again. "You are right, Miss Dobbs. I am haunted, and I will bear that cross for the rest of my life."

Maisie stood up. "You may wonder why I came today, to tell you what I have discovered when there is nothing I can do about it. I came because I wanted you to know that someone else knows what you have been part of, and that you had taken property from the dead before you even buried their remains. You should have been the moral anchor of the village, not of the hue and cry."

Maisie bid the vicar good day without further ado and left Hawkhurst to return to Heronsdene, where she intended to pack her bags and make her way to her father's house before going on to London the next day. It was unlikely that she would be able to see Sandermere this afternoon, given the police presence she had witnessed as she left the village this morning. She was looking forward to getting home now, to the city with its self-important bustle. If she were to remain faithful to her practice of ensuring that all ends of a case were tied before leaving, she would have to admit that there was more to do, but James Compton had not required her to bring all the guilty to account. He had asked her only to find out what was amiss in the village, and she knew more than enough to make her report. Yet such considerations did not sit easy with her, and she hoped, even now, that she might find a way to usher her work to a more fulfilling close.

• • •

FRED YEOMAN GREETED her as she opened the door from the street into the residents' sitting room.

"Good afternoon, Miss Dobbs. On your way this evening?"

"Yes, I think so."

"We'll be sorry to see you go. Not very busy for the next couple of days—mind you, when I saw the police driving through the village, I thought we might see some more outsiders, though we don't welcome newspaper reporters and the like in Heronsdene."

"Quite right. Are the police still up at the Sandermere estate?"

"According to one of the regulars who works in the gardens, they've been up in Sandermere's rooms talking to him, and there's been some sacks taken out of the stables."

"I see. I wonder what's in them."

"I reckon it's that missing silver. Probably them London boys hid it under his nose, thinking they'd come back for it later."

"You still think it could be the London boys? Even though they've been absolved of the crime?"

"Well, they can unabsolve them, can't they?"

Maisie realized she was shaking. "Have you considered that it might be someone other than a Londoner or a gypsy who has committed a crime? That the person might be at the house? Or in the village?"

"Well, I—"

"You, of all people, should know what Alfred Sandermere is like. The whole village knows what he's like. He's had every one of you in the palm of his hand for years."

The man flushed. "I better be getting on. I'm sure the police will sort it all out, whoever took the silver."

Maisie admonished herself for taking such a position, but she had felt her frustration rising to the surface. She packed her bag, checked the room to ensure she had collected all her belongings, and came back downstairs, where she rang the bell to summon Fred Yeoman. He stepped through from the kitchen, where he had been talking to his wife.

"I must apologize, Mr. Yeoman. I should not have snapped."

"And I shouldn't have tarred all Londoners with the same brush. I keep forgetting that you're one of them, if you know what I mean."

Maisie ignored the implication. "I've enjoyed staying here, at the inn. Thank you."

"And thank you again, miss, for saving our bacon on the night of that fire."

Maisie smiled and said goodbye. She packed her belongings in the motor car and drove toward the farm, once again passing the two police motor cars as they left the village. She saw no silhouettes in the back seats and guessed that Alfred Sandermere had not been taken into custody yet.

For the last time, Maisie parked by the oast house and walked out along the farm road toward the hop-gardens. Only a few gypsies were out today, but a full complement of Londoners were still picking, as were some locals. She breathed in the spicy air and reached out to take a solitary hop from a spent bine. As she crushed it between her fingers to release its fragrance, she thought of Webb and of his younger self, Pim van Maarten, and how it must have been for him to return to the village only to discover his family gone. The time of year must torment him so, for in the Weald of Kent it is in late September that the senses are teased more than at any other time, with the hops, sweet apples, and earthy hay. And it is in the senses that memories are summoned, so that a sound, a scent, or the way the wind blows brings a reminder of what has happened and when.

The Beales asked Maisie to stay awhile, to lean on the bin, to pick hops, and to pass the time of day before she left. As the sun began to slip down on its journey toward the horizon, she said she should be leaving, and after saying her farewells, she turned to leave. It was a departure that would be curtailed only too soon.

A sudden cry went up from a Londoner working at the top of the hop-garden, who pointed toward clouds of smoke belching from the just-visible roof of the Sandermere mansion.

"Fire! Up at the big house. Look, fire!"

EIGHTEEN

Women with children remained behind, as the hop-pickers ran en masse toward the estate house, some stopping only long enough to pick up an old bucket or other receptacle that might be needed.

"Quick, Billy, the motor. We'll cut across on the estate road."

They pulled out of the farm and sped toward the entrance to the Sandermere mansion, where they parked outside the gates and ran toward the house. They saw the groom struggling to lead two of the horses from the stables, in case the fire should spread and leap to the outbuildings.

"I'll go and give him a hand." Billy moved with as much speed as he could muster toward the groom.

Villagers soon began arriving, and when she looked up at the hill where, days ago, she had seen Webb gazing down on the mansion, she saw the gypsies clustered, watching. She stopped for mere seconds and saw Webb come to the fore, the silhouette of his hat distinguishing him from his people. Then, raising his hand to the tribe, he led them toward the house to help.

Staff were clustered outside the property, as flames licked up from the windows of the upper floors like giant tongues seeking sustenance. One side of the roof was ablaze and crackling, the flames that had caught the onlookers' attention leaping up in a fiery dance.

"Is everyone out?" asked Maisie.

The butler shook his head, his eyes glazed. "N-no. Mr. Sandermere locked himself in those rooms. He went up there in a black mood after the police came."

"Was he drinking?"

The man nodded. "Yes, yes, he was drinking. Called down twice for more wine and brandy."

"God!"

"Did anyone telephone the fire brigade?"

The man nodded. "Just before we all got out, on account of the smoke. The house may be made of stone, but there's the paneling, the curtains, the upholstery—it's all smoldering, giving off fumes, and burning like tinder."

Maisie ran back to the gathered crowd, who were already forming a line down to the water tap by the stables. This was how it had been at every fire, the villagers working together to extinguish the flames, thought Maisie. Every fire except one. *They'll never do it. They'll never stem this inferno.*

She looked back at the mansion, and as she scanned the windows, her eyes squinting against the smoke, she saw Alfred Sandermere standing, looking at the throng below as if in a trance. Then he fell forward and slowly began to slide down the panes of glass.

Together the Londoners, the villagers and the gypsies passed buckets of water back and forth. Maisie was close to the house, next to the butler, who was pointing up to the window, when Webb broke away and ran toward her.

"Is he still in there?"

Maisie nodded, coughing. "Yes, he's up in his rooms, on the first floor."

The butler explained what had happened and pointed to the windows.

Webb held his breath, his face contorting as he understood that Alfred Sandermere was likely unconscious, and would burn to death if not helped. Then he took off his jacket and his shirt. "I cannot let a man die like that, no matter how much hate I bear for him."

Paishey ran to her husband's side, and as others came closer, seeing the gypsy remove his clothes above the waist and begin to douse himself with water, Webb turned to his wife.

"I've got to find him. Give me your shawl."

Paishey pulled the shawl from her shoulders, immersed it in a bucket of water, and wrapped it, sopping, around her husband's upper body. It was then that Webb pulled off his hat. Maisie saw Fred Yeoman, who was standing nearby, put a hand to his mouth. Webb wasted no time; he held his wife's hand in his for a second and then ran into the holocaust.

No one spoke or shouted, but a muttering began between the villagers as Fred turned first to one, then to another.

"Did you see that? Wasn't that Pim Martin?"

"I didn't want to say anything, thought I was seeing things."

"Looked for all the world like Jacob."

"It was him, I know it was."

"No, couldn't have been. He's been dead all these years."

In the distance, the relentless ringing of the fire tender's bell could now be heard coming closer, as the people came together to wait for Pim Martin to walk from the burning home of the man whom, they knew, he would himself have murdered, if he could. No movement was visible as the flames bucked and leaped from floor to floor, and some of the onlookers screamed as the reverberation of a falling beam echoed through the house.

"They'll both be dead. The man was mad to go in, mad."

Two fire tenders screeched to a halt, their red livery reflecting another eruption of flames from the roof. Maisie and the butler spoke to the fireman in charge, as others pulled hoses and dug in their heels to brace against the force of water that cannoned out toward the eye of the fire. And still Paishey waited, as close as she could to the door through which her husband had entered the house. She neither keened nor cried but waited with her shoulders back, a vigil for her husband until he returned. Soon others gathered around her, both locals and outsiders, waiting, waiting to see if the man they knew only as Webb would walk from the blaze.

"I can hear coughing," a fireman shouted back to the chief.

Paishey called out, the first words she had spoken since her husband ran into the mansion. "Webb, come back to me, come back to me, Webb. I'n be waiting for you, my Webb. I'n be waiting here for you."

And then they saw him, the shawl gone, his torso seared with charcoal and dripping with black heat, one hand shielding his eyes, the other dragging behind him, by the scruff of his neck, the smoldering body of Alfred Sandermere.

"Webb!" Paishey was first to his side, as he leaned forward and retched, only letting go of Sandermere when Fred Yeoman touched him on the arm and said, "It's alright, we've got him now. It's alright, lad."

The gypsy men pushed forward to claim Webb, dousing him with water again and again, pulling him away from the smoke toward the air beyond the boundary of the fire's breath. Two firemen placed Sandermere on a stretcher and took him back, close to the place where the gypsies circled around Webb at the bottom of the hill. Soon another bell was ringing and an ambulance approached, followed by the doctor.

Maisie made her way over to the gypsies. "Is he alright? How does he breathe?"

Paishey looked up. "He'n be safe, now, miss. Webb's breathing alright, and we'll look after the burns." She pulled a pot of deep green cream from a pocket in her skirt. "Beulah's mixture."

Maisie nodded, knowing the people who had come together to fight the fire would now disperse to their tribes, would gather to be with their own. She moved across to the place where Sandermere was being treated. "Can I help?"

The doctor glanced at her, as he held up a syringe ready to inject painkilling morphine into Sandermere's body, for the man's deep mucus-filled moaning told of his distress.

"I was a nurse in the war, in France."

"Good, then you'll have seen your share of burns. I need your help to get him stable before he's taken to Pembury Hospital. Right, then, let's get on with it—my instruments and that swab."

The years contracted as Maisie doused her hands with disinfectant from the physician's case, placed a spare mask across her mouth and nose, and laid out the exact instruments that would be needed. Using forceps, she picked up a swab, snapping the instrument into the palm of the doctor's hand as she prepared another swab, then held scissors ready.

"Like riding a bike, isn't it? It all comes back to you when you need it." The doctor wrinkled his nose to keep his spectacles from sliding down, and Maisie reached across to push them back up again.

She took the soiled swab and handed him the scissors. She remembered the humor, the quips and jokes leveled at death, as he did his work at the same time as the casualty clearing station doctors. And she remembered Simon, that final day working with him, and his last words when shells began to rain down on the operating tent as they tried to save the life of another soldier: "Let's get on with it."

LATER, WHEN THE ambulance had left and the gypsies

328

had made their way up the hill, across the fields, and back to their clearing, Maisie found Billy among the Londoners trudging to the hopper huts.

"I thought we'd lost you, Miss. I'm glad to see you."

"You too."

"What about that for a turnup, eh? There's that Webb, showin' them all who 'e is. You should 'ave 'eard 'em, talkin' about it."

"I'm sure they were."

"They're terrified of what might 'appen now. There was talk of a meetin' tonight, at the inn. They want to get everyone together, to work out what to say to Webb when 'e comes. They know 'e'll come for 'em."

Maisie stopped. "Then that's where I'll go, to the inn."

"Miss, you're all spent. Look at you, you're wore out. You can sort them out tomorrow, they've been haunted this long."

She shook her head. "No, it's time. They know about Pim now—well, they've likely known all along, if truth be told, but now they have proof. And they know the piper must be paid. They have to tell him, to his face, what happened."

CLAIMING HER MOTOR car, Maisie used a clean handkerchief to wipe her hands and face, then started the engine and drove toward the farm, going as far as she could on four wheels before she had to continue on toward the gypsy camp on foot.

Webb was resting at the edge of the clearing where

the air was fresh with a crisp evening breeze that might help clear his lungs. Paishey sat with him, with Boosul on her lap, and together they watched Maisie approach. She saw Beulah's caravan moved to one side, farther away from the others, for the coffin containing her body rested within. The lurcher lay on the steps and did not stir.

"You were brave, Webb. You risked your life for a man you have every reason to despise."

He nodded. "I just couldn't stand there and do nothing to help him."

"You are hurt?"

"Not as badly as it seemed. Some skin singed, and my lungs are sore, but that will go in time." He looked at his wife and his daughter, then back at Maisie. "Will he live?"

"The doctor was not hopeful. The burns are extensive, and the risk of infection high. He will be drugged for days, for weeks to come, if he survives."

"It may be a small mercy, then, that my family perished. That they did not live with such pain."

A silence descended between them, the only sounds a gentle nickering to be heard, as horses grazed nearby, and a gypsy meal being prepared in the clearing.

"They know who you are, Webb."

"Yes. The hat has served me well, and the passing years have done their camouflage work on my face, though it seems I look more like my father than I thought, except for the hair. I have come to work here for many a season and have been taken for nothing more than the gypsy they saw me to be."

"It's like seeing someone you know in a different milieu. You don't recognize him because you don't expect to see him in a certain place."

Webb shook his head. "I wonder what will happen now?" He coughed, wincing and clasping his chest.

"I thought you would want to know that there is to be a meeting in the village tonight, at the inn."

"Ah, they don't know what to do about me."

Maisie came to her feet. "I'll be there, Webb. I want to hear what they say, and I want them to explain themselves, to tell what happened on the night of the Zeppelin raid. Just as you told me, in your words, how you came back here, so I want to hear their story." She turned to stroke a horse who had come close in search of a treat before she spoke again. "If you are well enough to come to the inn, I would have thought that you might want to hear their story too. It is, after all, part of your past."

Webb looked at Paishey, and she smiled. "If I'm there, I'm there," he said. "That's how it is."

Maisie looked across toward Beulah's vardo. "When will she be buried?"

"On Tuesday. The word's gone out, and I've seen the vicar, the one who comes to the village from Horsmonden. She'll be buried in the churchyard, with my people."

"Then back here for the afterwards?"

Webb nodded. "It's not as if Sandermere will be

here to complain about a bit of a singe on his field, is it?"

MAISIE PARKED THE MG close to the church and watched as villagers came alone and in pairs to the inn. Even though the evening was not cold, each and every one was wrapped as if winter's breath had settled upon the community and their bones had been touched by a sliver of ice. When those whom she knew had arrived, Maisie left the MG and walked across to the waste ground opposite. Gone was the chill of her earlier visit, the specter of the terrible night when the Zeppelin came and the van Maartens became the crucible who paid the ultimate price.

Pulling her collar up around her neck, she walked at an unhurried pace toward the inn. Was it on a night like this that the Zeppelin came over, its low drone lingering above the village? Had a light—perhaps embers from the smithy's fire—caught the enemy's attention, providing a new target? Here, in a place where sleep evaded those who had just learned that their sons were dead, Wealden boys killed on a foreign field and never to return home again, the Zeppelin had brought the war to a village in England.

She lingered for a moment or two outside the inn, looking through the ancient diamond-paned glass as the villagers came together, some seated, some standing at the bar. Fred Yeoman leaned across, resting his elbow on the counter, with his sleeves rolled up and a cloth in his hand that he absentmind-

332

edly drew back and forth across the wood as he spoke. From a seat next to the low inglenook fireplace surrounded with shining horse brasses, a man raised his hand to Yeoman and called out above the throng, loud enough for Maisie to hear, "Better get on with it, Fred. There's a lot of talk to be done tonight." Maisie took a deep breath, rested her fingers on the door handle for a moment, and entered the inn.

At first she was hardly noticed, then a woman glanced around to see who had joined them, and Fred Yeoman looked up from the counter, ready to pour another half-pint. The woman nudged her husband, who turned, and soon the hubbub of conversation died. The innkeeper broke the silence.

"Are you sure you wouldn't like to sit in the residents' room, Miss Dobbs?"

She shook her head. "No, thank you, Mr. Yeoman. But I would like a half-pint of the Harveys ale, if you please." She pulled off her jacket, a sign that she was staying, and looked around the bar. A man next to the counter stepped away and held out his hand toward a stool. She inclined her head and stepped forward, thanking the man for giving up his seat. Fred placed the frothy brew in front of Maisie, which she sipped before turning around. All eyes were upon her, the outsider.

She set down her glass and looked again at the villagers, weighing her words with care. She had no need to raise her voice; the crackle and spit of a fire in the inglenook was the only sound to punctuate her words.

"You've all seen me in this village, and you know I'm working for the company involved in negotiations to purchase the brickworks and the estate. And you know by now that my interest has been in the crimes, and more importantly, the fires that have occurred in this village."

Her words were met with silence. One man shuffled his feet, only to be met with a scornful look from his wife, who crossed her arms and turned away from him. Maisie continued.

"Heronsdene is a beautiful village, and I believe you are all good people." Again she paused, choosing her words with care. "But a secret cannot be kept for-ever—"

At that moment the door opened, and it appeared to Maisie that every single man and woman in the room drew breath as the man they had known before the fire only as Webb, the traveling gypsy, came into the bar. Maisie nodded and smiled, holding out her hand to the seat just vacated next to her. No one attempted to leave. No one made an excuse to depart, or coughed, or made a noise.

Webb joined Maisie and looked around the room, as if to remember every single face and to torment each villager with his silence.

"I was just saying," said Maisie, her voice low, "that a secret cannot be kept forever."

Webb cleared his throat to speak, but instead nodded to Maisie, who continued addressing those assembled.

"You came together this evening to decide what to do about this man, whom you knew as Pim Martin when he was a boy. He was from a family you understood to be of Dutch blood until the night of the Zeppelin raid, when you came to sense the power of doubt. Will anyone speak to this man of that night?"

There was silence for a moment. Then a woman began to sob and was comforted by Mrs. Pendle. One man stood as if to leave, but was stopped by another, who laid his hand on the man's shoulder and shook his head.

Maisie spoke again. "Pim Martin went to war as a boy. He fought for his country, as did the other sons of Heronsdene. This man, then barely fourteen years of age, saw death of a most terrible kind—" Her words caught in her throat, as she banished images of the war from her mind. "Then he came home to . . . nothing." She paused. "So I ask again—will anyone speak to this man of that night?"

Now the silence in the room was interwoven by more sobbing. Maisie watched one woman repeatedly punch her knees with her fist, as if to strike feeling into limbs that were otherwise numb.

The man she knew to be Mr. Whyte coughed and raised his hand, taking off his cap, then passing it from his left hand to his right and back again. "It's hard, to tell of what happened—"

Another voice joined in. "It was madness. We were all touched by madness and didn't know what we were doing."

"It wouldn't've happened if the boys hadn't been killed."

"Or if that Sandermere hadn't been drunk, the lying hound."

Now voices came from left and right, as if every man and woman wanted to speak at once, to confess and have the hand of absolution laid upon them.

Fred Yeoman raised his hand. "Miss Dobbs is right. We've got to tell, and it's no good starting in the middle and then going both ways at once. Someone has to start at the beginning, and it might as well be me, because I'm the landlord here. But first I'll put a glass in Pim's hand, if you don't mind."

"Webb. You can call me Webb now."

Yeoman nodded and pulled an ale, finishing the pour with a hearty head before passing it to the gypsy. Then he wiped the counter once again, threw the cloth to one side, and gripped the edge of the bar as he began to speak, looking down at his whitening fists, then up at Webb and the gathering in front of him.

"After you'd gone, after they'd taken you to the reformatory, there was change here in the village. We lost a lot of our boys, the first lot in '15, then others here and there, then a dozen all together in the summer of 1916. It was during the hop-picking that the telegrams with news of more lost were delivered." He looked at Webb. "You'll remember them. There was Derek Tovis, John Barham, Tim Whyte, Bobby Pickles, Sam Pendle, Peter Tillings—all gone on the same day. All our boys."

Webb nodded. "I remember them, each and every one."

"Word went round like wildfire, and it was as if we'd lost them all at once. Small village like this, and we'd lost nigh on all our boys."

Yeoman cleared his throat. Then George Chambers, whom Maisie had visited, looked directly at Webb, raising his hand to speak.

"All I've got to say is, that it got us all here, right here." He thumped his chest. "It felt like we had one big heart that was breaking, here in the village, and we didn't know what to do. How to get rid of the . . . the pain."

Maisie looked at Webb, at his fingers, curled and frozen as he clutched his glass, which she feared might break.

Whyte took up the story. "Then, that night, we'd all been in here. You know, Pim—Webb—you know how it was, how we'd always come here, to talk of village matters, sort things out. Well, we were here, talking of the boys, wondering how we would all get through it. And that young Sandermere was in."

"I refused to serve him, not only on account of his age, but by the smell of him he'd already been at his father's brandy," said Yeoman.

Whyte continued. "It's not as if anyone would ever listen to him, as a rule. Not as if he was respected, like his brother, Henry, and his father before him." He shook his head and brushed his hand across his forehead. "But he was going on about the Hun this, and

Fritz that, and we all sort of joined in. It was somewhere to put the—you know—the *hate*." He looked
around the room, his discomfort at such candor
causing him to shrink back against the wall.

Yeoman spoke again. "We was all talking, about the
boys, about the war and the Germans, when we heard
that drone. It was strange, a sort of muffled whirring.
Bill over there said, 'Can you hear that?' Then Sandermere stumbled outside and looked up and came
running back. 'It's a Zeppelin!' he shouted. Someone
said, 'Don't be bloody silly, boy, you're one over the
top. What would a Zeppelin want here?' The Hun had
taken enough of our boys over there."

"Then we heard it," said another man, who also took
off his cap as he spoke, looking with intent at Webb,
as if willing him to understand.

"The explosion," added Yeoman. "Down at the
smithy." He coughed and held his chest. "We all
rushed out, and the fire was already well out of control, but someone started running to the telephone
kiosk in the next village, to call out the fire brigade."

Whyte took up the story. "We had to do something,
so we all ran down to the smithy to do what we did
today, to put out the fire, which was in the barn next
door." He looked at Webb. "Your people were at the
bakery, son. Your father never came down to the inn
as a rule, on account of being up early to start the
ovens."

Webb swallowed deeply, his eyes watery yet his
gaze unflinching. He said nothing, but looked around

the room to see who might take up the story. Maisie turned to Yeoman, who spoke again.

"We thought the smith was dead. Couple of people had gone to his house, but there was no answer, so we thought he'd been in the barn—always pottering at night, the smith." He paused, then reached behind the bar for a brandy bottle and a tot glass. He filled the glass, downed the amber liquid in one gulp, and poured a second time. "Then that Sandermere boy started again, yelling about vengeance, about revenge. Then he says, for us all to hear—" He turned to Webb. "I'm sorry, lad, I am so sorry—are you sure you want to hear this?"

Webb nodded and reached for the brandy bottle, pouring a measure into his empty beer glass. "Go on, Mr. Yeoman. I'm listening."

"Sandermere said, 'Them *von* Martins called the Zeppelin to kill us all.' He kept screaming and yelling that you were really Germans, that you weren't Dutch at all, and that you'd avoided being sent to an internment camp because your father had lied. He said your sister Anna had told him that your name was really von Martin, not van Maarten, and you were spies." He choked back tears, and the villagers clustered closer together. "And we had no doubt, because our boys were dead, and our village had been bombed, that he was telling the truth. He just kept screaming to go and get them, that they must pay with their lives. It—it's hard to tell it now, but it was as if we'd been struck by madness. We weren't ordinary people anymore, we were one big monster, an animal out of control going after the enemy, who had to pay. And we let a drunken boy lead us, with his filthy ideas and his taunting, until we believed we had to make the enemy suffer, for our sons and for our village."

Webb did not look up but asked, in an almost whisper, "And what did you do?"

"We had fire in our hands, and we had fire in our hearts, and we ran, a mob holding pieces of burning wood from the barn, nothing but a rabble with Sandermere at the head, moving toward the bakery. And the terrible thing is, your parents were running down the street, to see if they could help." He choked back tears and put his head in his hands.

Whyte took up the story again. "Then they saw us coming, with Sandermere shouting, 'There they are, Fritz and his wife!' And Jacob put his arm around Bettin and ran back to the bakery. She was screaming for Anna, to go indoors—the girl was just coming out to see what she could do—and they all hurried inside." He stopped to take a breath, rubbing his chest as if winded by his memories. "I don't know where the paraffin came from, but soon the bakery was burning, and we bayed like animals, for the blood of the German family we'd been told lived inside."

Mrs. Pendle stepped forward, her voice low, as she spoke. "We were the devil himself that night. It was as if all the terrible things you ever thought in your life had made lunatics of us, and we could not stop. We are murderers, each and every one of us, because we killed an innocent family. It doesn't matter where they came from, they were innocent. And we are ashamed. *We are so ashamed.*"

Fred Yeoman spoke again. "I don't know when we came to our senses. The house had almost burned by the time the fire brigade came, and the men who were sent by the authorities had no questions for us. And the smith had been out on the railway lines, picking up coal for his fires, so he wasn't dead after all." He moved to place his hand on Webb's shoulder, then drew back. "The next day, we all saw the truth of what we'd done. It's been like a sickness ever since. A few have moved away, but it's hard to do with a village like this. You know your own, and you know where you belong. We'll never get over it, never. We'll bear that cross, all of us, forever, and there's not one of us that goes to bed at night and doesn't hear the screams."

"Then, the next day, we found out you were presumed dead," said Whyte. "And the lie went on, a whole family killed by the war. Soon we all began to believe the tale, though we never forgot that lunacy, that insanity that laid claim to every single one of us." He looked around the room, as if to dare a contradiction. "Then the fires began, each year, about the same time as the anniversary of the Zeppelin raid. And we believed we were being haunted, that the spirit of Pim Martin had come home to drive us into our graves, had come for his due. So we didn't report the fires, because we knew we had it coming to us. We deserved to die, if it came to that."

Silence enveloped the room. No one stirred, no one coughed or shuffled their feet. Only the fire crackled in the grate, the odd spark spitting out onto the hearth as the logs smoldered.

Yeoman was the first to move, pulling down tot glasses and filling them with brandy. He began speaking as he poured. "And the thing is, I never did find out—I don't think anyone did—why Sandermere went off like that. He'd been seen with Anna, was sweet on her, so why would he do such a thing? I never knew whether it was a mania or the drink that made him accuse like he did, that made him lie and cause death into the bargain." He set the bottle down and looked at Maisie, as if for help. "And he's had us by the throat since it happened, reminding us that we were all in it together and if one talked, we'd all be branded killers."

"You *were* killers," said Webb, breaking his silence. "You took my family, and they were good people. They came here to be part of this village, part of *you,* and you murdered them." He sighed and took up a tot of brandy. "But—" He paused and looked around the room, his gaze alighting upon each villager in turn. "But I have come to know something in the past few days, something I learned from my father when I was a child, except that somewhere in the middle I forgot. I have learned, I hope, that revenge can only take more lives, and this life of mine—my wife, my

342

daughter—is too precious for me to give it over to vengeance."

"Do you forgive us?" A voice barely more than a whisper asked the question.

Webb shook his head. "That is not for me to do." He finished his drink and rapped the glass back on the bar. "This business of forgiving yourselves is *your* work." He turned to Maisie. "Beulah was right; she said you would set me free. I thank you for your kindness—to her, to me, to my people."

Webb picked up his hat and left the inn, the cluster of villagers parting to allow him to reach the door, which he closed, gently, as he stepped outside.

Fred Yeoman turned to Maisie. "He won't come back, will he, Miss Dobbs?"

Maisie shook her head. "The gypsies will move on after Beulah's funeral, and they won't be back. They rarely return to a place where one of the clan has died. It's bad luck."

"I'm glad we talked to Pim. Can't call him Webb, not with him being the image of his father, now that I've had a good look at him."

"It's done now. It's out in the open and we've told of what went on, but it won't make us sleep easier in our beds," added Whyte.

The room was quiet once more, as if all assembled here were trying on their memories of that night to see how they fit, only to realize that they would wear their guilt forever.

Maisie was thoughtful before speaking again.

"Think of what Webb said, that there's no time for vengeance. I can't help you with your shame, your remorse, but I can make one small suggestion."

"What's that?" Fred Yeoman leaned forward.

"You've let their land grow wild. In law it belongs to Webb, and you never know—he may come to claim it one day or he may wish to sell. Look after it for him. Keep it well. People died there, so it deserves to be cherished." Maisie stepped away from the bar, reaching across to shake Fred Yeoman's hand. "Thank you, Mr. Yeoman. I have to be off now."

Once again the villagers stepped aside as Maisie left the inn. She stood outside for a few moments, and as she pulled her collar up she heard the sound of sobbing coming from inside and the low muffled voices of the villagers. She walked back to the MG, stopping alongside the land that once held the bakery where Jacob and Bettin van Maarten worked to raise a family and be part of a community. She thought she saw movement on the other side of the lot and stepped aside, so that the light from the church gate could illuminate the land. Michaelmas daisies had been strewn where once the threshold had been, where Jacob Martin, the baker, had been photographed holding a loaf of bread baked in the shape of his adopted country, surrounded by her flags flapping in the wind.

SOON SHE WAS on her way to Chelstone, but stopped when she reached the next village, to place a call from the telephone kiosk.

"B. T. Drummond speaking."

"I guessed you'd be there, waiting by the night phone."

"Maisie Dobbs! I thought you had gone to ground and I'd never get my story. If this is about that fire, then you're late. I already know, the story's mine, and I'm coming out as soon as it's light—with a photographer."

"The fire is only part of why I'm calling. I have your scoop for you, if you want it, though I don't think you'll be able to print it—but a promise is a promise and I said I would let you know."

Maisie heard a notebook flipping open.

"Right, then, go ahead."

"It's too long a tale, Beattie. Can we meet before you come down to Heronsdene tomorrow? I can see you in Paddock Wood, if you like."

"Right you are. Nine o'clock at the station?"

"Nine o'clock it is."

Maisie set the telephone receiver back on the cradle and returned to the MG. Settled into the work of driving, she sighed. No one, not even Webb, had asked why Alfred Sandermere had been so anxious, even in his impaired state, to see an end to the Dutch family. It was an omission that allowed her a measure of relief. She had been cautioned by Maurice Blanche during her apprenticeship to take care when handling truth, and she knew that such knowledge would have brought nothing but added distress to a man who had lost so much.

NINETEEN

Maisie arrived at her father's home late and tired, with black smudges on her forehead, her hair matted and slicked to her face. The odor of disinfectant and smoke was still clinging to her as she dragged her bag from the motor car and entered the cottage.

Frankie banked up the kitchen fire and brought the old tin bath from the scullery, setting it on the floor in front of the coal stove. As soon as the water was hot, Maisie filled the bath while her father walked across to the stables for his customary final check on the horses stabled at Chelstone. She opened the stove door so that heat from the blaze would keep her warm as she bathed, washing away the stench of fire and several livid red smears of Alfred Sandermere's blood that remained on her arm above the wrist. She was exhausted, the muscles of her neck and shoulders were taut and aching, and though she was keen to return to London, she knew that a day under her father's wing would be solace indeed. She would remain in Kent until Beulah Webb was buried and the ritual of the final farewell done.

Finishing her bath, Maisie dressed in a pair of old tweed trousers and one of her father's worn collarless shirts—not garb she would wear on the London streets but comfortable in his home and while she was at Chelstone. They shared a stew of rabbit and vegetables, and later, while Maisie dozed in an armchair by the fire, her father touched her shoulder.

"Better go up, love, you look all in."

She agreed, knowing that tomorrow she would have to be awake early, and on her way to Paddock Wood station to meet Beattie Drummond. She wanted to see Maurice, but the day had been too long already. She would see him tomorrow.

THE FOLLOWING MORNING, Maisie collected Beattie from the station, and from there they went to a small tearoom in Paddock Wood. The shop, constructed of white overlapping weatherboard in the Kentish style, offered low-beamed comfort as they entered, with a counter to the right filled with plates of cakes and pastries baked to tempt even the most sated appetite. There were drop scones and cheese scones and melt-in-the-mouth butterfly cakes decorated with marzipan leaves. There was tea bread, malt loaf, and walnut cake; chocolate sponge, rich fruit cake, shortbreads, filled rolls, and cream horns, as well as Maisie's favorite, Eccles cakes.

They chose a seat in the corner by the window and, when the waitress came, asked for a large pot of tea and two Eccles cakes, an order to which Beattie added a slice of malt loaf before the waitress left the table.

"I was at the newspaper until late—didn't have supper or breakfast. I am famished."

When the tea was poured and the cakes divvied out,

they leaned forward to talk. Beattie flipped open her notebook.

"No mention of my name," instructed Maisie. "And no direct words from me—understood?"

Beattie sighed. "If that's what I have to promise to get the story, so be it. Start anywhere you like."

Maisie sipped her tea and commenced telling the story as she would a child's tale, painting a picture of the characters and their sensibilities, fears, loves, hates, weaknesses and strengths. Beattie was silent as Maisie spoke, only interrupting to ask the odd question or to lick her finger, flick back through the pages of her notebook, and then nod her head for Maisie to continue. Almost two hours, one more pot of tea, and a fresh round of malt loaf later, Beattie leaned back in her seat and shook her head.

"I have no idea how I am going to write this story," she sighed.

Maisie poured more tea. "I can't help you there. I can only tell you what happened."

Beattie flicked through her pages of notes again, still shaking her head. "And Anna was expecting Sandermere's child?"

"That's what her friend said." Maisie looked down as she spoke.

"And that's what killed her family?"

"It was a catalyst for Sandermere's wanting Anna out of the way."

"But in situations like that, where there's an unwed mother with the wrong 'breeding,' it's not as if his sort worry, do they? At best they usually throw some money at the family—well enough to have the girl go away to have the baby, who's then adopted far from home to avoid any embarrassment over a rich man's offspring living at a lower station, just up the road."

"I have no more light to throw on this story for you, Beattie. Sorry."

Beattie Drummond shook her head. "No, no, you've given me a lot here, but as I said, I'll have to think long and hard about what to do and how I can make my mark with it—before someone else does."

"No one else has this amount of information, but by this afternoon much of it will be in the hands of the Compton Company. I have no reason to believe they will make any part of it public, though."

Beattie looked at her watch. "I'd better be off. I've to meet the photographer's train at eleven."

Maisie nodded and pushed back her chair.

"Are you going back to London today?" Beattie Drummond picked up her bag and walked toward the door with Maisie.

"No, I'm staying for Beulah Webb's funeral tomorrow."

"Tomorrow?"

"Yes, she'll be laid to rest in Heronsdene churchyard at eleven o'clock."

"Now that *is* news. A gypsy funeral—the village will be packed! I'm glad I mentioned London, otherwise I'd never have known."

"Oh, yes, you would, B. T. Drummond. You would

349

have found out, a terrier of the news like you."

MAISIE RETURNED TO Chelstone, where she would visit Maurice Blanche and, later, James Compton, who was now in Kent. He had informed her via a telephone call to her father's house that he would be at Chelstone Manor in the afternoon to receive her final report. He would later be in conference with his legal counsel and solicitors for the estate, to discuss the land purchase in light of the recent fire and current perceived values.

During the drive, she ruminated on the fact that she had withheld one small grain of information from the newspaper reporter, not an overt omission but more in allowing the reporter to make an assumption. When Beattie referred to "Sandermere" as the father of Anna's unborn child, Maisie had done nothing to disabuse her of that belief. Taken literally, it was not an incorrect conclusion.

Maisie parked the MG outside the Groom's Cottage and, knowing her father was still at work, went straight to the Dower House to see Maurice Blanche, who waved to her from the conservatory as soon as he saw her walking up through the rose garden. The housekeeper showed her through to where he was standing, waiting for her. She was pleased to see that he looked better and said as much.

"I confess I was dealing with matters of some concern when you came before, but now I am back to my old self. Sometimes the worries of the world give one pause for thought, and one wonders—especially someone of my antiquity—why history is not a more efficient teacher." He held out a hand, inviting Maisie to take a seat next to his in front of the bank of windows commanding a view that seemed to comprise only converging shades of green and blue, where Wealden fields and forests met a clear and distant sky. "Now then, tell me what has happened."

For the second time that day, Maisie recounted the events that led up to the killing of the van Maarten family, knowing she would have to steep herself in the narrative again with James. This time, however, she gave a complete report.

"So Anna did not consort with Alfred Sandermere?"

"No, she didn't." She shook her head. "Something did not sit right in the story told by Phyllis, that the child was Alfred's, though I am sure Anna made her believe it was so." She paused. "I didn't know her, but I knew enough *about* her, and I just could not see how a girl who was sweet on *Henry* Sandermere—a fine person, according to all who knew him—could throw herself at Alfred. Admittedly, I have no means by which I can confirm my conclusion, but I am sure it's right."

"So what do you think happened?"

"According to his military record, Henry came home on leave in early June 1916. He was keen on Anna, who by all accounts was quite a beauty. I suspect that when the young subaltern returned from service in France, he melted her heart, and they spent more time together than just the few moments it took for him to purchase a cake or two at the bakery. By the time his leave was over, she was with child. In July, shortly after his return to duty, he was killed by a sniper." Maisie sighed. "I suspect she panicked. Her brother had already caused much distress in the household on account of a Sandermere, and she probably wanted to spare her parents further anguish if she could. She was seen spending some considerable time with Alfred, who pursued her relentlessly—to him she was even more alluring because his brother had fallen for her."

"Despite her station."

"Yes, *despite* her station." Maisie paused, then went on. "I believe she told Alfred about her condition. She may have wanted him to propose marriage. It is my guess that she probably said she was going to inform his parents that she carried their dead son's child."

"And that signed her death certificate, though she didn't know it at the time."

"I doubt whether Alfred knew it at the time either, but he soon would have seen the writing on the wall, the possibility that his father would recognize the right of the child to the Sandermere name, which would put Alfred out of the line of inheritance. Henry's fondness for Anna was well known, and the family must have been aware that they were spending a great deal of time together during his leave—enough to fall in love."

Maurice nodded. "And in a time of war such parents

would perhaps turn a blind eye to the girl's lowly standing, imagining that after the war the chasm that divided their circumstances would drive them apart, and everyone would be in their place again."

Maisie flushed and pressed her lips together, her eyes filling with tears as his words struck a resonant chord. "Yes, that's probably exactly what happened." She wiped her eyes. "Alfred must have known that, for his grieving parents, such considerations—that chasm, as you say—would diminish with the prospect of their beloved older son's son growing up at the Sandermere estate, with a beautiful young woman whom they could mold, even though she would not have been their choice. Or they could have adopted the son, another recognition of his status." She paused, remembering the attack on Paishey. "The rank that went along with being heir to the estate was crucial to Alfred. He had stepped into the shoes of the popular and much-liked Henry and could not bear to risk the loss of what was, in effect, his foundation."

"And when the Zeppelin bomb hit, even in his drunken state Alfred saw an immediate means of dispensing with an embarrassing situation, an unwelcome claim to the Sandermere name."

"Yes. Shock can give new energy to even the most addled brain."

Maurice nodded. "An interesting case, Maisie. You must be glad it's over."

She gave a half laugh and was thoughtful before replying. "Yes, I'm glad it's over, all of it. But at least it gave me something to chew over after Simon passed and following his funeral. Now his death seems as if it were something in the distance behind me, as if we were at sea and he is vanishing into the mist."

"Yes, time is strange in that way, is it not? You will be glad to get back to London, won't you."

"But not until after the gypsy's funeral tomorrow. Then I'll go back."

They sat in silence for a while, comfortable in the quietness and solitude of their renewed friendship. Maisie had wanted to ask Maurice about his work, a question or two to follow his comments when she entered the conservatory, but she was aware of the fragility of their reconciliation. It was his secrecy—understandable, she now realized—that had led to their discord last year. Now, as time and the thread of forgiveness drew them together again, it was Maurice who began to speak.

"In some ways, Maisie, similar work has engaged us of late. We—my contacts overseas and my colleagues in London—are most concerned with a growing frustration on the other side of the Channel. The depression we find ourselves in here, and which is causing havoc in America, is allowing people to give weight to that which divides them, rather than to the shared experiences and elements of connection they see mirrored in their fellow man. There are those in Germany who would use discrimination to elevate their politics, which gives us cause for disquiet. And on the continent in Spain, inequities threaten to become incendiary. There are many people, Maisie—and I confess, I am among their number—who believe our peace to be only so resilient and who fear another war."

"I pray it doesn't come to that, Maurice."

"Yes, pray, Maisie. Do pray."

And as her beloved mentor regarded the vista before him, his hands clenched on the arms of his chair, Maisie reached across and placed her hand on his.

LATER, IN THE library at Chelstone, Maisie gave James Compton a complete briefing according to the case assigned to her when they met in London. She explained new facts she had gathered and recapped those elements already reported, concluding that there would be no more petty crime, and the fires would now cease. Webb—Pim van Maarten—would most likely never return to Heronsdene following the funeral of the woman who adopted him.

"Well, we know Alfred Sandermere won't be committing any more acts of burglary, on his own property or anyone else's."

"What do you mean?"

"Oh dear, of course, you wouldn't have heard." James sat forward. "He died in Pembury Hospital this morning."

"Oh, poor man."

"Poor man?"

"Yes, to be troubled, haunted in that way, since childhood. What a dreadful way to live—and to die."

James sat back in his chair. "I don't know if I can be

that forgiving. The man was a liability, a menace. The village will be better off without him, and—I hate to admit it—so will we."

Maisie frowned. "I would have thought his death might make purchase of the brickworks and the estate rather difficult."

He shook his head. "Following Henry's death, his father added codicils to the trust that would enable their solicitors to go ahead with a sale of the property if anything should happen to Alfred and he was sole heir at the time of his death, without a son to inherit. Essentially, the whole estate is now for sale and we are the buyers."

"What will you do with the house?"

"Demolish, then apply for permission to build several new houses on the site."

"Oh."

"Don't tell me you're one of those who doesn't like to see new houses go up."

"They can be such a blight on the land."

"We're in the business of construction, Maisie. And we've got a brickworks right there, ready to be improved with investment and an injection of new practices."

She nodded. "What about the horses?"

"We're selling all but one."

"Sandermere's bay?"

"How did you guess?"

"I'm my father's daughter. I know a good horse when I see one."

"He'll certainly have a better life. And I'm bringing the groom over to Chelstone. Your father will be his boss. I'm sure he'll teach the boy even more than he knows already."

"I'm glad. He was kind to the horses." Maisie paused. "James, when are you returning to Canada?"

"In a month or so. There's a lot to do here, so I expect I'll sail at the beginning of November—don't want to leave it too late. Those bloody icebergs make me nervous."

"Of course." Maisie nodded, then cleared her throat.

James Compton looked at her across the desk. "I've known you a long time now, Maisie, since before Enid died. And I think I know when you have a thing or two on your mind."

"It's something you said, days ago, about expanding the Compton Corporation in Canada, about looking at security for your company and your sites over there."

"Yes, it's all on the agenda. We have to prepare the company for expansion when the economy gains enough momentum to get out of this slump, and the surprising increase in house-building will help us. Why?"

"It's my assistant, Mr. Beale. He and his wife lost their small daughter earlier this year, and what with one thing and another he wants to emigrate to Canada, to give their boys a better way of life."

"You want to help him, even though you'll lose him?"

Maisie nodded. "They aren't getting over it. His

wife looks more drawn each time I see her, and I know they are saving for passage."

James picked up a pen and tapped it on the desk. "Nothing's going to happen overnight, I can tell you that. The markets are still depressed, so even though I have spoken of future developments, we cannot hurry that chain of events."

"I see." Maisie bit her lip.

"However, I have made a note here, and I know you can vouch for him. Wasn't he rather good with telephonic engineering?"

"Yes, he was a sapper in the war. He's been working for me for two years now, so he understands matters of investigation and security. And as he'll tell you, he can turn his hand to anything."

James nodded. "A fine reference, Maisie. I believe I might have a position for him in a year, perhaps two. I can speak to one of my staff about it."

Maisie smiled and nodded. "Thank you, James. I won't mention it to him, as I wouldn't want to get his hopes up, but I will write to you again next year."

"Good." James held out his hand. "I expect you have a bill for me."

"And my written report." She handed him a manila envelope.

James pulled her notes out of the envelope, glanced at the bottom line of the invoice, and reached into the inside pocket of his jacket for his checkbook. He unscrewed the top of his gray and black marbled fountain pen and began to write, using a wooden-handled blotter to dry the ink. "There you are. Good work. I am sure the company will use your services again."

Maisie took the proffered check. "James, I'm curious. What will happen to the Sandermere money? There must be a fortune there."

"Oh, the old man was very specific in terms of establishing a trust and how it should be used. He made it watertight so even Alfred couldn't change it. There's to be a new school built in the village, with a generous annual allowance for books and materials. A fund is to be set up to provide scholarships for those children who show promise either academically or in music. And there is to be provision made for improvements to the village, though there are protections in place to avoid overconstruction on the High Street. It wouldn't surprise me if you saw electricity in every house and on the streets of Heronsdene within a year or two. And of course there's the usual stipend for the church, to pay for repairs and to keep the war memorial in good condition. After the story you've just told me, and considering how Sandermere made the villagers' lives a misery, I don't know whether this is the perfect end or whether they don't deserve such luxuries."

"Let's just assume, James, that for Heronsdene it's all for the best."

AUTUMN HAD JUST begun to finger the trees, sending cool breezes to sway branches and cast leaves scudding down the street, on the day Beulah Webb, matriarch of her tribe, was laid to rest in Heronsdene churchyard.

When Maisie arrived in the village at half past ten, the High Street was already narrowed by vardos from near and far, jostling for position, lined up almost to the crossroads at the edge of town. Some gypsies came in old lorries, swaying from side to side along the country roads, while others walked across fields from farms close to Heronsdene. The women clustered together, clad in black, all color banished from their clothing. The ritual of a funeral, as at so many gypsy gatherings, demanded that the women and the men be parted, each to their own, for the duration of the day. As she walked closer to the church, Maisie could hear the cries and lamentations of those directly related to Beulah. Grief was expected to be voiced aloud, the pitch of each gypsy's wail in direct proportion to the mourner's relationship to the departed one. Paishey was surrounded by women, who held her by the arms as she cried to the heavens for Beulah to come again.

On the street, villagers stood and watched, most from doorways, standing back into the shadows to diminish their presence in deference to the gypsy throng. There were no complaints, no mutterings that they should go, or speculation as to what they thought they were doing, taking over the street. Word had gone round that young Pim Martin, the baker's son, who they'd all thought had died in the war, was with *them* now, had been taken in by the travelers, and the gypsy being laid to rest was the one who had saved him. Knowing their debt, the people stood back, giving their streets up for just one day, all signs warning NO GYPSIES having been removed for the duration.

Soon the crowd outside the church began to quiet, with one or two pointing to the road. The descending silence allowed the gentle clip-clop of horses' hooves to reverberate toward the church, as Beulah's vardo came into view, with Webb at the reins, dressed all in black and without a hat, his hair swept back. Next to him, Beulah's lurcher lay with her head across his thighs. As he drew up alongside the church, opposite the place where his family had met death in a fiery hell, men came forward to help unhitch the vardo, one of them taking the horse away until after the funeral. The weeping began again as Beulah's coffin was taken from her traveling home. With Webb leading the pallbearers, the rom, shoulders braced to hold her weight, carried her into the church for the service, which would be followed by removal of the coffin to the burial site. She would be committed to earth next to the graves of Jacob, Bettin and Anna van Maarten.

Maisie remained at the back of the church. Though she knew gypsies who were not of Beulah's tribe questioned her presence, she would see one of those she knew nod in her direction, to explain, and thought they might be saying, *Beulah made her welcome; she's a diddakoi, one of us on her mother's side.* And staring up at the stained glass windows, Maisie remembered, just, her grandmother's funeral. When

361

she died, her father had given word of her passing to a band of water gypsies, who had taken the news along the rivers and canals. On the day of her funeral, narrow boats came from near and far, her people coming to bid her Godspeed.

With the burial over, Webb hitched Beulah's horse to her vardo once more and led the gypsies back to the clearing, where a feast of *hotchi-witchi*—hedgehog—stew had been prepared. Maisie walked across the empty hop-gardens and saw, at the bottom of the hill, the Londoners waiting, as the locals had in the village, to watch the gypsies gather. Billy Beale waved out to Maisie and came to greet her, with Doreen at his side.

"We just wanted to pay our respects to the old girl. We'll go, once they know we've come. Most of us are packed up now, ready to catch the milk-train to Paddock Wood in the morning, then a hoppers' train to London from there."

"Webb will be glad that you're all here. I'm pleased you stayed."

Maisie turned toward the field where the gypsy horses grazed and watched one of the men move them down and into a corner, where he tied each halter to the fence to keep them in place. Webb maneuvered Beulah's vardo into the field away from the clearing, and as he alighted from the driver's seat and unhitched the horse for the last time, he looked down toward the Londoners. He remained still for a moment before raising a hand to acknowledge their respect, at which sign the outsiders began to walk back to the huts to complete their packing for the journey home, back to the bustle of London.

Paishey came to Maisie, taking her by the hand and bringing her into the clearing to sit with the women and partake of the funeral meal. Though the clearing was full of people, the talk was low, the natural throatiness of the language tempered in respect for the dead.

When the eating was done, and with no announcement, the gypsies started to make their way to the center of the field where Beulah's vardo had been left. A group of women remained behind, bringing out the bowls dedicated to the washing of china and cutlery, pots and pans.

Maisie looked for the lurcher and realized the dog was not with the gypsies—in fact, she had not seen her since the funeral. Webb seemed unconcerned, and as the gypsies gathered, he began to pour paraffin around the perimeter of the vardo, which contained everything the gypsy woman had owned: her clothes, her crockery, her bed linens, her crystals, the dowsing rod, and the last bunches of Michaelmas daisies she had tied, ready to sell door-to-door. Another man came forward, running with a burning branch from the fire. He handed it to Webb, who held the torch up high for all to see, then threw it upon the vardo with a scream of despair. Maisie flinched at the eruption, as flames tore through the wood, paint peeled back, and the china, glass and metal inside crackled and spat back at the inferno.

As they watched, Paishey brought Webb's violin to

him. Once more he gently opened the case and removed the instrument from its nesting place of golden velvet. He placed the violin under his chin, drew back the bow, and began to play, each soulful note of the lament carried up on the wind and cast across the fields and along the byways that Beulah had ambled for many a year. Maisie stared into the flames as Webb played, the music growing in intensity, the rhythm changing time and again in the way that life changes, so that, as the fire leaped and scurried around and through the vardo, each refrain became a tribute to Beulah from girlhood to crone. This was the gypsy way, this fire that marked the end of a life, when all that was owned and all manner of ties to an earthly existence were destroyed. Tomorrow, when the vardo's iron chassis was cold, the gypsies would take it with them, to rebuild. Another traveling home would rise from the remains like a phoenix from the ashes.

When the flames abated, Maisie said goodbye to Webb and Paishey. She did not tarry long with the gypsies. It was time for her to leave because, in truth, though a trickle of blood from the traveling folk ran in her veins, she knew she was not one of them. She was a Londoner, and it was time for her to go home.

As she walked through the village, she stopped at the church, where, as she expected, the lurcher was with her mistress, lying on top of the fresh earth and bounty of blooms that covered her final resting place. Maisie knelt down by the animal, who did not move but remained with her pointed nose between her front paws, eyes open wide, guarding.

"You can't stay here, jook. Your people are moving on."

The dog still did not even flinch, so Maisie remained awhile, stroking her coat and lulled by the sounds of the village—the birds on high, a horse being ridden along the High Street, children playing in the fields. Soon, though, Maisie stroked the lurcher once more, remembering the time when Beulah's dog had walked with her to the MG, her glistening diamond-like eyes reflecting the moonlight.

As she drove through Heronsdene, Maisie saw Beattie Drummond, notebook in hand, interviewing Fred Yeoman outside the inn. She did not stop, to talk or pass the time of day. She was going home.

EPILOGUE

In early November, Maisie decided that the ritual she referred to as her final accounting was long overdue on the Heronsdene case. In the interim, work had come in at a more pleasing pace, although the economic slump that gripped the country showed no signs of improvement, with evidence of a deepening crisis. Those of a certain station were able to retain the illusion that nothing had changed since the heady days of the early 1920s, and the increase in house construction remained baffling to economists. But for the poor, life became even more desperate, with labor lines growing, soup kitchens struggling to feed more mouths, factories closing, and the country in the grip of despair.

Along with that mood of hopelessness came the search for a scapegoat, with the finger pointed toward those who appeared not to belong, who were not considered "one of us." Oswald Mosley's particular brand of fascism was feeding upon the discontent, and it appeared to Maisie that people were beginning to take to their corners, ready for a fight. Thus she would not allow herself to breathe easy, feeling the weight of responsibility she had assumed, not only for her own financial security—as had many women of her age who would remain spinsters due to a war that had claimed a generation of young men—but for the weekly wage that kept the Beale family from want. Only when she had cleared her desk of urgent matters would she take time to reflect upon the month's worth of events that still caused her heart to ache.

"I won't be in the office for a few days, Billy. It's time to write my final notes on the Heronsdene case and put it to rest."

Billy nodded. He understood the importance of this time to his employer, and in his way was emulating her procedures, closing those cases she now allowed him to consider his own with a visit to each place of significance encountered along the way.

"I expect I'll see you on Tuesday or Wednesday, then. I've got me 'ands full with this woman who reckons the shopkeeper is thievin' from her, the one the police didn't want to know about. And there's that other woman who says her best friend is bein' blackmailed and will pay us to find out."

"Good work, Billy." She tidied her desk and collected her shoulder bag and document case. "I just hope the weather holds. This sunshine is lovely, but that wind is going right through me."

"And takin' the leaves with it—'ave you seen the square? It looks like every leaf in London came to cover the paving stones."

Maisie smiled as Billy opened the door for her. "You can leave word with my father, if you need me."

"Right you are, Miss."

HER FIRST STOP was not in Kent but in London. At St. Anselm's school, she remained in her motor car and watched from beyond the gates as the school's cadet force—an extracurricular activity for those who might one day wish to join the services—marched back and forth across the quadrangle. She thought back to the headmaster, and the way he talked about the school being an army where everyone had to fit in, play their part, and not rock the boat. As the boys clattered across the paving stones, their uniforms pressed and their boots seeming one size too big, she thought about those too young who went to war, the Pim Martins, boys treated as men when it came time to face the cannonade. After listening to the boy in charge shout, "About turn!" one last time, she pulled out into the traffic, on her way to see Priscilla.

Maisie was shown into the entrance hall of the house in Holland Park, just in time to see a gang of boys rush through in a boisterous game of tag. Tarquin, who was bringing up the rear of the unruly snake of boyhood that galloped past, greeted her in his usual manner, by leaping into her arms and kissing her on both cheeks.

"Tante Maisie, Tante Maisie, watch this! Stay where you are and watch this!" Still without his four front teeth, he clambered from her arms and ran to the top of the stairs, where he swung his leg over the banister and, holding on as if his life depended upon it, slid at some speed to the bottom of the staircase, where he promptly fell off and landed on his behind.

Soon his brothers and their friends had sprinted up to the top of the staircase, ready to slide down the banister one by one.

"Get off that banister and down those stairs immediately! You are nothing but a band of ruffians." Priscilla walked to the bottom of the staircase, her hands on her hips, then called out, "Elinor! Do something about these horrible creatures before I have to do it myself!" She turned to Maisie, grinning. "Better not let them see me smile. I think it's all rather fun—used to do the same thing myself."

Elinor emerged from the upstairs rooms to inform the Partridge boys and their friends that tea was ready in the nursery.

"We'll go into my sitting room for something a little

more grown up," said Priscilla.

Maisie accepted a glass of cream sherry, while Priscilla prepared a cocktail.

"Douglas is with his publisher this afternoon, hence the high jinks on the staircase. I daresay Simon slid down that very banister when he was a boy." She looked at Maisie as she sat down on the pillowed sofa next to her friend, each of them having claimed one end. Priscilla kicked off her shoes and pulled her feet up under her. "Make yourself at home," she instructed, before continuing. "Have you seen Margaret?"

Maisie shook her head. "I saw her just before she moved from London, and I thought I would drive out to Grantchester in a day or so. I'll be sure to call first, just in case."

"She'd love to see you."

"Yes, I know. I'll go, I promise." Maisie changed the subject. "Are the boys settling in at their new school?"

"Didn't you see that tribe out there? The school is popular with the families of diplomats, so it's like the League of Nations, with everyone speaking a different language—as well as English, of course. They leave school early on Fridays, and each of the boys wanted to bring a friend home for the weekend, one of the boarders."

"Will you stay here, in London?"

Priscilla shrugged. "I'm not sure. I was planning to open up the country house for weekends, but now I don't know."

"What do you mean?"

"I haven't decided if I like it here. Perhaps it wasn't such a brilliant idea to bring the family back to England just because I wanted to relive my childhood." She shrugged. "After all, that's what it was all about, wanting to see my boys doing the things my brothers had done, as if I could bring them back in a different way. But the fact is, my boys are who they are, their own little people. They've been brought up in France, on the coast, and they are each of them different. Even though they're in a good school, for them, we might all be better off back where we were, away from this country. Even Elinor wants to go back to France. Do you know that last week she was telling me that when she was in school they were whipped for speaking to each other in Welsh? They were *forced* to speak English."

Maisie sipped her sherry and was about to comment when Priscilla looked over at her, grinning. "In the meantime, before we decide whether to up sticks and scurry back to Biarritz, I am going to enjoy seeing more of you, for a start. I think I might have to take you in hand, Maisie."

"And I think I'm doing quite well, thank you."

"What about Simon?"

Maisie was quiet. "He's gone, Pris. And now, even more than before, I believe cremation was the best thing. Margaret made a wise decision, though difficult. It's over. He's free at last."

"And you?"

"I don't know. I can't say. It was as if he were

imprisoned in a room where we could see him but not speak to him, as if we were caught in a vacuum of silence even if we screamed."

"But you've never screamed."

"Have you?"

"At the top of my lungs, across the Atlantic Ocean, every day for months after the war, after my brothers and parents died. I screamed all the time."

"Oh."

The women sat in silence, comfortable in their friendship. Then Priscilla braced her shoulders and reached toward Maisie.

"I almost forgot. I have something for you."

"For me?"

"Yes. The furniture we chose to bring with us was delivered last week—what a performance, I shall be hard pushed to take it back with me—and I have a piece I think you'll love. I want you to have it as a belated housewarming gift. I'll have it sent to your flat next week."

"What is it?"

"Come and have a look."

Maisie followed Priscilla to the corner of the room, where an upright gramophone stood in the corner. The cabinet was of rich mahogany, inlaid with maple.

"Douglas has bought a new one, and this one is going begging." She bent over it. "See, you lift the lid here, and there's where you place the gramophone record. You wind it up with the handle at the side and then pull up the arm like this. And there's a cupboard below where you'll keep your gramophone records."

"I don't have any gramophone records."

"Don't worry, I've thought of that." She pulled out a record and placed it on the turntable, then held up the horn, ready to set the needle in the groove. "This man is one of Douglas's favorites. His music has been all over Paris, and he's in great demand in the *bals musettes,* you know, the small dance clubs. He's a gypsy—one of *les Manouches,* the travelers who live in caravans just outside Paris—and his music is quite wild and clever. I'm sure you'll love it."

And as the music surged into the room, Maisie smiled. "Yes, you're right, I love it."

MAISIE HAD DELAYED the journey to Kent until after her weaving class on Saturday. Once more, her spirits were lifted by the colors and textures around her, by swags of dyed wool that hung from the laundry racks, by the presence of Marta Jones, who had told her, in confidence, that she was considering reclaiming her family's original name.

"I think it will release something, some passion, something here." Whispering, she pressed her hand against her chest, then took up Maisie's bobbin to correct an error in her weaving.

"And what *is* your name?"

"Marta Juroszek." She smiled as she pronounced the word, rolling her tongue around the syllables as if tasting a new sweet pudding for the first time. "Yes, I am Marta Juroszek."

And though Maisie was concerned for her teacher—
the country seemed in no mood to demonstrate toler-
ance for those of distant cultures—she saw a sense of
belonging claim her.

"It's a good name, Marta, a strong name. And it's
yours."

A SURPRISE WAS in store for Maisie as she left Marta's
studio. Leaning against the wall inside the entrance to
the building, a visitor waited for her.

"Beattie, what on earth are you doing here?"

"Your assistant told me where to find you. He said
you would be finished by twelve."

"Come on, let's walk to my motor car. Why are you
in London?"

"I've been here for a couple of days. I'm going back
to Maidstone today."

Maisie pointed to the MG and opened the doors.
Once they were both seated, she turned to Beattie.

"Do you want a lift to Charing Cross?"

"Thank you."

"So, do you have that job yet?"

Beattie shook her head. "No, still at the newspaper,
I'm afraid."

"Then what have you been doing in London—hot
on a scoop?"

"Not quite. I've been seeing a few publishers."

Maisie changed gear to pass a horse and cart. "Go
on."

She shrugged. "I knew I couldn't write the story—

the one you told me about Heronsdene—for the newspaper. It was as if I had a lot of fabric and no sewing
machine or pattern. So I racked my brains until they
hurt, and I decided what to do."

"And what's that?"

"I decided that this newspaper woman would
become an authoress. I took the story and wrote it as
a novel—embellishing it a bit, you understand."

"And will it be published?"

"I went through several typewriter ribbons and eight
fingernails to provide manuscripts for three publishers, and—you will never guess what—I think one
of them will buy it!"

"Congratulations, Beattie, that's wonderful—and it
might help you get a job on a bigger newspaper."

She shook her head. "I'm not so sure about that."

"Don't rule it out. And you can always write more
novels. I'm sure your work has provided you with
more than enough *fabric*." Maisie smiled at her passenger. "Here you are. Charing Cross."

Beattie thanked Maisie for the lift and for keeping
her promise. As the newspaperwoman closed the passenger door and walked away, Maisie wound down
her window and called out to her.

"What will you call the book, so I know what to
look for?"

Beattie Drummond cupped her hand around her
mouth and shouted her answer above the throng of
passengers going in and out of the station, then she
turned away and ran for her train, the book's title

caught up in the melee. The only word Maisie heard was *revenge.*

HERONSDENE WAS QUIET as she drove through the village and parked the MG. She stepped out of the motor car, changed her shoes for a pair of Wellington boots, pulled out her umbrella in case it rained, and set off on a walk across the hop-gardens and up to the clearing. A moment later she saw the lurcher, standing by the entrance to the farm, watching her every move.

"Jook, what are you doing here?"

The dog loped toward Maisie, her head low, her tail tucked under, brushing close as if to feel the warmth of a human being.

"You should have gone with your people." Maisie looked up and around her. The dog must have recognized the distinctive rumble of her motor car and followed her from the village. "Do you want to come with me, then?"

The dog's ears flattened back, so Maisie leaned down, stroked her neck, and set off across the hop-gardens, which were muddy now, the spent bines heaped in brown, brackenish piles ready to be burned. She cut through the wood, across the field where the gypsies had grazed their horses, and up the hill toward the clearing. Everything around her was silent, with the bright silver sky a portent for stormy weather.

Blackened soil marked the place where Beulah's vardo had burned, and with it evidence of her sojourn on earth. All that remained was that which was carried in the heart. Maisie touched the ground, while the lurcher sniffed, pawed the soil, and then began to slink away to the clearing as if called. Maisie followed, almost expecting to hear the gypsies, but it was silent, with only the wind sifting through the branches and light reflecting off the bark of silver beech trees and muted by giant oaks. Walking to the center of the circle where the gypsies' fire had once crackled with life, Maisie remembered the night she danced with the women, the color and energy of their celebration reverberating through her bones, along with the sound of Webb's violin as his bow scorched back and forth across the strings, teasing out sounds she had never heard and might never hear again. Soon, the lurcher touched her hand with its nose, as if knowing there was nothing more to be said or done in this place.

The dog left Maisie at the MG, vanishing into the bushes on a shortcut to the village. Maisie knew she would see her soon enough. Pulling up outside the inn, she waved to Fred Yeoman, who was sweeping the street outside the residents' entrance.

"Miss Dobbs, didn't think I'd see you again."

"How are you, Mr. Yeoman?"

"Mustn't grumble. Bit quiet now, not so many day-trippers passing through."

Maisie nodded. "Stormy, today, isn't it?" She looked back at clouds gathering in the distance, then at the innkeeper. "Tell me, where does the gypsy's dog stay?"

He stopped sweeping and leaned on his broom.

"Strange old thing, that one. She stays with her mistress, sleeping on that grave as if the old lady were about to get up at any minute and walk off with her. I call out to her some nights, save a bit of broth for her, you know, put out a bowl here by the door. She'll come across, eat it up, then go back to her place. And the funny thing is, it's as if she knows we've done right by her, because I'll go out the next morning, and find a hare by the door, freshly caught, like it's her payment." He shrugged. "Whyte says he'll build a kennel for her, put it in the churchyard, but we've some cold nights coming, and she'll freeze. Mind you, she's used to it, I suppose."

Maisie glanced toward the church. "Yes, I suppose." She paused, then turned back to Yeoman. "I'd better be off. Remember me to the villagers, say I asked after them."

"Right you are, Miss Dobbs—oh, and before you leave, go down to the old bakery site. We've had a bit of a go at it, you know, in case he ever comes back."

She walked toward the church, stopping alongside the waste ground. The overgrowth had been cut back, old bricks removed, and a series of flower beds tilled. Copper markers indicated where bulbs had been planted, and when Maisie looked closer, she smiled. According to the markers, in spring there would be a profusion of tulips in this very place. She turned toward the church, stopping alongside the war memorial where Willem van Maarten's name remained among those of the village who gave their lives in the war. She thought of Simon and of the thousands of other young men who had returned wounded. *They are the forgotten*, thought Maisie. The ones who came home alive, to linger—perhaps for years—before death claimed them or they brought about their own end. She pulled up the collar of her mackintosh and went on to the church.

Lying across Beulah's grave, the lurcher wagged her tail as Maisie approached. She stopped briefly, with head lowered, in front of the graves of Jacob, Bettin and Anna, and saw that the headstone had been changed, with the name VAN MAARTEN now scored into the granite. Was it another grain of atonement on the part of the villagers, or had Webb paid for the alteration? She knelt down next to the gypsy's dog, ruffling her ear as she spoke quietly and with kindness to the animal.

"You can't stay here, jook. She's not coming back, she's gone. Come on, you've been here long enough. She wouldn't want you to stay longer."

Maisie came to her feet and, though the dog did not stir, she raised her head to be fondled.

"One last temptation for you, jook. I know a lovely man who would look after you forever, and I think you could look after him too."

Still the dog did not move. Maisie gave her a final pat and left the churchyard. She looked back at the gray clouds and, feeling a spatter of rain, began to run to the motor car. She opened the door just as the rain came down, shaking droplets of water from her hair as she started the engine. She was about to pull out, looking back to ensure that a tractor had not come around the corner, when she saw the lurcher running toward her. She clambered from the MG and opened the passenger door. The dog leaped in, sitting on the seat as if she belonged.

"Good, you listened to me. Now then, jook, let's take you to meet Frankie Dobbs."

Later, as Maisie sat by the fire, she looked across at her father, his newspaper opened to the racing pages as he squinted to read by the light of an oil lamp. The lurcher was settled at his feet, her head resting atop his crossed ankles. She had claimed her new owner and, following an initial element of doubt on his part, Frankie had taken her into his heart, already reaching down to touch the dog's fur with every turn of the page.

MAISIE HAD NOT visited the Lynch home in Grantchester since the night of Simon's party in 1915. Unsure of her emotions, she drove with care, rehearsing conversations and anticipating questions. But when she arrived, Margaret took both her hands in her own and made her welcome. The house seemed more cozy than she remembered. She thought her youth, and the fact that she had allowed herself to be intimidated by such an invitation, would have made even a smaller house seem like a mansion when she was eighteen. The room where she had danced with Simon was, admittedly, spacious, but Margaret had ushered her into a small sitting room overlooking the gardens.

They spoke of Simon, though not of his passing. Margaret told stories of her son's boyhood and youth, of the ambition that brought him to medicine, and his decision to join the Royal Army Medical Corps as soon as he'd qualified. Then, later, the women together made their way to the meadow, unlatching the gate that led from the gardens to the fields beyond. The late-afternoon light was rendered colorless, grained by a rising fenland vapor, so that to stare into the distance was like looking at a photograph taken long ago.

Margaret chose a place beyond the trees, where they stood for several moments. Then she handed a small pewter urn to Maisie. "Would you . . . ?"

Maisie looked up at the trees to ascertain the air's direction. She unscrewed the lid and set it on the ground. Then, with one hand on her heart, she reached out with the urn and carefully tipped Simon's ashes into a gentle breeze.

HER FINAL ACCOUNTING complete at last, Maisie sat back from the dining table at her flat in Pimlico, closed her journal, and set the cap on her fountain pen. She pinched the bridge of her nose to ward off fatigue, then walked to the window. It was late, dark, and as she stood looking out at the swirling pea-souper smog, she rubbed her arms for warmth. She remembered scattering Simon's ashes and reflected again on the burning of Beulah's vardo. She could almost hear once more the way Webb had first played a lament that day, then changed the tempo and changed it again so that, with each new tune, something of the gypsy woman's life was commemorated—her vivacity in youth, her laugh, her wisdom, the fields she called home, and her wanderings along the country lanes. Then it was done, the mourning not confined to that which was dark and shadowed by loss but also rejoicing in the life that must go on.

She ran her hands along the edge of the fine walnut gramophone given to her by Priscilla and then, almost without thinking, lifted the lid and began to turn the handle at the side. She took out her one record, by a gypsy now famous in Paris, a man who had blended French passion with the spark of the Roma. And as the beat began to reverberate around the room, with violin and guitar cutting through the silence, Maisie felt the rhythm in her feet, her body, and her arms, and she remembered the gypsies moving to the music, pounding the ground in a celebration of the spirit.

So, alone in her flat, Maisie Dobbs danced.

ACKNOWLEDGMENTS

To my friend Holly Rose—as always, thank you for being the first and most important reader of my work. Your thoughtful commentary and unfailing support are so deeply appreciated—thank you.

To my parents, Albert and Joyce Winspear—thank you for your wonderful stories about being "down hopping" and for providing me with the circumstances that formed my own memories of those good times. And to the Webbs, wherever they are, for the gift of friendship to two just-married escapees from post–WW II London who came to Kent to start life anew—you are remembered with great affection, and I have cherished my parents' stories of your kindness.

As with my previous novels, thanks must go to the staff of the Imperial War Museum's library and archives—a truly priceless resource.

To John Sterling, Maggie Richards, and the wonderful team at Henry Holt in New York; to Frances Coady and everyone at Picador; and to Roland Philipps, Heather Barrett, and the staff at John Murray Publishers in London—thank you for your support and your regard for Maisie Dobbs.

To my dear friend, wise mentor, and amazing agent, Amy Rennert—thank you for your support, counsel, and insight. I am blessed to be working with you.

And to my husband, John Morell—thank you, for everything.

Center Point Publishing

600 Brooks Road ● PO Box 1
Thorndike ME 04986-0001 USA

(207) 568-3717

US & Canada:
1 800 929-9108
www.centerpointlargeprint.com